The Temple of Frozen Fates

JENNIFER KAY

Contents

Content Warning

This book contains the following elements that may be sensitive for certain readers:

Alcohol Consumption

Explicit Language

Explicit Sexual Content including creative ways of using vines as restraints and light spanking

Violence

Suicidal Ideation in the form of self-sacrifice

This list includes but is not limited to all triggers, if you see something that should have been mentioned please email: authorjenniferkay@gmail.com

Pronunciation Guide

Aceus - (ay-see-uhs)

Ambrose - (am-brose)

Aurum - (ah-rum)

Caelum - (kay-lum)

Casimir - (ka-see-meer)

Dolan - (dole-lahn)

Galen - (Gae-linn)

Halcyon - (hal-see-yon)

Iris - (eye-ris)

Kusharian - (koo-sha-ree-on)

Leoni - (lee-own-ee)

Maya - (mai-uh)

Niklaus - (nee-ko-louse)

Riel - (ree-el)

Sumyre - (soo-mi-ray)

Tantal - (tan-tall)

To all who need a little more adventure and freedom, this book is for you.
Don't be afraid to embrace every part of yourself.

Chapter 1

CAELUM

"CAELUM, ARE YOU POSITIVE we're not lost?"

"No," I replied honestly, raking my fingers through the growing strands of hair on the verge of becoming too long. Even though I said otherwise for the last eight hours, there was nothing but rock and darkness. A pessimistic, sinking hope in my chest told me I might never see daylight again.

My compass had long since stopped working. The mineral deposits in the caves were so dense, it was shifting the needles north and south to east and west. I gave up using it entirely.

There was a pathway through here—ancient tales I pieced together from all over the eastern coast of Ambrose told of it. Apparently, this was a tunnel for safe passage when the Great War had begun; there was definitely a way *out*, because there had been a way *in*.

Unless time had eroded and blocked the entrances.

Well, that would be a problem for future me, and present me just needed to find the right direction.

"You've been marking our path so we know the way out, right?" I asked Iris, adjusting the straps which held a satchel and a small dagger across my chest. She grunted out an irritated "yes."

"Can you use your magic again?" a no-nonsense voice asked, and I turned my bluish-green Everflame torch to shine on Maya, her long black hair swaying in a tightly woven braid. Both of the women looked gaunt in the torchlight, their features shadowed from the darkness, the flame illuminating the smudges of dirt on their cheeks.

"I'm almost out." I shrugged. "Unless you have more of those potions...?" I waggled my eyebrows at her.

The longer we were traveling in here, the longer it would take for us to get back to civilization, so wasting those potions wasn't exactly wise. But if I could find the exit of these gods-forsaken caves, I needed to take it.

We were approaching five days underground, and none of us wanted to spend any more time in the dark, damp cave system that ran along the border of the mortal kingdom Tantal. If my calculations were correct, the exit would put us in Ambrose, but it would be cutting it close.

Maya sighed, rummaging through the pack she swung off her shoulder, before plucking out a small clear bottle with lilac liquid.

"I have a few more vials, but I would like to save the rest," she said, her thoughts clearly mimicking mine as she handed me the substance that would rejuvenate my magic.

I gave her a wink and swallowed the potion in one swig. *Gah.* Tasted like shit, but it got the job done. My body tingled as my magic regenerated.

It wasn't pleasant—in fact, it was borderline painful—and I sucked in air through my teeth. The more magic that needed to be replenished, the worse it was. Luckily, I was only beginning to tap out, not quite hitting the exhaustion that came with overextension, but it hurt just the same.

The potion settled, and my magic swelled inside me, my body instantly more energized, buzzing with eager anticipation.

"Okay! Let's do this" I shouted, my voice bouncing and echoing off the stalagmites and stalactites around us. Maya clicked her tongue at me, but Iris chuckled. We all knew there was nothing to fear around us—Iris would have known immediately.

Squatting low, I placed my hands on the ground and blew out a long breath to focus my mind and energy on my magic. These caves were finite—that much I knew—but each time I tried this method before, there was no sign of any exit or even so much as a change in scenery. Just layers and layers of hard rock.

Magic spread through my hands, the familiar sensation of heat writhing through my arms, reaching for an outlet. With my eyes closed, I could make out tendrils of magic—feeling for where the earth touched the roots of trees above, something more than just caverns and rock on all sides.

I kept pulsing my magic forward when I gasped. The moisture of clay extended into lighter topsoil and dirt of an earthy forest. No longer was there only the never-ending expanse of caverns and hard mineral deposits. Roots of flourishing trees and brush stroked against my magic like a gentle kiss of life.

I let out a relieved laugh, the exit clear in my mind.

"Only a couple more miles. We should be out within the day," I announced.

There was a collective sigh of relief from the women as I cut my magic off. My body sagged with the exertion, but my smile was wide. Maya rolled her eyes, hiking her pack higher before beckoning me to lead the way. Iris smirked, even though there was tiredness in her eyes.

Hopefully, all our efforts would be rewarded once we saw the sun again, because if the tales had been correct, there was an ancient temple nearby.

Once a place of refuge, it had long since been forgotten and never found again. A mystery lost to time.

The sky was dark when we finally found our exit, the stars winking at us in greeting through the tallest trees I had ever seen in my life.

Massive round trunks reached up to the sky at impossible heights, the branches nearly touching the stars themselves. The air was fresh and light, and after being in the cave system for so long, I tasted every shift in the wind, every piece of pollen from the blooming flowers that littered the ground. Moonlight illuminated everything in a faint glow, and I followed my instincts through the forest, slow enough for Iris to continue mapping our location.

"Incredible," I muttered as I swept through a portion of thick under-brush revealing astonishing, captivating, unbelievable ruins.

Tears pricked the backs of my eyes as my feet stepped on the solid stone that led to the entrance of this ancient, forgotten temple. I wasn't much of a crier, but seeing what I had been chasing for years had my knees weak. All my prayers had been answered on this humid evening.

Vines and overgrowth encased the temple exterior, but intricate carvings stood out, etched on tall pillars that precariously held up the temple. From the outside, it was clear time was not exactly friendly to the building, but it seemed—for the most part—structurally sound.

"Caelum," Iris hissed from behind me. Her tone was panicked, and it instantly had me turning on my heel and reaching for the sword strapped to my thigh, but my hand faltered as I saw her staring at the stars above, her dark brown face ashen.

"What is it?" Maya asked as she grasped Iris by the shoulders, trying to catch her eye. Iris looked at Maya before swinging her gaze at me, her eyes wide.

"We aren't just on the border of the mortal kingdom—we are *in* the mortal kingdom."

I shook my head, a lump forming in my throat as I darted to her side to look at the map. "There's no way," I insisted. "I was told by multiple sources that the temple was a greeting to Magi lands. It was a refuge for those escaping the clutches of the mortal army."

"Well, those tales are wrong. Or even if they were right, the mortals could have pushed the border back after the treaty went into place. Lost in translation and meaning through time. Regardless, we are trespassing. We need to leave before we get caught." She drew in a ragged breath, pointing at the sky above. "The stars and moon don't lie."

"Shit," I cursed, tugging on the roots of my hair before turning back toward the temple. Listening closely, I waited on abated breath for signs of anyone who might be around, but considering the state of the temple, I guessed it had been a while since anyone even ventured into this portion of the forest. "Are we close to the border of Ambrose? How far until we cross back in?"

Iris rotated her map and squinted. "It looks like the actual border is right around where we exited the caves. It was difficult for me to tell when we were underground, but now that I have the stars' location..." Iris looked away from her map, her eyes meeting mine with fear. "This is *bad*, Caelum. It's a death sentence if we get caught."

"Listen," I whispered, gesturing to the tall redwood trees around us. "Really listen. There's nothing but nature out here. No voices, no cities or towns. The temple is so overgrown it's likely no one's laid eyes on it in centuries."

This seemed to placate Iris, and the longer the silence was filled with the noise of crickets and the rustle of leaves from the slight breeze, the more her tense shoulders dropped.

Maya chewed on the side of her lip but said, "The border isn't very far. Nobody else knows we're here. If we find trouble, we just need to make it to the caves. We have enough provisions to get us through the night, and then we can look around tomorrow and leave."

I nodded in agreement. Iris still looked skeptical but nodded all the same. "Just because we are in Tantal and there are no Magi, doesn't mean our magic doesn't work. I can still feel it within me, just the same," she observed.

In fact, there was nothing other than Iris' map that made me feel as though we were anywhere other than Ambrose. There were rumors that when magic had been banned—outlawed—there was some sort of barrier that prevented magic from being used. Luckily, it didn't seem to be the case; it was just the words of scared people who hadn't been allowed to cross over in ages. "Why don't you use your magic, try to feel for anything," I suggested.

Iris shook her head, her long braids falling over her shoulder, before she clenched her fists and closed her eyes. A deep breath exhaled from her chest, and when she opened her eyes they were softer, the fear fading away.

"You're right. There's no one here but us—for as far as my magic can reach. Sorry."

She smiled up at Maya, who placed a tender kiss on her cheek and said, "There's no need to apologize. It's always better to be safe than sorry."

"I think we'll be safe for the next couple of days," I reassured her. "At least we can make sure this is a temple worth fighting for when we get back. I'm willing to bet there are tons of treasures within the walls."

Maya snorted as she unbuckled her bedroll from her pack. "It's always about the treasure with you, isn't it?"

"Usually, yes. But treasure comes in many forms. You know this."

"Do you think it holds the secrets of the *before*? When gods and humans coexisted?" Iris asked, her fear now quelled and instead replaced with whimsy and wonder.

I shrugged, but I couldn't wipe the grin off my face. "I hope it does—I really hope it does."

It was the reason I did this. A lifetime of archeology just to find out the long-lost secrets of the world. I was trained as a scholar once upon a time, but it wasn't enough to mollify my curiosity. All my life I'd heard the tales; now I wanted to see if they were true. Wanted to touch the pieces of our history as they were discovered.

Dirt and grime were the primal answer to finding where we came from. Ancient vestiges that were lost to the War held who we were, and why the Magi existed in the first place. The priceless jewels that we found were only a bonus.

And I hoped this temple held the answers to the questions all Magi had been asking once and for all.

Chapter 2

HALCYON

Duty. If my life could be wrapped in one word, that would be it. From the moment of my conception, it had been my destiny. I was bred for it, molded by my teachers, and this was the day I would accept it as my own. My father's perfect daughter—his rightful heir.

I stood in my appointed bedroom of Dolan's castle as Shara wrapped my body in swaths of blue and grey silks—the Forte house colors. Every smooth and luxurious layer pressed against my skin like lead weight.

"Smile, Halcyon," Shara admonished as she noticed the crease between my brows. "Today is a *good* day. You've been readying for this your whole life."

I could only nod as she guided me to a padded seat in front of an aged silver mirror. Her pale fingers threaded through my hair, tying the nearly white strands into delicate braids and wrapping them on top of my head with elegant expertise.

Shara's mother served my mother and it just so happened we were born only seven months apart. When we were younger, we were fast friends, but as time passed, she settled into her role as handmaid.

Although our friendship had gone from open childhood giggles and shrieking through the castle halls to gentle whispers behind closed doors, it still persisted, no matter how much it made my mother purse her lips.

Shara's own brown hair was plaited in the back, and I *wished* I could wear my hair so simply. I knew she didn't have an easy life, but I found myself envious just the same. She would not have a city to run, nor would she disappoint a thousand people if she failed.

"It never felt so real before," I said gently, wringing my hands in my lap, unable to meet my own gaze in the mirror. What would stare back at me would be the future leader of Dolan. A Lady who was meant to keep my region of Ambrose in line. As did my father, and his father before him.

As the eldest—and only—child of Lord Alastair Forte, it was my burden to bear, but not one that I quite processed. Not until the past few weeks, where I had been run exhausted with preparations to fill my father's shoes.

Shara dropped the hair she was holding and knelt in front of me, her hands warm as they grasped my own.

"You have nothing to fear. You are one of the strongest women I have ever met. For thirty years, you have been forged into a person capable of leading our city, and through those thirty years, you have proven worthy of the title." Shara's grip tightened as I shook my head in refusal. "I mean it. There is no one better suited for the role. Think about all you've done already."

"Those were initiatives set in motion by other people. What if I can't recognize those initiatives? What if I make a wrong choice and deny my people what they need?" I implored, gazing at my reflection and not quite recognizing the woman who stared back. Heavy diamond and silvered-gold earrings hung from my lobes, and my cheeks were painted pink. It was a mask intended to fool everyone, even myself.

"You've studied for years about our place in Ambrose. People Behavior was your highest subject. Need I remind you who was there when you fretted all night about tests?"

My throat bobbed, but I swallowed down my nerves, putting up a mental blockade against my self-doubt. She was right, of course. All of my credentials pointed to the fact that I was beyond capable. Gods knew, if my aging father—who never stepped a foot out of the castle—could do it, so could I.

Shara took my silence as confirmation and resumed placing pins in my hair. She adorned my strands with delicate silver chains and pearls, making my hair gleam every time I turned my head. There was a knock at the door, which had both of us pausing. I gave Shara a quick nod, to which she stepped back with her head down.

"Come in," I called, and the door swung open on silent hinges. Niklaus strode in, his black hair combed away from his blue eyes, further brightened by the azure cotte he wore. "Cousin." Standing, I greeted him with a nod of my chin.

"Are you ready, Lady Halcyon?" His lips turned up at the corner, giving me a smirk.

"Not in the slightest," I muttered as I patted myself down, smoothing my garments that needed no such thing. I nodded to Shara, who only bowed as I exited the room with Nik.

The looming presence of Aceus accompanied us as we strode through the expansive halls of Dolan Castle. His eyes wrinkled with age and sun exposure, but he was the highest esteemed guard in Dolan, and now, since I was to be the Lady of Dolan, I was kept under his watchful eye. I remembered when I was younger and he had a head full of hair, but that had long since fallen, only his carefully waxed blonde mustache still in place.

"It's only the dinner this evening. You won't be officially inaugurated until the end of the moon cycle," Niklaus reminded me.

I stared at Nik from the corner of my eye. He was always so attuned to my moods that it sometimes frightened me. He didn't even have magic of the mind; he was just extremely observant. Reading people was his strength, and it served him well in his role as advisor.

As my cousin, he had the choice of whether he wanted to serve on the Council, and I could never remember a time when he had any doubts. But then again, his position had been secured long before I was born. With our Magi bloodlines, our bodies aged much slower than mortals after hitting puberty, so even though we were nearly a century apart, we looked roughly the same age.

"I've never once claimed the title before. It's heavy," I said simply.

"You will get used to it, cousin. I have no doubts that you'll strike fear into the hearts of our people, as you often do with mine." Nik's smile widened, and I let out a burst of laughter. "What?" he asked. "You're frightening when you get angry."

I laughed, recalling the outbursts that had me freezing the halls and rooms when I was younger.

"I don't aim to strike fear in our people's hearts, no matter what my father might think," I said seriously.

Niklaus only smirked before shoving the double doors to the dining hall wide open.

Tables lined the ostentatious room that was my father's domain. Candelabras lit the stone walls with warm flames. Food was piled high on each table, and kegs of wine were scattered around the edges, easy access for the gathering.

Councilors and socialites crowded amongst each other, falling silent as Nik and I strode through the threshold. My father helmed the room from the front, his table facing the opposite direction so he could keep a watchful eye on the attendees. My mother sat to his right, her narrow face beaming. Her hair, silver like mine, fell around her in loose curls; a direct contrast to my father's cropped black hair, his cheeks rounded and red from wine.

"Daughter!" he bellowed across the hall. Standing from his seat, the chair screeched against the stone flooring. "Come. Sit by my side, for tonight we celebrate a new leader!"

Raucous cheers went up at his declaration. Men and women both slammed their tankards on the tables before them. My body was alight with adrenaline, every instinct begging me to run and hide, but instead, I smoothed my features and rolled my shoulders back in false bravado.

The cheering faded into boisterous conversation as I settled into my seat, careful not to wrinkle the fine silk fabrics which adorned my body. Niklaus sat next to me, his easy demeanor a welcome reprieve to my anxious energy.

"Smile, Halcyon," my father admonished from the side of his mouth. "You could at least pretend like you are eager for your role."

"Yes, father," I replied, forcing my lips to curve upward. It seemed to satisfy him well enough, and the night carried on.

Congratulations were offered by many as they passed through the hall, mingling and vying for attention. The candles burned at a snail's pace as I watched the wax dribble around them, begging for them to hurry so I could retire.

"Did you really fund that trio to go to the mortal kingdom, Alastair?" an older gentleman spoke to my father in a humorous tone. I jolted at his ridiculous question. No one ventured into Tantal. It was forbidden, and a death sentence.

My father licked his lips. His eyes were glassy as he raked them about the room. I recognized it as his way of looking for eavesdroppers, but his gratuitous wine pours made his voice loud, regardless of his intent.

"My dear boy, yes I did." He laughed, no remorse or fear in his voice. My stomach dropped to the floor, and the blood drained from my face. "They came in claiming something outrageous. Well, you were there after all. I figured if they were so keen on signing their lives away, might as well give them the satisfaction of thinking they had won." He shrugged, laughing, but horror gripped my insides. "And if they do, by chance, retrieve proof of whatever they were spouting and bring it back, Dolan will be all the better for it."

"Father," I cut in, unable to hold my tongue. "What are you talking about?"

He swung his head in my direction, surveying me before clicking his tongue. "A man came in practically begging me to give him and his troupe money so they could raid a temple they claim to have found in the mortal lands."

"And you just gave it to them? Without proof, or collateral?" *Not to mention, if they got caught, it would be treason...* Fear turned to rage as I realized at what he had done. If Dolan was found guilty of treason, then he would not be held responsible. I would.

He bellowed a laugh, far too loud to be genuine, and clasped a hand on my shoulder. His fingers pressed into my skin to the point of pain. Ice coated my fingers, and I balled my hands into fists in my lap, trying to banish my magic from revealing my mood shift.

"Oh, no. We have collateral. I am sending my best soldier to tag along. If they die, then they die. If they are liars, then they die. If not, then we will have some extremely valuable and coveted information, and not to mention, *treasure*." He shifted his gaze to the back of the room where Aceus stood, his broad shoulders stiff as he monitored the crowd.

"My bodyguard? You're sending Aceus? Why?"

"He's the best we have, and the only one I trust. He will be sure to bring them back, or die trying."

Blinking, I tried to clear my head from the buzzing that filled my ears, trying to process this decision. Without Aceus, I would likely get the next best bodyguard, but there was a gap of talent between Aceus and anyone else. My father was sacrificing Aceus' life to make my security more unstable.

"And where did you get the funds?" I asked with a tight-lipped smile.

"Used the library's pension. They are bloated with scholarship funds. It was rotting in there. Might as well use that money for something worthwhile."

Worthwhile? Disgust roiled in my stomach. The library was Dolan's best source of our economy. We weren't wealthy, like Aurum. There was no military like the Seaside Cliffs. We only held knowledge. Without the scholarships to entice new scholars—families who dedicated their lives to knowledge—our economy would stall. People would not be motivated to live here. And he placed that money into a trip to the *mortal kingdom*?

My breath hitched as I realized: I was never supposed to succeed as a leader. In one fell swoop, my father had used this as an opportunity to set me up for complete failure.

"IF YOU WILL EXCUSE me, Father. The candles have turned to nubs, and I must retire." Even though I directly addressed him, he ignored me and gave me a passing wave as I stood. The crowd was very drunk, and I took it as a chance to leave. I would not be missed.

I met a glance from Niklaus and tilted my chin, beckoning him to follow. Promptly, he excused himself from his conversation and followed me out. My throat ached to ask him about my father's newest investment, but I remained silent until we reached my living chambers. I closed the door behind me, lest there be prying ears.

"Did you know?" I whirled on Niklaus, letting my features contort into the outrage I felt.

"Know what?" Nik asked.

"That my father is trying to sabotage me? That he funded *treason*? How could you let this happen, Nik? Are you even loyal? Do you not care about this city? Or are you my father's man?" Once the words poured from my lips, I couldn't stop. Niklaus just stared at me in confusion. "Would you rather see me strung up and eaten by crows than watch me succeed in my father's position?" Pacing around the room, I wrung my fingers together. "I knew my father never liked me as his successor, but gods above, I did not realize how far he would go to watch me fall. And *you*. I trusted you! And you just sat aside and watched it unfold."

No longer could I manage my magic. Ice encased my hands and wrists until it reached my elbows. The floors creaked as the stone froze around my feet, but Niklaus seemingly ignored my power before letting out a heavy sigh.

He leaned on my bedpost and raked his hands through his hair, removing the neatness of the styling, before meeting my eyes.

"I had no idea he actually funded that excavation. He didn't even bother to ask for my opinion, in which case I would have told him '*no*'. As for loyalty, my loyalty always has been—and always will remain—with the people in this city. The people in this country."

I stared him down, watching every feather of his jaw, the sag of his shoulders.

"Can I trust you, Nik? How can I be sure you aren't trying to undermine me as well?" Nik gave a few passing glances to my magical outburst, weary as the ice edged toward him.

"You're going to have to trust my word, Halcyon," he stated simply.

"Your *word*," I guffawed. "Maybe I should throw you in a dungeon cell, so at least when Ambrose gets word of my father's crimes, I can tell them that I had already taken precaution and eliminated the threats to our country."

Forming a shard in my hand, I threw it hard enough to impale my head-board. A show of what would happen to him if he betrayed me. Not that I thought I could follow through with the threat, but I *had* been around my father enough to know that sometimes fear really was a wonderful motivator.

Nik's face paled. "Halcyon, please. I had *nothing* to do with this." His gaze did not waver, and I nearly buckled in relief from the honesty in his eyes. "Have I not given you countless reports of the meetings your father has been having without your presence? Have I not mentored you and brought you up to speed on all the current on-goings in Ambrose?" he asked desperately.

My rage cooled as I recalled all the times he had told me things my father refused to do.

He had even introduced me to Galen, the Dragon Rider who was currently undercover in the mortal kingdom. It was a way to get me to engage in more political conversations. I needed to know who was who in Ambrose, and Niklaus provided. It should have been my father introducing us, but my father heard how I spoke openly with educators. About policies other places in Ambrose had implemented, what worked, what didn't. My eagerness to change Dolan soured him.

Not that I ever *tried* to give him reason to hate me. I was exceptional in my studies. Friendships and relationships were sacrificed for my future role. On parchment, I was his perfect heir. Unfortunately for me, it was never good enough.

"I need to know if you are on *my* side with this," I reinstated. "Not my father's. I need to know everything he does while he still remains as Lord until I officially take his name." Ice crackled around me, solidifying, but no longer spreading, in my outburst.

Nik nodded. "Of course, my lady. I am at your disposal. What would you have me do?"

"Explain to me in great detail exactly what my father just spent our library's scholarship funds on, and what their goals are."

Niklaus bowed his head. "Yes, lady. Let's move to another chamber while I send for someone to clean this up. I'll gather all the information I can find. We will figure this out."

Chapter 3

HALCYON

The plush chair in Nik's room grounded me as I pored over the notes he procured from the meeting that this *Caelum Masters* had requested. I was shocked that my father even entertained him at all.

A Magi temple in Tantal, the mortal kingdom. This Caelum had figured that there were ancient materials and historical relics which could give us insight into our long-forgotten history. It was absurd. *Absurd*, but admittedly intriguing.

As much as the idea of an unexplored temple sounded tempting, it did nothing to change the damning situation that my father forced me to deal with. My head hit the back of the chair as I groaned, wiping the backs of my hands over my eyes.

The fire crackled and lit Nik's room with an orange glow. Everything in his room was dripping with opulence. Velvet cushions on oversized chairs were on the left, and a mahogany tea table sat across the fireplace in front of a dark blue velvet chaise. A white fur rug lined the stone floors and made the room feel decadent and cozy.

The door to the room opened and Nik walked through, looking as haggard as I felt.

"What did you find out?" I asked, sitting up taller. The chaise sank low when Nik plopped onto it, groaning.

"He's already given them their funds. The deal is done."

I figured as much, but it didn't make the dread any less potent.

"And when do they leave?"

"In three days."

Three days. The day of my swearing in. *Convenient, father*. "And Aceus is going with them?"

"Yes, apparently so."

Not a bluff then. "Is there any chance we can convince them otherwise? Give them another task? Somewhere in Ambrose?"

Nik shook his head, dark hair falling over his eyes. "Caelum is very persistent. They've already gotten their provisions and are tying up loose ends. There's not anything more I can do besides beg for them not to go." Nik glanced at me from the side of his eyes, telling me that begging was not on his list of things to do.

I sat up slowly as an idea sprang to mind. It was a harebrained idea, one of which could cause a mess of trouble, but if I was already going to be thrown to the depths of the Realm of Darkness, I might as well go laughing the whole way down.

My father, the conniving bastard that he was, no doubt expected me to take the brunt of my fall with gasping tears while I begged for mercy. I had always complied with him, but I hadn't lived under his thumb—nor in this castle—in twelve years. What he failed to realize was that he no longer had power over me. Instead, I held the power of the city under my reign.

"Tell them to wait one more day. That they will need to leave after the swearing," I said, trying to formulate this plan that would keep my name from getting tied to treason.

"Why don't you just have them arrested? What they are doing is illegal, after all," Nik suggested.

I shook my head. "They haven't committed a crime, not yet. I won't have my first act as Lady persecuting innocent people." But I did have an idea forming, a small thread that might actually work, and I sat straighter, a smile tugging on my lips.

Nik's piercing blue eyes narrowed on me. "What are you planning beneath that silver head of hair?"

"If my father wants me to be blamed for treason, then I might as well embrace it."

Nik grimaced. "Halcyon, this was *not* what I agreed to. We have to stop it, not encourage it."

I shook my head. "There is no stopping the plans my father set in motion. He was too thorough."

"What are you intending to do?" Nik asked once again, and I only gave him a vicious grin in return.

OUTSIDE OF THE SMALL hall where I waited, I could hear the roar of the crowd beyond the castle gates. Nerves took form as jolts of anxious energy in my fingertips and swoops in my belly.

Shara stood next to me, her hand entwining with my own, as her presence was the only thing that grounding me. I turned to her, meeting her deep brown eyes with gratitude.

"Please meet me in my chambers after the ceremony. I have a request, and need your input," I requested, deliberately not mentioning any details, but with the way her eyes widened, she knew there was more behind my demand than idle chitchat.

"Yes, my lady," she said and ducked her head before fidgeting with the sapphire necklace across my collar bone.

"Halcyon, it's time," Niklaus called, offering his hand to me. I thanked Shara quickly and placed my palm in Nik's, the silver bangles lined with sapphires jangling on my wrist.

The noise of the crowd erupted as I emerged on the mezzanine overlooking Dolan. My father was beaming as I stepped over the threshold, only the smug look in his eyes betraying his joy.

"Ladies and gentlemen, Magi and mortals of Dolan," his voice boomed over the crowd, the cheers quieting as he went on, "I present to you, Lady Halcyon of Dolan! May her reign bring in a new era to our great city!"

The people of Dolan howled in celebration as my father grasped my hand. His firm grip bit into my wrist as he wrenched it upward. I gave the crowd a demure smile. People jumped up and down, their arms flailing in the air. Surprisingly, there hadn't been an outburst of magic yet, but it was only a matter of time.

Father let go of my hand, and I gave the crowd one last parting wave before letting it drop and turning away. I had no reason to stand and bask in the attention of a thousand people who knew nothing about me. This was all a show. An act my father knew would placate the masses with a reason for them all to let loose and yell in the streets. My father followed after me, regardless that I had quickened my pace to get away from him.

"Halcyon!" he bellowed from behind me. I turned, making my features blank so he couldn't see how angry I was at him. The betrayal itself hadn't stung as hard as I thought it might, but Dolan would still suffer for his actions if they didn't go as planned.

"Yes, Father?" I curtsied before him, and his brow rose in disdain.

"Your mother and I leave this evening. You are the Lady of Dolan now. Start acting like one."

"I have already sworn my oaths. Dolan could not be in better hands." My confidence wavered as I was stared down by the same blue eyes I had, but somehow, so much colder.

My father's sneer turned into a bone-chilling grin as he stared down at me. A shiver slithered up my spine. But he didn't know that I already knew he had planned my downfall.

"I expect you will see us off tonight. I suspect it will be the last time we see you."

"No returning trips to see how your city fares under my command?"

He stuck his tongue in his cheek and veered his gaze away from me. "No, I'm afraid your mother and I will be too far to travel back."

"I thought you were just going south to Helos? That's not more than a five-day trip."

"We had a change of plans. Unfortunately, I have been called somewhere else. The kingdom of Elyea is asking for my presence."

"Elyea?" I gasped. The southern country was not quite as limiting to Magi as Tantal, but passage was difficult to acquire. And even more so, it meant that if any crimes were somehow led back to my father, there would be no way for Ambrose to convict him.

Ice-cold fear sludged down my body as he glanced at me once more. "Good luck, *daughter*. You're going to need it."

Chapter 4

HALCYON

My breath caught in my throat, and my mind reeled from the conversation that I just had with my father. The slimy, pompous bastard. And my mother...of course she would just go along with whatever he wanted. She never questioned him or his methods.

From a young age, I had known she married him for his status. There was never any love between them, even in the most intimate settings. But she fulfilled her duties as a wife and birthed an heir. Me.

Looking back, I knew my father wasn't happy to let go of his position. He never gave me any reason to think he believed I was the right person to follow in his footsteps. I mentally kicked myself. I should have seen this coming.

Once he had an heir, it was only until they completed their education when he would be allowed to rule. He managed to put off bearing children for so long, but once I was here, he couldn't prevent his daughter from ruling—short of murder—so he would have to find another way to bring me down and skirt the consequences. It was enough to make my blood boil.

I was sure if he had his way, Dolan would beg for him to come back and see me as an unfit ruler. Unfortunately for him, he was still at the mercy of old laws and a small Council who enforced them. I sighed heavily, releasing my angry energy, instead forcing myself to focus on the task at hand.

Shara was already waiting for me in my bedroom. She stood next to my dressing table, but before I even reached her, I started untying the knots holding my dressings together.

"Allow me, Lady Halcyon." Her voice was timid as she reached for the ribbons.

"Don't start with formality, now. We are still the same friends we have always been," I reassured her.

"You know that isn't true," Shara said sullenly, biting her lip, and I turned to her, taking her hands in mine.

"I don't want our relationship to change. I need you." And I meant it. Shara, who felt like my only ally in this lonely world.

Shara hummed under her breath as she flipped me around by the shoulders.

"You are my best friend, Halcyon, but you are the Lady now. Our relationship cannot be seen other than one of a handmaid and a lady outside these walls."

"I hate it," I confessed with a scowl.

"Me, too. Now, what did you want to talk to me about? I know damned well that you didn't just call me in here to undress you."

I sighed in relief as the silks fell off, quickly replaced with a breathable tunic. My heart beat faster as I turned back to her.

"I need you to do me a favor, and quickly."

"Anything."

"Go down to the kitchens. I need you to bring me more black walnuts than you can count, a large pot, and some lemons." If Shara thought my request was odd, she didn't let on as she nodded, her eyebrows drawn in determination. She was the truest friend, always willing to support my needs without hesitation.

Before she had a chance to leave, I called back to her. "Niklaus will be here by the time you get back, but you are not to submit yourself to him as you normally do. Today, he is your equal." At that, she inhaled sharply, but said no more as she turned to the door and walked out.

The silence from Shara's exit was a welcome reprieve. I took a deep breath. I wasn't entirely sure I was making the right decision, but I also knew I had never felt more motivated.

My father had never wanted me to be his heir, and I severely underestimated how far he would go to see me flounder. It was unfortunate for him that in his deceptive plan, I saw a new opportunity.

The timing was not ideal, but it made my heart race. My heart hadn't raced in ages. Not for my duty, not for a man, but these files Nik had left me made me *want* again.

I chewed my lip as I opened the curtains to the wide window, letting the reds and purples of the dusk sunset stream through. I loved how the sunlight cast across my room, bathing my bed canopy and all the fresh flowers I kept along the various surfaces in gold.

Niklaus didn't even bother to knock as he barged into the room, and I couldn't help but laugh at his wide grin. In his hands was a bottle of sparkling wine and two glasses.

"A big congratulation, cousin!" He placed a light kiss on my cheek before setting the glasses down on my white tea table.

"Don't celebrate quite yet," I told him.

"I know things are bad right now, but I'll make sure we get through this as smoothly as possible." The bottle popped loudly as he removed the cork. A sign of celebration, but I just couldn't feel the joy.

"No, you won't," I said.

Nik narrowed his eyes at me, and I took the glass of wine from his hand. I chilled it with my magic before sipping, the bubbles tingling my throat.

"I have a plan, but you will not like it," I admitted.

"Tell me."

Biting my bottom lip, I took a deep inhale. "You must swear that nothing I say leaves this room, and you must do everything exactly as I say."

"How can I, if I don't know what you are planning?"

I sighed heavily, watching as confusion crossed his features. "This is how you gain my trust, Niklaus. If you are not willing to do this for me, then I must insist I find a new advisor." It was a bluff. One I hoped he wouldn't call me out on because the truth was that I didn't want to find another advisor. I spent the last night tossing and turning as I thought all about how much Nik had really done for me, and I decided that out of anyone in the court, he was the one I could trust the most. Rage-induced doubts aside.

"Fine. Now, tell me what it is you need," he agreed and took a seat on my light blue chaise.

Shara arrived back in the chambers, two large pots in her hands filled with walnuts and lemons. She placed the pots near the fireplace and bowed in my direction before heading for the exit.

"Shara, you are to stay here. Remember what I said before you left?"

She nodded and turned back toward us, and I beckoned her to have a seat. She sat next to Nik, but keeping enough space between them to where I could feel the tension in her posture. Pacing in front of the fireplace, I gathered my thoughts.

"We have one chance—one that I can't guarantee will work—but in order to upset the path my father has laid down, we must ensure the safety of that crew, and my bodyguard."

"Halcyon—" Nik tried to interject, but I waved his words away with my hand.

"I have read the report so many times I have it memorized. My father may be trying to undermine my position, but he isn't wrong. If there is, in fact, a temple across the border, then we need to get our hands on it."

Pinning Niklaus with my most resolute gaze, I told him determinately, "I need you to cover for me while I travel with the crew. I have to go to the temple and see it for myself."

"Halcyon, this is insanity," Niklaus balked, his mouth falling open in disbelief.

"Three weeks. I need you to cover for me for three weeks." I held up three fingers just to emphasize my point.

"And what of our laws?" Niklaus steepled his hands on his knees, watching me keenly with eyes that never stopped thinking.

"The other Lords and Ladies of Ambrose will charge me with treason by giving them funds to go. If this will already reflect on my rule, then I may as well commit the crimes I am supposedly responsible for."

"It's your father who is committing the crime. He will be held responsible," Niklaus placated, but I shook my head.

"My parents are leaving for Elyea. Once they cross the border, I'll be the only one to answer."

Niklaus groaned, and I could see his teeth grinding as he pursed his lips.

"Lady, if I may," Shara cut in, her face pale. "What happens if you don't survive the trip or if you get caught by the mortal kingdom?"

"Then my name shall be one of an Ambrose traitor, and Niklaus will take my role as Lord of Dolan."

"What you're asking for is absurd!" His face contorted into confusion, his cheeks reddening at the possibility.

"I have no heirs; I have no siblings. Therefore, you *will* be Lord if anything were to happen to me. Or, leave it up to a vote as they do in Aurum." Inhaling through my nose, I centered my thoughts. I would have preferred an election, regardless. Surely, if Aurum could do it and find peace, then Dolan could, too.

"You're not entirely wrong on that point. I won't lie, I have thought about what would happen if I was to step in as Lord." Niklaus mulled over my proposition, his shock turning into intrigue. He couldn't deny now that I had been sworn in, there was no way for my father to legally resume his reign. So, if I died under rule—right now—Niklaus would have to step in, at least as interim. Then the council would make a decision from there. With my father out of the country, he was burning the city to the ground, dusting his hands of this place, and me along with it.

"Good. It's possibility that you need to take seriously. I am counting on you in more ways than just my advisor." Niklaus nodded, and I took a deep breath. "That being said, while I am gone, it is imperative the public does not realize I'm missing."

Nik snorted. "And how do you suppose we manage that?"

"With these—" I gestured to the items Shara had brought up. "Shara, I have never asked something so risky of you before, and you are free to tell me no, but I trust you and value you. I am begging for your help."

"What do you mean, Halcyon?" she asked, her eyes shifting to Nik as she spoke.

"I need you to pose as me while I am gone. Nik, I need you to make sure that in the next three weeks I will not be scheduled for any public appearances, and there will be no reason for anyone to question why I am not visible to the public eye."

"You just swore in, you are asking for an impossible task—"

"I'll do it." Shara's determination surprised me. Gratitude for my friend swelled in my chest, and I smiled back at her.

"No! Absolutely not. This is insanity!" Niklaus' restraint had finally snapped. His scowl deepened as he swung his gaze between the two of us. The hairs on my arms stood on end, and I lifted my brow as Nik momentarily lost control of his magic. Just as quickly, the feeling was gone as he managed to rein it in. "If the mortal kingdom catches you—catches a single *whiff* of you—then the treaty we have in place is null and void. War would be on our doorstep. Three rogue explorers we can explain away, but I *cannot* explain why the Lady of Dolan is in the mortal kingdom!"

"Nik," I placated, although I could feel my temper rising from his response. "This is why Shara will stand-in for me. I will not be going as Lady, but as someone else entirely. Someone whose identity does not matter. As far as anyone else knows, I will still be here." I paused, waiting until the redness faded from Nik's cheeks, but his hardened gaze never softened. "We are going to lighten Shara's hair, and she will make herself seen on the grounds, but not close enough for anyone to get a good look."

"This will never work! Halcyon, please. I am asking you to listen to reason." Niklaus stood, his height giving him an edge over me as he tugged at the roots of his hair.

The glass in my hand shattered as ice consumed it. I didn't even register that the glass had cut my skin, but red drops of blood fell to the stone floor.

Shara jumped up, off to get a towel, and I stared Niklaus down.

"I am nothing but a sitting duck waiting to be slaughtered by Ambrose's High Council. If I go, I at least will have the chance to give a first-person recount. And then I can be blamed solely, rather than Dolan becoming overruled with another Lord taking our land from us. If I stay, they will see me as unfit and as a traitor."

"If you go, they will see you as unfit and a traitor," he countered.

"If I go, and come back with evidence that the mortal kingdom is harboring *our* history, then I can convince them that—"

"You will end up convincing them of nothing," he snarled, bright spots of lightning sparking around his hands.

Ice flared from my body, encasing the floor beneath me. Nik didn't bat an eye, but Shara shuddered. "I am the Lady of Dolan, am I not?"

"You are, but—"

"Then I. Am. *Going*. That is my final word." We stood chest to chest, staring at one another, neither one of us willing to back down. I held Niklaus' gaze for several moments until he finally relented and sighed before taking his seat.

"Why do you want to do this so badly? We can send anyone. Why do you choose to send yourself?"

"Because I can't trust anyone else. They could take what they find to any other city and leave Dolan in the dust, and then we would have nothing to prove the venture was worth it. I am powerful enough with my magic to protect myself. I had high marks in both defensive and offensive magic. Besides, Aceus is already set to go, and he is sworn to protect me. If we must run at some point, we will be safer together."

I could tell that Niklaus wanted to keep fighting me on this, but I wouldn't allow him any more argument. Huffing out a breath, I said, "I don't know what else to tell you, but this is my word. Three weeks. If I am gone longer, then you may reveal this secret in the way you see fit."

In one of the large pots, black walnuts boiled in the fireplace. It smelled surprisingly like citrus, but it could have been from the lemons Shara was currently cutting and squeezing into another pot.

"That should be enough," I told her. She settled in the chair before my ornate mirror.

Generously, I applied the lemon juice to her hair, starting with the ends. I wasn't entirely sure it would lighten her brown hair enough to become silver like my own, but it would have to be passable enough.

"You said goodbye to your parents?" Shara asked, cutting through the silence. Nodding my confirmation, I kept silent, not willing to rehash their farewell.

It wasn't an extravagant affair, anyhow. There was no crowd, no procession to see them off. Instead, my father chose to exit quietly from the city he had overseen for the last hundred years. My mother pressed light kisses on my cheeks and wished me well, but there were no tears to be had. If anything, I thought she was more than ready to be released from the burden of her duties. Finally able to let this life go. It was her version of freedom, and I couldn't blame her for it in the slightest. Raised by servants, and then carted off to Neverwind for my studies, I felt as though I barely knew her, much less cared for her on a motherly level.

Golden strands pulled through Shara's hair as I worked it, and I breathed a sigh of relief. Once it was all applied, it was my turn.

"Are you absolutely sure about this?" Shara asked timidly.

"Yes. But you don't need to be. You can go to the library and seek refuge there if you would feel more comfortable." I met Shara's gaze in the mirror, taking in the sad smile she wore as she removed the pair of lambskin gloves from her hands.

She chuckled. "No, I would go to the ends of the world for you, Halcyon."

"I appreciate you more than I normally articulate."

"I know. It shows through your constant kindness. I see how other servants are treated elsewhere in this castle."

"You are more than a servant to me, and I don't ever want to be like my father," I muttered.

Shara patted my shoulder as she reassured me. "You could never be like him."

When we rinsed, I had never seen my hair so dark before. It gave my skin a pallor that washed away the starkness of my bright blue eyes.

Shara's hadn't quite reached the silver of mine, but it was a good, pale yellow. It was actually a lovely color on her and made her pink cheeks look even more cheery than usual.

"Well, you look stunning as both a blonde and a brunette," I told Shara with a grin. She only glanced at me, her cheeks turning tomato red at the compliment.

"I almost like it," she admitted, biting her bottom lip before cracking a smile. Eventually her smile turned into a giggle, and then we were both laughing at the ridiculous reflections that stared back at us in the mirror.

Being with each other like this, it was almost like we were back at the library studying together, and I bathed in the familiarity. It was finally something that felt normal before I made the hastiest decision of my life.

"HALCYON, IT'S TIME." SHARA stood over me, her voice soft as she woke me up from my restless night's sleep. We stayed awake far too late after our hair dyeing. Eventually, we held each other with tears streaming down our faces until I fell asleep.

"Thank you," I mumbled and removed myself from my sheets.

"I brought you a cloak, and Niklaus is with Aceus in the hall."

I nodded, pulling on dark travel pants and a brown top, and I gave her one last embrace.

"Thank you so much for this. I don't know how I could ever repay you," I told her as I embraced her, soaking in the warmth from her arms.

"You don't need to repay me. Just come back alive."

"I will," I promised.

Shara stayed in my room and nodded to me one last time as I exited, the cloak hood pulled over my head. My hair was dark, but I didn't want any reason for anyone to ask questions.

Aceus grunted in greeting, Niklaus having filled him in on the details already.

"It's time for you to go. Are you ready?" Worry lined Niklaus' eyes, and I nodded. "I can't say I enjoy this idea," he stated once again, trying to convince me to stay.

"Too bad you don't have a choice in it, then," I replied.

"Three weeks, Halcyon." He turned to me, stopping me atop the stairs that led us from the castle into the city.

"Three weeks," I agreed. He turned back, and I followed him into the city of Dolan.

How much had I given up for this city? Countless nights and weekends had been spent dedicating my time to the people. Rejected relationships and friendships lost in the name of fulfilling my destiny. This would be no different. It was just another way to serve and uphold my city.

Walking through the city streets in my disguise made my heart beat rapidly, even though the early morning was quiet. I kept expecting to see people stand and stare, kept waiting for the moment someone saw right through me and pointed out that I was the newly appointed Lady.

None of that happened, and eventually my chest loosened. Our footsteps crunched along the path were a peace bell and it allowed me to take steadying breaths. Was Niklaus right? Was I crazy for stepping outside my castle walls?

Doubt niggled in the back of my mind, but just as quickly, I locked it in a box and shoved it away. Dolan needed this. *I* needed this. And more importantly, my father would never control my fate.

Chapter 5

CAELUM

THE SUN WARMED MY skin as I stood in the same town square that had hundreds of people witnessing the new Lady's swearing in the day before.

I had watched the new Lady—Halcyon was her name—as I eagerly bit into a delicious pastry standing in the back of the growing crowd. When Lord Alastair announced his heir, I hadn't heard the words spoken so much as the roaring and shouting of the people in the city. Her silver hair gleamed against the sunlight, along with the silver, sapphires, and diamonds she was adorned with, and she looked like a long-lost goddess.

Her blue dress fluttered in the breeze, and while I couldn't see if she smiled, she bowed her head and waved. The crowd went wild.

Just as quickly as she had come out, she ducked back inside, and I found myself waiting to see if she would make another appearance. If only for another glimpse of her sunlit silver hair.

The public apparently loved Lady Halcyon. I had overheard a few mer-chants speaking about some outreach projects she had done during her studies. Her work was remarkable, but my only worry was that she would disapprove of the expedition. And she did.

The Dolan advisor, Niklaus, found me—along with Iris and May—at the tavern, where he tried to convince us this trip was a mistake. Unfortunately for him, I was having none of it. I was going to the temple, and they would have to kill me to stop me. No other city had even given us the chance to plead for our case. Any time they heard about the mortal kingdom, we were met with slammed doors and mockery.

He did, however, convince me to agree to wait another day so we weren't leaving on a day of such importance and fanfare. I had to agree, as the atmosphere was just teeming with celebration.

Laughter and singing rang throughout the city until late in the evening, and a small part of me missed belonging to a community. I hadn't called a place 'home' as far as I could remember. But now was not the time to long for something I couldn't have. There was still so much work to do.

Hidden behind an inn on the outskirts of Dolan was a small outpost where we took inventory and sorted through all our items. A lazy breeze drifted through the tall trees surrounding us, and the light chirps of birds sang the song of the early morning. I smirked against the dewy breeze, hope fluttering in my chest as it caressed my skin.

I liked Dolan, for the small time I had spent here. Having only ever been up to the library one time in the past, I only had the chance to delve into their many books and maps and artifacts, so I hadn't appreciated the beautiful landscape the city offered.

Dolan was near the sharp, treacherous peaks of the Jagged Border. The black rock, pointed and stacked on top of each other like knives spearing the sky, serving as a natural border between Ambrose and Tantal. The mountains were nigh inhabitable and was as much of a warning as it was a death sentence. Those brave enough to traverse over the peaks were often not heard from again, and it was deemed impassable unless you had a way to fly above it, or in our case, below.

"Cal!" Maya waved me down as I made my way toward our meetup spot. Her black hair was messy in its braid, and her dark eyes crinkled in a friendly smile. She sat amongst bottles and dried herbs, as she noted exact amounts of each before piling them gently into a crate her horse would carry.

I raked my hands through my hair and blew out a breath.

"Whew, this is a lot of stuff," I said as I noted crates of dried food Iris was piling into a small wagon.

Maya stood, placing a hand on her hip and nodding. "Well, we won't be able to get anything once we are over the border, so better to be prepared than starving." She dusted the dirt off her pants, stray bits of grass clinging to the dark fabric.

I laughed. "I doubt you would ever let us starve, no matter the circumstances."

"I'm a witch, not a miracle worker," she muttered.

"Same thing." I shrugged and handed Maya a small bag filled with pastries we wouldn't get for another while. They weren't exactly sustainable for travel, but when indulgences were as rare as they were for us, I never shied away from it. "Here, I brought breakfast."

Maya's eyes lit up as she dug in, taking a big bite before wiping a small crumb from the corner of her lips.

"You really know how to make a girl happy," she said with an expression of bliss on her face.

"Oh yeah? And how is that?" I asked, snagging one for myself.

"Chocolate." She practically moaned as she took another bite.

"Damn. If I had known it would be that easy, maybe I wouldn't be the odd one out anymore." Not that I minded being the third wheel in our little group, but I couldn't lie that the loneliness did hit me from time to time.

Maya smirked up at me. "We both know it's not the lack of chocolate that's keeping you perpetually alone."

"Please, enlighten me on why I'm destined to live my life trailing behind as I watch you and Iris make doey love eyes at each other constantly."

Maya swallowed her last bite and licked her fingers before standing. "Because you're too afraid of what will happen if you allow anyone in that stone heart of yours."

"Ouch," I muttered, rubbing my chest.

"You asked!" Maya laughed, and I gave her a playful shove on her shoulder.

Gravel crunched behind me, and I turned to see Niklaus emerge from the town path. Behind him was a hulking man with beefy arms and a bald head shining like a glimmering, polished gemstone. His long mustache was styled to curl on the ends, and it immediately made me smile. This man had to be the appointed chaperone they were sending us with, but I wasn't exactly sure how he planned on keeping his mustache in tip-top shape for three weeks.

On Niklaus' other side was a woman who looked like she could be his sibling. They both had dark hair, fair skin, and bright blue eyes the color of glaciers.

She looked vaguely familiar, but I was sure I had never seen her before. Either way, she was stunning, but as she pinned me in her gaze, I felt the prickling sensation of being appraised.

Niklaus offered me his hand, and I shook it with a firm grasp.

"Looks like you've got everything. Are you sure you're ready to cross the border?" Niklaus asked while I studied him. He was all harsh lines, but I thought I could see worry underneath it all, especially with the way he kept glancing at the woman.

"As ready as we will ever be." There was no backing out. The temple was too important, too precious to be left to the mortals who didn't have any need or want for it.

Leading them through our supplies, I explained a brief plan for our trip.

Niklaus moved through the crates thoughtfully. "This is a lot of weapons for a seemingly peaceful trip." He picked up a sword I procured. Unsheathing the blade, he studied it in the early morning sunlight, the bright rays gleaming against the metal.

"It's never a bad idea to be prepared." I shrugged. We all knew the potential dangers of this expedition, even if none of us were willing to voice them. Even treading through Ambrose could be treacherous at times, especially trekking through less traveled land. Dragons aside, there were plenty of beasts we could potentially run into. Some were more avoidable than others, but we had previously encountered bobcats, wild dogs, and even had an unfortunate run in with a bear.

Entering the mortal kingdom, though? I didn't particularly think we would see anything out of the usual from Ambrose—wilderness was wilderness after all—but there was the looming possibility of something more sinister. *Dragon Riders.* It made me anxious, but not nearly anxious enough to back down.

Niklaus raised an eyebrow at me and then glanced back down at the woman. She nodded tightly, and he sighed.

"There is one matter we have yet to discuss," he gestured to the woman, and she bowed her head in greeting. "This is Lydia. She is an impeccable scholar and should serve you well in your findings. The newly appointed Lady insisted she join you. Lydia—along with Aceus—will serve as both an asset and collateral. If they do not return unharmed, then you can expect Lady Halcyon will respond in kind. Starting with a warrant for your death across Ambrose."

I swallowed thickly, chancing a look at the brunette before me. Her blue eyes pierced through me. Was adding another person onto this team really the best idea? Probably not. Did I have another choice? Also, probably not. The most important question, however, was whether she could keep up with us.

Certainly, Lydia didn't look like the type of woman who had spent much time in wild forests. Her fair skin was smooth and free of blemishes, and she watched with her hands clasped in front of her as Maya and Iris flitted behind me.

Although, the way she held herself piqued my interest. She stood straight, determined to follow through with whatever orders her Lady had given her. There was no resentment on her face, only readiness and conviction. Maybe not just an extra body, then.

She swung her gaze around, mentally taking everything in before blowing out a breath. In another life, I would have tried to vie for her attention. Her beauty alone was captivating, her confidence alluring. But in this life, I couldn't even entertain the idea. No matter how those striking cerulean eyes threatened to drown me.

"We'll need another horse," I noted.

Niklaus clicked his tongue. "It won't be a problem. I sent for one on the walk over. As soon as it arrives, you'll be off."

I nodded in agreement, understanding that bringing Lydia would just be one more price to pay to find my answers.

Holding out my hand to him, we shook again, and I gave him a grin. Lydia stepped forward, and I smiled down at her, knowing my feelings had no influence on whether she was coming with us. She held her own hand out, curiosity written all over her face.

"You must be Caelum. I know it's last minute to have me come along, but I hope my expertise will be of value." Her hand was cold and soft as I grasped it.

Iris hopped out of the wagon, greeting us with a wide smile. She pushed one of her braids of black hair out of her face, smudging some dirt on her dark brown cheeks.

"Caelum," she called, "we're almost ready. Would you mind loading up this last of the crates? I'll get the horses." Before I could respond, Iris was off greeting the man who tugged a brown mare behind him. I shook my head, and reached for a box that held more weapons.

Iris took a lot of pride in how she handled the animals. It had been a long time since I had even questioned her methods. She was very particular with their treatment, and I knew better than to even ask if she needed my help.

As I stacked crates in the wagon, I noticed Lydia and Niklaus speaking in hushed tones. Niklaus was frowning, but Lydia looked determined. Meanwhile, Aceus seemed almost bored as he stood beside them, his gaze roaming beyond us like he was constantly surveilling.

"Everything alright over here?" I asked, dusting off my hands on my pants.

"Yes, we're fine," Lydia said, turning toward me and smiling, although it didn't reach her eyes. Her hands clenched into fists, but as if she noticed where my gaze had traveled, she loosened her palms. "Can you take me to the horses, please?"

There was a lilt of formality to Lydia's speech, and I wondered how long she had been a scholar, and for whom she served. If she came from the castle, it was likely she served the Lord or Lady, but seeing as the advisor brought her here...

My head hurt with the thoughts of the inner workings of politics, and I was more eager than ever to leave Dolan.

Lydia, Aceus, and Niklaus followed me to the horses, and I beckoned Lydia to the sturdy Kusharian. The bright auburn bay shook out her black mane as we approached.

Iris was checking the saddle as we walked up, and she greeted Lydia with a wide smile. "I'm Iris, animal caretaker and all-around smartest one of this group." She winked at Lydia, who gave her a shy smirk. Shoving her shoulder lightly, Iris laughed. "This is Calliope. She will be yours for the duration of our travel."

Lydia's eyes grew wide, and I couldn't help the smirk on my lips. "Are you able to ride a horse?" I asked.

"Yes," she said hesitantly, "it's been a while, but I'm sure the muscle memory remains."

"You'll catch on quickly," I reassured her, and I had no doubt she would. Given that most of this trip would be at the temple, I anticipated little heavy riding. If we were trying to cross the sands leading past Aurum, I may have felt differently, but with the wagon, we would be slow moving regardless.

Confident Lydia was settling in, her long fingers running against Calliope's coat as she muttered soft praises under her breath, I made my way to Maya once again, checking everything over. Iris followed me after she was sure Lydia was comfortable around Calliope, and her smile faded.

"Are you sure about bringing the girl?" Maya's rich voice was hushed.

Iris bit her lip as she looked between us. "Caelum, even I'm hesitant. Another person to add on is more risk."

I shook my head. "We don't have a choice," I grumbled, but they still looked skeptical. Maya slid her gaze from where Lydia and Niklaus were exchanging goodbyes. "I packed enough provisions, and she brought some of her own, so it shouldn't be a problem, but I won't play mother to her. She's your responsibility, Cal."

"I can agree with that." I nodded. "There's no reason to put your lives in front of hers. She has her bodyguard."

Iris tsked. "Chances are if something happens to her, we will all be in peril."

"Let's just pray to the gods for smooth travel, then." Not that I was especially religious, but with the mortal kingdom, I would take every boon available. We broke apart from each other, and Lydia and Aceus strode toward us. I greeted her with a smile, and she returned my greeting with a cold stare and a slight frown.

"Are you ready?" I asked with a smirk.

"As ready as I'll be," she sighed.

"Don't worry," I reassured her, placing my hand on her shoulder. She glanced down at it, but did not try to move away, and the small patch of skin on her neck was just as soft under my touch as it looked. I yanked my hand away, quickly brushing back strands of hair that fell in front of my face.

"We are going to go slow, and you have the rest of us if you need help. This is a team effort." I winked at her, and she seemed to relax, blowing out a long exhale before offering me a small smile.

Regardless of the slight change of plans, my mood didn't falter. This was the trip of a thousand Magi lives. To go into the mortal kingdom and come back with treasures that would tell us more about our history—possibly our origins. It could change the course of Ambrose forever.

Chapter 6

HALCYON

I SPENT THE FIRST two hours trying to adjust myself without squirming too much. Caelum's horse was too close for my comfort, and I could feel his rich hazel eyes watching me as though he was waiting for me to fall off. Every time I caught him looking, he would either smirk at me, or veer his gaze away with a quick rake of his fingers through his brown hair.

Gods, he was handsome. Far too handsome for someone who supposedly spent their lifetime with their head in a book or hands in the sand. I imagined if I lived a different life, I would be more than happy to spend time in his company. As it was, he was absolutely off-limits for someone with my title.

We kept riding, but now my thighs ached, my abdominals throbbed, and my back was tight with knots from trying to stay as upright as possible. Calliope was steady underneath me, dutifully following the lead of the other, larger horses. The handler who brought her over made a good choice. It was as though she wasn't bothered by unfamiliar riders at all.

We would have to stop at some point, but I wasn't willing to ask when. Already, I could tell I was an unwelcome guest, even though they tried to make it seem otherwise. They watched me too closely, and we were traveling too slowly.

The trees were getting thicker the longer we traveled, and even though the sun was high and the clouds were spotty against the sky, it was quite dark in the forest's shade.

A shiver wracked me as I fought to think of the last time in my life when I had been so far from my home. Of course, I had traveled to many cities across Ambrose, but those always promised a return. This felt more permanent. It was more like I was saying 'goodbye' rather than 'I'll be back soon.'

Neverwind Library was the farthest I had ever stayed for an extended time period, and it was less than a day's travel away. Seeing the dark limbs of the trees reaching above, covering us with spotted shade, only made me more aware of how far I was from the comfort of my castle.

The mortal kingdom terrified me, even if I would never allow myself to admit it aloud. Instead, I forced myself to place my worries in a small box, locking it up in the back of my mind, never to be opened again.

"Are you cold, Lydia?" Caelum asked, and I shifted slightly, trying to find a reprieve from the numbing of my rear end.

"No." I sighed. "I've never been so far from home, and I'm just now realizing it." I turned to see Caelum's face, and he gave me a small smile. His dark brown hair was shorn on the sides, but longer on top. Pieces would fall into his eyes, but I noticed he would push it back with his fingers frequently. He smiled casually, making jokes with the other women. A testament to how closely they worked together.

Caelum nodded with a softness in his eyes. He shifted on his horse, and I couldn't help but track how his muscular thighs flexed as he leaned toward me.

"It's really not so bad." Caelum's voice was low and quiet, his words only meant for me. "You'll see things you would have never seen otherwise, and living off the land is one of our specialties."

"What do you mean?" I asked breathlessly, surprised by the kindness which flowed from his words, and the reassurance he seemed to understand I needed.

"We've been traveling like this for years. You couldn't be with a safer crew." Caelum nodded at Maya, who was gleefully riding her horse, staring at the trees above. "Maya is practically a part of the earth herself. She knows all the plants, whether edible, medicinal, or poisonous. She can make a healing potion out of nothing."

"That's not true!" Maya shouted.

"Damn, woman!" Caelum cursed. "How do you hear so well?"

She laughed and trotted next to us. "It's my witchy powers." She waved her fingers in our direction and winked. "He's not as quiet as he thinks he is." I bit my lip at her joke, sparing a glance at Caelum through my lashes.

Caelum sighed and rubbed his hand along his chin. It looked like he had shaved recently, but there was a shadow of facial hair along his sharp jawline.

Iris shouted from her position on the wagon, "This is the best part about travel. It's so peaceful—"

"It's *boring*." Maya cut in with an eye roll.

I glanced back at Aceus, who was quietly riding along behind us. He winked at me, clearly not sharing the same apprehension I had.

I supposed it was pretty peaceful, but my thoughts hadn't quieted. Here I was, in the wild with complete strangers. Had I made a mistake? For a moment, I forgot about the danger of the mortal kingdom. Instead, the dread of the very real risk of being kidnapped by these people sank into my stomach. If they knew who I was...even an inkling could cause me very real harm.

Even if Aceus could fight them off, what were our chances of getting back? Aceus was an incredible fighter, but he was still mortal, and according to my father's files, the rest were Magi. Caelum had the power of earth wielding, a simple elemental power. Iris' powers were unique, and while the file was vague, it seemed like she could track animals. Maya's powers were listed as unknown, which I initially thought was interesting, but now it only struck fear in my heart.

Dense woods only furthered my dark thoughts. What if they killed Aceus, kidnapped me, and fed me to the bears and bobcats? I swallowed thickly, trying to banish the feeling of impending doom that coursed through my entire body.

The surrounding forest grew darker the longer we went on, and I was hyper aware of every sound that came from the mysterious trees beyond.

"The sun will set soon. We should find a place to camp out." Maya nodded toward the dark forest in front of them.

I lifted my eyebrow. "It's still early. We've barely been on the road for more than a few hours."

Caelum shook his head. "Because we are so close to the Jagged Peaks, it gets darker earlier."

My stomach turned with unease. We kept going until our shadows grew longer. Until the sky was purple and dark blue between the many leaves above us.

"We will stop here and make camp." Caelum slid out of his saddle with grace, and I studied him as he took in the surroundings. He pulled his broad shoulders back, and a smirk tugged on his lips, revealing a dimple in his cheek and a glimmer in his eye.

Atop the horse, I watched as the crew unloaded bedrolls and Maya set up a fire in a clearing between trees. She piled pieces of wood in a pit she dug and sparked a flame. Crackling and smoke grew, and a fire lit the area in a warm glow.

"Here, let me help you down." Caelum's voice made me jump. I had been so focused on Maya, I didn't even hear him walk up to me. With his hands held out to brace me, I inhaled deeply, accepting I had made my decision to be here, and now I needed to accept it.

Swinging my leg over, I made to hurtle myself from the saddle, but my legs were aching and I slipped. Before I could right myself, the world tilted on its side. Caelum's reflexes were quick, and he caught me by my hips with a small *oof*.

Wrapping my arms around him for support, his strength was evident underneath my touch. I stole the moment to glance at his lips—which looked so soft—and my cheeks heated. Clearing my throat, I pushed him away.

"Sorry about that," I muttered. Caelum chuckled, but didn't say anything else as he strode to the fire.

I patted Calliope, letting myself feel the soft brown hair around her eyes until Iris came over and took the reins to lead her to where she tied off the other horses.

The pleasant temperature of the day dropped to a chill, and I gravitated toward the fire. Maya was still there, putting fresh vegetables into a metal pan.

"You didn't use magic for the fire," I observed, not so subtly needling her about her abilities.

Maya looked up with a broad smile. The fire reflected in her dark eyes. "I don't have any magic." She shrugged.

"You're a mortal?" I asked, confused. The parchment my father had clearly stated she was Magi.

"I'm not." Maya grinned. The light flickered against her face making her whips of dark hair framing her round face gleam red. "I'm a witch." Her voice filled with pride. My mouth popped open, realizing the joke she made earlier was not a joke at all.

I regarded her with curiosity, but it made sense. She would have been a Magi from birth, but if she hadn't reported her powers after she manifested them, there would be no record of it. "Witches are rare. You gave up your powers? Why?"

Feet crunched behind me as Aceus plopped on the ground next to me with an audible *thud*. "Is she getting nosy?" The question was directed at Maya as he threw a thumb in my direction. She smirked back at him, her black hair swaying as she shook her head.

I glared at Aceus, but he only chuckled. Aceus may have been my bodyguard in the castle, but I hated to admit: I barely knew him. He was my father's guard up until I returned for my swearing in. He was always polite, but truthfully, I didn't mind seeing this bolder Aceus who knew he could get away with speaking his mind.

Regardless, I never met a witch before, and it intrigued me. The path required a Magi to give up their powers to gain a sort of wisdom instead. What kind of wisdom I didn't know, but I wanted to.

Maya's smile didn't falter as she watched us, but I didn't miss her gaze dart to the others before she finally responded to my question. "A story for another time." She went back to stirring her pot over the fire before announcing, "I hope you are all hungry. I made plenty of food for dinner."

The steam from the pot melded with the smoke from the fire, and I could smell spices in the air. Earthy and sweet, but not overpowering or unpleasant. Caelum appeared on my other side and handed me a water skin.

"Here," he said, "you should hydrate."

I took the water skin graciously, and poured the water into my mouth, not realizing how parched I actually was. The liquid ran down my throat and quenched the dry feeling underneath. I handed it back to him, thanking him quietly as Maya handed me a plate of hot vegetables.

Maya's dinner was absolutely delicious. Each bite was packed with unique flavors, even though she made it from threadbare items.

"You made this with only the stuff we could bring?" Dried meats and threadbare provisions were the only items I had seen.

Maya sat across the fire, taking nibbles of her own food with a small smile on her face. "I foraged the forest after we settled. The ground is ripe with aromatic herbs, if you know where to look. Even in the late seasons."

"You picked all of this yourself?" I gazed across the forest floor. It looked like a bunch of sticks, leaves, and dirt. I wouldn't know an edible plant if it ate me first.

Maya nodded, "I did. It's part of the wisdom the goddess bestows when you become a witch."

I scrunched up my nose. "The gods are all dead."

Maya's smile down turned, and Iris let out a scoff as she took a seat next to Maya. Her braids were tied back, and I noticed stray pieces of hay clinging to her black tunic. Maya handed her a plate, and she took it was a chaste kiss to her cheek. Caelum nudged his shoulder into my own.

"Asleep," he corrected, "not dead. If they were dead, then Magi would have nothing more than mortals."

"You think the gods are slumbering," I deadpanned. "Just taking a nap? And for what? So they don't have to deal with the constant nagging prayers from their children?"

"Or," Caelum grinned. The fire cast flickering reds and oranges over his face, making his smile look almost devious. Like he knew something no one else did. "They can't wake up. Trapped in a slumber, waiting for someone to wake them." He whispered it like a children's story made to frighten them into behaving.

Aceus nodded his head in agreement, and I couldn't help but scoff. I narrowed my eyes and shifted on the log underneath me. "Really Aceus?

You're falling for this, too? I've read countless texts about the gods. None of them mention anything about them slumbering."

Aceus shrugged, and his mustache twitched in amusement. I wasn't sure if he was jesting with me or being completely serious. Either way, it earned some appreciation from Maya and Iris, who both warmed up to Aceus while we ate.

"They don't mention anything about them being dead, either." Caelum pointed out, and I opened my mouth to refute him, but as I thought about it, I realized he was right.

"But if they are sleeping, then why haven't they woken up?" I asked with exasperation.

"That's what we would like to find out," Iris agreed, and Caelum's smile gleamed in the dim light.

Aceus' gaze roved over us all, his hand drifting over his bare scalp, interest written all over his face. When his eyes met Maya's, she bit her lip and glanced away from him. Was I seriously the only one here who didn't believe that the gods were still alive?

I hummed out a noise, considering Caelum's hypothesis as I returned my focus to my food. Iris and Aceus fell into a deep whispered discussion which I couldn't overhear from the crackling fire and cicadas. He let out a roaring laugh, and I had to admit I was glad our companions were pleasant.

I was acutely aware of how close Caelum sat next to me, his thighs nearly brushing mine. I tried not to flinch as I felt him look down at me. Content to ignore the tingling sensation of awareness that shot through me, I placed my now empty plate on the ground and dusted off my hands.

"So, how does one become a Lady's designated researcher?" Caelum asked, his brown eyes staring at me inquisitively, and it made me feel rather exposed. Was he questioning my credentials? Did he not believe the Lady of Dolan would have employed a researcher? My heart raced at the thought—because I certainly did *not*.

But what made my heart race even faster was the thought of whether he could possibly know I was an imposter. My ears burned, and I was grateful for the fire which heated my whole body, so he couldn't see the evidence of my lies in the flush of my skin.

No, he couldn't know. He was, of course, just asking to be polite—to know who he was traveling with.

Steeling myself, I shrugged. "I studied alongside her at the Library." I had put some thought into how I would respond if I was asked about my profession, and I decided I would keep it as close to the truth as possible.

There was no need to lie more than I needed to keep my identity a secret. I was an exceptional student, ranking at the top of my classes, so there would be no reason to believe I wouldn't be capable of maintaining an advisor's status.

"I specialized in politics, but my interests lie in history." Another truth buried beneath the lie.

Caelum's eyes sparkled, and he leaned closer to me, his thumb tracing his bottom lip in a way that had my mouth drying. "Is that why the Lady sent you with us?"

I smirked, quite enjoying the fact he didn't know who I was. "Lady Halcyon has her reasons. This trip is treasonous, you know."

"So she sent you here to, what? Make sure we succeed?" His brown eyes questioning Lady Halcyon's—my—motives. Guilt sank into my gut for the first time, but my feelings on the matter were irrelevant.

"Or make sure it doesn't lead back to her if you don't." I bit my lip at the small admission, but Caelum only leaned in further. My breath hitched as his eyes burrowed into mine. The hand he had slung over his knee brushed against my thigh and I shivered from the electric current his one little touch made course through my body.

"And what does history tell us about those who commit the crime of trespassing and become traitors to Ambrose?" he mused.

"Most of them are never heard from again, and if they are, then they are tried and punished accordingly." I squirmed under his penetrating gaze. My breaths became heavy, but as my body was leaning ever so slightly closer, he pulled away, leaving me bereft in the coldness of his absence.

"What about traitors who find themselves on the mortal kingdom's chopping block?" There was an untold question hidden beneath his words. *What would happen if the mortal kingdom captures us?*

I blinked, trying to think about anything other than the way Caelum's lips looked so soft in our closeness. Clearing my throat, I answered, "Most likely, executed. More probably, tortured and then executed." Caelum listened intently, and I found myself losing focus in the way the light sparkled in his eyes. "But there is much we don't know, considering we have been blocked from their ways for so long."

Caelum grimaced, as though he hadn't considered what the mortal king would subject us to if we were caught. Maybe the success of this mission was as much of a non-option for him as it was for me.

"No accounts from the mortals who flee into Ambrose?" He inquired with genuine curiosity.

I shook my head. "Frankly, there aren't many. The ones who try often don't succeed. And the ones who actually make it are smart enough not to say anything about it. We can't give them refuge. It would cause war."

"It seems like Ambrose is a willing party for the poor treatment of humanity," Caelum stated matter-of-factly.

I gave him a small grin. I hadn't had such an intellectual conversation since I had left Neverwind Library. It reminded me of the evenings I spent with Dean William and how we would pore over theoretical possibilities until the sun rose the next morning. The memory gave me warmth in my chest, and suddenly I found myself longing for my old life once again.

"It isn't that simple, unfortunately. Even though we have our powers, they have the dragons. It creates an even playing field, one which would end in slaughter on both sides."

Caelum studied me, mulling over my response before he asked, "Are you worried about crossing the border? What it would mean for you if you got caught?"

I swallowed down the lump in my throat at the thought. Truth be told, I hadn't let myself give it much thought. I refused to think about a lot of things these days.

"I will not be caught," I said resolutely.

"There is no guarantee," he countered.

"I cannot be caught. Under no circumstances," I stated firmly.

"Well," he said simply, clearing his throat, although his eyes never wavered from mine, and I could barely handle the heat I felt coursing through my veins, threatening to melt the ice inside. "We will do our best not to let the mortal army find us. We are lucky the temple is close to the border, so—"

"No. I refuse to even entertain the idea. I must make it back to Dolan. Otherwise…"

"Otherwise, what?"

My city would cease to have a leader. Niklaus would fill the role well, but if he had his way, I wouldn't have left in the first place. What I needed was to make sure Dolan not only survived, but thrived.

For years, I watched how my father let the city become a background noise to the other great cities of Ambrose, and I hated it. Father was content in being the ruler of his own little realm and left alone otherwise. Would Nik follow in his footsteps? I wasn't sure, but I refused to find out. I blinked, returning my focus to the conversation at hand.

"Otherwise, what's the point? I'm just as eager to find out what is in the temple as you are. If there are relics that predate what we already have in the libraries and museums around Ambrose, then what would it mean for not only Dolan but Ambrose as a whole..."

Caelum's grin was wide, and I found it contagious. I offered him a smile back, and I flushed red as his knee nudged against mine. "It would mean we were one step closer to understanding our origins and where the gods disappeared to."

"You really think they are still alive?" My voice was breathless as I asked, and I sat still, unsure if I should move, or if I even wanted to.

"I do. If they weren't, Maya's blessing wouldn't exist."

"That's true," I conceded. "So that's why you want to explore this place so badly? Because you want to know more about the gods? Why they disappeared?"

Caelum regarded me, a lopsided smirk appearing. He took my hand and twisted it to my palm, facing up. I tried to jerk out of his grip, but his fingers were an iron band on my skin. Gently, he pried opened my fingers, coaxing my hand to relax in his hold. I sighed, relenting.

Slowly, he traced the lines in my palm with his fingertip. Each stroke of his finger sent shivers down my spine, making my toes curl.

"What are you—"

"Did you know that each line in your hand represents an ancestor's life?"

His question surprised me, and I shook my head, unable to speak as his fingers kept gently stroking my hand. Gooseflesh broke out over my arms, regardless of the heat of the flames next to me. "It's a map of our bloodline. We all have countless lines, each one telling the unique stories of our ancestors."

He traced the small lines on the side of my palm, then each line on my fingers. "Eventually, with each generation, you will reach the apex of your ancestry. Which god was it who made us? Which god was it who gifted us with life? With magic?" He pressed his finger deeper, nearly scratching my skin as he traced a thick curved line which dominated the middle of my palm. It made my whole body tingle, aching for the smallest touches that I had been deprived of for so long.

Caelum's voice was soft as he spoke, his cadence captivating, and I felt myself leaning toward him, eager for him to keep touching me, to trace his fingers higher up to my elbow, to my shoulder.

"Do you know how much information we are missing because it is contained—or destroyed—by the mortal kingdom?"

"No," I whispered. Of course, I heard about the King ordering the citizens to turn in anything related to Magi. Knew we had lost an insurmountable amount of our history. But how much, exactly? Truth be told, I preferred not to think about it.

"It's so much that the texts we currently have only cover about half the lines on the palms of our hands."

"So that's why you're going to the temple in the mortal kingdom? To retrieve lost archives?"

"Don't you think we deserve it?" His brow raised in question.

I regarded him for a moment and let the thought really sink in. Did the mortal king really deny us so much?

"I think we are *owed* it," I concluded.

Caelum's face lit up, and he leaned close enough our breath mingled, and I stopped breathing.

"You are *fascinating*, Lydia."

I held my breath, my heart racing, afraid he was going to kiss me. Afraid he wasn't. I wet my lips in anticipation, my hand burning in his grasp. But he pulled away slowly, releasing his own shaking breath, and I slowly removed my palm from his.

My cheeks were flushed with heat, my body humming from the closeness of his, his pine scent washing over me. My thighs squeezed involuntarily, and I hoped it was too dark for him to notice how exactly his touch—his words—had affected me.

Never had someone touched me so intimately, with so much reverence. I also had never in my life had anyone called me *fascinating*. It was a lie. Surely as the sun would rise tomorrow—if he knew who I truly was—the last thing he would say about me would be that I was *fascinating*.

I needed to rein myself back in. Once again, I found myself locking yet another worry in another box and shoving it into another dark corner of my mind. Caelum would never find out my true identity, and it would never even matter.

Chapter 7

HALCYON

The next morning was a hustle and bustle of packing and organizing to get back on the road. Caelum had shaken me awake gently before the sun's first rays crested over the mountains, and I groaned from the restless sleep I had gotten. I wasn't used to the sounds of nature.

Each crinkle of a leaf and each breeze that shook the trees jolted me awake. When the rustling of leaves didn't wake me, my screaming muscles did every time I shifted. By the time I packed all my things and settled back on Calliope, I was less inclined to keep up my strong façade.

The air was thick with fog. Tiny droplets of rain coated my eyelashes as we slowly trekked through the woods. The trees became more sparse as we went, and the rocks of the Jagged Peaks—which distinguished the border between Ambrose and Tantal—started peeking through the grey clouds.

I wasn't sure if the cloudy day made them look more foreboding or if the claws that scraped the sky just radiated malicious energy.

Caelum shifted on his saddle and snapped his reins to make a sharp turn deeper into the woods. I grasped onto my reins with white knuckles as the horses followed.

"Where are we going?" I called, sharing a glance with Aceus that told me he was on high alert as well.

"Can't go over the mountain range, it's too dangerous. We have to go through."

My palms grew clammy and sticky realizing we were moments away from crossing the border. Untold dangers lay across those mountains, and once again I questioned my resolve. We trekked through the woods single-file, Caelum leading the way with a scribbled map in his lap.

We followed the trail into the untraveled forest, and I kept close to Aceus, not trusting the change of scenery. The trees seemed to hold their breath as we passed, not a single sound reaching my ears outside of the horses' hooves. The terrain became more narrow as we went on, our path hugging in closer to the tree line as rock sheared off the side. Not much elsewhere to go other than forward.

Calliope, who had been nothing but obedient and docile until this point, started whinnying and shaking her mane. I glanced back at Aceus. Seeming to notice the oddity, he observed the forest with pinched eyebrows.

A loud whistle from behind me had me jumping out of my skin, and my heart beat a little faster as Iris used hand signals gesturing toward the darkness in the trees.

I found myself flanked by Aceus, Caelum, and Maya. "Wolves in the forest," Maya whispered. "Usually they aren't interested in us, but up this high with the changing of the seasons, food might be scarce."

I gulped, refusing to acknowledge the roaring of fear in my ears. Aceus sat taller on his horse, and then we heard it.

A cacophony of howls and snarls came from the woods, and even though I twisted every which way, I could see nothing. The horses were uneasy, their feet stamping on the ground, manes shaking, and nostrils flaring and huffing about.

Caelum drew the sword he kept on his side, his eyes wide as he watched the tree line. He kept his left hand free, and I recognized it as a stance to summon his magic should he need it.

Maya held a short sword in each hand, and Iris, who remained with the wagon, pulled out a bow and notched back an arrow.

The horses Caelum and his team were on were apparently trained for this sort of situation—their feet solid on the ground—as they waited alongside their riders. Mine and Aceus', however, were not.

Calliope reared back, her cry ringing in my ears, and I toppled to the ground, only able to ease my fall with a quick call of my magic. There was a shock of pain, my ice cracking beneath me. Gritting my teeth, I stood. The other horses panicked, and shouts rang out as chaos ensued.

Aceus managed to dismount before his horse bucked him off. He nodded at me, confirming he was alright. I breathed out a momentary sigh of relief. A pang of guilt settled in my chest. Aceus was the only mortal here, and the one who would most likely get hurt out of all of us. He was an impeccable bodyguard, but was he really able to defend himself against nature's creatures?

A wall of earth rose from behind, keeping the horses from running. Calliope squealed as she found no other way out, unwilling to jump off the mountainside cliff. Caelum's quick magic succeeded in keeping most of our horses from bolting, but Aceus' horse managed to escape. Two towers of earth collided right as the horse's tail fluttered past.

Olympia reared, but Caelum regained control, his arms straining with the reins. Curses flew from Caelum's mouth, his focus on calming his steed.

White fur pounced toward us with an earsplitting snarl. Before I had the chance to react, blood sprayed my face as Aceus slashed his sword at the attacking wolf. It fell hard against the ground with a thud, and I froze. I had never seen an animal killed that way before, and the swiftness of it stole my breath away.

Another wolf leaped from the trees. This one managed to dodge Aceus' blade, and instead it knocked him to the ground. I screamed as he fell, tumbling with the wolf. He landed a fist to the wolf's jaw. With a loud yelp, the wolf backed off, but returned to snarling and challenging Aceus in a low stance.

Arrows whizzed from behind me. Iris' jaw was set, her eyes pinned on the wolf. Her arms strained as she aimed her arrows, but she missed as it darted from side to side. Two more wolves emerged from the trees, their teeth gleaming white with the need to spill blood. As one, they charged. I didn't think twice before letting my ice magic rush out toward the wolves, but it was too slow. The white wolf pinned Aceus down. I couldn't take my eyes off of them until I heard a far-too-close snarl from behind me.

Shouts rang out as the wolves attacked.

Gasping, I swung around as a wolf with a coat of ash grey rushed toward me. I screamed. Magic blasted from my palms. Daggers of ice speared into the wolf, and it fell with a yelp of pain. My heart rushed in my ears, the scent of blood overwhelming my senses. I covered my nose with my hand, my wide eyes scanning the area.

Maya handled her wolf with precision. Arcing down, she sliced the short sword into the wolf's flesh, but not before it knocked the wagon over. All of the contents spilled to the ground. I waited, preparing for another attack, but the wolf lay still. My hands clenched into fists.

Aceus stood next to the white wolf, now slain. He was alive. Dirty and bloody, but alive. I watched intently. Other than the squelch of Maya retrieving her sword from the wolf's prostrate body, I saw nothing.

"Are there others?" I asked, looking for the evidence of more animals.

"Those were the only ones I detected," Iris confirmed, as Caelum dismounted and walked over toward me. Olympia and the other horses finally quieted.

I released my magic, letting my ice fall to shards to the ground. My hands shook, and I blew out a deep sigh.

"You okay?" he asked, his hands solidly grasping mine. I clung onto him for strength before nodding. I allowed myself the indulgence of his fingers tight around mine. It made me feel safe and grounded. Something strong to hold on to while I breathed through my racing pulse.

"Should we go after Aceus' horse? What will happen now that she's loose?"

Caelum shook his head, and grimaced. "We don't have time to look for her now. She'll be long gone, and we are on a limited timeline."

"Oh." I could feel the tears threatening to prick the backs of my eyes, not realizing how much I had been holding it together. With a deep, trembling breath, I banished my tears and instead tore my hands from Caelum, shaking the anxious energy from my palms.

Caelum pulled back from me, looking at me with his deep hazel eyes, the brown swirling against green. A worried smile pulled on his lips, revealing the dimple on his cheek. "You didn't think a few wolves would stop us, did you?"

"I don't know…" I trailed off, for the first time really understanding that these people weren't just a band of travelers who were out camping for the joy of it. "Was it your magic that provided the barrier?" Asking more for confirmation that my father's intel was correct, but also to deflect my panic.

"Yes," Caelum ran his hand along the back of his neck, making the short strands of his hair on the back of his head stand up. "I just wish I could have protected all the horses."

"So, what do we do?"

"Someone can ride in the wagon," Caelum stated, but as he glanced toward the overturned vehicle, he grimaced.

"No," Maya called over, her hands full with provisions that spilled to the ground. "The wagon is broken." She gestured to the overturned wagon, where pieces of wood splintered from the side. "And we lost a tent." Shredded canvas fell from her fingertips, ribbons of cloth piling on the ground.

"Did we lose anything else?" Caelum asked, and Maya shook her head.

"Thank the gods for that," Caelum muttered as he adjusted Calliope's saddle. "We will just have to rearrange sleeping arrangements when we get to the temple."

I looked quizzically over at Aceus, and he only shrugged, clearly not bothered we had lost some of our supplies.

"It could have been worse," he said to me, and I raised an eyebrow at him. "We could have lost any of the food stores, the water store, or even weapons."

Aceus moved around and helped revert the wagon back on its wheels. The damage didn't seem too extensive, but the less weight it carried, the better. Which ruled out anyone riding in it for the time being.

"Keep all the scraps. I can fix this once we settle in," Aceus said, appraising the damage. "For now, I don't mind walking alongside if we go at a slower pace."

Caelum shook his head. "No, we need to move quickly. The sun will go down soon, and I want to be out of the forest by the time night falls. We managed to fight those wolves off, but there are still other creatures out there."

"Then Aceus and I can ride together," I suggested.

"Aceus, you don't have any magic, do you?" Both Aceus and I stiffened at Caelum.

Caelum smirked and shook his head. "It's not a problem, but we need to be strategic. Aceus, if you take Lydia's horse, she can ride with me. Niklaus was very clear we need to return the both of you alive, and I can protect Lydia with my magic if I need to. Iris has her hands full with the wagon, and Maya doesn't have defensive magic."

I glanced warily at Aceus. I couldn't argue with his logic, but it also didn't sit well with me.

"Aceus is perfectly capable of protecting me," I told Caelum.

"Oh, I have no doubts about that whatsoever," he smirked, and opened his mouth to say more, but Aceus lifted his hands in surrender.

"La—Lydia," Aceus stumbled over my name and my cheeks burst with red hot fear. There was a pause as we both held our breath, but Caelum didn't seem to notice the slip-up. Aceus barreled on. "He's right. The two of us together might be too much weight for your horse, and I have an injury from the wolf. Nothing too bad, but you would be safer with him." I peered at Aceus, once again noticing the line of red blood dripping from his elbow to his wrist.

"Maya has healing potions, if you would like one," Caelum offered thoughtfully, but Aceus shook his head.

"No, save it. We might need it for a more dire situation," he insisted before taking his shirt off and wrapping it around his injured arm. "It's nothing I haven't dealt with before." He winked, and I was very close to rolling my eyes.

After some time, the wagon was put together as well as it could be. The contents were placed back in an orderly fashion, and even though there were boards missing from the sides, it was still sturdy enough for travel. If Aceus really could fix it, then we would have no issues bringing things back.

"If we leave soon, we can make it to the river inside the caves before we grow too tired." Caelum tugged on Olympia's reins, and I allowed her to sniff my palm before stroking her nose.

Maya murmured her agreement before quickly checking the bags on her horse and climbing on the saddle.

Caelum's pine scent washed over me as he stepped up behind me. How his scent made my core tighten and shoulders loosen at the same time, I didn't know. Maybe it had just been too long since I had been around a man who had no desire to use my placement in society. Maybe I was falling prey to the idea of someone who wanted to protect me. Useless notions, of course.

His large hand settled on my shoulder. "We need to hurry. Normally, I would push for one more night of camping in the woods, but I think it would be best if we get into the caves as soon as possible."

I nodded in agreement and let him help me onto Olympia's saddle. His fingers pressed into my hips as I heaved myself over, and I sat ramrod straight as he settled in behind me. The fit was tight, his pine scent once again washing over me, and I let myself breathe it in.

There was an aura of anxiety as we trotted through the thick trunks of trees. Not a single person spoke as we raced as fast as we could—which really wasn't fast at all, considering the wagon was slowing us down. Even still, we urged forward.

Caelum's legs flexed around me as he steered Olympia further into the forest. His tunic sleeves were rolled up to his elbow, and I tried not to stare at the corded muscles of his forearms. I also tried to ignore how close his body was to mine, and I caught myself clearing my throat and shaking my head several times.

"Everything alright, Lydia?" he asked me quietly.

"I'm fine, just a little uncomfortable," I said hesitantly.

"You can lean closer to me, if you'd like," Caelum offered.

I didn't want to admit how much I relished the thought, my back still aching. Part of me was unwilling to allow myself any sort of comfort. I wanted to be perceived as capable, but the other part of me knew better. In the end, I leaned anyway—just a little.

He chuckled behind me, as though he could tell I was torn between letting him embrace my weight or flinging myself off the horse altogether.

As the sun disappeared over the crest of the craggy spikes of the mountains, I felt exhaustion pull me down, right into Caelum's warm chest. His entire body engulfed mine, and I had to admit, it was quite pleasant.

One of his arms wrapped around my middle, and I jerked in his grasp.

"If it's alright with you, I would like to hold you this way."

"Why?" I asked icily. Something in the back of my mind was telling me it was a terrible idea. Even indulging in resting on him was dangerous. I was already battling a minor attraction to him and needed no further reason to stoke that line of thinking.

"Because you're falling asleep, and I don't want to risk you falling off." He said it so matter-of-factly, and I had to wonder why my brain was so insistent on imagining his hand drifting lower, my legs clenching at the thought.

After a few bouts of my eyes drifting off without my permission, Caelum finally halted his horse. I sleepily leaned back into his warm chest, taking in the giant maw of a cave opening before us. The sun had made its descent past the mountains and the forest was nearly as dark as the cave.

"This cave tunnels through the mountains into Tantal," Caelum said confidently.

"Is it safe?" I asked. It was so dark all I could see was black. The slightest gust of air came from the entrance, and it wafted the smell of minerals and wet rock.

"Should be fine." Caelum said, his voice still held confidence, but his hands tightened against the reins.

Maya hopped off her saddle, and we waited while she rummaged for something inside the wagon. With a torch in her hand, she walked up to me, and I raised my eyebrow in question.

"We're going to need light to get us through, unless you somehow have fire magic?" she asked, and I shook my head. She smirked and poured a green liquid over the clothed tip, which ignited the torch in a blue-green flame instantly. There was no heat to it, even as I held it close to my face.

"What is this?" I stared at it in wonder.

"Everflame." Maya said. "It's a potion I concocted. Heatless. Doesn't catch to anything else but emits enough light to see by. Also, won't burn out easily."

"That's useful," I muttered.

We passed through the open maw of the cave, the imposing darkness embracing us as the light of the cave opening became smaller and smaller. The blue-green flame above me flickered along the walls, revealing a tall ceiling hosting jagged, sharp stalactites threatening to fall and pierce us straight through.

A scurrying of wings came from the dark, and I screamed as a flock of squealing creatures flew over my head. Caelum clasped his hand on my mouth so my shriek was muffled, and I shrank into his arms as I watched hundreds of these creatures fly overhead. The sound of their wings and screeching vocalizations deafening as they passed.

My heart pounded in my ears, and I shook. The wolf attack apparently set me more on edge than I realized.

Caelum wrapped his other arm around my middle, dropping the reins and holding me tight against him. "Calm down, it's just some bats. They are more scared of you than you are of them." His words were hushed and warm against my ear. Once he was confident I wasn't going to scream anymore, he slowly released his hand from my mouth, and I dragged in a long, deep breath.

"I just wasn't expecting flying creatures," I breathed.

"Best to expect the unexpected." He reached for the reins and Olympia continued to trot through the cave.

"Will there be more of them?" I asked, and I raised the torch higher, as if I could see any more small creatures that might try to attack.

Caelum shrugged. "Possibly."

"What about other animals?" If bats were in this cave, then I ventured to think about what other kinds of animals and creatures inhabited it.

Caelum stiffened behind me. "Possibly."

"I thought you said it was a safe passage?" I scoffed, my voice echoing against the never-ending grey walls. Thrusting the torch farther out, I leaned forward, trying to see as much of the cave as I could.

"We are still in the wild, so nothing is guaranteed. I promise I will keep you safe, though." I didn't have to turn around him to feel the way his grip tightened around my body. As though he meant what he said, but he also wasn't sure if it was a lie.

"And how are you supposed to keep me safe when you don't even know what's in here?" I hissed, unable to keep my fear locked in its prospective box.

"Can you just trust me?" he asked with thinly veiled annoyance.

"Not easily," I admitted.

"Too bad," he shrugged, and I heard the smirk in his voice. I wanted to argue, but it would be pointless. Exhaustion fueled my irritation, and Caelum was only doing his best with the given situation. But my fear had turned into irritability, and they both clawed at me from the inside.

"Iris will let us know if there's anything. Try to relax," he coaxed, and his reminder did help.

We continued to trek quietly through the caves with no end in sight. It was eerily silent, and there were no more creatures making themselves known. But the many alcoves we passed made me weary.

I wasn't sure how long we trod through the darkest depths of the mountains. There were no crevices above us that let in any sunlight. No birds or wildlife to give away any indication of the time.

It wasn't until Maya let out a low whistle for all of us to stop when I even realized my stomach grumbled with hunger.

My gaze continued to linger in the darkest parts of the cave, but thankfully there were no more surprises.

Maya got to work straight away with starting a fire. I started to protest, afraid the smoke would suffocate us, but the cave ceiling was tall enough to let the smoke rise. I couldn't even see the top, only the long, never-ending spikes that protruded toward us.

Caelum swung off Olympia. Grinning, he held out his hand for me to follow. I took it graciously and even offered him a small smile of gratitude. Compared to camping the previous night, I was confident I would have preferred sleeping in the forest.

The cave, while wide and tall, pressed in, making my chest tight. I didn't like the way the stalactites looked like they were ready to chomp down with their sharp teeth. The counterpart stalagmites grew from the ground, casting eerie shadows along cave walls. I also didn't like how there seemed to be no way to escape. My castle in Dolan was open, and the views were vast. This cave was downright oppressive.

Maya caught my eye as she wandered toward the fire with her hands filled to the brim with mushrooms. She immediately started her cooking process, chopping them up with a knife and board.

"How do you know those won't kill us?" I asked her.

She gave me a smirk and shook her head. "It's a part of the magic blessed by the goddess. I can feel the plants and wildlife. Know of their capabilities, either in food or magic."

"So, in theory, you could teach someone else which plants to use, and anyone could replicate your magic?" I thought about the potion that gave us the Everflame.

Everflame would be extremely useful in large quantities. Dolan and surely other cities across Ambrose would benefit from the recipe.

A heatless light source could save homes from burning by candles and torches. The long burn time would save on money and resources, which could go more into benefiting the community. Did Maya even realize she was sitting on a potential gold mine?

Maya shook her head. "It's also embedded with magic the goddess blessed me with. You could use the same ingredients, but the end result won't match up." She gestured to the herbs lying next to her. "I have to cast magic with whatever I make, otherwise it would just end up being an herbal stew."

I nodded like I understood. Sensing my confusion, she beckoned me to her. "Look at this." She pulled out a small bowl of salt. "Salt has cleansing properties, but it can also be restorative. If you or anyone without the goddess' blessing put this on food, it would be an ordinary meal—albeit a tasty one." She winked. "But if I call upon the goddess and imbue the salt with magical properties, I can enhance it to help with healing, among other things."

I scratched the back of my head. "But how—"

"Hush. If you want to see it work, just watch." She pulled the bowl into her lap and closed her eyes. I watched intently as she took a deep breath and exhaled slowly. Her voice was breathy as she chanted softly, placing her hands over the bowl with her eyes closed, her voice filling the stagnant air around us.

There was a definitive shift in energy, and I gasped as a silvery shimmer came from her palms over the salt. With a deep inhale and a serene smile, Maya stopped her chanting.

"There we go." She smiled with a sated look on her face and sprinkled the salt over the mushrooms which were now roasting over the fire.

"So what did you do?" I asked, my curiosity rearing and my desire to absorb this new knowledge itching the back of my mind.

"It's just a simple restoration spell. We've been traveling a while, and we still have a ways to go. This spell helps make sure we are all getting the fuel we need for the trek."

"So, you do this every meal? Isn't it exhausting?" I rubbed the center of my chest, where I felt the well of my power. I knew how taxing using magic could be, and I could only give as much as my body would allow.

Maya shook her head. "This particular spell is pretty minimal. I am experienced with many years of practice. A new witch might find this spell tiring, but I am no freshly hatched chick."

I wanted to ask more questions, but as I opened my mouth, Iris came and plopped herself on the ground next to me.

"How are you holding up?" She looked at me with her big brown eyes. Dark braids framed her round face and swayed with each movement of her head. Her smile was friendly. There was an air of freedom about her the others didn't have. Even after the attack, she was the most relaxed out of all of us. Maybe it had something to do with her magic, knowing if there was a threat or not.

"I'm fine." I told her and forced a smile on my lips that I hoped came off as genuine. The truth was, I was exhausted. The caves made me nervous, and without knowing which way was the exit, I feared I would get stuck here.

"There's a small pond just down the alcove over there." She pointed to a very dark portion of the cave, and I shuddered. "We should take advantage of it while we can. I'm so grimy. I need to get some of this dirt off of me before bed." Iris held her hands out in front of her and scowled.

"As long as you think it's safe." Maya shrugged and gave Iris a warm smile. Her response was light, but I felt the heaviness of perceived danger. It was a confirmation. The caves weren't as empty and easily trekked as Caelum had made me think.

Fear crept into my spine, but it was too late for me to back out now. I wouldn't be able to find my way out of these caves, even if I wanted to.

The gentlemen joined us around the fire, and Maya handed each of us some freshly roasted mushrooms with her special salt. It was divine. I marveled at how she got the flavors of the mushrooms so complimentary and how they practically melted in my mouth. Maybe I would have Maya come to the castle and train our chefs. Even if they wouldn't be able to wield witch magic, they made nothing half as delicious.

"LET'S GO GET WASHED up," Iris said as she placed her empty plate along the pile of dirty dishes that stacked up close to Maya.

"Do we need to wash those?" I asked, feeling a pang of guilt that most of the domestic duties fell to Maya.

Iris shrugged. "It's Caelum's turn tonight." She clasped me on the shoulder and turned me toward the darkness of the cave before grabbing a torch and lighting it once again with Everflame.

"Oh," I said, unsure if I should stay back to help him or not.

Like she could read my mind, Iris said, "Don't worry, you'll get your turn to clean soon."

We meandered to the wagon, presumably to get some clean clothes and a towel—gods, I hoped they brought towels—where we found Aceus crouched down at the wagon with a scowl on his face.

"What's wrong with it?" I asked, watching as Iris sifted through the contents of the wagon.

I tilted my head as I peered down to see the damage. It looked like some of the wood was broken, leaving a decent sized hole toward the bottom.

"Just some structural damage. I'll patch up what I can, but it will need more work once we get to our destination."

I nodded, chewing on the bottom of my lip. Iris reappeared by my side and handed me a small towel. I didn't have time to ask her any questions before she dragged me through the dark, wet caves. It was eerily quiet, our footsteps muffled by a constant dripping sound ahead of us.

"How do you know if it's safe?" I muttered under my breath.

"I can tell. Did my rounds when we stopped, checking for any manner of creatures or beasts," she replied, shrugging.

"How?" I rose a brow in skepticism.

"My magic isn't quite as blatant as yours or Cal's. I have a sort of sixth sense. I can feel whether there are living creatures around, be it animal or human. But it isn't anything I can use for offense, and I can't sense anything highly magical." She shrugged.

"Highly magical?" I asked, unsure what she meant.

"Magical beings, such as dragons, seem to evade my senses. Magi with concealment magic, too. I've been trying to expand my power, train more with it, because I think I have the potential, but I just haven't gotten there yet. Everything else, though, I can sense just fine. The good news is we don't need to worry about magical beings down here." She sounded confident in her ability, but I wasn't so sure.

We were essentially trapped, sitting ducks waiting for slaughter, if anything powerful enough could evade whatever magic she held.

A large body of water opened up in front of us. Steam rose from the ground, creating a humid blanket wrapping around my skin. The scent of sulfur stung my nostrils, and I wrinkled my nose.

"It's warm, which is a luxury we don't normally get to have," Iris explained as she placed the torch against a boulder and started stripping her clothes off. "You can leave your undergarments on if you like, but unless you have a way to pull the water out of them, it's going to be a bitch riding tomorrow—or you can ride without them. We aren't shy, though." She tossed me a small bar. "Soap. Use this to scrub down."

"We?" I looked behind me, confirming we were alone.

"Mhm. Everyone else will be here soon, so if you don't want anyone to see anything, I recommend getting in quickly."

Iris made quick work of piling her braids together at the top of her head, and as she tore the clothes away from her body, she left nothing to the imagination. She was petite, but her back was lined with defined muscles. Working with animals and being on the road all the time putting definition on her body.

Quickly, I removed my trousers and tunic, glad Iris was facing the opposite direction as she waded into the water.

The silt was soft on my feet, but I still couldn't see anything in the pond. I read books on fish who lived in caves—their eyes milky white from blindness, their sense of smell and taste heightened to make up for their lack of eyesight. Some sported poisonous spikes and sharp teeth. I shivered as I waded in further despite the heat radiating through the water.

The warm water spread over my skin and sank deep into my bones. I tested my magic against it and sighed as ice formed around me for the briefest of seconds before I let the water melt it away. Nothing had brushed against me yet, and the fear of the unknown drifted further to the back of my mind as I sank into the water. I leaned back, letting the water loosen the knots in my hair and wash the dirt which no doubt tarnished my now-brown strands.

"How's the water?" Caelum's low voice had me spinning around. I covered my breasts with my hands, although there was no need to do so with the dark waters around me. Even still, I coated the surrounding water in ice, just in case he could see something I couldn't.

"It's fine," I muttered back to him. Aceus and Maya appeared behind him, all three of them glowing in the blue-green light of Everflame.

Maya and Caelum started stripping unceremoniously, and I turned my head away to allow them privacy, even if they didn't seem to need or want it.

Aceus didn't question or protest the bathing situation either, and I envied how he seemed to take all of this in stride. He was a natural at every moment of this, and sometimes I felt like I was the only one who was struggling.

I accidentally glanced up as I heard them make their way into the water. All three of them had impressive physiques, cut from the work they did day after day.

Maya's curves were lined with lean muscle, Aceus' broad frame only more intimidating without his clothes. The flames bounced off his skin, his arms rippled with his bulky stature.

But my eyes snagged on Caelum, and I could hardly tear my gaze away. I had felt his arms around me, knew they had to be strong, but the clothes he wore hid his perfect physique. His long arms were toned, and the muscles on his chest kept going until they reached to a defined v-shape on his hips. The humidity clung to his skin, shimmering in the teal light.

If he noticed me staring, he didn't give any indication, and I veered my eyes away, but not before I got a glimpse of the impressive length he wielded between his legs. He wasn't even aroused, and I could tell Caelum was blessed by the gods in more ways than one.

My mouth dried at the sight of him, and I had the sudden urge to know what his toned muscles would feel like in my hands, what it would taste like to drag my tongue across his skin—

Biting my cheek, I was determined to veer my thoughts away from Caelum and his...well, everything. I pointedly ignored the way my stomach fluttered and my core clenched at nothing.

No matter who I portrayed, I had to remember: I was the *Lady of Dolan*, and under no circumstance would my wandering thoughts ever be appropriate.

"Ahhh..." Maya groaned in pleasure as she sank into the warm water, dunking her hair with a soft smile on her face. Iris had moved farther into the depths of the pond. I couldn't even see where she had gone.

"Over here, Maya." Iris called from the dark, and I went to follow, eager to be surrounded by two women instead of men.

Caelum caught my arm, and I jerked back. He chuckled. "I wouldn't go over there if I were you."

"Why not?" I asked, not fully trusting Caelum, and not fully trusting myself around him. Caelum grinned at me while he scrubbed against his skin and hair, and shifted his eyes to the darkness.

"It can get... lonely sometimes. With no other consistent companions other than ourselves." I glanced towards the darkness where the others disappeared.

Aceus moved past me with a small smile playing on his lips, heading to where the women were swimming.

"Where are you going?" I asked, a demand in my tone. He only gave me a smirk, his mustache lifting with the action.

"I had an invitation," he laughed as he made his way to them, and I could only stare with my mouth agape. Oh, I was going to have a nice chat with him the next time I got him alone. This was unacceptable and inappropriate on so many levels. Not that I had any room to talk with how desire flushed my body whenever I looked at Caelum.

A soft giggle echoed, followed by a small splash and a breathy moan. I swung my gaze back at Caelum with wide eyes. He chuckled knowingly and shook the water from his hair.

Sounds of sex began to fill the air, and I was stuck between horror and intrigue, and watching Caelum as he lathered himself with soap made my heart race and my thighs clench. The water was quickly becoming too hot, and I forced more ice around me in an effort to cool me down and try to focus on anything other than what was happening in this pond. It was impossible though, so I opted to dunk my head under the water and pray that by the time I came back up for air, everything would be back to normal.

Chapter 8

CAELUM

Lydia's face was in between horror and intrigue when she realized what Maya, Iris, and Aceus were doing. Her wrinkled nose told me she wished she could have been anywhere else, but her darting eyes held so many questions.

I couldn't help the chuckle that emerged from my throat as I watched her flounder with her next course of action. Moans of pleasure became louder, and she met my gaze with wide eyes and her mouth dropped in shock.

I almost bellowed a laugh when Lydia kept sinking herself down into the water, only coming up for brief sips of air.

The next time she emerged, I called out to her. "I'm all washed up. I'm going to head back to the base if you want to join me?"

Lydia nodded, following me out of the pond hastily. She encased herself in ice to cover her body, and I purposefully looked away to give her a semblance of privacy. Even covered in ice, she was devastating. The blue-green glow from the Everflame shimmered against her pale skin, making her look like the moon personified, and I had to shake myself out of a trance from staring.

I was hard pressed to admit, riding behind her gave me untethered fantasies. It was not the first time I had ridden with a passenger, but it was the first time in a long time that it ignited a thirst in me which no water could quench.

Seeing her practically naked fueled the fire within me even more. I let myself fantasize for a brief moment, lingering on how I wanted to mark her perfect skin with my mouth, my fingers digging into her thighs as they wrapped around my head. Her subtle curves and long limbs were like a siren's song, begging me to fall into her trap.

The best part about her, though, was her mind. I saw the thirst she had for knowledge and loved the way she challenged me last night. Even though I could tell she disagreed on certain facts, she listened and thought through her responses. She considered all possibilities, and it was a splash of cool water on a summer day.

But I couldn't let her know how much she affected me, and I glanced down at my cock as I tried to remind him of that, too. I handed her a towel and she wrapped it around herself as she banished the ice which fell into shards at her feet.

"Hopefully no one accidentally steps on those." I pointed to the shards, which were serated around the edges, their sharpness glinting in the dim light.

"By the time anyone leaves *that*," she nodded toward the back of the cave, "along with the heat of this alcove, the ice will be melted."

"Can't you melt it yourself?" I asked, drying myself off before pulling on my pants. There wasn't any reason to hide myself from her now. I took notice of the way Lydia's gaze lingered on me when I got into the pond, and I had to will myself not to get hard in response. I definitely didn't hate the heat I saw in her eyes as she stared me down, but I kept my mouth shut, knowing that if she knew I noticed, it would make her uncomfortable. My cock twitched just thinking about it, and I was instantly glad I covered myself up.

"I can, but it's not something that comes as naturally. I don't control water, just ice. It takes more of my energy to focus on it. Plus, leaving ice makes more of a statement than a puddle." She flashed a fiendish grin as she flexed her fingers out in front of her. It seemed Lydia had a flare of dramatics in her, and part of me wanted to see it for myself. There was another part of me which knew being on the receiving side of her ire would be a mistake. The way she fought against those wolves was testament enough. She was dangerous—if she wanted to be.

"Huh," I responded. Every magical ability came with its own set of strengths and weaknesses. I was able to sense things in the ground, but it typically took a lot more energy from me and was harder to focus. A lot of Magi had powers-within-powers. No ability was completely one-noted.

We padded through the cave, using the extra torch I brought with me as a light source.

Lydia cleared her throat. "So," she hesitated, and she turned slightly away from me, "is that a normal occurrence?"

"What do you mean?" I teased.

"Iris, and Maya...inviting Aceus? Really?" Her nose scrunched up before she shook her head.

I laughed. "Oh, it happens every once in a while. Like I said, we are pretty much with only ourselves and urges happen." I shrugged.

"Have you ever...?"

"Have I ever what?" I turned, lifting an eyebrow and biting back a smirk. I was goading her, of course. While I never got the sense that Lydia was naïve, she was certainly proper. Her face was turned down, looking at the ground beneath her feet. I stifled a laugh.

"Have you ever joined in?" Her words were rushed as they left her lips. This time, I did laugh.

"I have." I confirmed, and she whipped her face to me, trying to read if I was telling the truth. "Only once. Group sex isn't exactly my taste. And well, neither one of the girls comes without the other."

"Caelum!" Lydia gasped, and I laughed.

"I didn't mean to make a pun! Get your mind out of the ditch." I poked her shoulder with a finger. She swayed as though I had thrown her off balance, but her teeth gleamed in a smile.

"If they weren't an item, would you want to be with either of them?" Genuine curiosity laced her tone, and I had to take a moment to think about it. Could it be possible, though? Lydia was *jealous?* No, definitely not, even though I could have sworn I saw a flicker of it in the twitch of her lips.

The truth was, I had never really thought about it before. Maya without Iris, or vice versa, was such a foreign concept. It didn't even seem natural. Part of me wanted to see if I could play along, see how jealous I could make her, but I wasn't that cruel.

"No, I can't say I would."

"Oh..." Her voice trailed off, and I had no doubt her mind was whirling with exactly how each of us fit into the group dynamic. Really, it was always Maya and Iris. They were open to others joining, and Aceus happened to be the flavor of the week, but I always felt like it was too impersonal with too many people.

I desired to have something with just one person, ideally someone whom I could share my soul fully with. And as a result, I ended up resorting to one-night stands when the occasion arose. If I wasn't going to have a relationship with someone, I didn't care to share the experience and see them again.

Well, until now. I was telling myself I wasn't interested in anything with Lydia, but if I was being totally honest, she was tempting me like a fly nearing a spider's web.

The fire was still burning, but it was getting close to embers as we approached the small camp. Lydia inched her way closer to the flames, letting the heat dry the smallest drops of water that clung to her skin.

"Would you turn around for just a moment?" she asked politely, grasping the towel around her with white knuckles. I turned, allowing her the privacy to change back into her clothes.

We each grabbed a bedroll from the wagon, carrying them closer to the fire, but as Lydia went to unfurl hers, I stopped her with a hand on her wrist. She stilled immediately and swung her big blue eyes right into mine, and a shock zinged through me. My breath caught for one moment before I smiled down at her. I could have imagined it, but it seemed like she leaned closer, like if I wanted to, I could tug her toward me, but instead I let her go. The feel of her smooth skin lingered on my hand.

"Hang on a second," I told her as I crouched down, placing my palm on the ground. My magic surged from my chest as I coaxed fresh growth from the hard packed dirt underneath. Soft dirt and moss sprang up, and I pressed my fingers into it, feeling the strands grow and soften, my magic leaving a trail of pleasure through me.

"You manipulated the earth last night, too," she observed, and I nodded. "Do you do that every night?"

I scratched the back of my neck, suddenly feeling a little embarrassed. Lydia was surely used to plush blankets and soft beds. There was no way she would be comfortable on the hard stone, but I hadn't expected to be confronted about it. "I never do it, actually."

"Then why now?" she asked bluntly. Direct and to the point. I raised my brows, finding I liked it a whole lot.

"I just wanted you to feel more comfortable. You're pretty out of your element here—"

"Well, stop." She placed a hand on her hip and pointed those icy blue eyes at me. Her determination speared me right through my chest. "I didn't ask for your coddling, and I don't need it." With a huff of irritation that amused me, she took her bedroll, unfurling it right next to my mossy spot and placing it on the still rocky and hard-packed ground.

"You are going to regret it tomorrow morning," I told her with a small smile pulling at my lips.

"Regardless that this is all very new to me, I am not a princess, and I refuse to be treated like one." She sat on her bedroll and combed her graceful fingers through brown strands which were still dripping wet. Her eyes narrowed at me, like she was trying to figure out an unsaid question, and I cocked my head. She only veered her gaze toward the fire, leaving it unanswered.

I unfurled my bedroll on the mossy ground right next to her, and Lydia raised her eyebrow.

"No need to waste the magic I worked so hard on." It was a piss poor excuse, because the only reason I decided on laying so close to her was because I couldn't tear away from her proximity. I gave her a teasing smile, to which she only flicked her eyes back to how close our bedrolls were together and sighed in resignation.

"Do you miss Dolan?" I asked as I sat in my own spot, reaching my hands forward and letting the heat of the dying flames flick over my skin, warming my fingertips.

She hadn't talked much about living in Dolan, serving the Lady. I wondered what her life looked like. Did she stand in the Lady's shadow? Did she have a casual relationship with her, where she felt like she could speak freely?

"Why do you want to know?" Suspicion flashed across her face, and I shrugged in response.

"Just curious." I should have known better. There was not a lot Lydia disclosed, even with her friend, the bodyguard. At first, I thought she was struck by fear, but I was starting to understand. The woman just didn't like to bring attention to herself.

And damn if it didn't drive me crazy.

After she was satisfied with her hair, squeezing out the extra water outside of her roll, she climbed back in and wrapped herself up. I followed her lead and shrank into mine, our shoulders nearly touching.

"How much longer will we have to be down here for?" she asked quietly, like she didn't want to voice the question, like the question itself was a show of vulnerability.

"Only a couple more days." I adjusted my tone to make light of it, but the reality was: if the caves were driving her crazy now, she had a long way to go. Not to mention, the temple was underground in some parts. It would be dark, if not more imposing than these caves. "Don't worry, you'll see the sunlight again in no time," I promised.

My hand moved of its own accord as my knuckles brushed against her cheekbone, and I tucked one of her dark brown strands behind her ear. Her breath caught, and she looked at me through the side of her eye and frowned. She bit her lip, the soft pink flesh tantalizing me between her teeth.

"What's wrong?" I asked.

She shook her head. Her eyes glazed over, and it hadn't been the first time. After the wolf attack, she had become quiet and pensive as well.

Was it fear? Was it something else? Either way, I hated the way it made her eyes duller, and the way it pinched a frown between her brows.

She was the most beautiful woman I had ever laid my eyes on and while I warred with myself about how messy things could end up being between us, I was also tired of holding myself back.

How long had it been since I started denying myself connection? I couldn't remember the last time I even thought about wanting to know a woman on a deeper level. The way I wanted to know her. When she spoke about her studies or how she liked the challenge of my questions. When she clearly fought to keep her distance, but would eventually give in, like she did on the horse. It was enticing, and the temptation to let her swallow me up was too appealing.

"Nothing. I'm just tired, that's all." She shivered despite the warmth radiating from the fire, and I knew it was a damned lie. But she didn't want me to *coddle* her, so I decided to let the matter go.

Instead, I leaned closer, ignoring all the alarms ringing in my head. *Don't touch her, Caelum, because if you do, you might not want to let go.*

It was a warning I would not heed. She was too tempting, too captivating, and riding behind her today made me nearly lose my mind.

She gasped as I leaned toward her, but didn't pull away, and I grazed my lips over her ear before whispering, "You seem distressed, maybe I could give you a distraction?"

It was forward, sure. But something told me if I wasn't, I would never find out anything about this woman whose breath rapidly puffed against my neck. And I wanted to find out anything and *everything* about her.

"A distraction?" Her breath hitched.

My hands trailed up her arms, brushing her hair over her shoulder. She shivered at my touch, and my lips quirked, knowing I had a similar effect on her as she did on me.

"Mhm, something to take your mind off of the caves which press in on you so," I said, smirking, as I watched her pulse quicken in her neck. I licked my lips before pressing them to her soft skin, and she let out a breathy moan that went straight to my groin.

"We can't, we shouldn't," she whispered, but even still she leaned more into me, and I chuckled regardless that she was completely right.

Her skin was fresh from the soap and I inhaled deeply, relishing in this moment of intimacy. My hand moved up to her neck, tilting her head back, and I looked down, her eyes wide and her lips parted with barely restrained lust.

It was gentle, the way I placed my lips over hers, teasing my tongue over the bottom of her lip, and she moaned again, moving her hands to my chest. I paused, thinking she might push me away, but she only dug her nails into my skin, urging me forward.

It was all the confirmation I needed, and I thrust my tongue deep inside her, groaning as I tasted her, needing this, and needing so much more. It was like lightning had struck, and the rest of the world grew dim. I could kiss Lydia for hours and never grow tired.

"Wait," Lydia huffed through heaving breaths, pushing me gently, and I stopped immediately. She looked up at me, her blue eyes shining once again. That dull and distant look finally gone. "We really shouldn't be doing this," she insisted.

"I'm sorry," I said, shaking my head. "I'm sorry if I was too forward."

"No," she said abruptly. "No, I wanted it. I just…" she trailed off, her gaze shifting to the fire before looking back at me. "Now isn't the time. I'm sorry." She bit her lip again. Those damned teeth taking up the space where I wanted my tongue to be.

"No need to apologize for my actions," I said with a laugh. "I hope I didn't make you uncomfortable."

She smiled, even though it didn't reach her eyes. "You didn't. I promise. Let's just get some rest."

Lydia settled into her bedroll, turning so her back faced me.

"Goodnight, Lydia," I said with a small amount of guilt. It was hard to feel guilty, though, when the imprint of her soft lips was still seared into mine. She was quickly becoming a drug for me. I wanted to touch her, to taste her, to *know* her. And I knew I was treading dangerous territory, but I often found myself straddling the line of danger. How could a woman be more dangerous than crossing a forbidden border, anyway?

Chapter 9

HALCYON

CAELUM'S STEADY BREATHING WAS not nearly rhythmic enough to put me to sleep. The kiss he branded me with played on the forefront of my mind, and I couldn't remember the last time anyone had made my body react the way he did. It was like fire moved through my veins, from the tips of my toes to the top of my head.

The way his lips moved—controlling, sweet, and needy all the same—had me way too eager to lean in and let him take me.

Caelum thought he offended me, but that wasn't the issue at all. He didn't know me. Not even the fact that Lydia wasn't my true name. How could I allow myself to fall into his arms if he had no idea who I truly was? And if he did? Then he would look at me differently. Act differently around me, too. No. I couldn't allow him to get any closer. For his sake.

It wasn't a fair game. For him, I was just some girl who was forced to come on this journey. A nobody who meant nothing other than collateral. I shuddered, thinking about how much would change if he only knew.

Scratch. Scratch. Scratch.

Jolting, I grasped my bedroll and pulled it higher. Whatever made that sound, I didn't want anything to do with it. I squeezed my eyes shut, forcing my breaths to even out. I waited, my ears twitching at any sound.

Scratch. Scratch. Scratch.

My eyes slammed open, and I clutched my bedroll with tight hands, trying to listen harder. An animal of some sort, I was sure. But was it getting closer? Was it dangerous? And why wasn't Iris waking up? Did she know about this animal and was comfortable enough to sleep through it? The thought comforted me minimally.

Nevertheless, I held my breath, waiting for the sound to come again. Each drip from the cave jolted my senses into overdrive.

Scratch. Scratch. Scratch.

A low whine echoed around the cave, and I froze completely. The others didn't stir, and how they slept through the noise I didn't know.

The scratching didn't let up this time, and little by little, it seemed like it was getting closer to our group. I crept up from my laying position, cocking my head to listen harder. Should I wake the others? What if I woke them up for nothing?

I flexed my fingers out in front of me, debating whether I wanted to investigate. The real question lingered in my mind: if this animal was dangerous, was I going to be a passive victim or die fighting? I thought about those wolves, and how I barely had the chance to react. This would be different, would it not? *I* was the hunter.

Deciding I was more than capable of handling a stray animal, I left the warmth of my bedroll.

I stood up slowly, trying not to make any noise or jostle anyone awake. The scratching continued at varied intervals, each time making me pause and try to listen harder once more.

Grabbing a torch, I carefully tiptoed toward the sound with my other hand outstretched, in case I needed to call for my magic at a moment's notice. My breaths became shallow as I moved toward the sound. The scratching continued, and I stopped rigid. It was so close, nearly next to me, and I swung the torch down into a dark alcove. A long shadow appeared, and I inhaled sharply.

It looked massive, whatever it was, and even though my heart was beating out of my chest, I tiptoed closer. Ice coated the tips of my fingers, and I readied myself to blast it with all the power I had.

The creature whined again, and I took another step forward. Rocks crunched under my feet, and I froze as the creature swung its head toward me. I couldn't tear my eyes away as its neck elongated, and large green glowing eyes met mine. A lump formed in my throat, and I could barely breathe. I was staring right into the eyes of a *dragon*.

My heart raced in my ears as the dragon sauntered over to me. The black scaled creature gleaming dangerously in the Everflame.

Stepping back unintentionally, I skittered rocks and scraped the bottom of my boot against the cave floor. It was a miracle I hadn't tripped over myself, my mind completely blank. I held my hand out in a placating way, intentionally not calling on my magic.

Fear pulsed through me. I couldn't run. It would chase me. But I wasn't even sure what I *could* do. My magic was surely no threat to a *dragon*.

It limped toward me and I frowned. Larger than twice my height, its monstrous black wings filled up the alcove I stood in, shielding away the tops of the caves from my eyes.

The dragon came closer still, and I lowered myself down into a crouching position. Ice coated my arms and webbed across the ground beneath my feet. Maybe if the ground was frozen solid, it would deter the dragon's curiosity.

The thought of trying to freeze it and let it die crossed my mind...but I couldn't do it. Dragons were extremely intelligent. Revered across the entire world, and rare in the wild.

The dragon stepped on my ice and hopped back with a little whine, and I narrowed my eyes on it, taking in the dragon fully. This dragon had four thick legs the size of tree trunks, each tipped in razor sharp talons, one of which it was limping on. Its long neck bent down and sniffed the ice between us. I watched as the dragon spread out its wings, and I gasped.

The wingspan was huge—the tips reaching beyond the range of which my torch lit up. The tail, too long for me to see the end of, was slithering along the ground and sharp spikes ran along the creature's back, looking longer in the flame's shadow.

One long shiver wracked through the dragon's body as it licked the ice, and it let out a mewling sound before closing its eyes and running its tongue through its sharp teeth. The dragon made a strange noise, almost like a cat's purr—if a cat were a giant reptilian predator.

My heart didn't stop pounding, but I wanted to laugh when the dragon rolled over and wiggled across the ice. The position the dragon was in allowed me a better view of its leg, which had a large gash that—while not bleeding—was gnarly with white pus and had some sort of green viscous discharge leaking from it.

I bit my lip, still frozen from fear and indecision, but I gasped as I realized we had a witch! Maya would surely have something to help—a healing potion, salve, or at least *something*.

Slowly, I stepped back toward the way I came in. If the dragon noticed me moving away, they didn't care. They loved the ice, and rolled over it, coating the black scales in icy shards and melted moisture.

Once I was far enough out of the alcove, I poured magic out of my palms, sealing the alcove with ice, hoping it would be enough to hold the dragon in. I was sure if they wanted to, they could burst through, but I hoped the creature would remain distracted.

I followed the scent of the campfire back to the group and waved the Everflame torch over the group, trying to discern where Maya was sleeping. Recognizing Maya's long black hair, I tiptoed toward her.

"Maya?" I whispered hurriedly. She stirred before muttering something incomprehensible.

"Lydia? What is it?" She rubbed the sleep out of her eyes, and next to her, Iris stirred awake as well.

"I need your help." Panic started coursing through my limbs, making my voice waver. The ice would hold, but for how long? I should have just left the dragon and came back to the camp immediately. What was I even thinking? I was acting foolish. I should be demanding we pack up and leave. Sweat pooled in my palms, and I wiped them along my pants. I needed to save that dragon.

I looked at Maya. "Do you have anything that could heal an infected wound?"

She looked at me with eyes so wide I could see the whites of them from the glow of the Everflame.

"What's wrong? Did you get hurt?" She peeled herself out of the bedroll and made her way to the wagon before sifting through the supplies.

I shook my head. "No, it's not for me..."

She turned to me with narrowed eyes. "Who is it for, Lydia?"

"Can you get it or not?" I shot back at her. She pursed her lips, not happy with me evading her question.

"It would be helpful to know what you need it for, so I can be sure I give you the right stuff." She eyed me with skepticism.

"A large gash. White and green puss frothing from a wound."

Maya cursed as she rummaged around in the wagon, vials clinking together in her hands. "Sounds like it could be anything from an advanced infection to poison. Here, hold these." She handed me a long piece of fabric, presumably for bandaging, and a bundle of herbs.

She had a satchel of gods-know-what strapped to her when she hopped out of the wagon. Two short swords gleamed on her sides.

"We should wake the others," she whispered while Iris stood across the fire with her hands on her hips, ready to follow us wherever we went.

"Looks like they are doing it on their own," I said nodding to where Caelum was moving around as he heard our restlessness.

Aceus woke with a grumble, and I grimaced at the stir this was causing.

"What's..." Caelum grunted and sat up. I froze as he looked at us with tired eyes. His hazel eyes pinned on me, and he narrowed his gaze. I held back a groan and clenched my jaw instead.

"Well, come along if you must. I found an injured animal," I said, unsure on why I felt like I should have been hiding the dragon from him. The dragon was trapped by my ice, safe as far as I knew. My resolve wavered for a moment, considering Caelum might intend to hurt or kill the dragon himself, and a sudden roar of protection surged through me at the thought.

Everyone donned weapons before I led them to the dragon. My hands shook as I took a short sword for myself, even though I knew I would never use it.

We reached the frozen solid wall, and as well as I could see—which wasn't much by the Everflame—the dragon hadn't tried to force their way out.

"I don't feel any animal..." Iris' eyes pinned to mine, a frown creasing her brow.

"We need to get through," I demanded.

"And what will we meet inside?" Maya asked, her face serious. I grimaced, staring blankly at the wall of impenetrable frost in front of me, unsure of what to do next, or if we should have just left the dragon to their own devices after all.

I glanced between them all, worrying what would happen if I told them, and what would happen if I didn't.

Caelum tongued his cheek in thought, clearly noticing my hesitancy and rising panic. With a palm clutched to my shoulder, he shared a look with Maya, who had her hands clutching a sheathed sword on her hip. She nodded back, her gaze shifting to the ice wall.

He leaned over me, his lips brushing against my ear. "Can you melt it?" he whispered.

"Yes, just give me a moment," I panted, and Caelum only leaned closer. The scruff of facial hair along scraped against my cheek, and I gasped as each point of contact burned like flames along my skin.

I imagined my ice becoming water, the warmth of his voice enticing this different way of using my magic through me. I let myself fall into focus and held up my hand against the biting cold barrier.

Bit by bit, the ice cracked. The ice beneath my palms softened, and slowly, so ever slowly, it turned into water. Pushing my magic forward, I eventually made a hole big enough for us to walk through.

"Lydia," Caelum growled from behind me as he took in what stood on the other side of the icy barrier. I glanced at him, noting the way he processed the giant dragon I revealed. He wasn't angry or frightened. How he could remain so calm made me wonder what his life had entailed, how he became this sturdy, level-headed man in the eye of immediate danger.

There were a million possibilities shining through his hazel eyes, his jaw clenching as he pondered the safest course of action.

We all stood with our hearts in our throats, staring at the giant black mass that took up the cave space. The dragon was lying still, mud caking over the black scales as they huffed slow, steady breaths.

I turned to Caelum. "Please, don't make any noise. It's hurt, possibly worse." I threw a look at Maya, who looked sympathetic, but her jaw feathered just the same. My heart was racing so fast I thought for sure it would give out, but I stepped forward, determined to stick to my decision and help this injured creature. Caelum's hand grabbed my arm, but I pushed him off.

"Stop. I have to do this," I begged him. He gave me a pleading look, but I shifted my attention to Maya, beckoning her to follow me. We shuffled closer, both of us starkly aware of the sound each footstep made.

"Goddess above, save me now," Maya muttered.

The dragon shifted, and Caelum stood rigid behind me, his hand finding my shoulder and clutching to the point of pain.

"Back up," he breathed, "and block this back off. We need to go."

"No," I demanded. "The dragon needs help. I can't let this creature die because of our fears. I'll encase them in ice to keep them still. Maya, hand me the medicine." I shoved my hand toward her, but she pressed her lips into a thin line and shook her head.

"No. I'll administer the medicine—*if* you can immobilize it," Maya insisted. "If that dragon fights, we run."

I nodded with false confidence and pressed my hands to the ground, never taking my eyes off of the dragon. I willed my power to move through me, dragging it from my chest with the precision I knew I had. The ice webbed around the creature, getting closer and closer. The dragon stirred sleepily as I approached.

Fully aware of the sharp talons that could kill us all if I wasn't careful, I grunted, pulling on my magic more forcefully. Ice bent and folded as I weaved my hands through the air, shaping it to cage and freeze over the dragon. I wrapped it around the creature's middle, sealing as much as I could with the ice below. The dragon stirred awake, and upon realizing there was a band around the middle, started thrashing.

Maya and Caelum cursed, and I heard Iris pacing behind. Shards and chips of ice sprayed over me, leaving sharp cuts on my skin, but I didn't let it deter me from my goal.

Sweat beaded over my eyebrow and dripped over my eyelashes as I poured all my energy into my magic. Ice spread like a torrent with a crackled echo through the cave walls.

Careful to smooth the ice around the dragon, I made sure not to impale them with shards by accident. The dragon's wings were sealed to the ground, along with the thrashing tail, and I wrapped more ice over the dragon's long neck and teeth.

A bright green eye met mine, and I could have sworn I felt their fear and trepidation.

When the dragon realized they couldn't move, they grew still. The dragon's slitted pupil never strayed from mine, and my heart sank as I felt betrayal conveyed from the look I was given.

"It's secure," I panted as I peeled my eyes away from the dragon to meet two wide-eyed Magi and a witch staring back at me with their mouths hanging open. My chest heaved with exhaustion, but I still snapped my fingers impatiently. "I don't know how long it will hold, so you need to move quickly or let me do it."

Maya snapped her mouth shut and made her way toward the dragon's injured leg. "Are you sure this is strong enough?"

"No, but are you going to back out now?" I growled. She let out a ragged breath and straightened her shoulders. I veered my gaze back to the dragon in front of us. Purple smoke curled from their nose and I gave a pleading look, trying to convey every apology and good intention into my eyes.

The dragon's vertical pupil became larger when Maya placed her hand tentatively along their injured leg. We all held our breath, waiting for a reaction, but they only blinked. *What had this dragon gone through to accept their fate so quickly?*

I stepped toward those big, beautiful, green eyes when Caelum's hand wrapped around my bicep.

"What are you doing?" he hissed, his eyes wild with shock. I jerked myself out of his grasp.

"They won't hurt me." I took another step closer.

"You don't know that." He reached for me again, but I stepped out of his grasp. I turned back to the dragon, who was watching me with keen eyes. He was right. I didn't know. But for some reason, I could feel it. As much as I knew that the blood running through my veins was gifted from the gods, I knew this dragon would not harm me.

"It's okay." My voice was soft and as I approached. The dragon no longer blew out smoke, but a low whine came from their throat, and I glanced at Maya. She had her hand on their leg, peering at the wound and taking stock of the damage.

The dragon huffed out hot air, slightly melting the restraints I made around their jaw. I placed my hand on the impenetrable scales protecting the dragon's body. Pure black gleaming against my white ice. I felt the movement through the dragon's throat as they let out another whimper. Maya opened the stopper and poured it over the infected wound.

The dragon let out a horrid sound filled with pain and confusion. The wail of pain ricocheted through me, bringing tears to my eyes.

"Shh..." I stroked the dragon's long muzzle in between the ice. "Everything is going to be fine. We're just getting you fixed up."

They blinked up at me, their body moving up and down faster with quickening breaths. I tried my best to soothe them, and they stared at me, almost like they knew I meant no harm. At least, it was what I hoped.

"The medicine is applied," Maya stated, and as if the dragon knew she was done, they started thrashing about once again, trying to escape the icy shackles I had placed on them.

"So, what now?" I shouted a little too loudly, my hands shaking now we had finished what I had started. She let out a shaky breath and backed away from the flailing beast. The vial dropped out of her hand, shattering against the stone cave floor.

"We run." Maya darted for the small entrance I had carved from the ice, never turning her back on the dragon for a single moment.

"Wait—" I protested. The dragon was still encased in ice and they looked...scared. The same fear I saw in Maya's eyes was reflected in the dragon's. I couldn't just leave them here, encased in ice, with no way out. Making them break out seemed cruel.

I couldn't escape Caelum's grasp this time as he gripped my arm so tightly I was sure it would leave bruises. "Close it. Close it now or I will, and then it will be trapped forever."

I cursed. Caelum was right. With my magic they would eventually break free, but if he used his earth powers, the dragon might never get out—whether the dirt would be too hard packed to break free or cut off the air supply. I glanced back over at the creature. Cracks formed in the surrounding ice. Now they were fully healed and using their full strength to break free. I let my magic seep into my fingers, casting ice over the hole, all the while whispering apologies, hoping they would understand.

I wasn't sure why I felt so strongly about this beast. The need to protect them was so intrinsically ingrained, I had to make sure they would survive. But I had to survive, too, and letting an angry and scared dragon free to roam while we were still in here was suicide.

THE CAMP WAS PACKED with a speed and efficiency I had never seen. Granted, I had limited experience, but I imagined we set a record. I packed up my stuff without ceremony, shoving my bedroll into the wagon, and picking up any last utensils and supplies and throwing them in, while Iris and Caelum made sure the horses were all saddled properly. No one conversed, only giving out the occasional bark for help and last-minute reminders.

Caelum flung himself over Olympia and pulled me up in front of him, nearly taking my arm out of the socket. I didn't make a peep of pain, though. I knew this was my fault. If I had just ignored the damn scratching sounds, we wouldn't be running away like this.

"We can go this way!" Iris called as she led us through more caves in a different direction from where the dragon was trapped. A roar echoed from far behind us, but still loud enough for me to shudder in Caelum's arms. We were away from any immediate danger, but my guess was that the dragon had finally broken out of its icy shackles and frozen barricade.

We raced forward, Iris guiding us through twists and turns, the Everflame torches spitting green sparks behind us. I didn't know how we did it, but we navigated through stalagmites with relative ease, not even the wagon slowing us down. We jetted through the darkness, small rocks and stalactites bursting from our path, allowing the horses ample room to continue through.

It was then when I realized Caelum was using his magic to keep our route clear. I heard nothing but explosions from Caelum's will, the wind rushing past my ears, and my heart thumping violently in my chest.

Eventually, Caelum slowed Olympia, and Iris nodded back to him, letting us know we were in the clear.

"Are we safe now?" I asked, my voice tinny and more breathy than I had expected.

Caelum shifted behind me, and I hadn't realized how rigid he was until now. "We should be fine, but we will not stop until Iris is absolutely positive. She says the way the dragon affects the surrounding creatures lets her know the location."

Regardless of Iris' abilities, I was unsure if any amount of distance would make me feel safe in these caves any longer. It seemed like eons ago when I was only worried about a fish nibbling on my toes, and now we had a whole dragon chasing after us. Could they scent us and track us down? I shivered, not really wanting to know the answer.

Glancing back up at Iris, I noticed the lines between her forehead bunching. I wondered if she felt responsible, but in the end, it was all really me. If I hadn't woken up, would the dragon have just moved on?

"It's my fault," Caelum said, and I jolted at his words.

"How could you possibly think that?" I asked, with my heart racing in my chest.

"I normally insist we keep at least one person awake at all times." He sighed. "I figured it had been quiet, and we haven't run into any problems so far. I got too comfortable."

My breathing turned ragged. He thought it was *his* fault? I was the one who sought the dragon out. *I* was the one who insisted Maya heal the damned creature. If anyone was at fault, it was me. And it made me so angry. I didn't make mistakes like that. I didn't work on whims. It wasn't who I was...or was it?

Did I even know who I really was? Had I even had a chance to explore this part of myself before? My life was textbooks and public training, not gallivanting through caves and being chased by dragons.

My hands started trembling, and I breathed in uneven breaths as my head started feeling fuzzy. I clasped my fingers in between each other, but the shaking only transferred into my arms. I couldn't get my body to stop.

My shoulders trembled and my teeth chattered against each other. We had all almost been severely injured, or worse, and for what reason? Because *I* wanted to save the dragon—I needed to. And I couldn't for the life of me explain why.

"Lydia?" Caelum's voice was far-off. He kept saying that name, but it wasn't who I was. It wasn't me. Lydia hadn't endangered these people, Halcyon had. The Lady of Dolan had.

It was reckless and stupid, and if I couldn't make well thought-out decisions for a group of five, then how could I possibly make decisions for an entire city? Dark spots flashed over my eyes, and my body tingled with needles under my skin.

Caelum kept calling out, but I didn't want to respond. I couldn't respond. Instead, I took a deep, shaking breath in. My lungs burned with the expansion, and I kept inhaling and exhaling, in and out, relishing in the burn until my shaking stopped.

In return, every trepidation was locked tightly away. Everyone was in danger because of me, but there was absolutely nothing more I could do about it now. I piled that small box next to the other boxes in my mind and decided I would never open it again.

With one last long exhale, I shifted so I could look back at Caelum. I gave him a tight smile. "Apologies. I'm fine. Let's just get out of these caves."

Chapter 10

HALCYON

It was a never-ending sea of darkness and rock. I had long since resigned myself from asking how much longer it would be, putting my entire trust in Caelum to find our way out.

We trekked at a slow pace, and I could have sworn the caves kept getting narrower as we went on, until Iris held up a fist—a sign for us to stop. She looked exhausted. Her shoulders rounded in fatigue, and circles lined her eyes. Once again, I felt the guilt which threatened to take me under, and I shoved it aside.

"Our exit is this way, but it's blocked since we took a detour," she told Caelum. He shifted behind me, his large solid chest pressing against my back. With the reins gathered in one hand, Caelum held them out to me.

"Here, take these for a moment, please," he asked me softly, and I nodded, taking the reins from him. The leather was thick and warm in my palms. Caelum sucked in a deep breath, and an in instant, I felt the ground shaking beneath us.

I turned my face toward Caelum, but his eyes were closed in concentration. I watched as his hands flexed, making gravel fall from the ceiling of the solid wall we stood in front of.

Iris swung her horse around to stand behind us, and the horses whinnied and stomped their feet on the ground anxiously. A loud crack reverberated along the cave walls.

Caelum tensed his body, and I watched intently as the earth shifted and moved in accordance to his direction. His forearms flexed with his strength as he pulled and tugged the earth.

With one flick of his wrist, loose rock and debris were shoved to the sides of the cave, revealing a fresh path. The ground was clear of any fallen stone, and it was tall and wide enough for the wagon to pass through easily.

I sat in awe of Caelum's power. The man could literally move mountains. A burst of desire flooded through me, and for the first time since we had escaped the dragon, I felt something other than the cold emptiness of guilt.

Iris resumed leading the way as we turned into the new passage, and my ears perked as I heard noises. Noises I hadn't heard in what felt like days. Certainly not anything I had heard in these caves.

Birds chirping. Leaves rustling. I gasped as we made a turn and sunlight poured into the cave from an opening above us. Squinting at the onslaught of brightness, the light was almost painful, but my heart swelled all the same. It almost felt unreal, but I could taste the fresh air that drifted through the cavern.

The ground inclined as we went on, sunlight and fresh air embracing me in pockets. I felt my shoulders relax, and I leaned into Caelum softly, as I let the breeze drift over my skin.

"We are almost there," Caelum said in my ear, as we inclined further before a large opening revealed lush greens and trees so tall I couldn't see the tips of them from my point of view. Cave rock turned into dirt beneath us, and vines stretched out over the cave walls.

We exited through an enormous mouth of the cave and no longer was I staring at the bleak blackness of underground. Instead, I drank in the vibrant greens of the shrubbery and the striking blue of the sky.

Flowers bloomed in colorful contrasts of yellows, violets, and blues among the greens of foliage. It smelled fresh and wild and free.

It reminded me nothing of home, with our tall pine trees that overlooked deep mountainous crevices and rivers. Instead, these trees were immense in girth—some larger than the homes back in Dolan. Their colossal trunks, a deep burgundy red, supported the massive height of them as they scraped against fluffy white clouds above.

"Holy gods," I breathed. I had never seen anything like this. Did the mortals even realize they had this amazing world on their doorstep?

Caelum insisted there were no mortals nearby, but how could they keep away from something like this? It was as though the mortal lands held magic in their soil rather than their people.

"There is a myth," Caelum said, as though he could read my mind, his voice gruff in mystery, his stubble scraping against my head and catching in my hair. His arms tightened around me and I leaned further into him, soaking up his warmth. "When the border battle happened in the Great War, each fallen Magi sprouted into a massive tree. The blood they spilled fell to the ground, fertilizing it. Growing these trees—redwoods—in their honor. The more powerful the Magi, the bigger the tree."

I shivered, thinking about all those Magi who lost their lives, fighting against the mortal Dragon Riders, fleeing toward safety. Only to be met with a monstrous mountain range instead.

"Is that why mortals don't come close to the border?" I asked.

"Yes. The mortals regard the Magi as an evil entity. The King has rules barring mortals from places like this. He hides it under the narrative of safety, but we know it's just another form of control over his people. In reality, it's just too close to the border, and would be a simple escape."

"Living like that sounds awful. They miss out on so much," I commented.

Caelum hummed in thought behind me. "How would they know it's awful if they don't even know what they're missing out on?"

I let the question stew in my mind for a second. He was right. The mortals only knew fear when it came to Magi. If I had to guess, most of them probably didn't even realize this forest existed. Or if they did, it was a warning sign. The demons they feared were close by.

We slowly trudged deeper into the forest until the morning sun hung in the center of the sky. Stringy green vines became thick ropes, and the horses began to have difficulty traversing the forest floor.

"We're here," Iris called out, a huge grin on her face as she hopped off her horse. Caelum slid off Olympia, and I took his hand as he helped me down after him.

I stretched up, releasing my stiff legs, not hiding my smile. We made it, and even though this was the beginning of our quest, it felt like we already had a success.

"Where's the temple?" I looked around, staring into the thick nature around us, unsure how there could be a whole temple in a place like this.

Caelum lifted his pack off the horse, his arms constricting under his shirt with the weight. He brought the pack to his shoulder, and swung his head, trying to get the hair that had fallen into his face out of his eyes.

My mouth parted as his muscles rippled beneath the tight tunic he wore. Golden rays spilt between branches and cast his tanned skin in a bronzed light. I was rendered speechless, unable to move or tear my wandering gaze from him. He smirked at me, letting me see a small dimple on his cheek.

Caelum grinned harder and trailed my body with his eyes. Every point of contact he made coaxed my body to flush with heat until he looked beyond me and jutted his chin.

"The temple lies just through the brush behind you. Can't see it right now, but it's only a short walk away."

"Uh huh." I peeled my eyes away from him, only vaguely remembering my question.

Turning to see if I could spot the temple for myself, I sighed, resigning to the fact we had already come this far, and I just needed to trust Caelum.

Surrounded by the monstrous trees, we set up our camping spot. The sky was visible through a break in the dense canopy, and I breathed in the damp wood and fallen leaves which surrounded me. A river rushed somewhere nearby. The babbling of the water over rocks accented the rest of the forest playing its natural form of music.

We all pitched in getting the camp set up. This was to be our permanent spot while we worked, so we could make the camp more comfortable.

I helped Maya set up the tents. It was a struggle at first, figuring out the best way to hammer the stakes into the ground and untangle the ropes and cloth that would shelter us.

Maya didn't say a word to me outside of direction. She was rather upset at me, but I was perhaps hoping our secure safety would quell her anger. It was a bit naïve. I knew I had put everyone's lives in danger, and there wasn't really a good way for me to apologize. The words "I'm sorry" didn't quite seem to feel like enough. I sighed as I took a seat next to the fire Maya had lit, glad I could put my body to use. It was rewarding to feel the tiredness in my muscles.

The sun was descending through the trees. Deep ruby red and warm orange light bathed over the camp, showcasing little flying particles in the air. The breeze was cool against my skin, and I reclined back on my elbows, letting myself appreciate the outdoors once again.

An owl hooted low in the trees as Maya handed me a plate of her latest recipe. I glanced up at her, but she didn't even so much as look my way as she dropped the plate in my hands.

"Maya," I started, her back facing me, clearly ignoring me. "Apologies for the dragon incident. I wasn't thinking."

She stopped, her back rigid, and she clenched her hands by her sides in fists before breathing out a long breath. There was tiredness wearing on her face as she turned to me. With her hand on her hip she stared with her dark eyes, nearly black, pinned on me.

"I know you're new at this, so I will give you a pass this one time." She dragged her free hand over her features, trying to find the right words. "But in the future, all information needs to be disclosed before we charge in anywhere."

She scowled at me, and a lump rose in my throat. Maya had been nothing but kind, even when I had been less than desirable to be around. She bent forward, her face level with mine.

"I have a responsibility to this group. We all do. We rely on each other. Without a single one of us, we are probably all dead. So you need to remember that the next time you decide to rope any of us into anything without explaining yourself first. There will be times where we have to make sudden decisions, and our lives will be on the line, but use that pretty little head of yours and figure out the right thing to do in the moment."

Maya snapped back up and strode away. I blew out a breath, not really sure how else I could have expected her to react. I would have to make it up to her eventually, but I just wasn't quite sure how. Caelum slid next to me, both of us sitting on a log Aceus had pulled over earlier.

"That went well." The small dimple made an appearance again.

His presence was so calming, and I thought about how he had comforted me, even if he didn't realize he was doing so. My chest warmed as I looked into his hazel eyes, seeing the kindness seeping from them. I wanted to bathe in his energy. Cast aside all my doubts and reservations and just lean into his soothing spirit.

I sighed. "About as well as I would expect, to be honest." Maya came back with a plate for Caelum, which he took graciously before she went back to her post.

"How are we going to do the sleeping arrangements since we lost one of our tents?" I asked after swallowing yet another delightful bite of dinner, eager to change the subject.

"I've been thinking about that," Caelum rubbed his palm along his jaw, and once again I found myself hypnotized by his features. His long fingers pressed against his cheek, each finger putting a divot into his tanned skin. "I think you'll end up having to share with Maya and Iris."

I scowled. Not that I would have minded, but the tents were not built for three people, and Maya was clearly still upset with me. The last thing I wanted to do was encroach on her space. "I could share with you, if you wouldn't mind?"

Caelum bellowed a laugh, as though my suggestion was ridiculous.

"I'm being serious!" I frowned at him.

"You would be all right with that? I'm not going to pretend like I know anything about being a servant of a Lady, but wouldn't this compromise you in some way?"

I snorted. "Compromise me? We are in the mortal kingdom, surrounded by no one." I wanted to say, *It's not like I'm* the *Lady,* but I was, and I was only willing to lie so far.

Sleeping next to Caelum would have definitely been considered misconduct in Dolan. But I wasn't in Dolan anymore. And as far as anyone else knew, I wasn't the Lady. I could do whatever I pleased and Nik or anyone else would be none the wiser.

Caelum raised his hands in surrender, a bright smile making his whole aura shine. It instantly put me at ease. If I could ride in front of him on a horse for days, I could easily sleep in the same tent as him. At least then, we would have space between us. As it was, I already felt every single inch of the man when I sat between his thighs.

"I think you'll find it a rare day when I turn down sharing a tent with a beautiful woman." His gaze turned molten as he looked at me, and I found myself holding my breath as his fingers traced my ear before tucking a piece of hair behind it.

Caelum sighed before looking up to the stars above, and I couldn't help but stare at him.

The clear sky was tinging dark blue and purple. Stars were making their appearance, their light minimal in the twilight. Caelum's features were striking against the dusk sky. Flickering shadows from the fire accentuated the sharp lines of his jaw which carved into a soft smile on his lips.

"You've been waiting for this for a long time, haven't you?" I asked, intrigued to see someone with so much passion go to such lengths to get what they wanted.

Caelum nodded. "It isn't an exaggeration when I say Dolan was my last option. If the Lord had said no, then I would be forced to call it quits. And I was sure the day was coming, so for that I suppose I am beyond grateful."

I let out a dark chuckle. "Well, don't thank me yet. We haven't even started," I muttered.

Caelum gave me a quizzical smile. "Yes, I suppose I should also be thanking you for your attendance."

"Thank Lady Halcyon," I attempted to recover, not even realizing I spoke my truth, and I bit my lip, glad he didn't seem to catch on to my constant lies.

Chapter 11

CAELUM

One by one, everyone retired to their tents. The last few days had been grueling, and we were all ready for a solid night's sleep.

After the mad dash through the caves, blasting obstacles out of the way, my magic was getting low, and I desperately needed to recuperate. Maya offered me a potion and I took it hastily.

Unfortunately, it did nothing to sate my physical exhaustion. As much as I wanted to start sorting through materials and making a plan, I needed the sleep. It didn't matter how eager I was to get to the temple. Being back in these woods was a thrilling feeling, and my mind kept drifting to tomorrow's possibilities.

Maya agreed to take the first round of night watch. I was beyond grateful to her. She may not have had magic in the same sense as I did, but having her watching the woods was better than nothing.

My tent was near empty, save for a small lantern and the bedroll I placed in it earlier. I held my hand out to Lydia, gesturing for her to pass her bedroll to me.

Tentatively she obliged, and I wondered if she was really as on board with this idea as she let on.

Ambrose wasn't a particularly conservative country, but Dolan was notorious for being old-fashioned. The Lord had spent countless years making sure everything remained as he saw fit—the same as it had been for centuries.

It was one reason I never bothered going back before now. Dolan was stuffy and pretentious, especially when you started mingling with the socialites. Not my crowd. Not at all.

Lydia was different. She was smart; she was quick and was adapting to this lifestyle. I assumed it was because of her status. Not quite a ruling entity, working more like a servant to the Lady than of anyone with any decision-making power. And although she held an air of formality, she wasn't shallow or judgmental.

I was starting to think if she ever wanted to break away from castle life, then she would make a great addition to our team. Not that there was any *other* reason I wanted to keep her around. No, she was inquisitive and thoughtful, and that alone would make for a great asset.

Great asset or not, I couldn't help but indulge in every move she made, including how she was currently stretching herself down onto her bedroll. Her long brown hair swayed over her shoulder, and she kneeled on all fours. She moved her weight forward as she flattened the corners, her ass driving into the air, and my mouth dried instantly.

It should have been illegal for her to wear the pants she had on. They were tight over her rounded ass. The seam creased through the center. It took every ounce of restraint for me to avert my gaze.

"Caelum?" her sweet voice called to me.

"Yes?" I asked huskily, my desire overwhelming my senses. It had been so long since I had the intimate company of another woman, and here Lydia was tempting me with everything she was.

If she saw the heat in my eyes, she didn't show it. She smiled gently up at me and asked, "Aren't you going to get in bed? We should probably get some rest before tomorrow."

"Yes," I said, clearing my throat. I silently cursed as I realized I was in no shape to change out of my pants. My cock was hard, straining against the britches I was wearing.

Lydia shuffled around, finally settling herself in her bedroll. She rolled to her side, her back facing me, and I thanked the gods mentally. Turning away from her, I blew out a breath and ached for sleep to take me, because not only was I sleeping next to a woman I probably shouldn't touch, but now I couldn't touch myself either. This was absolute misery.

I laid as still as I could until I heard the deep rhythmic breaths which told me Lydia was definitely asleep. I rolled onto my back, drumming my fingers on my chest.

My brain refused to quiet as checklists ran through my mind. The anticipation of being able to thoroughly explore this temple set my thoughts whirring, no matter how fatigued my body was. Eventually, I dozed off.

Sometime later I woke with a start. The forest was eerily quiet. Too quiet. The crickets ceased to sing and the trees stood still, like they were holding their breath.

It was then that I noticed a shuffling sound from the outside of the tent, along with a large huff of air.

Immediately, my ears twitched, and I laid so still I hardly breathed. There was a beast on the other side of the flimsy material of the tent, and dread sank into my stomach. I had a feeling I knew what sort of creature was sniffing the tent. Right near Lydia's head.

Carefully, I crawled out of my bedroll, trying not to make any noise as I lifted the front flap of the tent. Maya sat on the other side of the fire pit, her gaze pinned on the creature with fear lining her features. She glanced at me and mouthed, "*Dragon.*"

Shit. Shit, shit, shit. Of all the obstacles we could have run into by coming into the mortal kingdom, wild dragons were *not* on my list.

I slid my gaze to where the creature was currently occupied by sniffing Lydia's scent, and I instantly recognized the black scales from the dragon Lydia saved in the cave. *Not good.* This dragon had returned, chasing down Lydia's scent.

Dragons were typically beasts of their own kind. They lived with each other, isolated from humanity. They weren't so secluded to never be seen, but normally they were only witnessed from afar. The creatures were considered dangerous enough that if you were close enough to one to see the scales, you were most likely the dragon's next meal. So why was this dragon sniffing my tent and not attacking?

Quickly, I grabbed my lantern and my short sword, just in case. I wasn't sure what this weapon would do against a dragon—if anything at all—but better to be safe than sorry.

I gazed down at Lydia, her breaths steady as she slept. She looked so peaceful, completely unaware of the beast who could swallow us whole if it felt the need to do so. But at this moment, it wasn't. It also wasn't interested in Maya or the other two tents in our camp.

Carefully, I placed my hands on Lydia's shoulders, shaking her awake.

"What are you—" Lydia mumbled.

"Sh." I covered my mouth with a finger, and she gave me a confused look before hearing the heavy breathing next to her head. Her eyes widened with fear, but before she had time to scream, I wrapped her in my arms and called on my magic.

The earth beneath us opened up, and I held Lydia close to my body, my hand covering her mouth. She thrashed wildly in my arms as I concealed ourselves in the hole I created underneath the tent. It was deep, and I willed my power to create an open sphere around us.

"What are you doing?" she hissed at me once I released my hand from her face. I didn't let my arms go from around her, enjoying how her body felt in my arms a little too much. Maybe I was acting selfishly. Not that I cared. "I can't see a damned thing."

"I just concealed us from the dragon," I said while I rummaged in my pockets to light the lantern.

"The dragon?" Her voice was high pitched, panicked.

"Keep your voice down," I hissed. "I think it's following you."

"Following me? But why?"

"Don't know," I muttered as I stepped around her, carving a tunnel deep into the earth. "But we need to move it away from the camp."

I hated the idea that I would essentially be using Lydia as bait, but I was confident I could lure it away from causing any damage. And hopefully, we could also escape.

Chapter 12

HALCYON

CAELUM LIT A LANTERN, and I rubbed my shoulders, trying to banish the chill wracking through me.

Caelum lifted the lantern higher, exposing the tunnel he had built so hastily. He barely paid me attention, sticking his hand on the earth next to us as he answered with distraction. "It was the same dragon as before," he explained.

"*Why* is it following me?" I repeated more firmly.

Caelum ignored my questioning as he used his magic to burrow to the left, leaving a gaping tunnel in the wake of his magic. "Come on, this way."

"Where are we going?" I followed him with haste, swallowing the lump formed in my throat. Again, he didn't answer, and my palms grew sticky with sweat.

He pushed against the packed dirt, creating a path for us. I didn't know where we were relative to our camp, but Caelum at least looked like he knew what he was doing.

He rolled up his sleeves, and dirt coated his tunic in streaks. We walked quietly for what felt like ages. There was no sun or moon to tell us how long we had been underground, and I once again started feeling the same sort of trapped as I did in the caves.

Even though the tunnel was wide and tall, there was a never-ending vast ceiling, and my chest began to tighten. I breathed through my whirling thoughts and instead tried to focus on anything else, but if it wasn't the dirt tunnel around me, it was the dragon who could be chasing us.

"Almost there," Caelum whispered.

"Almost where?" I hissed through my teeth, my patience running thin. When I signed up for this trip, I readied for an exploratory investigation, not getting chased in the cloying, suffocating earth by a fully grown dragon who wanted to eat me.

He grimaced in concentration, and the earth fell away from the touch of his hands. His long fingers sunk into the wall before us, and he grunted before a path exposed itself. But, instead of more dirt, we stepped into a large dark cave. No, not a cave—a room.

Caelum raised the lantern higher, revealing a large room made of marble and gold.

"Oh, my gods." I raised my hand over my mouth. "Where are we, Caelum?"

"I felt an emptiness, thought it was a cavern, but this..." His words trailed off as he took in the enormous expanse himself.

Large well-preserved pillars held up the tall ceilings, and as I walked further, Caelum's lantern bobbing dutifully behind me, I noticed a dais on one side of the room. A massive marble throne sat upon the dais. It had a pedestal on each side. One displayed a bow, propped up by a marble stand; the other, a tome. I could only guess that the tome was presumably a detailed recount of events of whoever reigned on this throne.

Dolan had several tomes written by scribes and historians, most of them kept in the Neverwind Library for safety. For one to be here, after however many years—and in what looked to be a decent condition—was nothing short of a miracle.

The Divine was potent in here, like the stagnant underground preserved godly energy. It thrummed through my body, calling to me, welcoming the magic in my blood like an old friend.

I sighed in wonder, taking in the opulent structure, and I tried to imagine what it must have looked like back when people were here. I could practically see the gleaming gold, could smell the offerings of incense and wine.

"We must be deep in the temple, but this isn't right. I went the opposite direction of the temple entrance," Caelum whispered. He made his way to the center of the room, and I felt infinitely smaller.

How had this massive place been so hidden deep underground? What sort of temple was this? This was a throne room—not a place of worship, but a place of ruling.

"Caelum, look…" I pointed to the pedestal where the exquisite bow sat, gleaming even in the low light of the lantern. I tilted my head in confusion as a strange noise seemed to emit from it, my feet subconsciously leading me forward. The bow…was it singing?

"Lydia, wait." Caelum strode over, tugging me back pulled me back toward him, and I looked up at him in confusion. I was supposed to touch the bow, supposed to hold it. As I pulled away from Caelum, his grip tightened around my arm, rendering me immobile.

"Let me go." I demanded, ice coating my fingertips.

"We don't know what that bow is," he hissed, his gaze bouncing between me and the pedestal. My blood boiled. I needed to get to it. I needed to know.

"Think about it," he pleaded. "It could be a trap."

I shook my head. The only thing that mattered was getting my hands on that weapon. It was embedded with magic. This entire room was. I could feel it pulsing in my veins, in my soul. Like a steady rhythm, the magic was slumbering, begging to be woken up.

"A trap from whom? We have to see." I peeled my gaze from the bow on the pedestal, which now seemed to hum louder and shine brighter, back to Caelum. "What if it's a message from the gods? Isn't this why we came here?"

I peered up at him with hope in my eyes, but as he looked at me, my heart sank. Wariness and frustration lined his features as his jaw feathered. His grip grew tighter, pressing hard into my skin.

I jerked myself from his hold and made to move closer to it when Caelum's broad frame blocked me from my goal.

He whispered darkly with warning, "Let's take things slow. We will get to the weapon, but we need to make sure we do this the right way."

I nodded, understanding that I may have been outside of my realm here. Caelum was the one who had experience with old relics and dangerous temples, and certainly he would know what to do.

I gave one last longing look to the bow, but as I did, the ache of need pounded in my chest harder. It was a restless, unrelenting beat beating in my chest and ears. Everything in my body and soul ached for the bow.

My feet moved of their own accord, and I felt myself drifting toward it. Caelum's protests fell against deaf ears as my legs propelled me forward. I needed to reach it. It was *mine*.

Each step I took was unhurried and deliberate. That bow held untold powers. Powers that I knew the mortal king would be eager to get his hands on. If he found this in his kingdom, it would be destroyed. It was my duty to safeguard this bow. My duty to wield it. I needed to protect my people. To protect Ambrose.

I couldn't help myself as I reached for it. A thrumming, banging pulse in my chest kept beckoning me toward it. As I neared, the song became louder, my soul crying and aching for the bow to be in my hands.

If fate existed, then this was surely mine. The temple no longer mattered. My father and his betrayal no longer mattered. I was supposed to come to the mortal kingdom because of this. I was sure of it. Everything clicked into place like the world stood still and waited for me with bated breath, and I smiled as I reached further, grasping for my true destiny.

Chapter 13

CAELUM

"LYDIA!" I SHOUTED, MY voice ringing off of the massive columns.

No matter what I did, she kept moving forward, reaching for the bow sitting upon the pedestal.

I raked my hands through my hair before chasing after her and grabbing her around her waist. She turned and snarled at me, her lips lifted in a sneer.

"I said to wait," I grunted out, but she was no longer listening.

Clearly, the weapon held her in a sort of trance, and fear gripped me as I realized there was no stopping her. Burning ice coated Lydia's arms, and I snapped my hands back in reaction.

"Fuck!" I cursed, my skin red from the contact.

I recovered, but not fast enough as Lydia ran to the pedestal, reaching for the bow with a fanatical gleam in her eye. Whatever was at play had Lydia in its grasp, and I didn't know how to snap her out of it.

Every time I neared, she surged her magic. Walls of ice blocked my path and obstructed my view.

My knuckles cracked and bled as I punched through the ice, failing to shatter it swiftly enough. Time after time, I put the full force of my body along with my magic behind each hit. My hands were coated in shards of rocks, striking until the last of the ice fell away.

There was no stopping Lydia as her outstretched arm reached for the bow. Her fingers brushed the dark wood, and wrapped around the grip.

Bright golden light filled the temple room. Lydia's mouth fell open with wonder, and I could only stare as a whipping wind encompassed her. An undeniable, unknown power girded her, and her brown hair whirled up as she raised her arms.

My heart beat out of my chest as I watched helplessly. She was shielded. The surrounding wind too violent, making it impossible for me to break through.

Behind me, a deafening roar had me spinning on my feet. I could do nothing except stare as the black scales and sharp white teeth burst out of the tunnel.

I was right. It was tracking her—hardly a comforting notion. Taloned feet scraped along the marble floor before launching toward Lydia. I yelled, not knowing what I could do to help. Whatever hold the bow had over her would pale in comparison to what would happen between the beast's teeth.

I charged the dragon, attempting to intercept it before it got to Lydia, but I was too slow, my magic too weak. My knees pounded against the marble floor as I fell. Leaping over me, the dragon's black scales gleamed against the supernatural golden light.

The dragon skidded to a stop. Lydia finally peeled her eyes away from the bow and met the dragon's fierce green eyes with tenderness. Her chest was heaving with labored breaths as she lifted her hand toward the dragon, who stood as still as a statue.

The golden light that bathed them grew brighter, and I squinted my eyes at the onslaught. Spiraling bands of gold drifted around them, binding them in this strange and alarming magic.

Lydia was ethereal, her skin glowing, and her hair even losing the luster of the brown and turning into a blinding silver around her shoulders. Silver hair that reminded me of someone, something that felt familiar, but I couldn't place how so.

Lydia's hand reached for the dragon's maw, and as it did, the dragon leaned in and closed its eyes. I screamed until my throat turned raw, telling her to get away, to come back to me, but it was useless.

The gold bands around them grew tighter, encasing their bodies in pure gold light before exploding outward and disappearing completely, shattering all of Lydia's ice magic and making the entire room black as night.

Only the light from the lantern in my hand remained.

"Lydia!" I shouted, scurrying up and running toward her as fast as my feet would carry. Each step felt slow and heavy, knowing my legs weren't long enough to cross over to her quickly enough, wishing that I had a power that made me run faster, push harder.

The dragon let out another roar before reaching out to grasp Lydia in its talons. She reached up toward it, not showing an ounce of fear, but that didn't keep me from yelling at her to back away.

Lydia's face slackened, and I watched in horror as she fell unconscious, the bow still clutched in her hands.

The dragon carried her easily as it pushed itself off the ground. Large wings snapped out and beat fiercely as it lifted them into the air.

"Wait!" I croaked, even though I knew it was futile. The dragon opened its large maw, letting out a stream of purple substance. Swirling purple haze gathered and formed along the marble ceiling of the room.

A reverberating click from the dragon jolted through me just before a loud explosion encompassed the room, and I clamped my hands over my ears. Pieces of marble shattered around me. I scrambled as quickly as I could to the safety of my tunnel.

I could see nothing but smoke and debris as the dragon carted Lydia away. Everything was startlingly quiet in the dragon's wake. No more magic. No more of that energy that pulsed from before.

Hastily, I ran back through my tunnel, tripping over rocks and vines as I raced toward the camp site. Without even thinking, I closed the tunnel behind me. The dragon and Lydia clearly took another route, but I wouldn't risk leading the dragon back to the camp, just in case.

Lydia was gone, and I was supposed to protect her. *Oh gods*. Aceus was going to kill me, and I wouldn't even be able to blame him for it. I had to find her. Maybe she was safe, maybe the dragon didn't rip her to shreds. But my doubts won over my optimism.

Eventually, I found myself back in my tent and clambered out. Whirling around in a circle, I peered through the trees, squinting through the long branches to see if I could spot any sign of the dragon and Lydia in its clutches.

The sky was lightening, lighter blue rays softening the sky from the harsh black of night. I could see nothing, but a distant roar made me bristle. Lydia was out there, and I needed to go to her as quickly as possible.

I skidded to the wagon, grabbing the first weapons I could find; slinging a belted sword around my waist and a bandolier across my chest. Strapping as many daggers as I could fit into the leather, I thanked the Lord of Dolan for his generous donation before turning to Olympia, hurriedly placing my saddle on her back, tightening her reins, and making sure everything was in place.

"What's going on?" a sharp voice called from behind me, and I spun around to find three pairs of eyes studying my hasty escape.

"The dragon, it took Lydia. I have to go find her."

Aceus stepped up toward me, a deep frown etched in between his eyebrows. "What do you mean a dragon took Lydia?" he growled as he flexed his arms, his face reddening with anger.

"Caelum." Maya's voice was harsh with resolve. "We came here to find more about the gods, not to chase after a *dragon*. You're being reckless."

"So I'm supposed to just let her die out there? I was supposed to protect her!"

"No," Aceus cut in. "*I* was supposed to protect her. And I have failed, but I refuse to believe she is dead. She *cannot* be dead." Anger swelled in Aceus' eyes. Maya exchanged an exasperated look with Iris, who only frowned.

"We have to find her," Aceus nodded at me, none of his anger fading, but instead, he honed it into lethal determination. He pushed me aside, sorting through a crate of weapons before strapping a sword to his side.

"Aceus," Iris breathed, "you can't. You'd be up against the dragon." Her palm met his broad shoulder, eyes wet with concern.

Aceus sighed, meeting her at eye level with a hand on her jaw. "Protecting Lydia is my duty."

"But—"

"No, this is why I came here. I have to help save Lydia. If not—" Aceus pressed a kiss on her cheek, before grasping Maya's hand as well. "Then I'm afraid of what the world will look like for you when you go back. By saving her, I'm saving you. The both of you."

My throat bobbed at Aceus' affection toward my two best companions. I turned my back, giving them some much needed privacy.

Even though my heart was racing, and my mind telling me to go *right now*, there was a very real possibility that neither one of us would come back to this camp. It wouldn't be fair to deny this closure.

Instead of peering in on their private moment, I double checked my weapons. Knots were tied, buckles snapped, and I was more than ready to find Lydia.

Triple checking Olympia's reins, Maya stepped beside me. Tear tracks lined her cheeks, even though her face was dry.

"Cal," she said with exasperation. "Be safe. Don't charge in against the dragon unless you know for a fact Lydia is alive, and you both—all of you—will survive." Iris wrapped her arms behind her, giving me a departing nod before I dug my feet into Olympia's sides.

I raced through the trees, urging Olympia to go faster, but with the uneven terrain there was only so much she could do. Aceus was close behind me on Calliope, the thumping of horses' hooves filling the morning air.

The sky was turning into dawn as I lifted my gaze, and I spotted a black-winged creature circling high above. Lydia, dangling above her certain death. I swung Olympia in the dragon's direction, praying to all the gods who existed that I wasn't too late. The dragon dived, going below the trees, and I lost track of where it went.

I cursed and urged Olympia toward where I had last seen the dragon, hoping and praying Lydia would be alive, and if I had to slay a dragon to get to her, so be it.

Olympia ran as hard as she could through the roots and rocks of the forest floor until up ahead, I noticed a purple haze floating across a massive expanse. The haze seemed to have no beginning or end. I grunted out a few choice curse words, realizing this was the same substance the dragon emitted in the temple room before it exploded the entire roof off.

I pulled on Olympia's reins, slowing her down and stopping just before the fog. There wasn't a doubt in my mind that Lydia was in there.

Horrific and bloody images were conjured in my mind. Lydia was in the grips of a dragon. Torn to shreds and barely breathing. I shook my head. I couldn't let myself fall trap to what-ifs until I knew her fate for certain.

A deep, guttural growl came from within the fog and I stepped back, crouching behind one of the giant tree trunks. The fog was unlike anything I had ever seen before. I didn't dare stick my hand through in case it was poisonous. I decided my best chance would be to go under and pray I could pass through the barrier.

"You try to look for a way in up here, and I will use my magic to see if I can worm my way in underground," I told Aceus as he slid off Calliope behind me. He nodded in confirmation before slapping a big palm on my shoulder.

"If you can save her, you must. She is more important to Dolan than you realize."

Lifting my brow in question, he handed me a small vial with lilac liquid. "I snagged this for you, just in case."

Cursing as I took it, I poured the liquid down my throat and let the potion replenish my magic. Smart man, that Aceus. Without any parting words, he strode around the perimeter, disappearing from my view.

Once my magic was full again, I buried my hands in the ground, and the dirt sifted until it buried me deep underground. I made the tunnel small, allowing myself to touch the top and feel for any tremors from the dragon. Movement caught my attention only a small distance away. I followed the movement with a lump in my throat.

If Lydia was already dead, I wasn't sure what I would do. Aceus was insistent she was still alive, and I clung to the hope the he had.

Roots and loose dirt brushed the top of my head, and I guessed there was a tree right above me, hoping it was large enough to hide me from the dragon above. I sifted through the ground and propelled myself up to the surface.

I had cleared the purple fog, but it surrounded the entire area, making a giant circle shielding the dragon. In the center of the circle, there was a large opening—free of trees—and in the middle sat the dragon curled up with its head under its wing.

There was no sign of Lydia, and I gritted my teeth. I needed to find a higher vantage point. If she was around here, whether she was alive or a pile of bones, I would find her.

Pushing myself up to the sturdy limbs of the tall tree next to me, I used my earth magic to create hand holds as I silently crept up through the foliage to get a better view. The purple haze reached up past the tops of the trees, and I could see now that it was an enclosed dome of fog, encapsulating this entire area of the forest.

I didn't see any sign of Lydia, and I felt panic rise in my throat. Only the dragon lay in the middle of the clearing, its head still tucked under its wing, body heaving in steady breaths. I gulped, running my gaze across the forest.

There was no guidebook on how to deal with this situation, and while I knew dragons were intelligent, I wasn't entirely convinced they weren't just wild animals at this point.

The dragon shifted, and it snagged my attention. Black scales shimmered as it moved its wing, and I had to double glance to make sure I was seeing everything correctly. A swath of silver hair feathered against the dirt, but it was no doubt Lydia's body lay curled up next to the dragon.

It wasn't eating her, and it didn't even look aggressive as the dragon poked at her face with its head. I stared in awe as this creature regarded Lydia. I swallowed thickly, hoping she was still breathing. Letting myself believe she had survived after all.

The dragon huffed in Lydia's face, blowing her hair back, but no smoke came out. I could have sworn I saw concern in its gaze as it looked at her, tilting its head one direction, then the next, and ever so gently prodding against her body.

I held my breath, not moving a single inch as I watched this creature take her in, and my eyes widened in surprise as I processed exactly what the dragon was doing. A whine left the dragon's throat, and it paced around Lydia in circles.

This creature had grown attached to Lydia, and it didn't want to eat her, it wanted to *save* her.

Chapter 14

HALCYON

I GROANED, FEELING SOLID dirt underneath me as I scraped my fingers, lodging the ground beneath my nails. The bow still hummed in my hand, but my head pounded, my eyes were heavy, and I remembered...

The golden light encompassing me. Enveloping me and the dragon. Warmth seeping through my skin, and a spiraling thread that was tethered to my soul, beckoning for acceptance.

Pure, unfiltered magic spread through and around me when I touched that bow, so bright it burned. The image of the dragon seared my mind, our souls meshing and combining...but it wasn't possible.

I shot up in a sitting position, gasping for air as the flood of memories rushed through me. I vomited, unable to process what had happened so viscerally. My silver hair draped around me, so all I could see was the dirt caked in my nails, and my sick puddled and sank into the ground. Somehow, the bow was unscathed in my right hand, and I clutched it in my fist tighter.

I panted, my hands shaking, and I threw myself back, away from my sick, and laid down on the ground facing the sky above. Except it wasn't right... Gone was the blue-black of night, and no stars shined. Instead, I could only see a hovering purple haze.

It was writhing like a fine mist, but it didn't smell like anything. In fact, I only smelled the dirt and trees around me. I closed my eyes and took in a deep inhale. My body shook, but I needed to find my way back to the camp. What had happened to Caelum? What had happened to *me*?

I felt a breeze on my cheek, then another, and another. It was strange, only one part of my body felt it, and it came at regular intervals. Like a breath...

I cracked my eyes open, only to find a large black snout huffing next to my face. Trying to calm the rapid beat of my heart, I dared another peek at the dragon lying next to me, breathing warm air onto my face.

In my memories, I saw the golden thread that seemed to tie us together...a choice...I had made a choice. A choice, and I knew what it was, but didn't want to admit it.

For the first time in my life, I followed my heart instead of cold logic and law. My soul was singing to forge the bond, but was it a mistake? Dragons were terrifying creatures.

And I chose to *bond with one*.

I held my own breath as the beast kept breathing on me, and a low whine came from its throat. It moved closer before opening its large maw over me.

I squeezed my eyes shut, preparing for the worst, imagining those sharp teeth sinking into my flesh, but instead I felt something warm, rough, and wet pressed against my cheek.

I slammed my eyes open. The damn thing had *licked* me.

It pulled back, and I got enough strength to shakily rise onto my elbows. The dragon blinked its large green eyes at me as I got myself into a full seated position. I stared into those eyes, knowing it was probably a poor choice to stare a directly at a predator, but something made me feel at ease.

Crouching on my knees, I inspected the dragon.

Reaching my hand forward, the dragon shifted toward me and sniffed my open palm. My breaths were shallow, my hands shaking with nerves. But when a loud trill echoed from the dragon's chest, and I had to stifle a nervous laugh. My panic eased, and while my heart was still hammering in my chest, it was now filled with exhilaration.

"Where did you take me? And why?" I asked, knowing she wouldn't be able to respond. The dragon inched forward.

This time I did laugh, as I tentatively put my hand between the two large spikes that protruded on the top of her head.

The dragon let out a sigh and closed her eyes, and as I placed my palm over the sleek scales, a tingling sensation took over my palm and worked its way up my arm.

A vision appeared, and I gasped.

I saw myself, lit with the teal cast from the Everflame, wide-eyed and scared, but I also felt fear from the dragon. Fear and pain. Her injured leg prevented her from exiting the caves, and she was lost...so lost.

The vision changed, and I saw myself again, comforting her through Maya's ministrations, and the pain mitigated. Confusion grew inside of me, and then an overwhelming sense of gratitude.

The next vision came, and towers and walls of ice erupted as I shielded myself with ice I had no recollection of casting. My hair blew every which direction, my hands white at the knuckles as I held the bow with a vice-like grip in the underground throne room.

I took a gasping breath as the visions faded, the dragon's emotions still washing over me. Gratitude, relief, joy. These were memories—memories from the dragon.

My breaths came quicker as I realized I could feel what lied in her heart. She shifted to lean further on me, my legs pinned under her long neck, and the reverberations from her chest were so loud that my teeth rattled.

I have finally found you.

The dragon's voice filtered through my mind, and I sucked in a sharp breath. It was strong and feminine, and if I focused hard enough, I could feel her contentment coursing through my own being.

A twig snapped from behind, and the dragon lifted her head with a vicious snarl. I jolted up, preparing myself to run if I needed to, but a handsome, rugged man emerged from the tree line, his brown hair disheveled and dirt smudged on his cheeks.

"Caelum!" I shouted. The dragon growled at him, and I watched as he stared wide-eyed at us, his hands held up in a defensive position.

"Woah, woah." I held my hands up to the dragon. "He's a friend..." I grimaced, realizing the dragon probably didn't know what I was saying.

She cocked her head at me, shifting her gaze between the two of us. My brain froze. Was it possible she could feel me, too?

I pulled up all the emotions I had regarding Caelum, the kinship we formed, the way I felt like I could rely on him.

"It's all right, Caelum," I called, hoping I was right. "She won't try to hurt you." I turned back to the dragon, who was no longer snarling at him, but still standing menacingly.

"He is a friend. There is no danger." I pulled on my magic, trying to coat my fingers in ice, but I was out, all of my magical energy sucked away.

"I'm out of magic, Caelum." He nodded in understanding before treading warily toward us. The dragon sniffed the air as he approached. But she stood beside me, stretching out her neck, the full length of her scales gleaming under the purple sky.

She was imposing and majestic and, judging by Caelum's face, intimidating. Taking a deep breath, I felt relatively confident Caelum was safe, and took two steps forward.

I sent the dragon a mental image of her staying where she was, trying to convey Caelum's fear. In response, she huffed out a breath of hot air and tucked her legs underneath her body to lie down.

"I don't know what happened..." I tried to explain, splaying my palms open. "She saved me..." I gave him a desperate look, and not for the first time on this trip, I felt at a total loss for what to do.

"*She*?" Caelum asked, fear etched on his face. His question sent a jolt through me. I wasn't sure how I knew the dragon was female. It was just something I knew so naturally, like it was a part of myself all along.

Sumyre

It was a whisper that brushed over my brain, one that felt foreign and familiar at the same time. I looked back at the dragon, only for her to give me a slow blink in return. "Sumyre saved me."

"She told you her name?" Caelum's question was a rapt whisper, but it was lined with fear, and if I wasn't mistaken, awe. "Did she tell you her name?" he asked again, his eyes darting between the two of us.

I nodded slowly.

Caelum closed the distance between us and grabbed my wrist, shoving my sleeves up to my elbows. Sumyre made a low hiss, and my whole body tightened.

Caelum's fingers traced along my forearm, a tingle of pleasure firing from his touch. I looked down and gasped. Along his traces were lines of gold embedded into my skin, two bands around the middle of my forearm, weaving through each other.

"Lydia." Caelum peered up at me, his eyes wide, mirroring my own shock. "You're bonded with this dragon..."

His gaze slipped from my eyes, taking me in fully, and noticing my brown hair was no longer brown, instead a white silver. The magic stripped it of its dye. He looked at me suspiciously, like he was trying to place exactly where he knew me from.

I looked over at Sumyre, who chuffed, and a wave of approval that wasn't my own moved through me. The full weight of what had happened struck me like a cold bucket of water on my head.

"It should be impossible," I muttered, but the memories of the golden light swam before my eyes.

Sumyre stood up, shaking out her wide wings, and she stretched her neck up, her head proud as she sat tall and cocked her head toward us. Caelum stood tall, but I noticed he shivered under her gaze.

"I just don't understand how, and what this even means." My heart was in my throat.

Caelum swallowed, his throat bobbing.

"The bow," I remembered. "I touched the bow—that's how I must have triggered the bond." Caelum and I only exchanged frantic and confused glances. I held the bow up for him, the humming long since ceased. His brows pinched as he reached for it, his fingers twitching as though he was unsure.

"It doesn't ring of magic anymore. It should be safe," I told him.

He took it tentatively, and then let out a long sigh of relief as he studied it in his palms.

"Halcyon!" A panicked bellow rang through the meadow we were in, and I grimaced, immediately recognizing Aceus' booming voice.

"Halcyon?" Caelum questioned, his eyes lighting up in recognition. I grimaced. "*You* are Lady Halcyon?"

"I'll explain later," I rushed.

I reached out to Sumyre with my mind, the bond between us tight and strong, asking her to remove the hazy barrier that separated Aceus from us.

She ruffled her wings before jumping, making me stagger backward. She was in the air in an instant, circling above us, and her wings produced a furious gale of wind that sent my silver hair flying in different directions. The smoke dissipated, revealing a pale-faced Aceus. He met my eyes and ran toward me. He skidded to a halt before me, falling to his knees.

"My Lady, I have failed you. I swore to protect you, and I could not."

"Rise, Aceus," I told him. "I am safe, and you are no failure."

Sumyre landed behind me, the ground shaking as she hit the ground solidly.

"You have so much explaining to do." Caelum pointed at me, his face a cross between anger and confusion. And explaining is what I would do. He deserved to know the truth, after all.

I gestured to the ground, seating myself, and waited. Caelum took two steps to his left, glanced and me, then took two steps to his right before finally settling on the ground himself.

I recounted my experience in the underground throne room to Caelum and Aceus, neither one of them looking relieved.

Caelum refused to meet my eye, and my heart sank as though I had deliberately betrayed him, and I supposed I did just that. I kept thinking about how tenderly he had kissed me, how his arm banded around me like I was the most precious thing in the world. It had all felt so real, but I hadn't been me. Not really. He didn't even know who he was kissing, and it was unfair of me to even allow him to do so.

"What I don't understand is why you lied to us? I would have never put you in any sort of danger or allowed you to come if I had known the truth," he told me.

"Which is exactly why I disguised myself," I groaned. "I had to come, otherwise there will be no way to protect you—or Dolan—if the truth of this trip was revealed."

Caelum nodded, turning his thoughts inward as he rubbed his palm against the scruff on his jaw.

"I should have resisted this arrangement further," Aceus said, his voice thick with regret. "Niklaus was against it, but I didn't question my orders for a moment."

"It isn't your fault," I told him, placing my hand on top of his much larger one. "You served my father for a long time. He would have never allowed you to question anything."

"You are much kinder than your father."

"You say that like it's a bad thing."

"It could be a weakness." Aceus shrugged.

"There is no weakness in kindness," I retorted.

"Weakness or not, this changes everything." Caelum's voice was stern, and as he looked at me, his brown eyes cold and calculated.

"No, it doesn't," I said, returning his tone. "My credentials are still the same. I *can* help you, and I will. Regardless of what my name is, I am still here and I am still me."

Caelum shook his head, standing and brushing the dirt off his pants. "You lied, Lydia. Or I guess I should say, Halcyon."

Before I could refute him once again, he walked away. Sumyre growled low in her throat, as though she could feel the fracture in my heart. I swallowed back the threat of tears that unexpectedly came to my eyes.

Hoping he only needed some time and space to digest this new information, I gave him his space. I needed a moment myself as well, to once again pull back on my emotions and focus on the end goal. Get to the temple and back to Dolan safely. Caelum could wait. The dragon could wait. They had to, because if I thought about all the repercussions all at once, I was going to burst.

Sumyre turned away from us before launching herself into the air. I stood with my jaw slack as I watched her circle above us.

"Amazing," Aceus whispered next to me.

"You're not afraid of her?" I implored.

Aceus chuckled. "What is there to be afraid of? She is your bonded now. Unless you want her to bite my head off, then I don't see any reason to fear." I studied him for a moment, taking in the absolute bravery and trust this mortal had in me. "She had plenty of time to maim and kill all of us, but she didn't. She's a part of you now."

Aceus' words echoed through my mind. I had never seen anything so majestic, so beautiful, so divine; and she was mine. And I was hers.

Being a Magi, I was a product of magic, the gods' blessed descendants, but I couldn't wrap my head around the dragon, a black mass in the sky who roared through the heavens. That was *my bonded*. I still didn't know what that meant, but one thing I knew was that this felt *right*.

ACEUS LED OUR WAY through the forest, Calliope trotting by his side. She was skittish around the dragon at first, but the longer we walked, the more comfortable she got. The forest was quiet as Sumyre pranced around me, her legs dancing as she spun around in anticipation. Her wings were closed, hiding the massive wingspan that lifted her high into the bright blue sky, and I couldn't help the smile that crossed my face as she nuzzled her head into my hand. I still held the bow in the other.

Worry settled in the pit of my stomach as we approached. How would the others react to this bond? Gods above, I didn't even know what to think of it myself.

Sumyre's tail swished along the ground behind her, pushing twigs and other forest debris to either side. I gently placed my hand on her neck, her dark scales feeling smooth under my palm. Pleasant warmth seeped into my fingers from where I touched her natural armor.

I expected her to jolt from my touch, to lean away, but Sumyre did none of those things. She was perfectly content to let my hands touch her, and the thrill of it shocked me. Here I was, one of the few Magi who had ever gotten close enough to a dragon to touch it in centuries.

Another vision flooded my mind, but it didn't distract from what I could see in front of me. It was like a memory, or a thought. The vision was in my sight, like I was there, but at the same time—I wasn't.

The vision was dark and cold. Either the cave we were in together, or another one, but I could tell this was one of the first memories she had. She felt young, freshly hatched.

Cracking filled the cave walls. Eggs. There were so many of them, nearly filling the entire space with unhatched and hatching dragon eggs of various colors. The air was stagnant and musty, and tiny mewls and cries from newborn dragons became louder and louder.

Outside the cave, a determined roar shook the walls of the enclosure. It sounded desperate and sorrowful, like there was no amount of pain greater than what the creature who made it was going through. Yelling voices followed the roar, but I couldn't understand what they were saying, only that they were distinctly human.

A bright light suddenly lit up the room, and the baby dragons all recoiled with small hisses. A tall shadow blotted out the light, and I knew it was most definitely human.

The vision faded, and a cry came out of Sumyre's throat. My heart was breaking. I had just witnessed a dragon breeding ground. Rage made me see the forest in red as I realized in what conditions the mortals were keeping these dragons, these near-godly creatures.

I turned back to her, a frown on my face as I pressed my hand to her tighter. I didn't know how she had escaped, and I could only imagine what these past few weeks had been like.

Terrifying. Hungry. Dark. Isolating.

Anger burned through me, and I winced, my magic desperately trying to form even though I was tapped out. It was an emotional reaction, and for once I was glad to be empty, otherwise the entire forest floor would be frozen solid.

"I'm so sorry, Sumyre," I cooed at her, feeling more maternal and protective than I had ever felt in my life. This dragon had gone through so much already at the hands of the mortals. I heard stories of how the mortal kingdom obtained Dragon Riders, but seeing it for myself was entirely different.

This was the King of Tantal's doing. The King had absolutely no right. It was *unnatural*, and if he was breeding these dragons in such conditions, how exactly did they bond them to mortals? Bile rose in my throat.

As we passed through a thick band of the wide trees, I heard low voices nearby. The camp was near, and it was time I faced the consequences of my actions.

"It's okay," I told her, rubbing my hand against her scales. "I'll be right back, I promise."

As I turned closer to the camp, I could feel the tension growing. The voices sounded angry, and I heard Maya's argumentative tone as I neared.

"*What do you mean she bonded a dragon?*" she hissed at Caelum, and I swallowed the lump in my throat.

I held my chin high, my face neutral as I strode into the campground. A fluttering breeze pushed my hair back, and I would have formed ice in my hands if I could.

Maya didn't know what happened in the forest, but I wasn't about to accept her tone. I had nothing to be ashamed of. I was blessed.

"Sumyre is the dragon's name, and she is *my* dragon." The group swung their gazes at me as I approached. "She isn't far behind, and she will be joining us while we work to find the relics we seek for the Library."

"Lydia?" Maya asked with wide eyes, hair loose from her braid, as though she had been running a hand through it.

"Halcyon, actually," I corrected, deciding there would be no more deception on my part. Maya's lips parted on a gasp, her gaze swinging between myself and Caelum.

Iris looked at me, her gaze hard, but she held more understanding than her partner. She tilted her head slightly, a sign of respect, but her eyes never left mine as she said, "We need to make sure that bringing a dragon to our camp is safe. Please forgive us for being hesitant. Especially considering if what Cal tells us is true, if it is the same dragon from the caves."

"I understand," I said thickly. A roar of protectiveness surged through me, and I staggered back at the overwhelming feeling. This bond...it was strong and it pulled me to protect every ounce of Sumyre.

I took a deep breath and filed the feeling away, pushing it down until I knew I would hold myself back from any biting remarks.

"Lyd—Halcyon, I mean," Caelum looked down at me, obviously still taken aback that I hid who I was, but there was also worry written in his features. "Are you alright? Maybe you should lie down."

I nodded, agreeing. I was bone tired. Everything had been drained from me, and I felt the exhaustion tug. "I need to reassure Sumyre. She's all alone out there."

The three of the troupe exchanged worried glances, only Aceus standing tall without reservations. For that, I was grateful.

Mortals could never have a dragon bond or a soul bond. At least they weren't supposed to. Somehow, the mortal king was able to circumnavigate the rules of natural magic. But either way, Aceus—raised in Ambrose—would have never even entertained the possibility for himself.

Some philosophers even wondered if that was a mortal's strength—not being subjected to a god's fate. Not that it mattered now the gods were gone. But the bonds they left behind were very clearly still alive. Staggering through the forest, I retraced my steps, realizing how easy it would have been to get lost. I was amazed that Caelum even remembered how to get back to camp in the first place. Then again, he was used to living in wild places. I was not.

My head turned every which way as I trekked, my heart rushing as I was sure I had wandered too far or in the wrong direction.

A low whine came from behind me, and I whipped around with a sigh of relief. Sumyre was crouched low, her bright green eyes blinking at me, and I felt her relief.

"Remove your fear, Sumyre. These people mean you no harm." I laid my hands on her snout, not caring about the sharp teeth hidden beneath. She nuzzled into my touch, and I sighed.

You are pushing yourself too far. Lean on me as we walk.

Sumyre's voice once again shocked me. I wasn't sure if it was something I would ever get used to. Suddenly, the weight of the bond worried my stomach into knots. Was I expected to have a dragon around at all times for the rest of my life? I stilled at the thought.

Was she going to come back with me to Dolan? What would Niklaus think? What would my people think?

I would bring her back to the camp. I would protect her, but there would be a day, sometime soon, where she would *have* to go her own way. She needed to be with her own kind, and it would be selfish of me to keep her away from them.

But even as it crossed my mind, we were tied together now, our souls linked as one. As much as logic told me it wouldn't work, I knew I would have to adjust in some way.

We strolled back, my hand on her, guiding her the whole way. The camp was silent, and I could feel an air of unease as we approached. Sumyre sniffed, recognizing this as the same place I had been sleeping hours before.

The group was all lined up together, but I noticed Aceus and Caelum standing slightly in front of the women, and I bit back a laugh. If they were trying to protect them from a dragon, I wasn't sure their fists or swords would really matter.

I can smell their fear, but no harm will come to them as long as no harm comes from *them.*

Her voice cut through my mind like an ethereal bell chime, and it sent a shiver down my spine.

Sumyre relaxed, a rippling chuff exiting her nose, and she shook off some tension as she shuffled out her wings. Her green eyes zeroed on Maya, and I heard Maya suck in a breath.

"She has no ill will to you. I can feel it." My words came out sluggish and exhausted. They needed to understand that this creature wasn't some mindless man-eating machine. She was smart, she was capable, and we were *each others.*

AFTER FINALLY CONVINCING MAYA and Iris that Sumyre meant no harm, I rested. Napping through the morning until the sun was once again lowering in the sky, my body and magic finally recovered.

Meanwhile, the group spent the rest of the afternoon preparing to enter the temple the next day. Gathering the proper tools, there was frequent discussion about which direction we were going and what everyone's plans were in case of emergency.

I paced through the campsite, watching as everyone kept their distance from Sumyre. She seemed to pick up on their hesitations and resorted to basking in the last remnants of sunlight a small distance from the tents.

There was so much more that went into these archeological trips than I ever could have thought. I raised my brow as I watched Caelum unpack a set of tools, each one with a specific purpose. There were fail safes, extra ropes and harnesses, tools I had never even seen before for dusting and extracting. Alongside everything were notebooks and blank maps Caelum was determined to fill out. For the first time since we started this journey, I finally understood why they needed extra funding to come here.

All the while, Sumyre lay on the sidelines, watching lazily with her green eyes darting between all of us.

I did what I could to help, regardless of the clear apprehension the others held around me. Everyone aside from Aceus. Eventually, Caelum softened back toward me, but it was a hesitant and slow process. He was pleasant, offering me tight smiles as I worked next to him, unpacking crates and asking him where I should put the contents.

Otherwise, he was completely in his own element, striding with confidence between the wagon and the tents, and I bit my lip, trying to push down on the heat that simmered through my body as I appreciated the level of care he held for his project. I knew our conversation was not over and that he felt betrayed, but I hoped he could at least understand why I did it.

The sun was finally setting over the horizon, peeking through the tree trunks with its golden light. Sumyre kept her green gaze on me throughout the day, but now I could see her eyes drooping with exhaustion. I couldn't blame her. I felt the same regardless of the nap.

Caelum still hadn't said more than a few pleasantries to me, and I meandered to where Maya was once again cooking over the fire.

After noticing my eagerness to help, along with my ability to take simple directions, Maya's attitude had warmed since the morning. She was still apprehensive, but I was no longer met with the same coldness as before.

Throughout the day, I caught her whispering to Iris behind trees, their words obviously not meant for me to hear, and I could only assume they were discussing me. Aceus had wandered to them, his voice low as well. No matter how hard I strained my ears, I couldn't make out their words.

"Here you go, Halcyon," she said amicably while passing me a plate. I gave her my thanks and eyed my food, noting the freshly harvested vegetables she had scoured the forest floor for, and bit my lip.

Maya took her seat next to me, and I was surprised she hadn't been so much as curt to me since revealing my identity. Even her wariness around Sumyre had faded as the day went on. Once Sumyre had left everyone alone, Maya relaxed exponentially.

"I'm sorry I lied to you about who I was," I started, but she waved a hand in the air, shaking her head.

"I don't want to hear it." She smiled tentatively at me as she took a bite of her food. I gave her a small smile back, and she swallowed before pinning her full attention on me. "I get it. You're a leader, you have to do what's right for your people, your status. I may not know the intricacies of politics, or why you do the things you do, but I know sometimes there are tough decisions that have to be made. Whatever your reasoning is, it doesn't matter to me." She sighed, looking toward Aceus who was smiling at something Iris said. "All that matters is that we are here, the temple is right there, and in a week, I'll have enough riches to get a place to settle down and have my own garden," she said, surprisingly satisfied.

"You want to stop exploring?" I asked, my eyebrow raised, and she nodded.

"It's been a while since I've stopped anywhere. How long have we been going at this now?" she asked Caelum as he slid to sit next to us. He squinted in thought.

"I don't know, fifteen years, I guess?" he said.

I balked. "You have been traveling for fifteen years? Straight?"

"No, not straight. But just about. Iris and I take trips back home occasionally." She pointed at Caelum. "He hasn't stopped, though. Always trying to find the next big discovery."

He smiled and ducked his head, but didn't refute. I couldn't imagine spending fifteen years roaming about the different parts of Ambrose. Three weeks already seemed like a lifetime, but a decade? More? It was unfathomable.

I couldn't help the hollow laugh that came from me. "And you're not worried about the dragon?"

"She's a liability." She sighed and gave Sumyre a side-long glance. "Having a dragon near us, bonded or not, is dangerous. It's a safety issue." I wanted to protest, but Maya raised her hand before I could get a word out. "I understand you are bonded, so you have to be together, but it puts everything at risk." She gave me an exasperated look. "We don't even know where she came from."

I bit my lip, because I knew exactly where she came from, and the truth might have been more liability than having a dragon here at all.

"The dragon stays," Caelum cut in, much to my surprise. He was staring at Maya with intensity as he spoke. "We still need Halcyon's expertise and funding. We have to compromise on this."

I gave Caelum a grateful glance, but he only looked away, his throat bobbing as he stared into the fire. After all that happened today, his dismissal was what hurt the most.

Chapter 15

HALCYON

THE NIGHT WAS LATE, and the camp quiet as I sat in front of the slowly dying fire. Caelum was still sorting through more last-minute items. I sighed, pushing myself up from the log we used as a makeshift bench, when Caelum came over with a small frown.

"Come on, Halcyon, let's have a chat."

He gestured towards his tent, and I swallowed thickly, readying myself for a truthful discussion. There was no way to read what was on his mind, and I prepared for the worst.

It reminded me of so many times when I had spoken to my father, and he would reprimand me for things—even when I felt I was in the right. Back straight, show no emotion. *State the facts and take whatever words get thrown your way, but don't let them hurt you.*

The tent was only tall enough for us to crouch, so I took a seat in a corner, while Caelum fiddled with his lantern.

"Caelum..." I started, but I wasn't entirely sure where to go from there. An apology seemed like it wouldn't be enough.

Kissing him, caring for him, was a mistake. I couldn't help my feelings, but I recognized I could have stopped my actions. The words I tried to say wouldn't come out of my mouth, so instead, I took a deep breath and swallowed.

"I wasn't sure how I wanted to talk to you about this, but I just want you to know: I get it," he said, and I blinked, because I had expected him to bear down on me with anger. With how he had been ignoring me all day, I assumed he would take his frustrations on me. It was my fault I let him kiss me, and I had led him on, all the while hiding who I really was.

"I don't like it," he continued. "In fact, I absolutely hate it."

Caelum finally faced me, his lips turned downwards, and his hazel eyes blazing with an emotion I couldn't place.

"I know. I'm sorry."

"No," he said, and I jolted at his expression. It was borderline feral, the way he looked at me. Like he wanted to hunt me down and eat me like a starving, wild animal. "You *don't* know. Believe me, I understand the need to hide who you are. You think I've gotten this far in life by being honest a hundred percent of the time?" He let out an indignant laugh. "No, *that* I understand completely."

He inched his way closer to me, and my breath hitched. The way he was crawling toward me, his face flashing in the flickering light of the lantern, made me feel cornered and helpless. Helpless, but not afraid. I wasn't even sure Caelum could make me feel afraid. But my heart still raced as he came close and sat on his knees in front of me.

There was a war in his eyes as he regarded me. He shifted his gaze from my lips to my eyes, blinking slowly before his jaw feathered. Whatever decision he had been trying to make was clearly made.

I didn't dare move as he took my braid—now silver—and removed the binding that held it together. The strands sifted through his fingers, and he sighed, his shoulders releasing tension as though just the act of touching me calmed him.

"I hate this," he whispered, his gaze flicking up to meet mine, "because I shouldn't touch you like this." I could barely breathe as Caelum flicked my hair aside, brushing his hand along my collarbone, making me shiver. I should have told him to stop, that what we had done before could not, under any circumstances, progress. But I couldn't. The words simply would not come out.

Caelum made me feel things I hadn't felt in a long time—if ever. He made me feel wanted, cherished. And he made me feel like that before he ever knew I was the Lady of Dolan.

He didn't want my title, my name. He wanted *Lydia*. Wanted the woman I was underneath all the layers of silk and precious jewelry. And it made me feel...alive. Alive and wanted, and not because I held a certain status, but for who I really, truly was.

"I hate this," he continued, pausing to wait for me to rebuff him, but I wouldn't. Not yet. "Because no matter how much I remind myself that I could be a better man, I'm not."

His lips pressed to my shoulder, and I shuddered. "Tell me to stop, Halcyon. Tell me and I will, but gods help me if you don't, I will take you right now and not give it a second thought. The Lady of Dolan will be underneath *me*, a petty adventurer who can only beg for his funding."

Gentle fingers trailed my jaw until he grasped my face, tilting it up so our eyes met fully, and a wash of desire ran through my body. My core clenched at nothing, and I couldn't even muster the will to squeeze my thighs to banish the feeling. "Tell me you don't want it. That you don't want to sully your name with a man like me."

My chest heaved as I looked at him. Those wild, feral eyes holding wicked promises lit me up from the inside out. I was too hot and not hot enough. Every touch of his hands burned my skin as though they were a brand.

"It could only ever be temporary," I choked out. I wanted him badly enough to consider throwing my defenses down, but now I knew the crux. What I had really been meaning when I told myself to lock away my feelings. My heart only ever lived in a cold hard box, never to be touched by anyone, and I somehow wanted to give him the key. As much as I didn't want to admit it, I was dreading the day this kind, caring man would end up leaving me, and I would return to the castle halls and assume my duties. Alone.

My life and his were so profoundly different, and I knew if I gave him my body, it would take a piece of my heart, too. I would be releasing a part of me to never be seen again, and I was too protective of myself to allow it.

Caelum's breath was hot as he exhaled on my shoulder, his hair brushing against my cheek. Threading my hands in his hair, I tugged him up to look at me.

"I know it's wrong," I amended. "And I am so, so sorry I let you kiss me under false pretenses. You have every right to be angry with me for that." Caelum's eyes blazed as I apologized. "But I can't tell you to not be a good man, because you already are. I wish things were different, Caelum." It took everything in me to tear my gaze away from his hazel eyes, swirling with heat and understanding.

Nodding, Caelum tilted my chin, his thumb brushing against my lower lip and I shuddered from the contact. I stopped breathing as he placed his lips on mine. It was soft and inviting, and I leaned in, unable to force myself apart.

But as quickly as he kissed me, he pulled back, frowning as he took me in.

"I at least wanted to kiss you. Even just once as the woman you are without a disguise to cloud my memory."

I woke up shivering, my teeth chattering and clanking against each other. The tent's flaps pinged and rasped against the metal bars that held it up from a blisteringly bitter wind that had moved through the night. It was still dark, not even a trace of light to be seen.

I had somehow shirked off my bedroll, leaving my body exposed to the frigid air that took the mountains, a promise of the coming winter.

I didn't even notice Caelum's arms snaking around me, to the point where he was almost smothering me with his body. Hovering over me, he took my face into his hands, and looked at me with a sort of medical precision.

Blowing out a heavy breath, he settled back over to my side, still looking down at me as he propped his head on his elbow.

I was forced to look at him with fingers grasping my chin, his eyes continuing to examine me. These weren't the same eyes he had looked at me with last night. Gone was the hungry and needy fire, and instead, concern filled his gaze.

He moved his hand from my face, but then wrapped my bedroll further up my body before tucking me in closer to him so we were wrapped in a tangle of limbs.

"What are you doing?" I said through chattering teeth.

"Hmm." He kept looking me up and down. "You were thrashing. Did you have nightmares?"

I went to shake my head, but stopped as I remembered clips of those nightmares—memories from Sumyre. Darkness and pain. Slashing and mind-numbing dizziness.

"The dragon bond..." I shook my head.

"What about the dragon bond?" he asked sleepily.

"I think Sumyre was having nightmares—memories, and I saw them." Flashes of her life before the caves swam through my mind.

I grimaced at the uncomfortable feeling of intrusion and the simultaneous feeling of wishing I could take away her pain and wipe those memories away.

Everything had been dark, but there were flashes of people scrambling and chaining her. Keeping her locked up and in the dark. Screams from other dragons formed from pain and fear. There was no light, no hope, just the soul-deep fear and need for survival.

Caelum raked his hand through his messy hair and shook his head before looking back down at me. I could see his medical gaze fading, and the lines of worry and helplessness sank into his eyes.

"That's interesting. I don't know enough about dragon bonds to know, but it would make sense. Your souls are linked now."

Warmth seeped into my extremities as I sank further into his arms, relishing in the heat. I still didn't know exactly where we stood with each other, but in this moment it didn't matter. Being entangled in him was beyond comfortable, and I wouldn't think otherwise until I had to. Caelum's hand found my cheek again, his palm leaving a scorching heat in its wake.

He was so warm, and I was *very* cold. Colder than I would ever even mention out loud. His heat pulled me in, and before I knew it, I was curling into Caelum's chest.

He smelled like nature and pine with the slightest hint of sweat from being outdoors, but even if he smelled of dung, I would have clung to him. His body heat was melting me from the inside, and my chattering lessened with time. Caelum embraced me, tugging me further into him, and I sighed.

I should be pushing him away. I didn't need him to take care of me, but after the exhausting events of yesterday, it was all I could do but melt into him.

His muscular arms braced me and ran up and down my back in a soothing motion.

I fell back asleep, but when I woke up to the pockets of dim sunlight filtering into the tent, I still felt the tug of exhaustion.

Caelum was still asleep, and I was beginning to feel smothered, so I shoved out of Caelum's arms without a word. I didn't even look back as I pushed through the tent flap.

A light frost had settled over the ground, but the sky was gradually lightening with the coming sunrise, and it was only a matter of time before it turned into dew. The forest was quiet in the early morning, a sort of peace saved only for this time of day. It was a promise of new beginnings, new discoveries, and untold possibilities.

My thoughts drifted as I rubbed the sleep out of my eyes, and I wondered how Sumyre slept, but as I did, I noticed the camp was missing one black dragon.

I whirled around. I could see tracks in the ground where she had swished her tail, indents where her feet had stepped, but she was gone. My first thought was to make sure she hadn't slaughtered the other tents, and I blew out a sigh of relief as it didn't look like they had been so much as touched.

I stilled myself, clenching my fists and forcing myself to take a deep breath. She was a dragon, after all. She could take care of herself well enough. But I didn't like the unease that settled in my stomach.

I shook my head and made my way to the wood pile to attempt to re-start the fire. This bond, or whatever it was, was severely messing with my head. The nightmares, the worry; it was overwhelming.

As soon as I had calmed myself down, I got a vision in my mind of the forest, teeming with morning life, and a dragon's eager playfulness at hunting small creatures. She was out hunting. I grinned. She was an early riser, too, then.

I was grateful she chose to hunt small animals instead of my friends, but would she have hunted us if she wasn't bonded to me? I suppressed a shiver at the thought.

Humans make for stringy meals.

How would you even know? I shot back at her, unease prickling in my stomach that she had possibly eaten a human before.

Sumyre's snapping teeth rang in my mind, but it was lined with humor, and I forced myself to shake out my hands, realizing I didn't really want to know the answer.

I placed a log on the hot coals which were slowly turning to ash and waited. Shouldn't the fire catch? I watched Maya light these fires, and it didn't seem difficult, but nothing was happening. I crossed my arms and stared at the non-fire, willing it to catch with nothing but the curses that slipped from my tongue.

Caelum emerged from the tent, and he strode over with a sly grin on his face. I narrowed my eyes at him as he started prodding the logs with a stick. He only chuckled at me in return, and I rolled my eyes as the wood caught, and a small flame picked up in the pit. Ever the knight in shining armor.

While I waited for everyone else to wake, I retrieved the bow I had felt so drawn to. I sat by the fire, toying with it as I took in the innate strangeness I felt from it. The grip warmed in my palms, and I lifted it to study the black gemstones embedded in the edges. They glistened in the early light, not like regular gemstones, but like they held life inside of them. I traced my fingers along the diamonds, and a shiver went down my spine.

"What do you think this bow means?" I asked Caelum as he sat down close to me on the log, his knee brushing against my own.

"I've never seen anything like it," he said. "May I?"

I handed him the bow, and the emptiness in my hands settled into my bones.

"For something that has been underground for so long, it's in incredible condition." He ran his hands from the tip to the center.

"It's stunning, too." I reached my fingers along the diamonds. "I've seen ancient relics, studied many of them at Neverwind, but this craftwork is incredible. And for it to hold up for so long without tarnishing," I clicked my tongue, "it's almost like it was made by the gods."

I let out a humorless laugh, but Caelum only stared at me, wide-eyed.

"You don't think…" He peeled his eyes away from me to take in the bow in front of him.

"Think what? The gods actually made this?" When he didn't answer, I could only laugh. "That would be preposterous. The bow would have to be at least three thousand years old."

My smile faded, the humor falling short.

We both stared at each other, taking in the bow, wondering if it really could be as old as the gods. The throne room was underground and untouched, and it wasn't a part of the temple that Caelum had discovered the last time he was here.

It didn't escape me that when I touched it was when the bond between Sumyre and me formed. Maybe there was some truth to the gods making this bow after all.

"Regardless," he sighed, "we need to keep it safe and take it to the library for further study. Whatever it's made from, and whoever made it, needs to be solved. I'll put it back in the wagon." Caelum went to get up, but I wrapped my hand around his arm.

"No." My heart was beating out of my chest. *The bow belonged in my hands, and my hands alone.*

I shook my head. He was right, it belonged somewhere else, and it *wasn't* mine. Caelum raised his eyebrow at me, and I looked away from him. "I mean, of course. Just make sure it's in a safe spot. We don't want to damage or lose it."

Caelum nodded as he went to put it away. I blew out a breath, shaking my hands out, and ignoring the little voice in the back of my head that told me to retrieve the bow—to keep it.

Everyone else made their way out of their tents once the sun's golden rays struck the forest. The fire was fully crackling, and I continued to bathe in the warmth of the flames. Maya cooked us breakfast once again, ensuring all of our bellies were full.

Caelum strapped himself with bags and weapons, and I watched with rapt interest as he slung leather bindings over his broad shoulders. His muscles flexed with each movement, my cheeks growing hot as I appreciated Caelum's physique. I instantly averted my gaze. Blinking quickly, I once again found myself banishing those wretched, naughty thoughts. They would serve no purpose today.

Caelum called to me and beckoned me forward with a jerk of his chin and a serious look on his face. I strode to him, where he bent down on his knees and wrapped a leather strap around my waist.

"What are you doing?" I asked as he yanked the strap tighter, and I wavered on my feet from the force.

There were all kinds of things hanging from it. Ropes, a small bag, a sort of latch system. His hands lingered on my thighs, his fingers tightening on my leg for the barest of moments, and I sucked in a breath at the contact.

I told myself I would not dwell on my attraction to Caelum. Put him out of my mind completely, but his touch shattered my resolve, and my core twisted with hope he would touch me again and again, but before I knew it, he pulled away.

"This is for safety precautions. The temple is old..." his gaze went behind me for a moment before he turned back to binding me with the straps. "And it's far larger than what we initially anticipated. If anything happens, you'll at least have some sort of preparedness." He yanked it one more time, and I gasped at the tight leather against my skin. He smirked at the sound, his eyes filling with a blaze of heat, and his fingers brushed against my hips for the briefest moments before he pulled away, leaving my body humming from the barest contact.

"There," he sighed, nodded at his own handiwork, "you should be all set. When we go in there, I need you to stick beside me. Don't touch anything, and just...try to be cautious."

I nodded, and flicked my head to the side, trying to distance myself from those hazel eyes. "I'll do whatever you say. It's your profession, after all."

"Good." He grinned and stood, giving me a heated look before checking his own straps, confirming the buckles. Two straps hung over his shoulders and there was a rope tied to the front, making his shirt tight over his chest, letting me take in all the rippling muscle that lay underneath. I bit my lip, determined not to let the sight send warmth into my core, although it wasn't working.

"Where's the dragon? Thought she would be back by now."

I shrugged, but as my thoughts reached out to her, I got a vision of woods, and her need to be outside while we traversed the temple. "She's close by, but wants to stay here."

Caelum nodded, satisfied I wasn't begging to bring Sumyre along with us.

I followed Caelum as we traversed away from our camp, the entire crew of us stomping through the thick trees before they opened up to reveal an old stone ruin covered up to the roof in thick vines and greenery.

The temple was ancient and looked so much worse for wear than the room we discovered only yesterday. Aceus stood close, his shoulders back in a protective stance as he hovered around me. I wanted to insist his proximity was unnecessary, but he was only trying to make up for the last two times he wasn't around to do the very thing he had sworn to.

Spindly vines and green shrubbery encased the stone structure, like it was overtaking and eating its way through the old architecture. Thick vines weaved over the entrance, and I wondered, how we were supposed to get in.

"I thought you had been here before?" I called over to Caelum. He strode over next to me and chuckled.

"We have." He winked before closing his eyes and taking a deep breath. Placing his hands on one remarkably thick vine, he pressed his magic forward, and I lifted an eyebrow.

With a slow creaking sound, the vines pulled back. Dirt fell from them, coating my silver hair with brown. I watched in amazement as the vines retreated, revealing the wide-open arch of the entry way. Caelum's magic peeled away every vine and leaf until we were standing in front of a stone archway leading into a dark corridor.

Caelum dusted his hands off and grunted in approval before turning back to me.

"I wrapped the surrounding vines before we left last time, in case someone else were to stumble upon it," he said simply. As though it was only common sense.

"Moving dirt and cave, and now vines. What can't you do?" I teased, and he gave me a wicked smile in return. It felt good seeing this side of him once more. The distance between us had become rigid, and I missed the sidelong smirks he tossed my way.

"I can do many things, Halcyon. You just have to use your imagination." His voice was low, and I licked my lips as my core heated.

I took a step toward the temple, pointedly ignoring Caelum's flirtations, and my mouth popped open in awe. As we got closer, I noticed intricate designs on the stone. Carvings of lines and patterns I couldn't quite make out. Whoever made this temple went to great lengths to pay attention to all the detail. I was already awed, and we hadn't even gone inside yet.

"Who do you think made these markings?" I wondered aloud. Iris stepped up to me and grinned as she pulled out a piece of parchment and charcoal.

"Not sure who made them, but they are great, aren't they?" She placed the parchment against the stone and ran the charcoal over it, replicating the pattern onto the paper in a negative image. "This is one of the few temples we know of that hasn't already been scoured by Magi or mortals. Who knows what secrets we will reveal?" She said excitedly, a gleam in her eyes.

Caelum ushered us toward the entrance, where darkness loomed. He lit a torch with Everflame, bathing the temple in blue-green light.

"Stay by me, Halcyon." His voice was filled with command, all earlier flirtations gone, and I obeyed, keeping up right behind him.

The flame flickered over the stone walls, revealing more of the delicate etch work. Iris was behind me, sketching on parchment. She made a map of the temple, each new room and alcove marked. But for all we passed through, it was empty.

I thought Caelum might be disappointed, but he just kept trudging forward, his feet light and cautious as we delved further in.

We went through passage after passage, taking us down steps underground. The steps were uneven, and I had to watch where I placed my feet.

A large open archway stood in front of us and beyond was only darkness. Stepping inside the cavernous room, I strode carefully as my feet crunched over debris and rocks.

The Everflame torch Caelum carried only lit so much around us, but from what I could see, we were under a massive, vaulted ceiling. The structure seemed to be similar to the throne room Caelum and I found, but this one was far smaller and weathering of age.

Underneath all the dust and debris were hard stone floors. Wooden beams supported the structure, but some of them were rotten and broken. It smelled stale, like not even the air had been altered in the hundreds of years it stood here alone.

"Amazing," I heard Maya sigh from behind us, my thoughts echoing her.

"This way," Caelum called, his voice ringing through the room. He led to a dark passageway off the side.

"Do you know where you're going?" I asked, my pulse spiking at the prospect of going in further.

"Not in the slightest." Caelum grinned wide, the fire gleaming off his teeth, while a trickle of fear moved through me. I really hoped Caelum knew what he was doing.

Chapter 16

CAELUM

The musty air, the darkness, and the exhilaration of the unknown were all feeding into the blood that pumped through my veins. Exploration would always be my first love. As a kid, my mother used to scold me for getting into places I wasn't supposed to be. And now, I got paid for being in places I wasn't supposed to be.

Or I *was* getting paid until we discovered this place and no one wanted to pay us...except Halcyon. She took the risk—*she* gave me this opportunity.

Well, maybe her father did. But she could have stopped us if she really wanted to, and she didn't. My heart swelled with gratitude, because without Dolan, this place would have been left to rot with no one but myself, Iris, and Maya knowing it was even here.

The passageway continued to go down, but I didn't think we were as deep as Halcyon and I were when she bonded with the dragon. If we kept following these pathways, I hoped we would find the same room once again.

My mind kept drifting back to the throne room. I was so caught up in the events from yesterday, I forgot there was another pedestal—one with a tome on it. I didn't know what it recounted, or if it was dangerous, but I would stop at *nothing* to find out.

The possibilities of answers held in those pages were endless, and if that bow was as ancient as Halcyon suspected, then the tome could be the same. My hands itched with anticipation. It would be Ambrose's next greatest discovery.

"Cal," Iris called, her voice soft. "Can you wait just a moment? I need to plot this on the map."

I nodded, even though my feet urged me to keep going forward. Lifting the torch so she could see her map, I looked at what she had already drawn. The temple looked like a maze, with the big room in the middle. If I had to guess, the temple extended much farther underground than what we originally thought, and we had only just started to breech it.

After Iris made sure all the details on her map were up to her standards, I kept leading them down further when I heard a soft sigh behind me.

Halcyon was keeping up, but she looked worse for wear. After the dragon incident, and a fitful night's sleep, maybe bringing her with us wasn't the best idea.

She appeared haggard. Still stunning—her silver hair was much more suitable than the brown—but the frown she wore was deep-seated, and her eyes looked tired.

"Why don't we take a little break?" I handed Halcyon my water skin, which she took immediately. The group settled in the hallway, sitting on various steps, removing snacks that were packed in their bags.

Getting used to referring to Lydia as Halcyon had been a small hurdle. I had to keep reminding myself yesterday as I tore through my warring thoughts. She had promised everything she had said other than her name was true, and I had to say the evidence pointed in that direction.

She was clearly well-educated. And I had no doubts she was excited about the prospects of this journey. That helped me make my rash decision last night. I had promised myself I wasn't going to get any more involved with her, but when she sat so prettily in my tent, I knew I was done for. Then that same far-off glare reached her eyes when I asked her to talk. I nearly lost my mind.

Halcyon, apparently, was no stranger to shutting away her wants and desires. I decided then and there I never wanted to be shut out. She may have been the Lady of Dolan, but would it really kill her to allow herself an indulgence? Allow *me* to be that indulgence? I hadn't imagined the way she looked at me, the way she leaned into me and allowed those swift moments of desire to pass between us. There was definitely an attraction from both of us, but she was far stronger than I was.

I knew I had seen a goddess on the top of that castle in her swearing in. What I failed to see was that she was *my* goddess, and I wanted to worship if only she would let me. If I got only one kiss from her for the rest of my life, then so be it. I wanted more, gods knew I wanted more, but if one kiss was all she was willing to give me, then I would cherish it as it was.

Halcyon sat down and threw her back against the wall with a huff. As the wall took the brunt of her weight, I felt something shift in the earth. I whirled around, trying to find the source of the movement, the light from the Everflame flickering against the stone walls.

The ground shook, and bits of debris started falling from the ceiling as we all scrambled next to each other. I pulled Halcyon by her arm, tucking her into my side as I saw the wall behind her shift. Aceus grasped his sword, taking up the other side of Halcyon. I should have known with the way he protected her that she wasn't just some random scholar from the castle.

No, I should have known better when he stood in front of that wolf from what seemed a lifetime ago.

We all held our breath as the wall before us swung open, revealing a hidden staircase that led downwards. It was dank. Staler than where we currently were, as though only ancient souls had ever passed through here.

The steps were even more aged than the ones we had already passed through, and if I had to guess, this passage was forgotten long before the temple itself was.

Dirt continued to drift from the ceiling and dust made the air difficult to breathe. I pulled a handkerchief out of my pocket and wrapped it around my mouth and nose before pulling out another one and handing it to Halcyon to follow suit.

The staircase was narrow and went down in a spiral. I led the group as we filed down one-by-one. Under the cloth, I beamed as I questioned what secrets this temple held.

It took everything in my willpower not to run down the stairs. The structure was most likely compromised, but the adventurer inside of me didn't care. I needed to be careful.

"Cal," Iris whispered, and I turned around. "This place is very old, and revealing a secret passage could be dangerous. We need to take caution."

Everyone paused, their eyes on me, and I shrugged. Were they really questioning whether a small hidden part of this temple would stop me from finding the truth? I just chuckled and shook my head. Iris and Maya, at least, should have known better.

"Come on, let's keep going," Maya said, seeing the resolve in my eyes, and she nudged Iris forward. Halcyon only frowned, like Iris' hesitation set her on edge. She shifted closer to Aceus, and I couldn't blame her. If I wasn't so set on exploration, then Iris' statement probably would have deterred me, too.

We kept spiraling down deeper and deeper into the ground when the stairs stopped at a small archway. A wooden door hung on broken hinges, the wood rotted and falling apart. I reached toward it, pushing on it with my palm and it swung open, surprisingly not deteriorating from my touch.

Tall wooden beams arched above us, a room smaller than the first room we walked into, with vines stretching across the floor and walls.

"Gods above," Maya gasped. The room was filled with small alcoves with statues, all surrounded by riches and trinkets.

Rubies, emeralds, sapphires, gold, and silver all laid scattered around the little wooden statues carved into various animals. The value of the treasure was immeasurable. Rings and necklaces, vases with aged and cracked paint; all offerings for whatever these statues represented.

Aceus tore off his bandana and crouched down by the nearest statue and reached out to one of the large rubies near it.

"Look at all of this," he marveled. "This room alone must be worth a small city in Ambrose." He let out a low whistle, and I was tempted to follow suit.

"Neverwind's archeology selection is about to be a lot bigger," I said, picking up a small trinket from the ground and rotating it in my hand.

Halcyon wandering around the room, her eyes wide. She removed the cloth from her face, and I moved behind her as she took everything in.

"A coin for your thoughts, Lady?" She scowled at me, and I laughed. Drop the title, then. Got it. Her features softened, and she rolled her eyes before turning back to the treasures.

"This is amazing. These statues must represent different gods. Look—" she pointed to the statue that looked similar to a tall cat with a long tail wrapping around its body. "That must represent Aurora. She is the goddess of new life, physical and spiritual. Look at her offerings." She bent down, sifting her fingers through a bowl of blue gems. "These crystals represent new beginnings. I learned this a few years ago for a project at the Neverwind Library."

Maya moved next to her and pointed to a small wooden carving. "This looks like a rabbit. It symbolizes fertility."

Halcyon turned to me, her eyes wide with excitement. "Imagine what this information could do for the knowledge of Ambrose. Shrines aren't rare in Ambrose, but for there to be this many, and all in one place...it's amazing."

She smiled, a real, vibrant, beautiful smile, and I inhaled sharply. Her pink lips parted on a breath as she took in another statue, and it took everything I had not to move to make her repeat that look in my arms.

She looked back up at me with complete awe and wonder in her eyes, and it stole my breath away. "We need to document this. Where is your parchment? I'll write down what I can."

"Incredible," I muttered, and she nodded, but I wasn't talking about the riches. I shook my head, attempting to clear my thoughts.

"Iris, please give some parchment to Halcyon. She will help document what we find."

We settled into documenting, but my head wasn't in it. I was too busy watching Halcyon flit through each of the shrines, trying to identify which statue belonged to which god. She smiled freely at Maya and Iris as they recognized different offerings.

Halcyon blossomed in this temple like a flower that was blooming in the first light of spring. Her silver hair shined as she tossed it over her shoulder, and it took everything in my power not to reach out and run my fingers through it. I liked her brown hair, but her silver hair was an ethereal halo, a color that could only fit Halcyon. Only her.

Halcyon picked up a small statue that lay on the pedestal of the shrine of Perses and turned to me with a frown.

"Caelum, can you hold this and tell me what you feel?"

I frowned in confusion as I took the statue from her. The marble was heavy and smooth, carved into a beastly dragon with four tails. Carved with expert precision.

"It feels heavy. Cold." I shrugged and handed it back to her. She furrowed her brow and bit her lip. "Why?" I asked.

"I swear," she sighed, "I can feel something in it, something more. Like it contains a sort of magic, but I'm not sure." Her fingers ran over the marble, tracing lines along the ridges as she flipped it in her hands. She placed the statue back where she found it and shrugged.

I grasped her wrist as she pulled away. "Take it back with you."

"Really?" she gasped, her blue eyes wide, and I nodded.

"Take it, and if you feel anything similar, take those, too. You never know."

Her grin was the sweetest image, and I memorized every line in her face as she radiated her joy. She stuck the dragon into her satchel quickly before returning her attention elsewhere.

Meanwhile, I drifted through each of the shrines, marking the items, and trying to figure out the logistics to taking some of the bigger items back. The shrine pieces alone would be worth a thousand stories. I wished we could bring them all, but we didn't have the room.

Raking my fingers through my hair, there wasn't a doubt in my mind we would have to come back for a second trip. If we could somehow navigate it.

After what seemed like a couple of hours of documenting and packing back up, we set off back up the spiraling stairs back to the main temple. Iris led the group this time, one hand carrying the torch, the other holding her map which would direct us out. I took up the rear, with Halcyon in front of me.

She clutched a quiver in her hand, and I frowned. I grabbed her shoulder and pulled her to face me.

"Where did you find that?" I asked, peeling her fingers away from what looked to be a leather quiver with six arrows that didn't look like aged a day.

I raised my eyebrow, and she shrugged in response. "It was in between shrines. I didn't feel any magic the same way I felt it in some of the other items, but I thought this would be a good addition to the bow."

"Why are you still thinking about the bow?" I implored.

Apprehension flashed over Halcyon's face, but a small smile that left me breathless quickly replaced it.

"I don't know, but it feels like these belong with it." She pulled the quiver from my hands and slung it over her shoulder before turning around and following Iris.

Concern flickered through me, but I kept a close eye on Halcyon. She wasn't acting strange or making rash decisions, so I held back any opposition.

I tried to put the magical blast that Halcyon had gone through behind me, but with anything unexplained, I couldn't just dismiss any oddities. Including the items that Halcyon felt a magical pull toward. But she was lighter than I had ever seen her before. The last thing I wanted to do was dim her brightness.

Before I even realized what I was doing, I brushed my knuckle along her other shoulder and playfully tugged on a strand of silver hair. She lifted her head back at me, a frown crossing her face before she broke out into yet another smile. Not nearly as wide as it was in the room below, but enough for my stomach to flip, and my pants became uncomfortably tight.

I cursed under my breath, trying to banish the thoughts of her silver hair wrapped around my wrist, and her pink lips wrapped around my cock.

"I must say, that was room was incredible, Cal," she said, and I stood still behind her. My body heated with the one word she had just muttered. Her voice echoed with my name on it over and over in my head. *Cal. Cal. Cal.*

Maybe it was a sign of trust, a sign she was falling for me the same way I was falling for her. Maybe it meant nothing at all.

My chest warmed and my fingers twitched with the urge to reach out to her. She frowned in concern and stopped with me while the rest of the group went on, not realizing they were leaving us behind.

"What's wrong?" she asked as she looked me over.

Before I let myself think about it, I grabbed her by her shoulders and pressed her back against the stone wall of the passageway. Logic be damned. Here I was in the company of an incredible woman, with only our titles making a fissure between us. I didn't care. None of it mattered to me when my heart was so full it threatened to burst.

"What are you doing?" she gasped, but she didn't push me away.

I placed my arm on the wall above her, caging her in, pressed my lips to hers, and groaned. Her lips were soft against mine, and I took control of the kiss, pinning her against the wall with my leg between hers and my free hand resting gently on her throat, angling her for me to take her deeper. Our tongues met and intertwined, and it was like tasting the most delicious berries.

She was fierce and delicate, and I wanted all of it. Her hands rested on my shoulders and she grabbed my shirt, wadding it in the palms of her hands.

I could take her right now, and damn it, I wanted to. Instead, I broke the kiss with a smile of my own on my face.

We broke apart, both breathing heavily in the darkness, and I ached to see how red her skin was, how her chest looked heaving with desire.

"You called me Cal," I breathed.

"Everyone calls you Cal," she countered, and she pushed me away, her footsteps moving away from me as she followed the wall to the exit.

I held back a groan. Hearing her call me 'Cal' pushed my already depraved fantasies into the forefront of my mind. I wanted to hear her call me Cal while she was naked underneath me, writhing with pleasure.

"Not you." I caught up with her, placing my hand on her shoulder as we carefully dredged through the darkness. She hesitated at my touch, slowing her tracks, but she didn't push me away.

"Well, after you had that reaction to it, I'm not sure if I want to keep calling you Cal or not." She breathed a laugh, and I gave her one last press of my lips against her ear.

"Please do, Halcyon," I breathed huskily, and I felt her shiver underneath my touch.

We kept going up the stairs, our hands brushing against the walls for direction, and eventually found the exit where Iris, Maya, and Aceus were all standing waiting for us. Aceus looked concerned, but his shoulders loosened as soon as we emerged.

"What happened to you two?" Maya asked with her brow raised.

I removed my hand from Halcyon's shoulder and shrugged, already missing the contact with her.

"Got held up with...my shoes." Halcyon said, but her face gave everything away with the pink that tinged her cheeks. I chuckled and stepped around her. She bit her lip, sparing a glance at me under her lashes. With that one look, she could refer to me as a shoe for the rest of time. Halcyon wanted me. There was no doubt about it, and I was determined to make her see it herself.

Chapter 17

HALCYON

THE BRIGHTNESS OF THE morning sun had me groaning awake. I felt like I had just fallen asleep, having slept like the dead since my head hit the ground.

The temple and the shrine room, with all of its riches, refused to leave my mind. There were so many, I was seeing gemstones and treasures in my dreams. That room alone made the entire trip worth it, and it made me wonder just how many hidden treasures were lying in the mortal kingdom, waiting to be discovered.

Niklaus had been so hesitant for me to embark on this journey, but he would never know what he was missing out on. Artifacts beyond the ages of our ancestors were lying dormant underground doing nothing but collecting dust. All given freely and then forgotten.

All of my doubts about the credibility of this excursion faded when I saw those walls lined with alcoves dedicated to different gods. Scribes could write about the temple for decades, given the chance.

"Good morning, Halcyon," a husky voice murmured behind me. Strong arms were wrapped around my middle, holding me close to a large and very strong body. My mindless pondering was cut off as I sank deeper into Caelum's embrace. I felt so comfortable. Like there was nothing in the world that mattered as long as I lay here forever.

I took his hand in mine and brushed along the calluses on his palms, noting where my own were smooth. He pulled me gently closer to him. His other hand rested on my clavicle, and I could feel my pulse under his thumb where he rubbed it back and forth.

But it wasn't right. I didn't deserve to be in his arms. Not when I had lied and deceived him. Not when I had a duty which made it impossible for my heart to get entangled with someone—with anyone.

I went to shove Caelum's arms away, but he only held me tighter.

"No, no, no." He *tsked*. "You don't get to push me away now." He chuckled, and I could feel a hardness against my behind. Rough hands drifted over my stomach, warm and inviting, as Caelum's fingers toyed with the hem of my shirt.

"Caelum." I meant for my tone to be demanding, but the words left my mouth with an air of breathiness. His laugh breezed over my ear, and I shivered and arched my back into him. He let out a hum of satisfaction, and suddenly, I wanted to hear more.

"We can't..." I trailed off, my body fighting against logic, not wanting this to really end, but knowing it should just the same.

"Why not?" His fingers lifted my shirt lightly, finally coming into contact with my skin and making me shudder in his grasp. I fought to hold on to my train of thought, telling myself this was most certainly not a good idea.

"You know why." I sucked in a breath as he played with the band of my pants.

"Because I'm nothing but a shoe?" he breathed, his voice low with remnants of sleep.

I laughed, remembering my flimsy excuse to Aceus. "No," I swallowed, "because I am a Lady, and…" my voice trailed off until I gathered enough courage. "And because I lied to you."

Caelum hummed in my ear, and the vibrations coursed through me. "I already told you I forgive you for that."

"But it's not right…"

"Then tell me to stop."

"I can't," I confessed. "I can't tell you no. You make me feel like another person. Like I can do whatever I like without consequence. I can't stop you. I won't."

My lips parted to say more, but the words were lost. In his powerful embrace, with his scent of pine smothering me and his hands drifting across my skin, I found my willpower fading more with each passing second. Every touch left tingling shocks everywhere, and I almost didn't mind that I would be leaving a shard of myself with him. At least I knew he would protect it, savor it.

"I don't want you to stop, but I am terrified of what happens when it's over," I admitted. "We can't keep this going forever. As soon as I'm back home, it's done."

"I know that," he said, but I thought I heard a crack of heartache in his voice. He knew this couldn't last, and maybe by pursuing this further, he was giving me a piece of himself, too. "But if this is all we get together, then don't you think it will have been worth it?"

Did I? How different was this moment compared to the rest of this trip? Knowing I could never find Caelum or another temple ever again. Would I be able to move on with my life without knowing how far this week would take us if I only dared?

"Yes." I answered, even though I felt so very conflicted. My mind was telling me to be logical, but my heart and my soul refused to deny myself this pleasure. I desperately wanted to feel what it would be like to be loved for once in my life.

As quickly as he stilled, he curved back into me, his hands continuing to roam across more flesh as he pulled my tunic higher and higher. His soft lips pressed against my neck, and I gave up on all my pretenses as I relaxed my head, giving more of myself to him.

"Take this off." He tugged at my top, and I removed it, exposing my whole top half to the chilly air. My breasts pebbled in the morning air, but before I could feel the chill, Caelum's warm hand squeezed my flesh, while his other hand roamed lower, seeking the band of my pants.

"Is this alright?" he asked, his hazel eyes intent on mine, looking for permission, asking for me to accept him.

I wanted Cal with every fiber of my being at this moment. The voice protesting grew quieter with each press of skin against mine. I nodded, staring down at where his hands met my breast, his thumb idly stroking my nipple.

Caelum leaned into my ear and whispered, "I need to hear you say it."

"Yes." I moaned and Cal's hand drifted lower, sinking a finger into my center. I gasped at the contact, and it had been so long since someone had touched me I nearly came from the contact alone.

Caelum did a sharp intake of breath as he touched me. "What were you dreaming about, Lady? You're soaked."

"I wasn't dreaming about anything," I said with a shiver, and I felt his smile on my ear as he ran his finger along my seam and I let my legs fall open for him.

"This is all for me, then?" He pulled his hand away from me and lifted it to his lips, where he stuck his finger in his mouth and groaned. I stared wide-eyed at him, unblinking as I watched him revel in my taste.

It was absolutely filthy, and my face heated as I realized I *liked* it. He pulled his finger out of his mouth with a small *pop* and continued his descent back to where he found me wanting. One finger slid inside of me again making me shudder with a moan I couldn't hold back.

"*Gods*, you feel delightful." Caelum pressed his lips on my neck, and I held back a moan as his tongue traced my skin. Caelum relaxed, and he moved inside of me once again, making me moan aloud from the pleasure, my rapid thoughts becoming muddled with ecstasy.

He hitched my leg over his, granting him easier access. His palm grasping my breast gripped me tighter as he pulled me flush with his chest. The hard lines of his abdomen met my fingers as I slid an arm behind me, until I was met with the band of his own pants. Skipping the teasing, I sifted my fingers through the fabric, meeting the flesh of his hard length. Caelum growled in his throat and cursed. I ran my thumb over the tip, smearing the bead of moisture that had collected there and making small circles as he groaned.

"Halcyon," he hissed. "Keep doing that and this will be over far too soon."

I smirked, instead taking it as a challenge, and I wrapped my hand around his thick length. It was smooth and large.

Caelum withdrew himself from me, leaving me gasping. He shouldered himself up, making me lose my grip. Before I could argue otherwise, he shirked off his pants and moved to place them in the corner, leaving himself completely exposed.

I couldn't help myself from drinking every inch of him in. Kneeling in front of me, he really was carved from the gods. Legs thick like tree trunks led up to perfect round buttocks I wanted to dig my fingers in. His back was bedecked with muscles, and as he turned around, I held my breath. On his muscular abdomen, he had a slight dusting of hair that led down to the thick cock I was just holding.

I lifted myself up to meet him on my knees. A hiss of pleasure left his lips as I grasped his length. My stomach fluttered, and I wet my lips, bending down just low enough to lick the tip.

He was smooth like silk along my tongue, and I moaned, wrapped my lips around him. A hand rested on my face, and I fluttered my eyes open. Caelum's jaw was slack as he beared his weight on his arm behind him. I gave him a grin, or as much as I could with my mouth full of him, and flicked my tongue.

He gripped my hair, tugging ever so slightly, and the sting felt pleasurable as I swallowed him as much as I could. Tears sprang from my eyes as I worked him, and he threw his head back in pure ecstasy.

Watching Caelum let himself get lost in the throes of pleasure ignited a fire in me. Even though I was on my hands and knees, I felt like a queen from this position. The world could have been burning around us and he would be none the wiser.

I was the one in control, regardless of the position we were currently in. The thought only spurred me on, taking him to the back of my throat. Absolutely obscene noises filled the tent, but I loved it. My thighs clenched as his groans turned into moans, my need coursing through me, urging me to go faster.

"Gods, Halcyon. I'm going to..." His words slurred, and he groaned as he tensed, his fingers tightening against my scalp. The pull of my hair and the snap of his hips as he lost control had me moaning around him, swirling my tongue around him with every thrust. With a violent shudder, Caelum tensed and released himself down my throat. I drank down every drop and licked away every piece of evidence like it was the last water on the earth.

"You weren't supposed to..." Caelum's thumbs wiped away the tears that sprung loose on my cheeks while I grinned with mischief and glowing with triumph.

"Lie down." He commanded, and I obeyed this time. Resting on my forearms, he tore my pants away. I bared myself to him, inviting in the challenge. The cool air did nothing to deter me. The heat from giving Caelum pleasure pumping through my veins was enough to keep me warm.

Could he make me feel as good as I just made him feel? I was dying to know and growing wetter by the second just thinking about it.

Hovering over me, he raked his gaze along my exposed body and licked his lips. Our eyes met, our breaths mingled, and he pressed his lips to mine. He forced himself in with his tongue, taking control over the kiss before marking my skin as he moved his lips down to my neck.

He pressed his fingers in between my legs, making me moan as he rubbed my clit in small circles. I could feel my climax building, aching for release, and I undulated my hips in rhythm with his fingers.

One finger slipped in, and then a second, and I gasped at the fullness and the pleasurable stretch that came along with it. Curving his fingers up slightly, he hit a spot I wasn't sure I ever knew was there, and I shuddered around him.

Caelum chuckled and his pressed his lips to my torso, the stubble on his jaw gently scratching the sensitive skin as he pumped in and out of me with his hand, expertly extracting keens from me.

My body was shaking and my breaths became heavy. Gone were the tender touches of the morning, instead a carnal need took over with loud squelches that filled the tent. I lost control over my limbs as pleasure poured over, and I came so hard I saw stars.

I grasped the bed roll, clutching the fabric for any sort of purchase. My legs shook ferociously as my core squeezed and I lost the power to breathe. I cried out, unable to control the noises coming from my mouth, unable to control anything.

For once, I didn't care. I needed this release, needed it as bad as I needed air to breathe.

Warm, wet liquid coated my thighs, dripping down along the crevices of my body, creating a puddle beneath me. I screamed so loud I was sure birds took flight from the trees, and I didn't even mind. My body was locked, and as I caught my breath, my limbs continued to tremble, and I wiped my palm against my cheek, finding tears I didn't even notice had fallen.

"What just happened?" I gasped, my mind gradually coming back to my body.

Caelum laughed rough and low. "The peak of a woman's pleasure, Halcyon."

His body collapsed beside me, the both of us heaving with heavy breaths. I shot him a glance out of the side of my eyes, and he gave me a sly smirk. It certainly had been the most pleasure I had ever felt at once, so I couldn't argue with him.

Morning was in full swing when we finally roused ourselves, my bedroll tucked under my arm. Maya was hovering over the fire and her cast iron, cooking something that smelled absolutely exquisite. I looked around the campsite; the morning sun bright through the leaves. The chill in the air stung my skin, and cooled whatever was left of the heat from this morning.

"I need to wash in the river," I told Caelum, and he nodded before he called out to Maya to let her know where we would be.

Twigs and dead leaves cracked under our feet as we made our way to the river, Sumyre not around. I reached out to her with my mind, confirming she was indeed catching her own breakfast.

The riverbank was clear, and I dipped my toes into the water, testing the temperature. As I expected, it was bitterly cold. I could manage a few minutes in, but I guessed Caelum would probably want to bathe as quickly as possible.

Quickly, I dipped my bedroll in the water and scrubbed at the mess Caelum made of me, my core already warming at the recent memory.

I shed the clothes I had hastily put on, uncaring about my modesty now that Caelum had seen me in the most intimate of ways.

He followed suit, and I had a hard time peeling my gaze away from him as he exposed his body. He smirked as he took notice of me watching him undress, and I quickly averted my eyes, instead choosing to focus on washing all the sweat and sticky fluids off of me.

I stepped into the river, its waters lazily flowing around me, rinsing my skin with its tendrils of current. The air was crisp as I breathed it in, my magic feeling fully replenished from my long sleep and the cool water along my skin.

Caelum climbed in after me, and I bit back a laugh as he hissed a breath and his teeth clattered against each other. Dipping my hair in the river, I combed my fingers through the strands, releasing any leaves or dirt that may have built up.

I chuckled as I handed him the soap and pulled myself out of the water.

The morning sun was warm against my chilled skin, and the towel Caelum had snagged for me was soft as I cocooned myself inside of it.

"You're staying behind with the dragon today?" Caelum asked through chattering teeth, confirming the plans we had made the night before.

"Aceus, too." I reminded him. As much as I wanted to explore more of the temple, Sumyre's bond was too important to put off. It also gave me a chance to put Aceus good to his word. He was my bodyguard, and I had been loath to admit I was neglecting his duty.

Mortal or Magi, I should have never assumed his ability. Not that he seemed resentful, with Iris and Maya around to keep him occupied. But there was a reason he rose in the Guard ranks, and a reason he had protected my father all these years.

Caelum pulled himself out of the river as fast as he could, rivulets of the water dripping between his goosefleshed muscles. He shook the water out of his hair, reaching for his towel.

"I wish you were coming with us," he admitted quietly. I bit back a smile, my stomach swooping. No matter if I was Lydia or Halcyon, or if my hair was brown or silver, Caelum truly enjoyed my company. There was no obligation for him to say such things. In Dolan, the people around me were there because of who I was—my position. Even Shara, my closest friend, was forced to be around me. She never implied she didn't want to be, but Caelum wanted to be near me simply because it was what he wanted.

"Sumyre is too important," I replied, touching the gold band tattooed on my skin.

"I know." He pressed a chaste kiss to my lips, far too brief for my liking.

A roar sounded from above as Sumyre flew over the trees before diving into the wide river.

The water rose in her wake. A gigantic wave cascaded from the center of the river and headed directly toward us. I squealed, and at the last minute turned my head away from the onslaught of the wave. Caelum wasn't so lucky, and I let out a bellowing laugh at his dark expression. His hair was flat on his head, his lips down turned into a scowl.

"Well, this is useless now." He held the now sopping towel in hand and then slapped it against the ground before strutting stark naked back to the campsite.

"At least the view is nice," I called out to him, to which he turned with a raised eyebrow before throwing me a dark look.

In three long strides, he swept me off my feet, my initial scream turning into laughter. He slung me over his shoulder, my hair swaying back and forth as he marched back to camp.

"Put me down!" I shouted, raising a hand and smacking it against his perfectly round buttocks. A hungry growl emerged from his lips.

"Oh, I'll put you down, and then show you a really nice view," he laughed, and I clutched my towel tighter around my chest, my body heating at the growl in his voice.

"You can't! You have to go to the temple today," I told him, and he sighed, but not before he gripped my thigh, his fingers dangerously close to my core.

"Later, then," he promised, and my body buzzed thinking about all the ways he could make my body sing.

When we arrived back at the camp, Maya spared us a single glance. She huffed a laugh as I gave her a small upside-down wave, but then shook her head and resumed her task. Not an ounce of embarrassment or modesty overcame Caelum as he waltzed with heavy footsteps.

With a surprising gentleness, he set me down and smirked before darting into the tent, the flaps flinging against each other.

Caelum emerged from the tent fully dressed, and I didn't even try to hide my appraisal. While he was impeccable to look at while naked, I appreciated him with clothes on just the same. His shirts were always tight around his arms and chest, and he wore a holster around his back and chest. It just made me want to sigh into his embrace while I gripped on it for support.

Heat prickled across my cheeks as he leaned toward me, brushing his lips against my ear and whispered, "Freedom looks good on you, Lady Halcyon."

Just as quickly, he pulled back, not giving me a second glance as he strode toward the fire for a helping of food.

I pressed my hands to my cheeks. Freedom? What was that supposed to mean? I *was* free. But those words rang through me as I slid my legs through my pants. A single article of clothing I never would have worn while ruling Dolan.

Chapter 18

CAELUM

HALCYON BECAME ALL I could think about. The way she walked with her head held high, the way her silver hair gleamed in the sunlight, the way she smelled—like jasmine and fresh spring. She was quickly becoming an obsession—an addiction—and I was at least a little glad she decided to stay behind. As it was, I barely took notice of the temple as we retraced our route. I raked my hair out of my eyes, trying to force her from my mind, and I cursed.

I turned behind me, catching Iris' eye. "How does everything feel right now?" I asked, double checking for the fifth time. She rolled her eyes in response.

"All is normal right now, Cal. I told you I would let you know *if* I sense any changes."

With a nod and an approving grunt, I rolled my shoulders back. I held up a hand, a signal for the group to pause.

"Let me feel the ground, see if there are any other tunnels we don't know about."

Before I could hear any objections, I crouched down low and spread my palms. I pulled on my magic and sent it out through the dirt and stone beneath us.

Detecting the earth was more difficult than just wielding it, and it had taken me painstakingly long years of practice to manage it. Even then, it still wasn't perfect, but I was confident enough to get the job done.

I closed my eyes and focused. As usual, I could feel the stone of the temple, the dirt and earth surrounding it. Tree roots and rabbit holes.

I dug deeper down with my magic, like tendrils racing through the ground. Sweat beaded on my forehead as I kept diving further down, where I finally felt the temple's inner workings.

It really was like a maze that Iris had drawn...and then further down there was...nothing. Nothing at all. No ground, no trace of the throne room. Just a void.

I cocked my head, trying to send my magic further, pressing through the strain, and I felt my body caving from the pressure.

"Cal." Maya's voice was barely audible over the rushing in my ears. "Cal!" She shouted, and I jolted myself from the connection. I was breathing heavily, like I had just sprinted. My magic was still accessible, but barely.

"What just happened?" she asked as she rummaged around in a bag she was carrying.

"There's nothing down there," I stated between breaths.

"What are you talking about?" She tilted her head to the side as she handed me a small vial with light purple liquid.

"Everything was as it should be, and then nothing. No ground, no temple. Not anything. It's like a giant void. And the more I pushed into it, the more it took from me." She stared at me before sharing a glance with Iris. "We have to go down there." I insisted.

"Cal..." Maya groaned, and I shook my head.

"No, we have to go down there. We need to know why my magic isn't detecting it, why it drained me," I insisted.

"Caelum." Maya's stern tone cut through any victory I was feeling. "If there is truly a void down there, we have no way of protecting ourselves. It's too dangerous. Will your magic even work down there? We could be completely defenseless."

I mussed my hair, tugging on the roots. The void felt similar to how it felt when Halcyon and I found that bow. My magic hadn't waned then, so I didn't think I had any reason to believe it would block me from using it now.

"I think the temple is just shielding itself," I said. "We were rummaging around in the shrine room just fine yesterday. I want to find any more secrets that lie beyond." More so, I wanted to find the direct route back to the throne room. I took in the two, tough women before me.

They had been through the thickest, most dangerous parts of Ambrose with me. I just had to remind Maya why we came here in the first place. I could tell the dragon incident freaked her out, but I wasn't about to let that deter us from our mission.

"We came here because we knew we could find groundbreaking information about the gods and our origins. If this is a piece to the puzzle, we can't just leave it for the mortals to find," I said as I leaned on the stonework, and crossed my arms over my chest, unwilling to budge until we agreed to explore more.

Maya grimaced, her jaw flexing as she grated her teeth. "No, Cal. We came here to find something that had long been forgotten, something we could take back to Ambrose—safely, I might add—collect our money, and move on to the next one. This quest was to reinstate our *name*. But if it's going to cost our lives, it's not worth it."

I scoffed. Maya was right, but she was also wrong. It wasn't *just* our reputation on the line anymore. Of course, we needed to get backing from

Dolan, to prove we aren't just some crazy team willing to delve into Tantal for the sake of it, but there was more at stake now.

There was power, there was *magic*, in the mortal lands. Magic no one had even seen before, and *we* found it.

"Maya," I sighed, and clasped my hand on her shoulder, to which she shrugged me off. "If we can solve this mystery, then we won't just reinstate our names into good graces. We will become *legends*. Everyone will remember us as the ones who uncovered magic in a magicless land."

Maya didn't even acknowledge me. Instead, she turned to Iris. "What do you think we should do?"

I bristled at her ignorance, but Iris stood there wide-eyed and with her mouth hanging open.

"I-I'm not entirely sure. I see both sides of this. Caelum is right. This is a groundbreaking discovery, but you're right, too. I..." Her eyes bounced between the two of us.

"Spit it out, Iris." Maya was biting with her tone.

"I think we should go." She raised her hands at Maya's attempt to counter argue with her. "I'm just saying, let's go check it out. If we see any evidence of danger, we leave immediately. We were fine yesterday. The chances of something happening today seem to be slim."

Maya groaned and rubbed her forehead with her hand.

"Fine. I realize I'm outvoted, so drink that replenishing potion and lead the way, Caelum."

Her reservations were justified. It could be dangerous...and this magic felt like it was something more than pure Magi magic. I unstoppered the vial she gave me and tipped it back. Warm liquid ran down my throat, and a soft burning sensation radiated through me. It was painful enough to make me grimace.

"You're welcome, by the way." She rolled her eyes as she snatched the empty vial from my hands.

"Thanks," I said dryly.

Just like the day before, all was quiet as we made our way to the shrine room. Nothing had changed, and even the air seemed to be the same air we breathed yesterday. As we descended, I kept pressing my magic through the ground, tracking where the void was relative to our location.

We were well within the barrier now, and it unsettled me knowing there was no evidence of anything down here magically, but I had seen it with my own eyes.

Maya gave me three magic replenishing potions before admonishing me. "I think we can confirm that it's safe for us in here, but you need to stop using so much of your magic. These aren't unlimited," she grumbled as she handed me another vial.

I searched the west side of the room, looking for stones that might move, while Maya and Iris took up the other side. I couldn't feel *anything* beyond the walls of the shrine room, and I grunted in frustration.

"Anything on your side?" I called to the women, and I sagged my shoulders as they denied finding anything of importance.

Rolling my shoulders back, I huffed out a breath and continued my tedious search. The blue-green light of the Everflame did little to make my search any easier, and I felt my patience wear thin.

Until I spotted a stone that didn't quite fit in with the others. It was polished, slightly rounded, and bulging from the wall. As I peered closer, I noticed another intricate carving that matched some of the ones at the entrance to the temple. It was barely visible, and if I hadn't been scouring every minute detail, I would have missed it completely.

"Hey!" I shouted, my voice ringing through the empty room. "I think I found something!"

"What is it?" Iris asked excitedly, and even Maya's face looked surprised and eager.

"I think..." I didn't finish my sentence before laying a hand on the stone. It was completely smooth under my skin, and I had to wonder if there was a similar one where Halcyon had accidentally bumped into when she revealed the passage down here.

With a grunt, I pushed my palm into the stone. At first, it didn't budge, layers of dust settled through the cracks making it difficult, but then a groaning came from inside the walls.

Clicks reverberated across the room, and I stepped back and watched as a crack revealed itself. Up and up it went until the roaring of stone grinding against itself was so loud I clamped my free hand over my ear.

The stone swung open, revealing a tall archway into complete darkness. My heart was racing, and I bellowed a hysterical laugh.

I couldn't see much, even with the Everflame torch above my head, but as soon as we crossed the threshold, I could feel the change in the air. The floor was more solid, and as I swept the flame close to the ground, it was the same marble as in the throne room Halcyon and I had found.

Steps led us further below ground, and down and down we went. I was starting to second guess following the staircase when we finally hit the bottom. My steps echoed, signaling we were in a room much larger than what we had been in before.

"Damn," I cursed, "I wish I could see better."

"Caelum!" Iris called from my left, and I strode over to her. She stood in front of a metal basin. There was wood in it, but as I held the Everflame torch above, nothing happened.

"Everflame won't catch, remember?" Iris asked me, a little snarky smirk on her lips. "You got any flint?"

I dug into my pockets, finally grasping the little piece that I always carried around with me and handing it to Iris.

Sparks lit up in the basin, and it wasn't long before the wood—long since dried with age—burst into flames. Smoke rose from the fire, and it lit up the room, but it was barely more visible than what our Everflames could reach.

"Maybe there are more basins around," Maya suggested, and I turned to start searching.

Iris gasped, but before I could voice a question, fire spread from the basin, headed straight down the massive hall we stood in. Candles flared to life, igniting one right after the other, illuminating the space. High vaulted ceilings towered above us, bathed in an orange and red glow. The fire continued moving, lighting everything in its path.

It was all we could do but stop and stare at the expansive castle we now stood in. Castle was the only word I could use to describe this place, but it felt like too small of a word for it. It was a palace.

White and black marble columns that were as tall as the redwoods above us held up gleaming gold ceilings embellished with large decorative spirals and swoops, like an artist's paintbrush against canvas. The hall was so wide that dragons—plural—could fit comfortably. My hands shook, wondering if that was the exact purpose.

"Incredible," Maya breathed next to me, and I agreed wholeheartedly.

We continued down what I could only describe as a hallway, quietly taking in the decadent fixtures as we passed through.

"This has been under here this whole time?" Iris asked, her brown eyes wide with amazement.

"I bet it leads to the throne room Halcyon and I found," I said.

"Only one way to find out," Maya agreed. Her past reservations seemed to have dissipated, or at least they came second to our discovery now. I was glad I had pushed her to delve further. Leave no stone unturned, and all of that.

There wasn't much in the way of trinkets, but I was no longer interested in the treasure we had marveled over not so long ago. It all felt so small compared to this architectural wonder.

Our footsteps clicked in the otherwise silent space, not a single one of us wanting to break the peace that had resided here for so long. At the end of the hall, we took a left, where the fire had continued to flow, as though it lit everything up from that single basin alone, and I had a feeling it really did.

What sort of people had lived in a place like this? I doubted the mortal king himself even had this amount of decadence in his castle walls.

As we went further into the palace, I noticed more hallways than I could count. Was this a place that had previously been above ground? If so, why was it buried so deep? And how?

We walked for what seemed like hours before coming to a double-arched doorway. It was made from frosted glass, two doors framed with gold, and a blue glow came from inside.

I paused, wondering if this was the doorway to the throne room, and I had somehow missed the entryway in the chaos.

Before I even considered voicing my actions, I made my way to the doors and pushed. They swung open with my added force, and I stumbled inside. What stood before me was not the throne room, but something so much more.

I fell to my knees, my heart lurching in a way that made me want to cry. What I saw I could barely comprehend.

It was clear this had been some sort of conservatory. Giant leafy plants somehow continued to grow in this underground climate. Embedded in the walls and high-reaching arches were bright, shining opals, amethysts, tourmaline, and other stones I didn't have a name for, that glowed with an unearthly light. The brightness from those gemstones cut through the darkness of the rest of the room. I wasn't sure how the plants were sustained this deep underground. Only the gems bathed the foliage in light. If I had to form a hypothesis, there was old magic at play.

The conservatory continued deeper than I could see, the massive expanse smothered with nature and vines crisscrossing over the rich dirt beneath me.

This was nothing like I had ever seen, and I had seen the bioluminescent oceans of Gorana. It couldn't even compare to the golden sands of Aurum which glowed in the sun and moonlight. Nor could it compare to the bright purple and green lights that appeared in the far northern sky of Hemera.

I dug my hands in the ground, feeling the soil between my fingers, and I could have sworn there was a touch of magic in it, but as I grasped to reach it, it disappeared like trying to hold on to a single grain of sand.

This had to be what Halcyon had felt when she touched some of those artifacts. What she felt toward the bow that called her name in the throne room. How I wished the palace hadn't been cloaked. Even still, I tried to use my magic, but sensed nothing once again.

Maya placed a hand on my shoulder, and as I glanced up at her, I noticed tears streaming down her face.

"This was no castle for a Lord or a King," she whispered on a choked sob. "This was made for a god."

"I need to find that throne room," I decided. "There's a tome in there. And whoever lived here, god or otherwise, had records. We need to bring it back to Ambrose."

We left the conservatory room begrudgingly. I wished I could have taken a piece of it with me, but there was no way a single piece would do it any justice.

Not only that, but it felt like a sacred space, like whoever went in there was there to enjoy it at that moment, and the treasure was the experience itself.

I wished Halcyon could have seen it. I would have loved to see the look on her face as she took in all the life and majesty of it. Tomorrow, I would bring her, regardless of finding the throne room or not.

Iris placed an x each time we made a turn as we made our way deeper into the palace, and I had to be grateful for her foresight. This place was a labyrinth. Hallways led to other hallways and more rooms, but none to the throne room. At least not yet.

"So, you and the Lady of Dolan?" Iris asked conspiratorially, and I swung my head in her direction, smirking as I remembered how close we had truly gotten behind closed tent flaps. Just thinking about her had my lips pulling up at the edges. "Are you sure it's a good idea?"

"Of course," I balked. "It's not like we have any sort of future together. This is just for fun." The words felt ashy against my tongue, like the lie I kept telling myself would solidify if I repeated it to others.

"Since when do you do 'just fun'?" Iris questioned, and I sighed.

"He never does," chimed in Maya with a flat tone.

"I know that after this, there will be nothing for us. It's just for now—while we can—and then we will eventually go our separate ways. It's how it has to be."

"And you're good with that?" Maya asked, and I winced at the question.

"Sure am," I replied, even though I wasn't sure if I was satisfied with it at all. The two scoffed simultaneously. "What?" I demanded incredulously.

Maya shrugged. "Just means that we will have to pick up the pieces when we get back." There was a sadness in her tone that I wasn't sure I liked hearing.

"Don't worry," Iris said. "You'll be in good company."

I nodded, but I knew that no matter what company I held after this, if I wasn't with Halcyon, a piece of me would be missing. But I was glad I got to feel whole once, even if it was fleeting.

After hours of searching for the throne room, we came up empty. The palace was far larger than I had anticipated, and my feet were aching.

"Let's head back. We can try again tomorrow," I told them, and they nodded.

My disappointment must have been apparent because Iris grabbed my bicep, halting me in my path.

"Hey, you were able to dig to that room, right?" I nodded, eyeing the excited gleam in her eye. "Do you think you remember where it is? We could just get to that room that way."

I shook my head. "Unfortunately, I closed the tunnels on my way out. It was chaos, and I didn't want the dragon following me back, just in case."

Iris looked crestfallen, but Maya's face lit up. "The dragon!" She exclaimed with a snap of her fingers.

I snorted. "What about the dragon?"

"What if she could lead us back there? Do you think we can get Halcyon to communicate with her to find it for us?" Maya asked thoughtfully.

I turned around and gripped Maya's face in my hands, squeezing her cheeks together. "Maya, you godsdamned genius. You're so smart, I could kiss you right now!"

She responded by pulling her face out of my grasp and feigning disgust. "Please, don't. Let's just go back and see what Halcyon and her bonded are doing."

I laughed, feeling lighter in my steps now that we had a plan.

Finally, we made our way back to the threshold, and a large gust of air blew through the doorway, making me stumble. All the light that lit the underground palace up was gone. Now it was back to the awning abyss of darkness.

"Well, that answers that question," Iris muttered.

"What question?" I asked.

"How hasn't the place burned down the above temple already?"

I chuckled as we continued our ascent to the campsite. "Magic?" I guessed.

"Magic." Maya and Iris confirmed.

Chapter 19

HALCYON

I BLEW OUT A long breath as I took stock of everything we had recovered from the temple. Trinkets and artifacts were stacked in crates and wrapped in linens around the wagon. Shuffling items around, I kept sifting through everything before I found the bow. It was also wrapped delicately in linen, saved for donation to Neverwind Library.

My hands tingled as I reached for it, and I sucked in a breath. With extreme care, I unwrapped the linen revealing those stunning black diamonds that lined the edges. They felt warm in my palms, and I grinned.

Just the singular thought of grabbing the bow set my heart racing. Not that I thought I was doing something wrong—or even that I cared if I was—but it jarred me because it felt so *right*. The weapon and its pull unnerved me. I had never been one to cling to objects, but this item called to me.

Frowning, I looked around the wagon for some string, wondering where Iris may have put hers. The bow warmed in my palm, and I gasped as a thin golden strand appeared. I fingered the string, finding it was whole and strong. Grinning, I let out a nervous giggle.

The bow is rightfully yours.

Sumyre was opening up to me more now the group had gone into the temple, and I found that having a dragon in my head wasn't quite as grating as I thought it would be.

I don't suppose anyone else would think the same way about it, though? I dripped sarcasm through the mental bond, knowing I would have to give the bow to the library, and Sumyre's answering laugh rumbled in my chest. Of course, I knew a dragon wouldn't be able to laugh the same way I would, but the way it reverberated into my soul was perplexing.

Dragon bonds were only ever recounted in stories and historical texts, so I knew they had the same level of intelligence as people—if not more—but experiencing the bond first-hand was something that could never be recounted on paper.

It does not matter what the humans think. It is what we *know.*

Quickly, I snagged the quiver and arrows and hopped out of the wagon. Aceus stood, waiting for me with a single brow lifted in my direction.

"I thought I might try some target practice," I said with a grin, holding up the bow for him to see. He only shook his head and laughed.

"Whatever the Lady wants, the Lady gets."

"You're getting awfully casual these days," I told him with a mocking reprimand. His face turned red, and he deliberately looked away from me. "I'm only joking. I don't mind, really."

Placing a hand on his arm, he glanced back down at me, apprehension written all over his features. "I'm not my father," I bit out.

"That you are not," he replied with a twinkle in his eye.

Sumyre trailed deep into the forest, away from the camp. I could feel through the bond that she wanted us to follow.

"Come on, old man. Let's go shoot some arrows. Maybe I'll even let you try a few." I grinned at Aceus.

"I'm not old," he grumbled under his breath, and I laughed.

The large red trees surrounded us with their never-ending canopies. Birds chirped from way above and sunlight spotted the ground in patches of bright light. We came to a small opening, and I stepped around Sumyre, breathing in the scent of bark and leaves decaying on the ground.

Aceus leaned against a redwood that was easily the width of my bedchambers back at the castle, and he tossed me a grin.

"For what it's worth, Lady Halcyon, I think you have far more courage than your father ever had."

I scoffed, pulling the bow from my shoulder. "You've barely been around him for enough time. There's a reason he's had Dolan fall in line for a hundred years."

Aceus shook his head, gazing at the clouds above. "I may not have the life span of you or your father, but I know what a leader looks like. Can I be frank with you?"

"Please," I offered, placing a hand on my hip. I wanted to know what he truly thought about my father's reign, and my future one as well. Aceus ran a hand along his head, his eyes averting my gaze.

"Alastair hid in his castle, using his council as a shield. From what I've heard from older Magi, his father did the same. Neither one of them would dare to leave their city—much less travel to the mortal kingdom—for the good of their people." Aceus sighed, and I shot him a doubtful look from the side of my eye as I fingered the bow string. "I'm not sure what happened to have raised a woman like you. Just making the decision to come here to protect your city is more than I ever saw from your father."

I scoffed. "Maybe it's because he didn't raise me." No, that was left to the servants and teachers my father hired.

"All the better for it. And I know I'm not the only one who sees it," he said with a far-off grin.

"What do you mean?" I asked, dropping the bow, meeting Aceus' gaze.

"Your servants, for one. We see the way you talk to them, how you treat them. Even your handmaiden. Word travels fast in the bowels of a castle."

My lips pursed, considering that my friendship with Shara could mean so much to the others in the castle. Respect was something I consistently valued for those who had less than desirable jobs, but I truly wasn't sure if it had made a difference.

"And for second?"

Aceus' mustache twitched in a sly smile. "I think there's a certain man who sees you for who you are, too."

I couldn't help the smile that tugged at my cheeks, nor the flare of heat in them as I thought of Caelum.

"But I must say," he continued, pausing as though he wasn't sure if he had tread too far already with his commentary. I gave him a wave for him to keep talking, and he ran his hand along his chin. "I hope you know what you're doing with his heart."

A nervous laugh escaped my lips. "And what of you with those two women? I haven't missed the hearts in all of your eyes."

He shook his head, smiling. "Nice deflection," he prodded. "It's just fun, Halcyon."

"Yes, Caelum and I are only having a bit of fun, too," I replied with a flatness in my voice which gave away my lie.

We both veered our gazes away from each other, knowing there was a chance we both were in over our heads with our feelings, but refusing to admit as much.

As if on cue, Sumyre nudged me from behind, and I stumbled forward. Her nose breathed on the arm that clutched the bow, and I stared down at it. The black stones gleamed, and for a moment I got lost in the beauty of them. Whoever crafted this bow had a gods-given talent.

With a deep sigh, I lifted it up to aim at a tree. I hadn't notched any arrows in it, but I ran my finger over string just the same.

Considering I hadn't practiced archery in ages, I doubted I could even aim properly. I released the bow string with a loud twang and watched as it vibrated back and forth.

The arrows.

I turned to Sumyre, who was now lounging on the ground, lazily watching me with her green eyes.

Letting out a *hmph* in determination, I grabbed an arrow from the quiver strapped over my shoulder. The action of sliding the arrow and locking it into place still felt familiar, even though I hadn't touched a bow in ages.

Archery had been something I had done in my youth, but it was for recreation. Once I got old enough to study for my position, my father had forbidden any more of it. I resented him for that, but I resented him for a lot of things. Things I continually refused to think about.

At least until this trip. It was like as soon as I crossed the border, I was forced to examine every part of my life that I purposefully locked away.

Aiming at a wide tree trunk, I took a grounding breath and pulled back on the string. The muscle memory came back well enough, but my arms shook from the tension. I kept my eye on the made-up target, a large piece of bark that was slightly darker than the surrounding bark.

It had been so long since I last shot an arrow, I was positively sure I would miss my mark. But when I let the arrow fly, it whizzed through the air, and I held my breath as it hit the tree bark dead in the center.

I gasped, running toward the arrow. My feet pounded the dirt underneath me as I neared where the arrow was firmly stuck in the tree. A perfect shot.

My mouth hung open in disbelief, and I glanced back at Sumyre, whose smug feelings pulsed through the bond, and I could have sworn her lips curled up in a smile.

Aceus, who had taken to leaning against a tree passively watching, stood up straighter as I pointed to my mark.

Do it again.

"Again?" My mind whirred as I plucked the arrow out, needing some force behind the pull. Bark shards flew out as I tugged it free and I flipped it in my hands. There was nothing assuming about the arrow, but the bow in my hands pulsed.

Reaching back to where I stood before, I rolled my shoulders back.

Farther.

I shot Sumyre a quizzical look, but stepped back two enormous steps just the same.

Farther.

"If I go any further, I won't be able to hit the mark. I'll barely be able to see it," I told her.

If Aceus was concerned I was talking to myself, he didn't show. Instead, he only watched me, a frown tugging his brows closer.

Farther, she demanded.

I narrowed my eyes at her before doing as she said, anyway. I walked farther and farther back until I was sure Sumyre would find my distance acceptable.

The piece I hit before was barely visible, but I lifted the bow regardless and notched an arrow back. My arm strained with the string, pulling it back toward my ear.

Sumyre shifted around me, her four legs lumbering along the ground, crunching twigs and leaves beneath her.

I didn't let my eyes stray from my target as she came up behind me and huffed a breath of air that blew strands of my hair around my face.

Trust the bow. Let go.

And so I did. I let the string go, and with it, the arrow pierced through the air until it *thunked* the long distance away. I couldn't even see where it landed, squinting my eyes, trying to discern where the arrow sank into the earth.

Sumyre bristled behind me and lowered her neck, beckoning me to get on top of her.

Get on.

I narrowed my eyes at her as she lowered the wing closest to me. Climbing on, I grasped at her smooth scales, finding divots in her muscles that made it easier to grasp. My legs settled on either side of her, fitting myself in the crevice that joined her long neck to the rest of her body.

"Lady Halcyon!" Aceus shouted, his face going from intrigue to concern. I waved him off.

"It's all right! Just trust me." Underneath me, Sumyre stood up jostling me from side to side, and I gasped at the unfamiliar motion. Aceus had his hand on his sword, ready to unsheathe it at a moment's notice, and I had to wonder what he expected to do against a dragon. The brave fool.

Sumyre trotted toward the tree that held my mark, my body swaying side to side as she walked. It wasn't entirely dissimilar to riding a horse, but the link we shared allowed me to expect her movements, allowing me to adjust accordingly.

I grinned, my nerves about riding her shedding from my mind. My confidence grew, and I let myself bask in the delight of our bond.

We neared the tree, and Sumyre crouched low enough for me to slide off easily.

The arrow lodged in the same spot it had the first time, and I gasped. It didn't even land aside from the original hole by a mark.

The bow never misses.

I turned to Sumyre, my mouth unhinged, my eyes wide.

"It shouldn't be possible."

Sumyre chuffed.

Neither should our bond, and yet here we are.

"There has to be some limitations. There's no way it could hit every time," I breathed, talking more to myself than to the dragon. Grabbing the arrow from the tree, I yanked it free and stashed it back into the quiver.

I turned to Sumyre and gave her a conspiratorial grin.

"I have an idea," I told her, and she chuffed in response while lowering herself so I could climb on her once again.

SUMYRE SPED UP AND slowed down at random intervals as I continued to aim and shoot my arrows at the same mark. Each arrow hit, but as we went on, I could feel myself tiring.

Taking a seat on an old tree stump, Aceus plopped next to me, more relaxed now he had grown used to seeing me riding a dragon. *A dragon!* Even though the bond hummed through me comfortably, I could still hardly believe it.

"It's siphoning my magic," I said as I blew out a fatigued breath.

"Do you think it could be dangerous?" he asked, looking like the last thing he wanted to do was touch the bow.

I shook my head. "I don't think so. No more dangerous than a regular bow with impeccable aim."

The black diamonds shined brighter as I used it, and I figured they must have some sort of magical property which ate away at my magical reserves.

As Sumyre and I tested it with different speeds, I realized the faster Sumyre was, the more magic it used. So at least, I knew the aim was finite. As finite as my magic, anyhow.

Sumyre's maw rested on the ground near my feet, and I could feel her hot breath as it ruffled my pants. I reached forward and placed my hand on her head, brushing along the black scales between her eyes.

Sumyre huffed out another blast of hot air and closed her eyes, pleased with the current position of being curled near me.

The thought of flying seemed exhilarating, but also terrifying. I had ridden her easily enough on the ground. Would it be the same up above?

Humming as I stroked her scales, I pressed my mind out to reach her. The mind link, or psychic path—or whatever we shared—was becoming stronger.

It only took a gentle tug, and I could feel her as easily as myself. I could definitely see how the bond would be useful in instances such as battle, but it would be a wintry day in the sands of Aurum if it ever came to anything such as that.

The sound of the ground crunching under footsteps formed behind us, and I whipped my head around.

Caelum, Sumyre whispered in my mind, and she removed herself from the ground, shaking herself free from leaves that got stuck on her underbelly.

Brown hair and a rugged face peeked out around the foliage, and he smiled as he approached us. Dirt smudged his cheeks, and he wore a grin wider than I had seen from him yet. Considering he smiled nearly all the time, it made my heart patter more quickly.

"Is everything all right?" I ached to reach for him, to inhale his pine scent.

Everything in my body called for him, and it took every ounce of willpower for me not to run into his arms. I had to admit, there were a few times today when I turned to call on his guidance, and when I realized he wasn't there, it stung.

Aceus was right beside me, nodding at Caelum in greeting, and then they clasped their hands together. A smile broke along Aceus' face, relaxed and friendly. Maybe I wasn't the only one feeling more at ease in this forest than we did at home.

"Yes, but I need to ask your dragon for some help." Caelum's smile faltered for a moment as he shifted his gaze toward Sumyre.

"What kind of help?" There was no way I would let him put her in any kind of danger. Not that I didn't think she couldn't take care of herself, but now we were bonded; protectiveness overruled logic. It was surely a defense mechanism for us both to survive. Ancient instincts roaring to life.

"We need to find the room we were in when you bonded with Sumyre," he told me with bright eyes.

Sumyre's head lifted at his request, and I gave Caelum a questioning glance.

"Why? You weren't able to find it when you were down there?" I angled my head in question.

Caelum gazed up at the quickly darkening sky and smiled freely. "You should have seen it, Halcyon." I smiled at the way his eyes sparkled. His excitement filled my body with warm butterflies.

"There's an entire castle there. A palace! It's more incredible than anything I have ever seen. Columns and pillars of gold. Doors larger than anything in Ambrose. And there's this room…" He sighed wistfully. Meeting my gaze with his warm hazel eyes, the green shining brighter in the light, I practically melted. His joy was oozing and infectious. "There's a massive room, like a conservatory. Plants with leaves larger than I had ever seen. Crystals glowing in every shade of color imaginable."

A nesting cave.

I reared at Sumyre's conclusion. Her ears flicked against the spiraling horns on her skull.

It's a true dragon nesting cave, she repeated.

How do you know? I looked at her with an inquiry.

Sumyre didn't answer, instead trailing further behind me. She sniffed the ground before shaking her wings and settling into a curl. There was curiosity at the forefront of our bond. But more than that, there was longing and sorrow.

"I have to take you down there." Caelum's excitement distracted me from the threads of Sumyre's thoughts, and I grinned back at him. "But first, we need to find that room. The tome is still there, and if this place is what I think it is, then we definitely want our hands on that book. Especially because we don't want the mortal king to have or destroy it."

"How is that possible?" I asked, gesturing for him to keep going. "A whole castle beneath the ground? It doesn't make any sense."

"I don't know. I'm not sure we will ever know, but the only chance we might have to learn anything is if we can read that book." He raked his hands through his hair, tugging on the roots. I made my way to him, placing my hand on his arm.

Caelum's arms wrapped around my waist, his warm body engulfing mine, and I tentatively wrapped my arms back around him. Inhaling as he pulled me in, his scent of nature overwhelmed my senses. I nearly groaned. Aceus shook his head at the display of affection, and he tipped his head.

"You've got her from here?" he asked Caelum, who nodded. "I think I'll head back to the camp." And with that, it was only Caelum, myself, and my dragon.

"Do you think Sumyre can find the room again?" His words were muffled in my hair as he grasped me tighter.

Sumyre bristled through the bond, as though she took offense. Of course she could find that room again.

"I think that dragon could do just about anything," I replied with a touch of smug pride.

"Great," he sighed, his body relaxing into mine. "We can talk more about it tomorrow, but for now—"

Caelum's lips crashed into mine, and I whimpered at the contact. Our tongues intertwined, slowly at first, before becoming a battle for dominance. My body immediately responded, and I arched into Caelum's chest, grasping at the leather straps of the holster he was still wearing. Caelum broke off our kiss, resting his forehead against mine, both of us panting.

"I've been wanting to do that all day," he said, lust making his voice thick and low. His hands digging into the small of my back, fisting into my shirt, and I pressed closer to him, feeling his hardness press into me.

He groaned, and I flattened my hands against his pectorals, relishing in the hardness of his body beneath my fingertips.

"I could take you right now," he murmured in my ear, making gooseflesh rise on my arms, and my nipples peaked, aching to be touched.

Sumyre made a chuffing sound, and it immediately broke the spell. Laughing, I nudged myself away from Caelum.

"Sorry, I didn't mean to be indecent in front of company," he said. I gave Caelum an apologetic look, but it didn't stop him from beaming down at me, his eyes ablaze with promises of later.

I gestured Caelum to lead the way back to the camp, but Sumyre huffed, her giant nose bumping into my back, nearly making me stumble over.

"What?" I turned as asked, and she motioned her neck behind her. An image flashed before my eyes, one of me climbing on her back and riding through the air. She leaned down in the same way we had practiced this afternoon. Riding on her back and walking through the woods was not on her mind, though.

My heart skipped a beat. I didn't like to admit how much fear had gripped me just thinking about taking to the skies.

Caelum stared wide-eyed and let out a humorless laugh. "I think she wants you to get on."

"I… I don't know if I can." Glancing back at Caelum, panic gripped my chest. We had spent all day trotting around the forest floor, but that didn't mean I wasn't still terrified of *flying*.

Caelum shrugged. "You're going to have to learn at some point. Might as well be now."

"I don't know," I lamented. "What if I fall? It would be instant death."

Cal clenched his jaw in thought. "You're right. Maybe we can try flying another day. When the sun is bright, and we have some safety measures implemented."

A growl echoed through the trunks of the trees where we stood. Sumyre's green eyes narrowed and a plume of purple smoke ejected from her nostrils.

As if I would allow you to fall.

Clenching my fists, frost coating my knuckles, I said, "I'm going to try to ride her. Gods above, I'm going to do it."

"Halcyon, if you don't feel comfortable…"

Determined to jump out of my comfort zone, I glared at Cal with determination.

"No. Like you said, I have to do this, eventually. Might as well start now." I reached out and put my trembling hand on Sumyre's neck. My heart raced, and my fingers tingled.

With one big gulp of air, I reached over Sumyre's wing, feeling the thick skin where the membranous wing turned into a scaled joint. I slipped my foot on it and pulled myself up.

Large spikes protruded from her neck and stopped right where it met her body. I shimmied as close to the closest spike as I could, my knuckles white around it. My knees dug into her sides, the scales smooth under my pants. Up here, Caelum looked smaller, and he grinned at me.

Sumyre huffed another breath of hot air at Caelum and he wafted it away, confused. She swung her head back toward me.

"She wants you to get on, too." I said, noting the relief in my chest as I spoke. "You already know how to ride a horse. How different could it be from riding a dragon?"

It was very different, I already knew, but I really wanted him to join me. The safety of his arms around me was still fresh in my mind from our ride here, even though I knew it was a false sense of security.

"Halcyon, I really don't think I should. Isn't your first time riding a dragon supposed to be, I don't know, special or something?"

"What? Like taking my dragon riding virginity?" I deadpanned. Caelum's face turned beet red.

"What? No, I just thought... I don't know..." As Caelum fumbled over his words, I couldn't help but let out a bark of laughter. Cal narrowed his gaze, but a small smile pulled at his lips. "There's magic we haven't seen in hundreds of years happening right in front of us, Halcyon. I don't know what it would mean if I rode with you."

Releasing my fingers from the spike, I crossed my arms over my chest.

"It would mean that you got to ride a dragon alongside a Dragon Rider. Get on the damn dragon, Cal."

He looked out into the forest as though he was about to get in trouble for doing as I told him. He let out a heavy sigh and climbed on behind me, his grace still better than my own.

I leaned back into his chest, letting myself relish in his warmth before grasping the spike once again. Caelum wrapped his arms around my middle, clinging to me.

"Okay," I breathed. "Let's do this." I turned back and gave him a small smile, mustering up as much bravery as I could.

Caelum, looking less confident than I had ever seen, called out, "Sumyre, if you let us fall, I will haunt you and kill you myself."

Sumyre huffed out another plume and chuffed—her way of laughing—and I squinted my eyes, preparing for whatever was to come next.

I gasped, and Caelum gripped me tighter as Sumyre stood on her legs, making us sway from side to side. I let out a bubble of nervous laughter as Sumyre spread her wings wide, the sharp black points on the tips of them gleaming in the last rays of the sun as it set through the trees.

She pushed her massive wings up, and flexed them, wind batting the loose strands of hair out of my eyes before she pushed off.

My stomach lurched as she jumped into the air, narrowly missing branches and leaves as we rose higher and higher. Caelum's grip around me was suffocating, but my eyes couldn't get wider, and I couldn't have felt more *free*.

We broke out of the forest, catapulting to the clear skies above. The tops of the trees created one giant green, orange, and yellow blanket over the land, and I stared down in awe.

I could see where the forest gave way to rolling hills and rivers twinkling with gold in the slowly sinking sun. The skies were a bright canvas of oranges and pinks chased by the dark blues of night over the large, serrated edges of the Jagged Peaks. Leaning forward, I drank in the never-ending view, trying to take in everything I saw and commit it to memory. Stars were beginning to make an appearance, white and yellow twinkling dots scattered above.

Sumyre's wings beat in a steady rhythm beside us, and she flew us over the forest until a familiar clearing opened below. Caelum was hunched over, his head buried in my neck.

"Cal, look." I nudged him with my elbow.

"I can't," he cried in my ear.

I groaned. "Stop whining, and *look*."

I could feel him peel his face out of the crook of my shoulder, his stubble scraping gently over my skin, and I couldn't help the wave of desire pooling in my core. I cleared my throat, banishing the thought of his stubble between my thighs, and instead nudged him once again.

"Holy gods…" he murmured in my ear. His grip never lessened, but the slowing of his heartbeat against my back made me smirk.

"This is incredible," I breathed as tears pricked the back of my eyes, and I felt a hum of satisfaction from Sumyre.

"I can't deny this is incredible, but Hal, it's terrifying and we still have to go down. I'm beginning to think this was a terrible idea. You shouldn't be up here at all."

I scoffed. "What are you talking about? This feels so natural, it feels…*perfect*." There was no word to describe exactly how I was feeling, the warmth in my chest, the freedom of being in the sky like this.

The world was full of unknown opportunity, and this was but a glimpse of it. I shook my head, giddiness hazing over the goal of this experiment. Sumyre flew in wide circles before hovering over an area of the forest with an enormous crater in it, so deep I couldn't see the bottom.

"Cal, see that crater? That's got to be where the chamber is." I lifted a hand off the spike and pointed unafraid of the vast space between myself and the land. Caelum, however, didn't feel the same, and pushed me forward until he also wrapped his hands around the spike.

"Yes," he hissed, "I see it. Hold on to the damn dragon, Halcyon."

I laughed, the sound coming easily out of my mouth. There was no word to describe the feeling bubbling through my stomach. My body was buzzing, my eyes threatening to water. If the gods were still alive, this is what I imagined it would be like to meet one.

Sumyre let out a raucous roar so loud the limbs on the tops of the trees shook beneath us. A plume of lilac fog erupted from Sumyre, filling the sky with swirling clouds of purple. As we passed through, I lifted my hands. It felt the same as air, not tangible in any way. As soon as I grasped Sumyre once more, a click sounded from inside her throat before bright flames erupted into the sky. The fire wasn't close enough to burn, but I felt the heat the same. Bright yellow and orange flames crackled in the sky around us like our own personal sun. When the flames dissipated, the world darkened, showing the twilight stars once more.

My cheeks hurt from smiling so widely, and Cal shuddered against my body as Sumyre swung herself back around before rushing to the camp.

The wind flew through my hair, the chilly air cooling my heated flesh. My heart lurched from amazement, and I whooped as she declined, throwing my body back against Cal, both of us gripping the one spike in front of us. Adrenaline pumped through my veins, but for the first time, the adrenaline felt *good*. Flying with Sumyre was the first thing that felt right in a long, long time.

Sumyre landed with grace, barely jostling us as her taloned feet hit the ground. My legs shook as I slid from her, my whole body buzzing from the flight.

Caelum, however, crumpled onto the ground, burying his hands in the dirt.

"I have never...been...so grateful...for land..." He heaved between his words. I bent down to his level, resting my shaking hand on his back.

"You're alright. Here, let's get you sitting up." I pulled on his shoulders, my hands still shaking from the flight. His body was too big for me to lift, and I grunted at the effort. He tried to push himself up, but his arms gave out.

"Just leave me here. I'll be fine," he mumbled into the dead leaves pressed against his face.

"Come *on*." I pulled at him again and finally got him to sit upright. "Put your head between your knees and take a deep breath. It'll help, I promise."

He nodded weakly, and I frowned at his ashen face.

Internally, I understood his fright. But that ride... It was the most glorious experience I ever had. I only wished he could have felt the same joy I did.

"What happened to you?" Iris' pleasant voice startled me, and I jolted back from Cal.

"We went for a test ride," I explained. "Do you happen to have any water? I think Caelum is a little shaken."

Caelum let out a nervous laugh that sounded almost like a giggle, and I bit my lip to keep from smiling at it. I wasn't trying to laugh at him, but the overwhelming feeling of glee had overridden any other emotion.

"A little shaken is putting it lightly," he said as Iris handed over her water skin. His arms trembled as he brought the skin to his mouth, and I placed my hands over his, guiding it so the water wouldn't spill.

He took small sips and when he was done, he rested his head, leaning against a tree, and blew out a long, deep breath. I used my thumb to wipe away a dribble of water on his chin.

"I'm sorry. I didn't know it was going to be like this for you," I apologized.

"No, I don't think I knew either." He let out a long breath, his shaking starting to subside.

"Well, shit." Iris looked between us and the dragon, who was now curled up on the ground, her eyes lazily roaming over all of us.

"We know where the underground throne room is, though," I said as I handed Iris her water back.

"Well, shit!" Iris repeated but her voice inflecting with impression. "We should tell the others. We can go in the morning!"

"No," Caelum croaked. I whipped my head back at Caelum in surprise. "I think I need—*we* need—a day to rest and regroup."

Iris sighed, and I turned back to him, placing my hands on his cheeks. His hands covered mine, the rough texture of callouses rasping against my soft skin.

"I just need a break. Plus, it will give us time to go over what we've already learned." He was stalling for time, and not because we needed to gather more intel, but because the flight had exhausted him down into his soul.

"That won't be a problem, will it?" I asked Iris.

Iris rolled her eyes with her hands on her hips. "No, it won't be a problem. I just hate adjusting timelines, that's all." She stalked away from us, leaving me and Caelum to ourselves. I grimaced at Caelum, knowing Iris was disappointed, but he gave me a weak smile.

"Thanks for sticking up for me," he said, finally flashing me his grin I loved so much.

"You don't need to thank me. I feel awful for making you fly. You were right. It was a bad idea to bring you along."

Caelum shook his head and pressed himself up off the ground, the color returning to his face.

"No, it's okay," he let out a small laugh, "I just can't believe it. I—*we*—rode a fucking dragon." He turned to me, grabbing me and pulling me into a warm embrace, his arms banded around my waist. "That was the most terrifying thing I have ever done, and you're an absolute natural. You're incredible."

Caelum's lips were close to mine, his brown eyes wide as he regarded me. As though he saw me, not as the Lady of Dolan, but as a gift from the gods—a rare gem, painstakingly dug from the depths of the earth, and polished to gleam.

"Caelum, I know I'm incredible, but it doesn't take me riding on the back of a dragon to make me so." I smirked at him, unable to calm the insistent tumbling of flutters in my stomach.

He grinned before pressing his lips to mine. His touch was soft as his hands dug into against my back. Slowly, he pulled away and his gaze dipped from my eyes to my lips.

"That is entirely true, Lady Halcyon. Dragon riding is only the beginning of your incredibility."

Dinner that evening was the most enjoyable dinner we had as a group so far. Laughter was rampant, and I swore Maya must have put some of her magic in the food to remove our stress.

We were all huddled around the fire, Iris' head on Maya's shoulders. Aceus sat on the other side of Maya, his arm placed behind her as he causally leaned toward her. I had a hard time wiping the smile off my face as Caelum retold his dramatic rendition of what our trip on Sumyre was like.

"As soon as I climbed on Sumyre's back, she shot up into the air with astonishing speed!" he exclaimed. I shook my head, giggling. "I swear, I only blinked, and we were in the sky with nothing between us except unimaginable heights!"

"Caelum!" I covered my mouth while I finished chewing before shoving my shoulder into his. "It did *not* go like that. Sumyre was plenty gentle. *I* was the one who had my eyes open the whole time, after all."

Everyone around the fire laughed as we spoke. Aceus, surprisingly, had the most questions.

"What was it like? Being so up high? Could you see the end of the world?"

Maya threw a pinecone at Aceus' head, which bounced off, and he grunted at her. "What was that for?"

"The world isn't flat, you big dolt. Of course, they couldn't see the end of it!"

I bit my lip to keep from laughing. Instead, I leaned my head against Caelum's shoulder as it bobbed up and down. He wasn't withholding his laughter, and soon I was giggling just from the movement of my head on his shoulders.

We all broke out into silly laughter, Caelum once again exaggerating the flight, and how Sumyre "whirled around the forest before plummeting to our sure deaths, only to come to a halt at the very end."

I looked back at the dragon in question, who curled up closer to our group tonight. Her eyes were closed, but I saw her scales ripple whenever she was mentioned.

You did good today. I told her through the bond, and I received a happy vibration in my chest.

We did good today. Her voice was clear as a bell in my psyche, with an edge of an ethereal chime around it. *That one did not.*

I barked a laugh, and of course it was in a lull of silence. Everyone turned to me.

"What's so funny?" Caelum wrapped his arm around my waist, pulling me into his side. I stiffened in his embrace, peering at the eyes of everyone around us.

Public displays of *anything* went directly against everything I was taught. I spent my whole life becoming unobtainable and training to command respect. In the past I never cared if I was well-liked, but as I looked around, taking in all the expressions Maya, Iris, and Aceus wore, I found myself caring a little more.

"Nothing," I mumbled as I tugged myself out of Cal's arms. "The dragon said you're pathetic."

The camp roared with laughter, and Caelum shoved me on my shoulder. A friendly, playful gesture.

"She didn't!" Caelum swung his gaze, pinning narrow eyes on Sumyre.

"Not in so many words," I shrugged, allowing myself to smile. "But the sentiment was just the same."

The jokes and banter continued until the moon was near its apex. The sky was clear, and stars glinted brightly through the tall, tall limbs of the trees. Sumyre had long since been snoring, and Iris and Maya retired to their tent, with Aceus not-so-subtly following them. Caelum stood up, stretching his back before holding his hand out to me.

"Lady, shall we excuse ourselves for the evening?" he asked with mock decorum.

I took his hand gingerly, and he pulled me up from the log. Wrapping his arm around my waist, he tugged me closer to him before lifting the tent flap open and ushering me inside.

Chapter 20

CAELUM

Halcyon often captivated me, but after today, she enthralled me completely. The walls around her heart were softening. When she laughed out loud, it was like the sweetest music to my ears. I wanted to capture her sounds and carry them with me everywhere I went.

It was dark, but the moon and stars were bright enough to illuminate us, and I watched appreciatively as she spread out her bedroll.

She hadn't bothered with tucking away the silver strands fraying out of her braid, and pink still tinged her cheeks from where the cool wind stung it. It was a far cry from the time I had seen her standing on that mezzanine, with her hair pinned in a perfect braided crown, her body clad in azure swathes of silk.

Both versions of Halcyon were beautiful, but I enjoyed seeing her this way. She was lighter, revealing the real Halcyon who wasn't thinking about her obligations to a city. I could only imagine what that sort of responsibility would do to someone. The expectations she was supposed to achieve, especially following in her father's footsteps. I never asked her directly about it, but I could see how she filed information away, how she weighed her options. It was as though she was constantly thinking of everyone else, willing to put away all her fear and comfort just to do what she thought was best for her city.

I was standing and staring, taking in every bit of her perfection, when she asked, "What are you doing, Cal? Aren't you going to come in?"

Ducking in the tent, I stepped out of my pants and felt the heat of her gaze sweep over me. Her eyes stalled just a moment longer over my cock before she looked away. I grinned and settled into my bedroll, relishing the soft warmth of the wool.

"You could do the same. It would be more comfortable."

Halcyon bit her lip, watching as I pulled the bedroll over my stomach. She let out a sigh and then pulled her clothes off as well, removing them under the cover before tossing them aside.

"Damn. I was looking forward to the show," I chided.

She breathed a laugh. "I know you were, which is why I didn't give you one."

She lay on her back, staring at the top of the tent, her long lashes blinking shadows along her cheek as she lost herself to her own thoughts.

"How did it feel?" I asked, unwilling to let the conversation die. Knowing the moment we rested our eyes, the joy of the night would be over.

"Hmm?" she responded, her thoughts drifting elsewhere.

"How was it, riding Sumyre today? You didn't say much about your own experience." In fact, she had said little at all tonight. Only interjecting as I told my story and laughing along with the rest of us.

She blew out a long breath and turned her head to face me. "It was the most incredible experience I have ever had, and..." Her blue eyes drilled into mine, lit up with excitement and a smile on her lips that took my breath away.

"And, what?"

"I can't wait to do it again tomorrow," she whispered, and I couldn't help myself from reaching out to press my thumb along her soft cheek, tracing the plump skin that grew taut every time she smiled.

I committed the feel of her skin along the pad of my thumb to memory, knowing this wasn't going to last forever. Her eyes lowered, and I didn't even know if she had realized that she leaned into my touch.

I pressed my lips to hers, gentle and soft. Her hands wound around my neck, her fingers playing with the hair on the nape of my neck. I was never going to cut my hair again. If we only had these fleeting moments together, then I wanted to remember them forever.

Slow and patient, our tongues danced together, and I clung to her every movement, every slight shift she made as she inched herself closer. I slid my arm underneath her, feeling each point of contact with her smooth skin, as I banded my arm around her, pulling her tighter to me. Her breasts pressed against my bare chest, and my cock jerked in reaction against her thigh, unable to hold back the effects being near her often had on me.

One of her legs slid in between mine, and she ground her heat against me. I groaned at how wet she was against my thigh. I had yet to claim her, and I wanted to—I ached to make her *mine*.

Breaking our kiss, I jolted at the thought. There was never a time in my life where I wanted someone so fully. Sadness and guilt fell to the pit of my stomach. She could *never* be mine. Maybe Halcyon had been right all along, and doing this with her was a mistake. I already knew I was in too deep. As soon as we got back to Ambrose, my heart was going to shatter into a million pieces.

Halcyon's chest heaved against mine. Her lashes were thick against her cheek as she licked her plush, pink lips. I brushed my thumb over her cheekbones, where my hand had yet to move from her face.

"We should get some sleep." I pressed a kiss to the top of her head as she nodded, her breaths slowing as she relaxed. I moved to snake my arm out from under her, but she gripped me around my neck tightly.

"Can you hold me like this?" she asked, and I stilled, my resolve quickly shattering. I should have told her no; I could feel myself drowning in her, and I was desperately clawing for air. "Please?"

That one word—the one plea—cracked me. I pulled her into me further. Relishing the feel of her up against me, I memorized all of her while she breathed against the crook of my neck.

She found comfort in me, and I had to wonder how long it had been since she ever found true refuge in someone else's arms. If she ever had at all. Halcyon's hands trailed over my chest, my skin burning wherever her soft fingers touched. I sucked in a breath as she trailed down my abdomen and over my ribcage.

"Hal…" I breathed in her ear, and she pressed herself up against me, her hips ever so slightly rocking on my thigh. My willpower was hanging by a thread, and with each press of her heat against me, it frayed. "If you don't stop, I'm afraid I won't be able to keep my hands to myself."

I expected her to stop, and I warred with myself about if I wanted her to. Before I could muster enough willpower to push her away from me, I hissed as her fingers wrapped around my cock. She pumped up slowly, in a swirling motion that had me biting my lip in ecstasy.

"I don't want you to," she said, voice husky with lust. I groaned, unable to stop her, unable to stop myself. Instead, I clung to her, digging my fingers into her back with the arm underneath her, my other hand skimming down until I reach the swell of her ass, pinching and groping until I found her wet center.

She arched at my touch, moaning, "Gods, please."

I smirked, committing to this act, and I pushed away the fear of my future—with or without her. I was granted this gift, this small blessing from the gods, and I was going to take it.

"So needy, aren't you?" I whispered in her ear, and she whimpered at my teasing touches. I prodded my fingers against her core, coating them in her desire. She kept working me, and I groaned as her hands expertly played my cock like it was her own personal instrument.

She pushed against me, rolling me to my back and lifted herself on top, straddling her legs on each side of my hips.

"Oh, fuck, Hal. You look so good up there." Her pert, pink nipples tightened in the cool air, and she bit her lip in a way that had me aching to thrust into her. This woman was a force to be reckoned with, and I wanted to face her head on.

She rocked herself along my cock, drenching me, coating me with the lust pulsing through her body. I ached to sink into her. Instead, I grasped her hips and pulled her over my face.

She shrieked, and I laughed as I licked straight down her slit, her hips quivering from the contact. Sweeter than I could have imagined, I moaned as I did it again, eliciting a surprised jolt as she hovered above me, her blue eyes wide and pinned to mine.

"Cal... Caelum..." I stared up at her, getting the perfect view of her breasts peaked in the night air.

"Sit down, Hal," I demanded, and her eyes widened, apprehension written all over her face. I grabbed her hips and pulled her down, forcing her to put her weight on my face.

She moaned, a little louder this time, as I tasted her and drank her in like she was the world's only water source. Her legs shook around my head, and I couldn't help the grin forming on my lips as she cried out.

"Oh, *gods*!"

I slapped her on the ass with my palm. She jolted. Her eyes were hooded as she looked down at me. I lifted her ever so slightly, removing my tongue from her center.

"There are no gods in this tent, Halcyon. There is only me. You will cry out *my* name. Understand?"

Halcyon drew in a sharp intake of breath and then nodded slowly.

"I need to hear you say it."

"Yes, Caelum. I understand."

"That's right, Hal." Before she could respond, I pulled her back onto me, my tongue diving into her core. I moved to her clit, swirling circles around the tight nub. My fingers made their way to her entrance, and I sank two of them into her.

"Oh g—Caelum!"

My laugh was muffled at her correction. I pumped my fingers into her tight channel, my cock twitching in anticipation of sinking into her warm, wet center itself.

She was so incredibly wet, but no matter how much I wanted to plunge myself into her, I wanted to see her shaking with pleasure first. So I swirled my fingers inside her, the same rhythm as my tongue, stretching her and then curling them into the soft spot inside.

Halcyon's moans and cries grew louder, as though she could no longer control herself. She was perfect always, but I needed her to relinquish her control. Let me take the reins so she could experience the rare moment of unrestrained bliss.

I didn't relent as her legs shook next to my ears, and she fell above me, bracing her arms on the ground. She clenched around my fingers, her orgasm pulsing through her and strangling my digits as they continued with their ministrations, her release dripping down my wrist. When her breathing slowed, her hair falling into a silvery curtain around us, I pulled out of her and lifted her off my face.

The remnants of her release coated my lips, and I eagerly licked it away. There wasn't a flavor in the world better than Halcyon, and I couldn't get enough of it. I shifted her back to where she was straddling my hips, my still hard erection pressed against her back. Halcyon's body was languid, her chest rising and falling as she stared directly into my eyes. She placed her hand on my chest and lifted herself up before guiding me to her entrance.

"Halcyon..." All of my restraint was quickly flying out the window. It took everything in my body not to buck into her. "We don't have to do this. It's not a trade-off."

She smirked at me, a devilish, mischievous smirk filled with bad intentions, and I had never in my life seen a creature more stunning. My heart raced in anticipation, but I couldn't give any more protest as blood rushed through my ears.

"For once, I'm going to do something because I want it. I want your cock inside of me, and I'm going to ride it harder than I rode the dragon this evening."

Fuck. "You have a filthy mouth underneath all of that prim exterior, Lady."

Her eyes narrowed at the title I used, but I returned with another smug look of my own.

She sank down slowly, her pussy gripping like a vise around my thick cock. I threw my head back as I groaned, and she kept sinking lower and lower until I was sheathed to the hilt.

Gods.

I could just live the rest of my days in her like this forever. She was hot around me, and I could feel every pulse, every quiver of her body, shifting around me in tandem with her heartbeat.

Halcyon braced herself with her hand on my chest, using it as leverage as she lifted herself slowly, adjusting to the way I filled her. Her eyes fluttered closed and her mouth hung open, her pink lips forming an o as she felt every inch of me inside of her.

"*Cal...*" she moaned as she started shifting up and down, tilting her hips back and forth in a slow but steady motion.

"Yes, Hal. Use my cock, make yourself come around me." She gasped and shivered at my words before her pace picked up.

Her movements went from methodical to more erratic with each thrust, and I couldn't stop myself before I gripped her hips, pressing my fingers into her soft skin hard enough to leave bruises.

I slammed into her, her tight wet cunt sucking me in as far as it could go, before I started unrelentingly bucking into her.

My magic wrestled under my skin, and I let it trickle out, calling vines to do my bidding as they snaked into the edges of the tent. Halcyon didn't notice until a vine wrapped around her ankle, and she gasped. She squeezed around me at the contact and it made my lips curl, knowing she enjoyed it.

"Let me have you at my mercy completely. Give yourself to me," I demanded. She nodded, a bead of sweat sliding between her breasts, and I licked it voraciously. Vines crept higher around her legs, holding them open around me, and her body shook, her cries of pleasure spurring me on as I rammed myself into her.

My head was in space, the sound of her cries and keening music to my ears. She felt more divine than I could have ever imagined, and I never wanted it to stop. She shuddered around me, her pussy gripping me and her body convulsing around me as she cried my name over and over.

Grasping her hips, I continued my relentless pace with her cries of "yes, yes, yes," resonating in my ears. Her release squeezed me tightly, making me cry out my climax as I poured myself into her. Halcyon's arms finally gave out as she collapsed onto my chest. I stroked her back in long, leisurely brushes, relishing in her weight on me.

"Holy gods," I breathed between heavy breaths. Halcyon sat up, her eyes hooded from pleasure and exhaustion.

"I thought there were no gods in this tent?" she laughed, but her smile faded as I took her face in my palms, cradling her chin and pulling her to me so I could stare into her big blue eyes.

"I was wrong," I whispered reverently. "You are a goddess, and I am an unworthy being who wants to worship you for the rest of my days." I hadn't meant the admission to slip from my tongue. The high of my release pumping through my veins made my words loose. But I had never spoken truer words.

I was beginning to fall for this woman who I could never have. In a nutshell, I was *fucked*.

Chapter 21

HALCYON

My arms strained as I pulled on the golden string of the bow. I lined up my aim and let the arrow fly, once again hitting my mark. Sighing, I flexed my free hand in front of my face.

"The release of magic is minimal, but I can still tell it's siphoning it away." I shrugged to Caelum, who was standing by my side with his jaw tight and eyes wide. "Would you like to try?"

I handed him the bow, and he took it tentatively. He turned it in his hands, studying the intricacies of the weapon before holding out his palm to me.

"An arrow, please?" he requested with a tone of determination. I found I quite enjoyed watching Caelum when he was focused on something. His brows always formed a v in between them, and his jaw feathered, like they were in time with cogs clicking in his mind.

"Have you ever used a bow before?" I asked as I handed over an arrow.

Caelum shook his head, more in disbelief than an answer to my question. "A few times in my life, but it's not my weapon of choice."

He notched the arrow and aimed for the same place I had sunk my last arrow in. Iris was on the other side of the small open area we stood in, retrieving the arrows I had already shot from their respective targets.

Placing my hands on my hips, I blew out a deep breath as I watched Caelum. The black diamonds on the bow still glimmered, but somehow they looked duller in his hands. The golden string, dimmer.

He exhaled slowly before notching the arrow and pulling on the string. His shot was strong, but it went wide, missing the target by a meter.

"It shouldn't be possible," he muttered under his breath.

"What? You missing your mark?" I huffed a mocking laugh.

"No." Caelum turned to me, his hazel eyes showing more green in the bright sunlight cascading over him. "You hitting your mark every single time, from a distance like this. I also don't feel any release of magic. It's like it won't take it from me. I even tried pushing my magic into it, but it didn't feel any different to me than any other weapon."

"Are you saying this bow *chose* me? Like it has sentience?"

He hummed under his breath in thought. "Have you tried hitting a moving target?" He asked, completely avoiding my question.

"I don't see how I could." I said with a shrug.

Cal gave me a lopsided grin, and I narrowed my eyes in confusion. He placed his hands on the tree closest to us, and I watched as he used his magic to peel the bark off the tree, pieces of red dropping to the forest floor.

With a coy smile, Caelum picked up one piece of bark and tossed it in his hand.

"With my magic, I should be able to launch this high in the air. Would you like to give it a try?"

I gave him a shrug, but I wasn't confident I could hit the flying targets at all. I hadn't lied to Caelum when I told him my experience with a bow were minimal. And I certainly felt those nervous jitters when trying something I knew I wasn't—or shouldn't be—good at.

"Let me know when you're ready, and I'll throw the first piece."

I nodded in acknowledgement and lifted the loaded bow.

"Go." I ordered.

The bark flew high in the air, and I sucked in a breath as I watched it arc up into the tall canopy of the surrounding trees. I exhaled, not realizing my heart had quickened, and released the bow on pure instinct.

Caelum and I both stood still as we watched the arrow streak through the air, following its path as it pierced the bark dead in the center, red bursting in the air from the impact.

"Holy gods above," he muttered.

Iris ran toward us, her smile bright and her eyes in awe. "That was amazing!" she panted, out of breath. With shaking hands, I took the arrows from Iris.

"Again," I demanded, turning to Caelum with cold, hard determination leaving a lump in my throat. One shot was luck, surely.

He only nodded at the command before tossing another piece of bark. It burst into a million tiny wooden shards as the arrow pierced it.

We went on until the sun was high enough in the sky to blind me as I aimed, and every single arrow pierced the things Cal threw into the air.

Iris had long since excused herself to find Maya, leaving me and Cal to keep practicing by ourselves. Caelum would use his magic to detect where the arrows fell, and we would repeat the process over and over again. Sweat beaded down the back of my neck, and I plopped on the ground unceremoniously.

I flexed my fingers around the bow, noting my magic felt a little tired, but not altogether depleted. The black diamonds swirled with the sunlight, and I wondered if they were swirling with my magic, too.

Cal handed me a water skin, and I took it graciously. The water was smooth against my parched throat as I took long, languid gulps. The cool liquid quenched my dehydrated lips, and I sighed in contentment. Caelum stared at me with a smile on the corner of his lips.

"What?" I asked indignantly.

"This is proof." His hazel eyes sparkled with satisfaction.

"Proof of what?" I chuckled.

"The gods...they aren't dead. *You* are proof."

I wanted to laugh at the absurdity. I wasn't proof of anything. "No," I replied. "It's not. Everything—the bond, this bow..." I held the bow out in front of me, once again marveling at the craftsmanship. "It's a fluke. A remnant of energy from the temple. Nothing more."

I had replayed the moment of Sumyre's and my bond over in my head countless times. There was no denying there was magic at play, but that alone didn't prove anything. It wasn't like there was anything special about me, nor was there a reason other than finding this temple to trigger the bond.

Caelum reared back with an incredulous look. "How can you possibly think that? For a thousand years we've had nothing. No dragon bonds, no bonds of any sort, and now look—you're here with a dragon. A dragon *and* a weapon that only works in your hands. What else would you call it than what it is? The gods are waking up. It's *fate.*"

The word rolled off his tongue with awe, and I couldn't hold myself back from laughing. Caelum was being ridiculous. But when I looked at him, with the serious pinch between his eyebrows once again, my laughter turned into a sigh.

"That's not true." I turned from him, instead choosing to focus on the four blades of grass stuck together in front of me.

"What do you mean?" He leaned closer to me, his thigh pressing up against mine. I could feel the heat from him searing straight into my bones. Rather than leaning into him, I shifted my body so he couldn't see the fear clutching my heart at the prospect of being fated.

"I can't be *fated* to any of this. I have a duty, I have responsibilities. Realistically, I can't be bonded to Sumyre or this bow. How am I supposed to run a city and fulfill a Dragon Bond?" The words tumbled out before I could even think about what I was saying. For days, I thought about how I was going to mold my life around Sumyre. It wasn't easily feasible, and I sighed in exasperation.

Caelum's hand grasped my chin, forcing me to meet his hazel eyes swirling with warmth, his lips downturned, and he brushed his fingers against my lower lip. There was a deep empathy in his gaze, and I suddenly wanted to hide from him, the urge to run pounding in my chest.

"Do you even want to be the Lady of Dolan?" he asked imploringly. There was no judgment in his tone, nothing underlying to suggest he had ulterior motives for asking, and it took me by surprise.

I opened my mouth to refute him before taking in his features and shrugging. "It's what I was born to do. If anything, *that* is the fate I am destined for. It's everything I know."

Caelum gave me a sad smile, and I cocked my head in confusion.

"I didn't ask how you became a Lady," he said. "I asked if you *wanted* it."

My throat tightened, processing the meaning of his question. It was never something I even allowed myself to ponder.

I was always supposed to be a Lady. It was my birthright. There was never a chance for me to ask whether I liked it, whether I wanted the position.

Suddenly my muscles squeezed too tightly, my body too small for the feelings rushing through me so fast I became dizzy.

I choked on the small word that nearly fell from my lips. I wanted to tell him 'no', and I wanted to scream it at the top of my lungs, but I couldn't.

Tears threatened to stream down my cheeks, and I stared at Caelum, fighting against the urge to break. I quickly swiped my palm against my eyes, refusing to let the tears rush down.

For the first time, I let myself admit something I could never voice before. "I'm not so sure anymore. I'm not sure I ever wanted it in the first place."

Caelum was so close to me, our noses nearly touching as he hung onto my every word. He pressed his forehead to mine, his hand wrapping around the one I still had clutched around the bow.

"You don't have to be, you know," he growled. I gasped as his thumb traced the bonding mark on my wrist.

I laughed humorlessly. "Yes, I do. It's my duty. Sumyre will fit in somehow. I just need to figure it out."

He sighed, pulling himself away from me, and I felt the distance like a gust of frigid air, but his eyes never left mine. They were filled with honesty and an overwhelming tenderness which I knew was reserved for my eyes only.

My heart skipped in his gaze, like he could see every crack, every chipped piece of me. I never let anyone see me like this. Not even Shara knew how broken I felt inside. I wasn't even sure if *I* knew how broken I was until this moment.

He shook his head, peeling his gaze away from me, and focusing on where our hands linked, studying the bond mark.

"You were chosen for a reason. I can't tell you what the reason is, but I can tell you that there's a possibility that you can change your path. You just have to embrace the change, otherwise you'll be forced to live in a world of bleak darkness."

"I don't know what you mean," I scoffed, but he was right.

I already carried a darkness. Never had I questioned where I was supposed to be in life. I gave up all opposition by the time I was old enough to understand. My father left no room for resistance, and I had even wanted his approval at one point in time. Eventually, that need for esteem gave way to resentment, which drove me to succeed. Not to gain his approval, but so I could remove him from my life. The pieces of me I locked away, the forced smiles and concession. It was a blanket I used to comfort myself because it had been all I had known for so long.

Caelum's words were like a flickering candle in the bleak abyss, and for once, I didn't try to lock it away. Instead, I pushed it to the side, allowing myself the possibility of coming back to those feelings later.

"I haven't seen you at your castle, but I've seen you here. I saw you when we left Dolan the first day, and I—" he cleared his throat, and I saw the uncertainty in his eyes, afraid he would step out of line.

We weren't *in* Dolan, I had no jurisdiction over him, and I didn't want to either. I craved his honesty. He was the only one I could trust who would give it to me, anyway.

"I can't, in good conscience, let you go back there without telling you that there is so much more for you. If you let yourself take it."

"I can't leave my position, no matter if the gods have called me to or not."

He shook his head. "I'm not asking you to do that. Just to take things as they come, and don't shut out the possibility of your own happiness."

I nodded, unable to voice a response. Instead, I became desperate to change the conversation back to something more comfortable. The golden band burned under Caelum's touch, and I slowly pulled away from his grasp.

"There have been bonds before me." If Caelum was hurt or surprised by this change of subject, he didn't show it. Instead, he leaned back, his curiosity getting the better of him.

"The Ambrosian Dragon Rider?" he asked.

I nodded, humming in agreement.

Caelum couldn't help himself but implore, "But no one knows how he got the bond, or even where he is right now. He hasn't been seen in almost a decade. He's a fairytale at this point." I peered at Cal out of the side of my eye, giving him a mischievous smirk. "You know where he is, don't you?"

"Yes," I hesitated, unsure if I should keep divulging more information, but finding I didn't really care. He had already looked at me with all of my broken emotions as if they were written plainly in text. "It's supposed to be classified, but..." I sighed, "he's working undercover in the mortal kingdom."

Caelum's face was one of astonishment and intrigue. It was hard not to smile at his investment. There was so much at play here, and divulging Ambrose's best kept secret felt heady.

I didn't forget that Caelum was only a citizen of Ambrose, and no amount of treks through hidden temples, or pretty words, would change it. He wasn't privy to this kind of information, no matter how badly I wanted to tell him.

Regardless...we were out in the woods, in the mortal kingdom. A kingdom we had no business being in. One that if *our own* government found out about would cause direct implications, possibly to our very lives.

I had only been privy to this information myself when I had stumbled into my father's study one night and overheard him discussing with another Lord. I wasn't even sure if my father even realized I knew. It made me wonder how much my father truly kept from me, and how many secrets were there for the sole reason that he wanted to see me fail?

Niklaus knew, of course. I asked him about it a few days later and he told me that under no circumstances was I to repeat it. Once I started living back at the castle, Niklaus had told me of several confidential instances, so I was sure there were other things my father kept from me. But Niklaus had always been as honest as he could be.

"I met him one time." Caelum raised a brow in surprise. "It was long before he left for his mission. He was researching something at the library. We spoke a handful of times. There's a lot of people who pass through, and Niklaus advised me to make the connection." Caelum looked at me with admiration in his eyes. "There's something else, too."

Caelum sat up straighter, leaning into me and clinging on to my every word.

"There *has* been another bond. A soul bond," I told him. Cal didn't respond, but his eyes were wide. "A couple in Aurum. The lead general and his wife. They became bonded around the same time Galen left."

"Galen?" Confusion crossed his features as I explained.

"The Ambrosian Dragon Rider." I nodded.

"How do you know all of this?"

I scoffed at his question. "Why wouldn't the future Lady of her region know the goings on of her own country?"

Caelum's face dropped, and he blinked, shaking his head. "It's just a lot to take in—"

A loud roar rang through the trees, and I jumped to my feet. This conversation was over, at least for the time being.

Caelum was right behind me as I raced through the forest, following the sound of Sumyre. I reached a clearing, skidding to a halt as I saw Sumyre crouched and growling at a heavy breathing Aceus.

"Sumyre!" I shouted, but she wasn't listening. Instead, she jumped toward Aceus with a loud snarl.

Taloned claws missed him by mere inches as he tumbled into a roll, dodging her attack. He held a broadsword, and I watched in horror as he lifted the blade into the air. He pulled it back, putting all of his weight into a swing, and I screamed.

Sumyre's head whipped toward me at the same time hands wrapped around my arms, holding me captive.

"Maya? Iris?" I jerked in their grip, and my heart skipped a beat, hearing their laughter while holding me back. I heard Caelum curse from behind me.

Ice coated my hands, pulsing through my body in confusion. I needed to protect her. Caelum stepped into my field of vision, smiling down at me.

"Calm down, Halcyon," he said, placing a palm on my cheek. "Look," he moved for me to see, pointing in their direction. "Everything is fine. I should have told you Aceus had mentioned wanting to spar with Sumyre."

"And you don't think that's something *he* should have told me?" I snarled.

Caelum shrugged. "Sorry, I thought he already did."

I blinked as the cling of Aceus' sword hit the ground, and he grunted a slew of curses.

"That wasn't how I wanted to win, dammit!" He turned his gaze toward me, his blond brows pinched, and I swore his mustache twitched in aggravation. He pointed one finger at me and shouted, "You distracted her! I was going to win fair this time!"

Sumyre chuffed, a puff of purple air dispersing in front of her, her wings ruffling out on each side.

"You haven't won a single time," Maya called back to him. "It's highly doubtful this would be the one."

Iris chuckled beside me as she released my arm.

"They were just play fighting?" I asked, brushing my palm against my cheek.

"Couldn't you tell through the bond they weren't serious?" she asked.

"I..." I hadn't even thought to check, but now she had said something, I could feel she was right.

Caelum came up beside me, his hand resting on the small of my back, sending sparks through my spine. Guilt wracked through me. Feelings I didn't even know I had came through when I thought Sumyre was in danger.

He leaned down to my ear and whispered, "Looks like we need to work on those instincts to check the bond more often." There was humor in his eyes, and I eased and released a breath.

"Well, at least she's getting some fighting practice in," I muttered, sending Aceus an apologetic look. He sauntered over to me and Cal, his face softening as he approached, even though his mustache still twitched from his false victory.

"I have something for you." Aceus motioned us over back toward the camp and we followed.

Rummaging around his tent, Aceus pulled out a large contraption with belts and buckles and ropes tied in various positions.

"What is it?" I asked, as I held out my arms to receive the massive contraption.

"A saddle. It's not the best by any standards, but should get the job done. Sumyre let me take some measurements, and I worked on it when I couldn't sleep. Used the tent scraps from the wolf fight." He shrugged, as if it was nothing to create a *dragon saddle*. "Probably why I forgot to mention sparring. Can you forgive me?"

"Thank you, and there is nothing to forgive," I whispered through bubbled emotions. The need to protect her was still lingering in my limbs, and the force of the emotion was jarringly strong.

Caelum was right. I needed to default to the bond. Hopefully, it would become easy with time. For now, I would have to make a more conscious effort.

After a quick meal, I found myself alongside Aceus, helping sort tools for the next day. I wiped sweat from my brow, leaning on a makeshift table Aceus had improvised from an old tree stump. My fingers drifted over the many rings within the wood, each line telling the tree's story.

"Are you almost done, old man?" I jested.

His golden mustache twitched as he placed his sword back in its sheath after polishing it to gleaming silver.

"I'm not old," he scoffed.

"Old by a mortal's standard, aren't you?"

He bellowed a laugh. "I'm thirty-seven!"

"Alright, old for a guard, then," I said my eyes crinkling in amusement. When he didn't laugh back, I tilted my head in question.

"I am old for a guard. Most mortals retire by thirty—if they live long enough."

"Indeed, you are an esteemed fighter," I agreed. "And rather good with your hands." A blush crept up Aceus' face at the compliment. "I mean it, the saddle fits Sumyre perfectly."

"It's nothing," he replied, banishing the notion with his hand. "You'll need to get one fitted for her properly back in Ambrose. She deserves better than what I made with tent scraps."

"Truly, thank you. If there is any way I can repay you for all you've done here, you have my word. As Lady of Dolan," I said seriously, and Aceus turned away from me, his hands clutching the sheathed sword.

"I think I *would* like to retire after this is all said and done," he peered back at me, a grim look lining his dark eyes.

I pushed myself off the stump, my heart lodged in my throat. "Whatever for? Did I do something—"

"No," he chuckled, and my heart slowed, "nothing like that."

I followed his line of sight to the fire where Maya and Iris sat, conversing with one another, bright smiles on both their faces.

"If anything," he sighed, "I feel like I owe you for not calling this trip off. I would have never found them otherwise."

"Maya and Iris?" I asked.

"My people, my heart," he confirmed.

"You love them?" Tears welled in my eyes, my own heart thumping with unsaid feelings of my own. Aceus said nothing, but I caught a small nod.

"Have you told them?" I asked curiously. I had seen them together, how Iris looked at Aceus with hearts in her eyes, the same way she looked at Maya. How Maya brushed kisses along his cheek before the nights were over. There was definitely lust, but something more, too.

"Not in so many words, but I'd like to." Aceus strode over to the wagon, placing his polished sword inside before stepping back to meet my eye. "But I don't want to do that unless I have permission to pursue them when we get back home. And I don't think I can do so from Dolan."

"You should—" I choked. "Tell them, I mean."

Aceus grinned, bright white teeth under his mustache. "You're serious? You would let me retire and leave Dolan?"

"I would have to find another guard, but I think it's manageable." I nodded. How could I deny him? After all, one of us should live our truth.

Aceus flourished a low bow, and I couldn't help the laugh that rattled from my chest.

"Stop being ridiculous." I tugged him up from his shoulder. "Go over there and tell those women how you feel."

"Thank you," he said, his hand clasping my shoulder.

I watched them keenly from the shadows of the trees. Iris scooted on the log bench to make room, leaning on his shoulder as he sat. Aceus' large arms wrapped around the both of them, pressing a kiss to each of their cheeks.

Attempting to wrap my own feelings deep inside, I tugged on my bottom lip with my teeth. I may not have had the power to change my own future, but I was glad to use what I did have to grant Aceus' request. Maybe it hadn't just been my destiny that changed when we walked into the kingdom where magic shouldn't exist.

I squinted through the bright sun's rays as cool, crisp air cut against my face. I sat on top of the makeshift saddle Aceus had crafted, a separate rope wrapped around my waist for added safety.

Sumyre gracefully flew us through the skies, sweeping around in large circles, moving up and down, and I adjusted to the feelings rather quickly. With our mental bond strengthening, she moved in tandem with my expectations, and I was never surprised by her movement.

A big puffy cloud hung above us, and Sumyre flapped her monstrous wings as we raced toward it. My laughter was wild as the gray abyss engulfed us, moisture clinging to my skin. The smell of open air and cool humidity enveloped my senses, smothering me with a sense of freedom and wild abandon. Something I had never indulged in before.

Satisfaction pulsed between the bond as Sumyre rose higher and higher. We broke out of the cloud in a sudden burst, the bright yellow sun greeting us with gentle warmth. I inhaled the clean air, relishing being so far removed from anything and everything.

Up here, nothing else existed. Nothing else mattered. I wished I could have stayed up here forever, never once returning to the cold halls of Dolan, where only routine awaited me. Up here, I was free.

Today, Caelum was going to show me the nesting cave they found, even though he insisted it was more room, less cave. The way he had described it seemed too magical, too unreal, so I was eager to see it for myself.

But first, he wanted to go to the throne room we had found previously. With Sumyre's help, we finally located it, and Caelum had been digging another tunnel down all morning.

Sumyre hovered before taking a sharp downturn, my body became weightless, the rope the only thing tethering me to her as she sped straight toward the earth. My fear was non-existent. I placed my faith in my saddle and in Sumyre, lifting my hands above my head, hollering as the force of the drop made my stomach flip and my eyes water.

Nothing, absolutely *nothing*, compared to flight. Whether it was the bond making me feel this way, or I was suddenly addicted to the thrill, I knew no matter what happened, I wouldn't be the same person who I was when I left Dolan.

We barreled through the sky until the treetops became larger and Sumyre swung herself back up, taking a wide arch over a pit leading to the underground throne room.

Caelum stood next to the clearing, a wide smile stretching over his face as he saw us approach. My heart leapt into my throat at the sight of him, even though I willed myself not to let it. I knew he had grown attached to me, and I begrudgingly admitted I was attached to him, too. But I couldn't let him see it, because no matter what happened here, we would inevitably end.

I never regretted anything that happened between Caelum and myself. In fact, Caelum was quickly becoming a beacon of joy. His talent with his hands, mouth, and body were enough to make my eyes crossed, but he was beginning to take up space in my heart and mind. Constantly, I reminded myself that our time was finite. It was a bitter thought, but something I needed to remember if I was going to eventually walk away.

Sumyre hovered above the ground before sinking her large talons into the dirt and tucking in her wings. I untied the rope around me, and slid off her back, beaming at Caelum. I couldn't even remember the last time I smiled so easily, my cheeks becoming sore from the act.

Caelum greeted me with open arms. Jogging towards him, I fell into his embrace. He was the warmth of the sun, and his pine scent grew addicting as I ran my hands around his back.

"Ready to go back down there?" he asked, pulling away from me. The rest of the group sauntered toward us, the three of them deep in conversation.

Aceus grinned down at Maya, and Iris smacked him on his arm. He laughed, pulling her into his side.

The tunnel was dark as we descended into the earth, and as the green-blue flickering Everflame illuminated dirt and roots around us, the anticipation of what we would find pulsed hard through my veins. When the dirt turned into stone, I gasped. Treading slowly through the throne room, I took in the vast space like I had the first time.

My heart beat in my ears and I tensed, readying myself for any of the same energy I felt last time. But nothing came. Even as I walked toward the dais, the energy was empty. Almost stale. When Caelum and I stumbled upon it the first time, there was a life to it, an essence, one that he admitted to feeling as well. But regardless, the room was just as stunning. Massive columns lined the room, now illuminated by sunlight seeping in from the space Sumyre blasted away.

Maya zeroed in on a basin, her path to it undeterred. I stared at her in confusion until she struck a piece of flint and it immediately caught fire. In seconds, the chamber was lit with flames. Sconces flared everywhere, and I stumbled back at the sudden onslaught of light.

"How did you know that would happen?" I asked curiously.

"There's another basin just like this one where we were the other day. It was an educated guess."

Educated guess or not, it was incredible. Peering down at the basin, I studied how the path of fire was engineered to light the rest of the room. Was there a substance like Maya's Everflame which made it easily transferable? Either way, it must have taken ages to build.

Now the room was well lit, I wandered easily. The marble floors clicked under my feet, and I swept my eyes around. Other than the giant hole Sumyre had made, there was no evidence my magic had ever touched this place. No water from my ice; only the rubble from Sumyre's explosion was out of place.

"Look at these!" Iris called us over as she pointed to a small offering table where more trinkets lay, the dust caked on top of them like a blanket.

"The shrine room above is ancient, but these"—she brushed one finger over the table, smudging the dust in a single line—"predate those artifacts by, if I had to guess, three thousand years?"

"How do you know?" I asked, cocking my head to the side, seeing if I could find the year created inscribed on it somehow.

"This pattern matches similar places in Ambrose. I would need to confirm it, but yes, I think this throne room was potentially where the god of this region ruled. Until they disappeared, that is."

"But how did it get so far underground? Why hide something so massive?" Caelum asked, and I turned to find him with his head raised as he took in the column's height in front of us.

"Aren't there places like this in Ambrose?" I asked, trying to recall my studies of Ambrose's ancient temples.

"Not like this," he muttered.

"Not unless those, too, are hidden," Maya commented.

I looked around the room, feeling smaller than I did the first time I was down here, and made my way to the dais, where the two pedestals were erected on each side of the throne. One was empty—where I had taken the bow—but the other one still held a massive book with pages yellowed with age.

I bent down, placing myself at eye level with the pedestal. Carefully, I reached toward it when Caelum's hand wrapped around my wrist. He shook his head as he pulled me back.

"Don't touch it," he demanded. I wasn't used to the sharpness in his voice and gulped. "It looks harmless right now, but do I need to remind you what happened the last time you touched a random item in here?"

"Sorry," I whispered, a little disturbed that he was right.

I chewed on the corner of my lip anxiously, aching to peel open the book.

"I'll get a wrap for it, just in case," he told me.

Maya and Aceus were behind one pillar, out of my line of sight. Tapping on my knee with my finger, I waited until Cal meandered toward them.

Iris was consumed with her parchment, scribbling notes, comparing diagrams. My gaze slid back to the massive leather-bound tome in front of me, itching to see what was written inside, just waiting to be discovered.

Maybe it held the answers to the Dragon Bond, or it told us the exact reasons some of us were blessed with magic, while others weren't. Insurmountable untold secrets could be held inside those pages.

Unheeding Caelum's advice, I stretched my fingers toward it, coating them in ice for an extra protective measure, and ran one long finger down the bound leather. Nothing happened, and I released the breath that I had been holding.

Banishing my magic, I took the tome into my hands. Dust coated my fingers, and I found my hands shaking.

"Caelum!" I called him over. He looked at me with a quizzical eye, and then his eyes widened.

"I thought I said not to touch it," he admonished, and I grinned.

"Well, I have it now. So, what are you going to do with it?" I asked eagerly.

He tugged it from my grasp, his breath catching as he turned it in his hands.

"I'm going to give this to Maya for safekeeping, and then we are taking it to Neverwind. I need to see the words on the page firsthand." His face was beaming as he cracked the book open, skimming the first page and touching it with a satisfied reverence. He passed the book to Maya, who took it with a gentle grip before placing it in the satchel she wore on her side.

"Come on, I want to see if I can find that nesting cave." Caelum beckoned me to follow him, and before I could even question the fact we were about to delve into a palace made for the gods, he stopped in front of a set of massive double doors.

Gold embellished the white marble doors with swirling designs and patterns. Caelum strained as he pushed against the door, and I thought it would never budge, until the groaning, creaking sound of stone grinding against stone made me wince.

The door didn't swing very wide, but Caelum managed to push it open just enough for us to slip through. Fire continued to light the palace, and we stepped into a hallway that could easily fit three of Sumyre side by side.

I tugged on the bond as I thought of her, getting used to this open line of communication. She had been quiet since we got down here, but I could still feel her up above patiently waiting for me to get back.

Caelum and I meandered through the halls that seemed to go nowhere and everywhere all at once. The castle I had grown to call home was nothing compared to this. Even through the ages, it was lavish with marble and gold.

I couldn't even comprehend how much money and time had gone into creating this place. It was a marvel of its own. What had it been like when it didn't lie forgotten, buried deep in the ground?

Caelum's calloused hand brushed over mine before he threaded our fingers together. "I hope it's around here somewhere. I feel like it never ends."

"You remember the way back, right?" I asked, alarm suddenly making me whirl back around. He chuckled before wrapping his arm around my shoulder, holding me close enough so I could feel the warmth of his skin beneath his clothes.

"I've been marking our path," he said confidently as he waved a piece of chalk in my face.

"Oh, good." I let out a sigh of relief as we continued onward.

After a few more turns, Caelum stood still. I opened my mouth to ask what was wrong, but he stared down at me, pointing at the large,frosted doors a few paces away from us.

"That's it," he breathed. "Come on, let me show you."

Caelum upped his pace, and I found myself jogging to keep up with him. I was vibrating with excitement as we neared the doors, and Caelum's beaming smile made my stomach swoop.

Pushing on the frosted glass, Caelum's muscles rippled under his shirt. With a final grunt, the doors swung open, and I peered in with a grin. What I saw was incomprehensible.

My hands clasped over my mouth. Bright purples and blues, oranges and greens, winked and sparkled from high above. Thick greenery blotted out the ceiling, and I twirled underneath gemstones shining as brightly as stars. As I stepped further into the nesting cave, tears pricked the back of my eyes.

Caelum didn't wait for me to step in further before taking my hand and leading me through the overgrown shrubbery. Somewhere far above us a dragon roared, and I pulled on the bond to feel Sumyre. There was sorrow and I couldn't help but feel guilty as I thought that she should have been here with us.

I should have been raised here from the beginning, she told me. Rage consumed me as another roar bellowed. We were far from her, but I felt it as keenly as if she was standing right here.

"Gods, Cal," I whispered. "What the mortal army does to those dragons, it's awful."

Caelum narrowed his eyes. "What do you mean?"

I recounted what Sumyre had shown me. How the mortals chained the dragon mothers and forced them to breed. How they didn't allow the dragons free rein. It was grotesque, and Sumyre kept pumping her memories into my mind as I let my words flow. I told him everything. Everything Sumyre showed me.

Caelum listened intently, worry etched on his face. He only nodded, processing all the information I was giving him. Hands caressed my cheeks, wiping away stray tears I couldn't control. Gently, he placed a kiss on my forehead.

"She found you. You are giving her a life outside of that."

I nodded in agreement, and my chest eased as he pulled me into an embrace. His warm hands gripped me tightly, and my breath caught at the firmness. Fingers threaded into my hair, loosening my braid as he tugged, forcing me to look up into his eyes.

How did he know exactly what I needed? The comfort for my sorrow, the prickling pain for distraction. He smirked and my knees nearly buckled. My tongue darted out, wetting my lips, and heat flared in Caelum's eyes.

His mouth crashed into mine, hot and all-encompassing, and I moaned into him. Fingers in my hair clutched tighter, and I greeted the stinging sensation with a shudder of breath. At the adjunct of my thigh, Caelum's fingers skimmed my core that was drenched beneath my pants. He lifted me, and I squealed.

A raspy laugh came from him as he melded his lips to mine, devouring the sounds I was making. He took me further into the cave before gently laying me down beneath him. His lips never left my body as he pressed kisses to the corner of my mouth, then my cheek and throat.

I panted his name as he licked and sucked on the small patch of skin below my ear until I was writhing and begging beneath him.

Letting myself bathe in Caelum's soft kisses and wandering hands, I gazed at him with all the desire and need coursing through me. The gemstones shone brightly behind him, casting rays of purples and pinks and blues through the foliage, and I gasped as I noticed we were surrounded by tall, vibrant flowers, all blooming in different colors.

Caelum grasped my chin, realizing I had gotten distracted, and plunged his tongue into my mouth. His kiss was possessive and I reveled in his dominance. There was no question about what he wanted, and I would give him everything.

Our clothes were quickly discarded, and I ran my hands along Caelum's chest, loving when there was a hitch in his breath as I drifted my fingers lower.

There wasn't a chance to explore him further as he took a nipple in my mouth, sucking and nipping on it. I cried out when he pressed his fingers into my center, finding me beyond wet for him.

"Caelum," I panted his name with a thousand meanings behind it. I wanted him, I wanted to keep him. More than that, I never wanted to let him go in any capacity. "I need you."

He groaned into me, sliding himself home, and my body shuddered. I was so full of him I could barely breathe. There was no hesitance in the way Caelum took me, his hips thrusting with such force I had to remember to breathe. We were lost in each other, joined together in this place of reverence, like we were meant to be together all along.

Sweat dripped down Caelum's chest, and I reached up, licking it off him. Caelum stuttered in his movements, gazing down at me like I would disappear as he gave one final thrust, and I shattered. My legs shook, my chest heaved, and my bones melted as I came.

We lay there in the dark meadow of giant wildflowers, our arms wrapped around each other, breathing each other in for as long as we could. Once I gathered enough strength, I peeled myself away. Caelum watched as I dressed, and I tossed him his pants. He didn't try to catch them, though, and they smacked him in the face.

He pulled them away with a grin, and I laughed. "We should probably head back before the others start to worry."

Caelum nodded his agreement and dressed, but not before he planted a wet, sloppy kiss on my lips.

A loud bellowing roar sounded from above, louder than the rest had been, and panic seized me. I took a deep breath, suddenly realizing the panic was not from *me*. It was from Sumyre.

"We have to go," I told Cal. His brown eyes widened with worry at my change of tone, and I tugged him along as I bolted for the exit.

Chapter 22

HALCYON

We ran through the halls, the flames on either side of us seeming to urge us forward as Sumyre's panic only grew by the second.

We have intruders.

Sumyre's voice cut through my mind, my heart leaping into my throat.

We were supposed to be alone. This was a forgotten part of the kingdom. Who found us and how?

Show me. I demanded, and Sumyre sent me a visual of three dragons, all still small along the horizon, but there was no mistaking the people on top—Riders.

Gods above, have mercy.

The risk of running into Dragon Riders was low, so why were they finding us now? My heart raced at the possibilities, landing only on one dragon-sized explanation that would warrant their search this far out.

I'll meet you outside, I told her as we skidded back into the throne room.

"We have a problem!" I shouted, my voice echoing through the columns. Maya, Iris, and Aceus looked up, confusion worrying their brows. "Dragon

Riders are approaching. They are still a ways away. There's no telling how long it will be before they find us."

"Fuck," Caelum cursed. "Okay, everyone, pack everything up and we will head back through the tunnel."

We rushed back through the throne room, and as I stepped into the tunnel, I took one last look behind me. A whoosh of air nearly pushed me forward, and all the flames were extinguished. I didn't have time to be shocked. Not when Riders were making their way directly to us.

Stumbling over roots and rocks, I raced to the surface. There was only one thing on my mind—Sumyre's safety. We emerged from the tunnel, and I squinted at the sudden light of the sky. Sumyre's beating wings from above made me look up as her vision overtook mine. The Dragon Riders were closing in, and I could now make out scales of vibrant blue, deep black, and gleaming silver.

Sumyre shifted and dove to the ground, landing in front of me with a resounding thump. I was terrified of what would happen if the Riders found her. She was *not theirs*. And if they took her away from me, there would be no stone unturned to find her. If they killed her, then there would be no fury brighter than mine.

We made our way back to the campsite, the trees blurring as we ran. A dragon's roar boomed through the forest behind us. It was ten times as loud as what I had ever heard from Sumyre, and it felt far too close for comfort.

Caelum cursed behind me as he jumped into the wagon, strapping a sword to his side. He tossed a crate of weapons on the ground and hopped out before passing a sword to Aceus.

"If it's a fight they want, it's a fight they'll get. It's too late to run now." He turned to me, his hand cupping my chin. "You can still get away, though." His eyes glistened. He spoke low enough only I could hear him. "You should ride Sumyre back to Ambrose. I don't think we will get far in this fight, but you should take the book and go."

"I can't leave you here." My throat tightened at the prospect of leaving them—leaving Cal—behind. My magic swelled within me, rearing for a chance to exert itself. "I *won't* leave you here," I reiterated.

Cal's throat bobbed, his eyes hardening in acceptance. If we were going to fight, we would fight together. After a chaste kiss to my lips, he reached behind him and handed me the black diamond bow. He slid it into my palm, slinging the quiver filled with arrows over my shoulder. With a tight nod, he stepped back and Sumyre leaned toward me, beckoning me on her back.

It was after I swung my legs over her, tying the saddle straps to my body, and the thumping of her wings took us into the brightening sky, when I realized: the gods chose me for a reason. This bond with Sumyre wasn't something that was bestowed upon just anyone.

I was born for this. I was blessed by the gods so I could protect my friends, protect all of us. And protect them I would, even if it cost my life.

Brisk early-morning air stung my cheeks as Sumyre launched us into the sky. Clouds in the distance marred the otherwise clear blue sky, where three dragons screeched as we emerged from the tree line.

They approach.

A viscous snarl greeted us as three massive dragons hovered in our line of sight in a V formation. The dragon in the front's cobalt blue scales shimmered as they bristled and bared their sharp teeth at Sumyre.

There was a smaller silver dragon in the back, and on the other side was a massive black dragon similar to Sumyre's scale pattern, with deep green undertones. The Riders were all clad in black leathers—Tantalian riding leathers.

I swallowed down the large lump formed in my throat. All the riders looked like surly men, but the front rider himself was unnaturally huge. Bigger than Aceus—wider and taller—and I wondered what sort of training Tantal made their riders go through. He had golden blond hair tied up into a topknot, and his scowl deepened the lines in his face from sun exposure and clear signs of aging.

"That dragon is ours. Dismount, so we can take it back." His voice bellowed across the expanse between us. In his hand was a long cone, and he held it to his mouth as he spoke, amplifying his voice.

I gritted my teeth, and Sumyre growled. "She belongs to no one, and least of all to mortals like you."

How *dare* he assume Sumyre belongs to anyone, like an inanimate object to be purchased or sold?

I had never thought of the people in Tantal as something other than the people who lived across the border. They lived their lives, and I lived mine. But staring at the Riders of the mortal army in front of me made disgust swirl in my stomach. Was this how all of Tantal thought of dragons? These amazing, intelligent, sentient creatures with more magic than Magi, who were once revered as the gods were?

Ice formed on my fingertips, coating my hands as I reached for my bow. The Rider's eyes widened and the dragon he rode on hissed, smoke curling from their nose.

"That dragon is the property of the Tantal Kingdom, and you are trespassing. The King will have your head for this," he shouted.

The blue dragon's mouth opened, revealing a very sharp set of teeth. Air stilled as the dragon breathed in with a sucking force that had me turning my head away.

"Fly, Sumyre!" I shouted, but she hardly needed the reminder. Her wings beat forcefully as we rose higher in the sky, evading the dragon's direct shot.

A crackle of energy followed closely behind us, the hair on my arms standing on end. I instantly urged Sumyre to drop us toward the ground.

A blast of lightning boomed through the clear morning sky, and I clenched my teeth as we barely scraped by from the shot.

Sumyre bellowed a roar, her purple smoke shooting out from her and encompassing the dragon riders. The riders were successfully blinded. But we were, too.

I clutched the bow in my hand and notched in an arrow. The black diamonds shined brighter in my hands, eager for the blood they were about to shed.

Wind blew my hair back as Sumyre circled within our haven. I felt like I could see everything and nothing at the same time. I could hear the dragons circling around us. Their wings beating furiously. Their snarls and roars a deadly threat.

Lightning from the blue dragon flashed around us. The haze flashing with light. Another dragon's blazing fire streamed from above, but Sumyre dodged nearly clipping her wing in the fire.

My arms strained as I pulled back on my bow. The golden string as taut as ever. My legs shook as I tried to keep myself on Sumyre, but I held all my trust in her and the saddle crafted from Aceus' hand. The arrow sang as it cut through the sky, piercing the fog around us. I held my breath as I watched it disappear through the purple cloud.

A pained roar screeched through the sky, and I winced.

You hit the rider; the dragon is merely reacting to their injured rider.

I blew out a breath of relief I didn't know I needed. I didn't *want* to injure the dragons if I could help it.

Hold on.

Sumyre swung herself through the air, making me slide back on the saddle. There was no telling which direction we were flying, but I didn't falter as I reached for another arrow.

With the arrow in hand, I poured my magic into it, coating it with ice. It made it heavier, and my arms shook at the added weight. Exhaling slowly, I held steady. Sumyre flipped, only the straps holding me to her.

A clear shot revealed itself to the rider on the smaller silver dragon. Blood smattered and dripped down his arm in rivulets. The arrow I had shot earlier impaling him through his shoulder.

Make it rain blood and men, Sumyre's voice snarled in my mind with poison.

I pulled back on the bow as far as I could.

These were her captors, her torturers. This wasn't just about protection and defense. This was vengeance, and her need fueled my determination. I was being granted this chance to avenge her, and I would give it to her.

Sumyre's mouth opened wide, that loud click of hers aimed at the giant purple cloud above us. The sky lit with fire, burning and cackling as the arrow I let loose whizzed through the air.

Blood sprayed in time with the exploding sky as it pierced the Rider through the chest. Ice tore through the man's torso. The power behind the bow blew through his body. As the arrow emerged from his back, it left a gaping hole in its wake.

The silver dragon screeched an awful cry, and the rider's body tumbled forward. Strapped in his own saddle, the dragon was forced to carry the dead rider as it flailed and spun without direction.

A pang of guilt speared through my heart as I wondered what a Rider's death means to a dragon. Did they feel the pain? Would the dragon die too? Maybe killing the Rider would release the dragon from their imprisonment?

Either way, the silver dragon didn't attempt to attack us again. Instead, they disappeared under the canopies of the trees.

My attention turned to the two remaining dragons and their very much alive Riders. Before I even registered what I was doing, ice was already coated over another arrow. My vision sharpened, and I aimed at the Rider on the black dragon.

Wait.

I started in the saddle, Sumyre's single word jarring me from the focus I had built.

"Why—"

Sumyre darted downward, tucking her wings in until we were headed toward the forest at breakneck speed. The two other dragons followed us as they chased us with their fire and lightning. Lightning grazed my skin, burning, sharp, excruciating. My saddle shackled me as I screamed. My body's magic too slow to heal the immediate shock of the dragon's power.

Sumyre roared, spewing purple smoke in her path as we continued our descent. Explosions sounded around me as she shot each plume. Lightning streaked after us. Everything was unbearably loud, and I couldn't move; my body too busy healing itself from where the lightning had touched.

Sharp talons collided with the earth. I barely noticed our landing until I realized we were in the forest's opening.

Caelum, Maya, Iris and Aceus all stood together staring up at the sky. Each of them gripped their weapons as the two remaining dragons hurled their way down.

Iris held her bow and was already firing arrows at the dragons. They pinged off of their protective scales. Fire brushed the tops of our heads as we all ducked, my skin feeling the heat far too close for my comfort.

I pushed ice out of my hands, spears aimed at our attackers as the ice sizzled in the blazing heat. The fight was hard-pressed. The dragons too agile, and my ice too slow.

Sumyre shifted underneath me as she once again pushed off the ground. With us low to the ground, I turned all of my magic behind us. Spear after spear flew from my palms, only to shatter against the dragon's scales.

A scream had me faltering in my concentration. Iris yanked a throwing dagger out of her leg, blood arching in the air as she flung it from her body.

Rage was written all over her face as she yanked an arrow from her quiver. Her eyes pinched as she aimed for the rider on the black dragon.

Fury was thick in the air as she fired arrow after arrow, piercing through the air. One of Iris' arrows had made its mark, hitting the rider on his leg. Blood poured from the sky.

The blue dragon swooped down, its massive wingspan shadowing the sun.

The dragon's mouth opened wide, sharp teeth gleaming. Caelum stood as the dragon's target, and I stopped breathing. There was no time for him to move. I couldn't reach him fast enough.

A scream escaped from me, so loud my throat turned raw. I had the bow in my hand at impossible speed. Aiming an icy arrow at the dragon, I pulled on the string. Before I could fire, the dragon roared in agony as one brawny, bald mortal sliced through the belly of the dragon.

Deep crimson blood coated the forest floor, and the taste of copper filled the air. Aceus roared as his sword slashed through the soft spot of the dragon. Caelum leapt back, breaking his own fall with a well-timed vine.

The dragon faltered in its flight, losing too much blood, and I screamed. Aceus was standing directly underneath, unable to scramble away in time. His feet faltered beneath him before the dragon fell to the ground with a resounding thud.

The world ceased to exist as I watched the man who swore to protect me get crushed beneath scales and wings. The ground shook in the wake of the dragon's fall, and the forest stilled. I waited on abated breath for any movement, any sign of Aceus at all, but there was none.

My focus shifted when the Rider on the back of the dead dragon shouted a stream of curses. With no regard to the man he just killed, he quickly unbuckled himself from the saddle and ran toward Caelum.

Sumyre pumped her wings, and we rose higher. I lost sight of the Dragon Rider and Caelum beneath the canopy of trees. I whimpered, praying Caelum would not meet the same fate as Aceus.

Focus, Sumyre snarled in my mind.

There was too much happening. My hands wouldn't stop shaking. I felt my magic start to wane. My gut clenched in a prayer. I hoped would still have enough magic to fight.

Purple clouds shot out in front of us as Sumyre coated the sky in her explosive fog. With three beats of her wings, and us within inches of the black dragon, Sumyre's throat clicked, setting the sky ablaze.

Purple fog turned into a massive sky of orange fire. I braced for the burn, but Sumyre pulled a twisting motion. With her wings tucked, she spiraled, protecting me from the explosion. Black wings blocked my field of sight, and my heart raced as I put my full trust in her.

Blinking, I could see through Sumyre's eyes. Like a vision within my vision, I could see the black dragon ahead of us.

The explosion didn't deter the dragon as it reached higher and higher, the sky a never-ending expanse of space.

Sumyre's protective maneuver slowed us down, and the black dragon made headway before rearing back to face us. I was rigid as the Dragon Rider above pointed at me, his brown hair freeing itself from his long braid.

"Cease the attack and we will let you live! We only want the dragon!" There was strength in his voice, but I caught the underlying fear. My back straightened, and I blinked away my remorse for my friend, shoving all thoughts aside for the man right in front of me.

Fire, Sumyre. Now is our chance.

I can't. There was a small whine in her voice, and it caught me by surprise.

Why not?

There was a beat of silence before she answered. *That is my mother.*

Shit.

We hung in the air, face to face with the other dragon. The rider was grimacing. I couldn't be sure, but it seemed like the dragon had her own hesitations. Her head tilted from side to side, as though she was attempting to shake the rider from her thoughts. Lightning arched in the sky. Clouds gathered beneath us, humidity gathering from the sudden heat.

"Do you trust me?" I whispered to Sumyre aloud.

Yes.

I urged her to bank around and down toward the clouds. She obeyed, her thoughts eerily silent, giving herself to me entirely. Every thought urged Sumyre in the direction I pointed at her, and I guided us through the quickly darkening clouds below.

The cloud cover was frigid, and I let it coat every part of my body. Beads of water collected on Sumyre's scales, and I pushed my magic to freeze them, adhering to us in an armor of ice. Her scales were shining, nearly blindingly, the ice creaked along with her movements. I reinforced them with as much magic as I could, my body trembling from exertion.

The bow in my hand was also glazed in ice, but the string remained pliable, and I loaded in an ice-encased arrow before unbuckling myself and flipping around the saddle.

I honed in on the rider. Memorizing his grimacing face, the wrinkles around his dark inset eyes.

I pulled back, my arms straining. The bow warmed in my hands. The shimmer of the last of my power was poured into the black diamonds, gleaming brighter in my peripherals.

I let the string go with a determined grunt. The arrow cleaved through the air, the whistle music to my ears.

Time slowed, and I watched with wide eyes as blood sprayed, staining the mist around us pink. The big black dragon screeched, but didn't attack.

Instead, she tumbled backward, folding her wings back, letting herself free fall back to the earth below.

Her rider was dead, and with him all the fight she was wielding. At the last moment—before she crashed into the earth—she spread her wings and buffeted against the surrounding air. The rider had fallen, his drop too far for me to see where he had landed.

I braced myself for an attack, but the dragon only turned away from us and flew into the clouds without a second glance.

Sumyre swung back around with a roar, making me lose my grip on her. No longer having my rope to protect me, I was launched up. There was nothing more between me and the hard ground but the wind blowing my hair back.

I should have panicked. I should have screamed, been fearful, anything, but I was falling through a grey void with no way to tell which way was up. So, I just let myself be. My magic was depleted, my arrows were empty. I had done all I could to protect those around me, and even then, it wasn't enough. But I trusted Sumyre, and maybe—just maybe—Aceus survived.

Foolish human, I will catch you.

A familiar snarl in my head shook me out of my reverie, and I barely had a chance to brace myself as Sumyre's black wings snapped out under me. My knees took the brunt of the impact on her leathery wing. It may have looked delicate, but her wing was sturdy as I pushed myself up and swung myself back on my saddle.

Sumyre's heartbreaking roar had me whipping my head back as we broke back through the clouds, but there was no urgency from her in the bond. Only sadness. Sadness her mother had attacked, that we could only kill the rider to free her. Sadness and pain. Sharp pain that wasn't from my body. I jolted. Amidst all the chaos, Sumyre had been hit.

She aimed for the clearing, where three bloody figures stood heaving next to a prostrate body and a dead dragon.

Sumyre faltered as she landed, talons scraping along the ground before tumbling forward, throwing me off her back.

I screamed, my arm breaking my fall as I hit the ground. My only saving grace was the ice that was still armoring me, shattering as I fell. I hoped I didn't break any bones in my arm, but even so it would be a small price to pay for colliding with the ground so forcefully.

Footsteps rushed toward me. I tried to push myself up even though my whole body protested. Hands grasped my shoulder, pulling me up, and I groaned with my bruised body.

Warm hands cradled my face, lifting my chin as I met hazel eyes filled with concern.

"What the hell was that, Hal?" Caelum's voice was crazed with worry, and I grimaced in his grip.

"That was Sumyre's mother. The Rider is dead. Sumyre couldn't kill her."

He shook his head as his jaw feathered. "I'm not talking about the dragon. Why did you remove yourself from the saddle?"

"To kill the Rider."

"And yourself? Are you *trying* to die?" The question stung, but for a moment, I considered it a possibility. A probability.

I stared into Caelum's hazel eyes, the green brighter in his muddied face. "If it meant you got to live, I would pay that price a thousand times over."

Caelum only stared at me with his mouth hanging open, and I shook myself from his grip.

Pain from my arm was still pulsing through my body. My body wasn't healing in any capacity—my magic completely tapped out.

I turned to stalk away from him to Sumyre, who was now lifting herself off the ground, and shaking herself out. A throwing knife was still lodged in her, right at the juncture of her wing. I breathed out a sigh of relief. It didn't seem to be a fatal wound.

"Hal!" Caelum grabbed my arm, and I hissed at the contact. He removed his hand quickly, as though my skin burned him. "Gods, I'm sorry I didn't mean to hurt you, but please, listen to me." I turned with a brow raised. "I understand you want to protect me, I really do. But you cannot do that again. My life is not worth the price of yours." His eyes were watery, and I wanted to soothe his fears. But I couldn't lie to him. I would die a thousand times to save him.

Instead, I deflected. "Where is Maya? Sumyre is injured, and she needs help."

"I'm right here." Maya stood with her hands on her hips, blood speckling her cream-colored tunic, her braid fallen and her long hair flying freely behind her.

"Tell me what to do," I demanded, the adrenaline from the fight still pumping through me. Sumyre was injured, Aceus was dead. And I couldn't help but think it was all my fault.

"Iris will have to help you with this one," she muttered, averting her gaze.

Iris crept toward me and Sumyre, her hands splayed in front of us, as though to placate Sumyre's irritation at the knife stuck in her. She approached, and even as she put her hands on Sumyre's scales, Sumyre didn't do more than growl.

"I'm really sorry, Sumyre," she whispered to the dragon.

Her hands grasped the knife's length as she tugged it free. I was right, it wasn't lodged deep, but blood still pooled on the dirt. Iris' hands pressed into the wound, attempting to staunch the bleeding as her arms shook from applying pressure. Sumyre huffed in annoyance, but practiced being the perfect patient.

"There's not much more we can do," Iris said. "Luckily the wound didn't damage much more than her skin, so she will just have to heal on her own time. Not sure how long—"

Blood ceased to drip, and the wound sealed itself shut within seconds. I raised my eyebrow in surprise, but it made sense. Dragons were magical beings, her wounds being able to heal quickly seemed to be part of her biology, just like us.

"And Aceus?" I asked, my voice cracking. The three of them exchanged sorrowful glances before Caelum shook his head.

Tears streamed down my cheeks, and I let out a tormented sob that felt too big for my body. Caelum wrapped me in his arms. I sobbed into him, allowing him to take the brunt of my weight. I barely got in another breath as another bellowing call of a dragon echoed through the trees.

"There's more of them?" Maya hissed, and we looked up to see two figures approaching quickly. One veered another direction, and I assumed it was to recapture Sumyre's mother.

Dread pooled in my stomach. I was out of my magic, and from the looks of everyone else, they were teetering out, too. Nevertheless, I tugged for more magic. Instead, was met with emptiness and ache. With one more stubborn shove, pins and needles filled my limbs and I hissed. I was well and truly out of magic. If I pressed anymore, I would only cause myself more pain.

Sumyre's head pointed to the sky, with her eyes tracking the dragon above us. A low, vicious growl emanated from her, recognizing the imminent danger.

I reached to grab onto the saddle, but my arm screamed in protest, and even then, the straps were torn and the saddle slid off Sumyre's body. I grimaced through the pain and turned to Cal.

"What are we supposed to do?" I asked him, new nervousness making my head buzz with fear and anticipation. "Should we make a run for it?"

"Run? From one—potentially two—dragons?" He looked down at me with so much love and fear for my life, my heart threatened to crack in two.

I swallowed the lump in my throat. "I don't see much else of an option."

Cal looked over all of us, all tired, and I was certainly not in any shape to fight.

"Fine. We go. I'll need to retrieve the book first."

I had forgotten completely about the book, but even as I wanted to be upset it was still on his mind, if the mortal king got his hands on it, whatever was in it would be lost forever.

"You two, get the horses and back to the cave system. Avoid that other dragon at any cost. Hide, run, I don't care. Just be sure to survive."

He turned to me with a fire in his eyes. "You and Sumyre will come with me. They want her, so that dragon up there will most likely follow. At least with Sumyre we stand a chance of fighting if we need to."

"But what if the Rider attacks? If you don't survive, then we're leaving *everything* behind, including the Lady of Dolan," Maya protested.

Caelum sighed, his palm cradling my cheek, and he looked down at me with so much love in his eyes it was nearly overwhelming. "I won't ask you to do this if you don't want to. You still have a chance for escape—"

"No, I'm coming with you. Like you said. Sumyre is your best chance of survival. I already let one person die today. It won't happen again," I told him.

Maya cursed, but quickly grabbed Iris' arms and ushered her away. With no time for argument, Maya was quick to catch on.

Caelum nodded, his eyes glassy as he took me in. "Then let's hope for the best, and we can escape the Dragon Rider's grasp."

Chapter 23

HALCYON

My feet pounded against the dry leaves and dirt as I chased behind Caelum. Sumyre followed us, one eye on the skies above. The Dragon Rider made no attacks as we ran, but Sumyre assured me he was still following.

Unease sank through me. The forest was quiet; only the heaving of our breaths made any sound. Even though I knew there was a dragon somewhere above within the low-hanging clouds, it was silent.

Fronds and branches brushed against my shoulders, scraping along my arms as we delved more into the forest toward the temple. My breaths heaved with the labor and adrenaline until we were finally met with the temple walls.

It stood as dilapidated and worn as it did the first day I laid my eyes on it, but now it felt sacred. More sacred than normal, considering we were leading one of the mortal kingdom's soldiers straight to its doors.

What would happen if the Rider saw this temple? Would he be hell-bent on destroying it? What would happen to the contents which rightfully belonged to Ambrose? Would they find the palace beneath and raid it, too? Riches and history would be destroyed, sold, and forever forgotten in Tantal. My eyes watered as I thought about the potential destruction of what we considered so precious.

Caelum skidded to a stop in front of the temple and took a moment to take it all in. He turned to me with a melancholy gaze.

As if he was the one who could read my mind, he said, "It's a shame I had to hide it here. I wish I would have been more thoughtful. I can't imagine they won't try to destroy the temple."

Up above us, the whooshing of wings grew closer. Our time was up. The bow on my back practically burned through my clothes, and I armed myself, pointing directly at our mysterious Dragon Rider. My arm throbbed in the motion, but I held strong.

White scales nearly blinded me as they broke through the clouds. Even though those scales were one of the most beautiful shades of white I had ever seen, they looked dull and pallid. Several gashes were embedded on the side of the dragon, and I wondered exactly what this dragon must have gone through to get those types of scars.

Broad shoulders stepped in front of me before I could study the dragon any longer. Caelum hurriedly cast a wall of earth and vines in front of us. He grabbed me by my good arm, tugging me into the temple entrance as I placed my bow back on my back. Sumyre followed, her large body barely fitting in the tight chamber.

"Why did you hide the book in the temple?" I hissed.

"Where else was I supposed to hide it? I thought we could shake the Dragon Riders off easier than this. If only they didn't have backup..." Caelum shook his head, trudging deeper into the temple.

I glanced back at Sumyre, fearful she was going to get stuck in these halls, but they moved around her. I stared, confused, until I saw Caelum's palms pressed against the walls as he walked, widening the passage for her.

Darkness pressed in on us, Caelum using his magic to feel for the entrance into the shrine room. As soon as we entered, a blue-green torch of Everflame greeted us, next to where Cal had placed the book on one of the pedestals.

Without hesitation, he snatched the book and the Everflame and led us back up through the temple. We entered back into the large worship chamber, and Caelum slowed to a stop.

"We should destroy it ourselves," he said while studying the room's beams and ceiling.

"What?" I squeaked. The only explanation for Caelum's sudden revelation was insanity. He strode over to me, handing me the tome and using his hand to lift my chin to meet his gaze in the flickering light.

"The mortals are going to destroy it, anyway. Once we leave here, we can never come back. I should destroy this temple, so they have nothing left to gain from it. Sink it so deep into the ground so only we will know it ever existed. Just like the underground palace. Locked away from unwanted forces for eternity."

I inhaled deeply as I took in the room's expanse. Sumyre shuffled her feet behind me and let out a solemn huff of hot air.

"Can you even do that, Cal? I'm not trying to say you aren't strong, but...this temple is huge."

He grabbed my hand, squeezing it. "I can do it. Pray to the gods this is something they want, too." I nodded slowly, seeing the logic in his argument. Calloused fingers brushed away a tear from my cheek.

"Just make sure we get out of this alive," I told him determinately.

Soft lips met mine and Caelum's arms wrapped around me in a kiss which felt awfully like a goodbye. He held me as close to him as possible, pressing his palms against my back, his fingers drifting until they found my scalp pulling me in deeper.

The ghost of his lips remained seared on my skin as he pulled away and met his forehead to mine. He tugged a vial of lilac liquid from his pocket and inhaled sharply before pouring it down his throat. Groaning, he flexed his hands as the magic in his body was replenished.

"Sumyre," he called to her without taking his eyes off mine. "You get out first. I'll keep Halcyon safe, but you need to distract the other Rider. Get him away from here."

He peeled away from me as he met Sumyre's green gaze and bowed low. She chuffed at his show of respect before rearing back and jumping over us, disappearing through the temple halls.

I wanted to scream at her to stop, to not put her own life at risk for my own. Confidence pulsed through the bond, and I knew no words or feelings could stop her.

"Stay near me, Halcyon. We're going to be alright," he promised, and I clung to his words like my last lifeline.

He crouched down low, releasing a long breath of air as he concentrated. Creaks filled the silence of the temple and dust fell from the ceiling, settling all around us, dusting my shoulders and hair.

Caelum grunted, adjusting his stance as he pushed all of his power into the temple. Wood splintered and stone cracked and shattered as the temple began falling apart around us.

The ground rolled beneath my feet, and I clutched Cal's shoulder to keep myself steady. The shaking ground grew more violent. Beads of sweat dripped down Caelum's reddened face. The temple was tumultuous, and the ensuing carnage put us at a severe risk of injury.

Sweat dripped from his forehead as he pushed himself up. Not giving me a chance to say anything, he grabbed my good arm again and tugged me behind him as we ran toward the entrance.

The book was still clutched in my hands. The throbbing in my arm paled into comparison of the panic in my chest. My nails pressed into the tome's leather, confident it would never leave my side.

The temple continued to cave in behind us, rocks and debris somehow narrowly missing us as we ran ahead. My heart was beating so fast, it felt like it would jump out of my throat, and my thoughts were on one thing: survival.

Finally, we reached the temple exit, and I flung myself out, leaping into the air as I pushed off the last step.

I landed face down in the dirt. Mud and grass caked in my mouth, and my arm screamed in pain, but I didn't care. I peered back just in time to see the earth swallow the temple, only leaving broken stone and columns in its wake. A booming collapse behind me was the final indication that our deaths had been a certain probability.

I ROSE ON A shaking arm, but stilled when a pair of boots entered my line of vision. Black boots. Expensive black boots that led up to Tantalian leather pants.

A hand clenched around my hair, pulling me from the ground up, and I screamed. The last remnants of my magic formed ice around my fingers, but it was all I could do before cold metal pressed into my neck.

Caelum was crouched on his hands and knees next to me, and I recognized his stance as the one where he was about to pull on his magic, but the man who held me only laughed as if he knew we were both tapped out.

I looked into the face of my captor. Sharp cheekbones led to an equally sharp nose. Light brown hair dusted along his forehead, and if he wasn't wearing a sneer so harsh it could cut glass, he might have even been handsome.

My heart raced in my ears. Dread pooled in my stomach as I saw a mass of black scales in the tree line. Sumyre was lying unconscious on the ground. I tugged on our bond, but there was only a faint pulse, and it took everything in me not to lash out against my captor.

Tearing my gaze away from her, I forced myself to scan the ground for the other dragons, but instead, a dark shadow passed over us. I didn't need to look up to know his dragon was hovering above.

The man yanked on my hair, and I yelped.

"You destroyed those ruins. I'll destroy your dragon." He nodded behind him, where the temple was no more. "Tell me what was in there." His gaze slid down to the tome in my hands, and his eyes flared.

"The King's dragon, bonded to a Magi." He spat at me, and I flinched as his saliva slid down the side of my cheek. "Despicable. A disgrace. Which is why I poisoned it. And I did the same to the others. Too weak to keep their riders alive." His haughty laugh slid like oil down my spine and raw fear gripped my body.

He bent down to my face, his nose nearly pressed to mine, and I stole a glance at Caelum—his own eyes wide with fear—unable to help with a blade pressed to my throat.

"Helpless without your magic, aren't you?" The rider scoffed, a sinister grin pulling at his lip. I gave him no answer, shaking from rage in his grip. "Do you know why there are no Magi riders?" The rider taunted, venom coursing through every word. I only glared at him. He couldn't rattle me. I was made of ice, and ice was what he was going to get.

"It's because you have no backbone. You rely on your demonic magic, and that seems to be enough. Mortals aren't tainted with magic. But we need some sort of leverage against you." He glanced in Caelum's direction and sneered. He dropped me, my knees cracking against the hard ground.

The man stalked over to Caelum, and crouched down to his level. I watched with wide eyes as I hoped Caelum had a shred of magic, but the tiniest of head shakes told me he also used up the last of it destroying the temple.

He swung his gaze back at me, landing on the tome clutched in my arms. His lips turned into an ugly smirk, and something lit behind his eyes.

My fingers tightened around the leather, as if it would help shield it from his gaze. "I'll make you a deal. You tell me where you found that book. Then you'll give it to me, and I will give you the antidote to the poison. You can save your precious dragon."

I spat at him, and he scowled back. I would kill him and take the antidote from him.

The man clicked his tongue, pressing the blade against Cal, a trickle of blood seeping down his neck and onto his chest. "You make any sudden movements and I will slit his throat so you can watch him bleed. The King wants any found Magi alive, but one is better than none."

Nothing I had ever felt before compared to the absolute rage I felt. Cal did *nothing* to earn this man's ire. My body vibrated from the vitriol I held for this man—for these riders of Tantal—who did nothing but enslave these dragons and use them as some poor excuse to feel better about their shortened mortality.

I watched with wide eyes as the man took his knife and sliced along Caelum's cheek. Cal hissed, and I saw red. The man only laughed, a true psychopath, and he *sniffed* Cal's blood. Then he raised his hand and smacked Caelum on the side of his head with the pommel of the blade, knocking him unconscious.

I screamed. The man shot over to me, his hand wrapped around my throat, his fingers biting into me, cutting off my air.

His other hand pried at the book, but I only clutched it tighter. My arm screamed in pain as he fought me for the book, but he would have to cut my arms off if he wanted it.

Black spots dotted my vision, and I kicked my leg back and delivered one powerful blow to the man's groin. He pulled back, yelping in pain, while I collapsed on the ground.

Oxygen refilled my lungs, leaving my head dizzy, but I was far from done. The man stalked back over the Caelum, but I pulled my magic from the deepest well of my soul, searching deep for any dregs I could muster.

Panic threatened to claw through me as I realized the no amount of digging for my magic could make me form any ice. I stole a glance at Sumyre, who was entirely too still. If there was a chance I could pull more on the bond, maybe Sumyre would wake up.

I tugged hard. Yanked until sweat broke out over my forehead. It was weak, but it was still there; proof she was still alive. I needed her to stir and rise and eat this man, no matter how stringy he might be for her palate. Wake up just enough to land a single snap of gnashing teeth on this man. When I sat there, panting and she remained still, I decided I would reach for my magic once again.

No matter the cost.

My lungs seized, my heart pounded as I pulled with enough force to break me. I felt every sting of the depleted magic trying to pulse through my body and coming up empty.

My cheeks grew wet with tears. The strain was too much to bear, but I would bear it. For Sumyre, for Cal, for those two dragons who had no chance to live if I didn't succeed.

The man either didn't realize I was trying to push myself to kill him, or he didn't care. He only glared down at me as he yanked Cal up by his hair. Cal was still unconscious, his body limp underneath him. He raised his blade to Caelum and...

Nothing. I could see *nothing*.

Dread clawed its way through me. My ears were ringing, and pain radiated through my limbs so fiercely I thought I was burning from the inside out.

Two long golden lines pulled taught into the darkness in opposite directions. One was bright and thick, sturdy in every way. The other thin and spotty in places, frayed threads meant to be together as one.

A thread that had not yet been woven with fate. I wanted to inspect it. See where it led to, but now was not the time. I could only guess, but if I was right, I wondered if that thread would ever be complete.

I reached for the larger, the more sturdy rope and pulled through the tearing of my muscles. Too much magic, I had used too much. I could feel it eating away at my body, but I pulled on that line, the hard cord, tugging it, desperately hoping this was the answer to the predicament we faced.

Wake up, Sumyre! I called into this void, my voice nothing and everything all at once.

I kept pulling, feeling myself drifting toward a bright shining orb, and as I got closer, I could make out its shape.

A dragon.

The light pulsed slowly, and I pulled myself closer still.

It was Sumyre...a perfectly glowing replica of Sumyre! This was her magic, her *soul*.

Our souls tied together, bound by magic and sealed in fate. She was barely alive, but here I was, keeping her tethered to life. To me. I reached my hand out, brushing against her. As soon as my fingertips brushed against the shining dragon, her glowing soul light erupted.

My lungs expanded, and I breathed in a full breath of air. As though no time had passed, the man still held his blade to Caelum with an evil, wicked grin.

Immense power flooded through my veins. My body burned with it, too hot and freezing cold all the same. My teeth were clenched so hard I thought they would crack.

Behind me Sumyre stirred, and out of the corner of my eye I saw her stand and shake her head before she let out a bellowing roar.

The rider's eyes widened, and he stood stunned for a moment before grimacing. His own dragon answered Sumyre's call with another roar, and I didn't have time to yell out a warning before the dragon nosedived straight for her.

The white dragon descended, and my heart leapt into my throat at the sound of teeth snapping and claws swiping. Lavender smoke poured from Sumyre, engulfing them and hiding them from our view. Only the sounds of screeching and clawing and scraping let me know she was still alive.

I surged my magic to the ground below, webbing across the dirt, turning the autumn leaves into frigid blue icicles. For once, the rider looked afraid, but he steeled himself and held the blade to Caelum tighter.

"Give me the book!" he yelled, and I responded with a shout of my own.

Raw power erupted from my hands, freezing everything in my path. Blades of grass turned to hard frozen daggers, tree limbs grew heavy with ice, creaking under the weight. The temple ruins blocked in ice.

Everything that was once green and brown and flush with life, was now blue and white and cold. And in the middle of my ice was an undulating lavender mist...Sumyre's and my power combined.

Fear radiated from the Rider's eyes, and he dropped the blade beside him, as if he knew I spared him for the slow kill. He backed away from Caelum, letting him fall to the ground, but I wasn't satisfied.

Caelum stirred, and I let myself feel a slight relief before turning back on the Rider. A malicious smirk spread across my face and my fingers twitched at the fear the Rider showed me when his eyes widened and face paled.

"You threaten me, you threaten my dragon, you threaten my *soul-bonded* for a book that *doesn't even belong to you*. And you think I will let you live?"

Malice and rage simmered under my skin, as I summoned a sharp blade of ice in my palm, heavy and lethal.

A cry from Sumyre nearly made me lose my resolve, but I steeled forward.

Take the fight to the sky, Sumyre. We can hope to save that dragon. Once the other riders were dead, the dragons fled. This one could, too.

I had to convince them to flee, she responded, sounding tired and battle worn.

Then convince this one to flee, too, I growled at her mentally.

A burst of air blew around me, dispersing the purple smoke, and Sumyre shot into the sky, her maw biting at the white scales of the other dragon's neck, baiting him. The dragon snapped back and chased after her. His large alabaster wings beat against the ground, throttling him up after Sumyre.

"No!" the rider shouted, but he lost his balance on the ice-covered ground, falling on his knees.

The dragon, too preoccupied with Sumyre's snarls and growls, ignored his rider for the immediate threat. They leapt to the skies, leaving me and this mortal dragon rider alone. I grinned, relishing in this man's fear.

With a flick of my wrist, I bound him in the ice, ignoring his pleas and apologies. It was too late for that. I spun the blade in my hand.

The ice felt good in my palm. Solid. It was mine to yield, made from me, my ire, my anger at this slaver.

"Answer me, Dragon Rider, why do you, and by extension the King, desire an old book that belongs to the gods that your nation is so hell-bent on demonizing?"

"Fuck if I know!" he spat at me, but something flashed in his eyes. He did know something; he just wasn't telling me. I would *make* him tell me.

I stood over him, the ice pinning him down to the ground below me. With a sneer on my lips, I grasped his chin in my icy fingers. He tried to jerk away, but it was futile.

Pressing my blade on his heart, the ice punctured through his leathers.

"I don't like to repeat my questions." Every single box inside of me that was full of rage, disappointment, or fear burst wide open. It was a Purge of all the things I had kept to myself for so long.

My father's betrayal. My mother's willingness to allow his tyranny. Every time I had submitted to avoid conflict. Aceus' death.

It was like a dam broke, and I refused to back down and shy away from who I was any longer.

Unrelenting.

Unapologetic.

Decisive.

The rider's eyes widened, and his breathing turned ragged. Any fight he had was long gone now. His only saving grace, his dragon, was far up in the skies still battling with Sumyre.

"I–I don't know. He studies the ways of the old gods. Loves that old shit, says it gives him defense from Magi."

I quickly slashed my blade along his face, giving him an identical cut to the one he gave Cal before I pressed the blade into the spot where I knew his soulless heart lay beating. Blood dripped from his chest, rivulets rolling along his leather.

"It's how we bond the dragons," he whispered, and I squeezed my blade tighter. "There's old magic the king can use...he finds it in pieces that belonged to the once-gods. It's how he binds us to the beasts. Once mortal riders die, the dragons can't bond a new rider, so he needs the magic to reproduce new dragons and bond them to mortals. Otherwise, our army would cease to exist."

My eyes widened, my heart thrummed in my ears.

I wanted to scream, my cheeks getting red with anger. Before I even registered my actions, I thrust my blade into the rider's chest, letting out a hollow shout which echoed against the tinkling icicles around me. As I expunged my anger, the ice exploded around me. Daggers speared into the man's body from every direction leaving nothing left but a pile of meat skewered with shards of sharp ice.

An answering screech mimicked my scream from above, and I startled as red blood fell from the sky like a gruesome rain. I began to panic, fearing the worst, but Sumyre's voice cut through my rage.

It is done.

She killed her foe as I did mine. Two dragons fell from the sky. Sumyre, hanging onto the dead and bleeding one between her teeth. Her black scales soaked red with blood.

He would not listen, she said mournfully.

I FINALLY PEELED MY eyes away from the carcass of the man I executed without hesitation. There were stories I read in the library which said killing would elicit certain emotions. Soldiers who recounted how they had gotten sick after their first kill, that taking the life from someone feeling so unnatural that it made them ill.

But I felt nothing.

This man had regarded dragons as nothing more than objects, and Magi as demons. He paid for his crimes, even though the real person responsible was much farther in this country, most likely guarded by his prisoners.

But despite that, seeing his lifeless body, riddled with ice to a pulp, in front of me did nothing to make me regret or feel remorse for my choices.

Without rage clouding my thoughts, I took a look around the mess I made.

Ice towered through the forest. The sun was setting, casting rainbows through the winding and complex fractals that etched themselves into my magical sculptures. A slight breeze made the weighted-down branches sway, and the icicles hanging off of them rang and tinkled against each other.

I was surprised by the tranquility of it. So much havoc and violence to trade for this peacefulness after.

"Halcyon, the other dragons are still alive but barely." Caelum shook me from my reverie, slowing as he came back from the edge of the forest. He had gone to scout for the other two dragons the man had claimed to poison, and with Sumyre's help found them not too far from our campsite. Arrows coated in poison were lodged between their scales. One of the poisoned dragons was her mother, and the bellow she made threatened to break me into pieces.

"He said he had the antidote," I explained as I searched the dead man's pockets. Weapons and darts with what was presumably poison fell out. I found a small money slip with papers of Tantalian currency, but there was no sign of the antidote anywhere.

I cursed loudly, and even Cal jumped. "He lied. He had no antidote!"

I closed my eyes, trying to think, when an idea came to me.

Can you communicate with people other than myself?

Sumyre let out a chuff like it was the most ridiculous thing she had ever heard. If she could have rolled her eyes, I figured she would have.

Of course I can.

Well, then why haven't you spoken to anyone but me?

Why would I want to do that?

I groaned.

Find Maya. Tell her we need an antidote or, even better, bring her back. I paused, recalling the last time I asked for her help in healing a dragon.

And make sure you tell her every detail of what is going on. She doesn't like surprises.

Sumyre took off, her wings beating a breeze so hard that ice crackled and groaned as it threatened to snap.

"Where did she go?" Caelum asked, and for a moment I forgot he couldn't hear our conversation.

He nodded after I told him, and he raked his hands through his hair. "Good thinking."

"Thanks." I stood and stared at Caelum. Dirt and sweat coated his tunic, more sweat and grime smudged on his cheeks and forehead. We had come so close to death today, and by some form of sheer luck, we both survived.

I thought about that thread that had started to weave itself into existence. The way it was still frayed, half-formed, and while I was positive it was Caelum on the other side, it was still only a guess.

I loved him. I wasn't sure when exactly I had realized that what I felt for him was love, but I knew now. Knew even more now that I assumed he was my bonded. The thought had my knees weak and my head fuzzy.

However, our situation hadn't changed, no matter the experiences we just went through. I would still go back to overseeing Dolan, and he would go back to...wherever his life would take him. It wouldn't be right for me to declare my love for him now. Not when we both had our own responsibilities to uphold.

He would be praised for this expedition, and then asked to lead other—hopefully safer—expeditions, wandering across the world. My heart skipped a beat when I remembered that he wanted to study the book at the Neverwind, but even then, it wouldn't matter. I was not going to be there. I would be in the cold castle walls, pretending to know how to command a city.

Regardless, I reached out for him, and he instinctively pulled me in. I inhaled his scent, the pine still coming through underneath the grime. As soon as his arms wrapped around me, I crumpled.

Tears cascaded down my cheeks as I sobbed, my legs shaking underneath me, as if I had been holding it in, remaining strong for this specific moment. No one had ever seen me break like this, but with Cal, I knew there would be no judgment.

"Oh gods, Halcyon." There was weariness in his voice, and I looked up at him. His brown hair stuck to his forehead, and his hazel eyes reflected the worry that I was sure I held in mine.

He brushed a piece of hair behind my ear and muttered, "I thought you...when he held that knife to your throat...I was so glad he walked away from you, and then he knocked me out. I was so worried when I started to wake..." His words were thick and as incoherent as my thoughts.

"I was scared too. For you. I don't know how I did it, but I pushed through a barrier of sorts. Sumyre's power and mine connected. It gave me a huge magic boost. I still don't really even know what happened. But I couldn't stand and watch you die."

Recounting my experience in the void to him, he took every word I said with complete seriousness, and only as the words tumbled out of my mouth was when I started to realize how mad it all sounded. But he took it all in stride, believing everything I told him.

It was a relief. I left out the portion about the smaller thread, not willing to make any more acknowledgment of it. Not because I wanted to shy myself away from that reality, but because I didn't want to force Caelum to make any sort of rash decisions. Bonded or not, he was still his own man, and I wouldn't sway his decisions based on a possibility that had not yet been solidified.

Caelum frowned, but he sighed in my arms as he took in the icy fortress I had made.

"And your arm?" he asked, gently wrapping his fingers around my wrist, but I shrugged.

"Fully healed, along with my magic."

His hand snaked up my shoulder and cradled the back of my head, holding me close to his chest. Tenderly, he circled his thumb behind my ear, making me shiver and embrace him harder.

"I don't know what any of that could mean. I've never heard or read any accounts that could be similar, but you did what you needed to save all of us." Warm lips pressed against the top of my head. "You are every bit as powerful as I knew you were," he paused, "although you are absolutely terrifying."

I couldn't help the laugh that tumbled out of me. "That's not the first time I've heard that."

Chapter 24

CAELUM

Two enormous dragons circled above us. One with recognizable black scales, the other with bright flame-red ones. Halcyon tensed, frost lining her fingertips for a brief moment. As the ice melted away, she looked up at me with her big blue eyes, a smile lining her lips.

"I know who it is," she laughed as she pointed at the dragons approaching. "Sumyre with everyone in tow. And a friend I haven't seen in a very long time."

The dragons landed on the ice with grace. Maya and Iris were riding on Sumyre, looking more anxious and paler than I had ever witnessed. Iris sat behind Maya, her arms gripping Maya so tight I could see the whiteness of her knuckles.

A man I had never seen before sat on top of the red dragon. The red one was twice the size of Sumyre, and I swallowed thickly as I took in how vicious it was in every way, gleaming with violence.

"Galen?" Halcyon called to the man with excitement radiating from her body, and I rose a brow in confusion.

She smiled brightly, and a pang of jealousy washed over me. I grimaced. This must be the Dragon Rider she told me about in the forest what felt like a lifetime ago.

"Halcyon?" the man with dark brown hair and deep blue eyes asked. I couldn't help but scowl at his muscular frame, and his smile that shined like the sun.

He hopped off his dragon easily before giving Hal a slight bow. I eased at his show of formality, finally understanding his respect for Halcyon.

"Halcyon, what on the gods' green earth are you doing in the mortal lands?" He was still smiling, but he was clearly confused.

"A simple research mission gone very, very poorly." Halcyon grimaced and looked back at me. She spoke differently to this *Galen*, more formally, and it made me almost want to smile. "Galen, this is Caelum. He is the head of research for the troupe."

Galen smiled at me, but I puffed up my chest, offering him a handshake I may have made too hard. Oh well.

"Well met, Caelum. I'm Galen, Ambrose's Dragon Rider." He shifted his gaze to Hal before returning to me with a smile. "Well, I guess I'm not the only one anymore. I work undercover for Ambrose in the mortal kingdom." He chuckled and brushed the back of his head...like *I* sometimes did. I scowled. Halcyon threw me a questioning glance and I cleared my throat.

"Well met. Nice dragon you've got there." I glanced at the red dragon with sharp pointy teeth, like those stalactites in the cave. The dragon let out a low growl, and I backed up a step. Galen only laughed.

"That's Casimir. He's, uh, not in the best of moods right now."

I swallowed a lump formed in my throat.

"Oh really? Why is that?" I regarded the dragon with unease seeping through my limbs.

"He rarely likes young ones," Galen whispered to me while throwing a thumb in Sumyre's direction. "A bit of a grump."

I jumped back as Casimir gnashed his teeth at Galen. He was a bit of a grump alright, and one that I did not want to be on the bad side of. Galen only laughed, though it didn't set me any more at ease.

"Stop bothering the dragon, Sumyre," Halcyon admonished her and shook her head as she helped Maya and Iris off Sumyre's back.

"We have two poisoned dragons," she told Maya. "I'm not sure what they used as poison, but I was hoping you could help. After they wake up, the dragons could talk to each other and convince these two to flee over the border."

Galen clicked his tongue. "It's probably Naria extract. The mortal army uses it to euthanize un-bonded dragons. It takes a while to complete the process since they are enormous creatures, but even the smallest amount will kill them, eventually."

"Because once a mortal rider dies, they can't bond again?" I asked, my curiosity rearing back up as I barely grew more comfortable.

Galen only shook his head, melancholy overcoming his features. "It's not that they can't. It's that they *won't*. Once a rider dies, the dragon is released from whatever mental hold they have over them. And instead of working with the dragons, they force them to become breeders."

Halcyon grimaced, and I nearly followed suit.

"However, if a dragon is particularly uncooperative—or if they are too far to drag back to the breeding camp—they opt for killing them."

Maya sighed, tugging items out of her bag and laying them on the ground. "I really could have gone without knowing they were mass-murdering dragons. I have a few items I can use in the antidote, but the rest of what I need, I don't have. Iris and I can scout the forest. Hopefully it'll have something I can use."

"No need." Galen pulled two bottles of clear liquid from his satchel. "Once I found out about the mortal king's methods, I started carrying the antidote with me."

Halcyon followed Galen as he administered the antidote, asking him questions about dragon riding. I listened in, keeping myself to the sidelines. I *was* jealous, but I swallowed it as best I could. She would need a mentor after all of this was done. So who better to get her familiar with dragon riding than Ambrose's only Dragon Rider himself?

Besides, Halcyon and I were never meant to last. It wasn't like I could make a claim on her, even though the thought of her with anyone else threatened to rip me apart.

"Sorry to break up this party," I interjected. Halcyon's eyes softened at me, and with that one look, my jealousy melted away, and my shoulders relaxed. "But what, exactly, are you doing here?"

Galen turned back to me, clearing his throat.

"A lot of what I do is confidential, but the gist is: I infiltrated my way into the ranks of the Tantal army. A dragon got loose a couple months ago…" Galen's eyes bounced back toward Sumyre. "It may or may not have been me and Casimir that freed her." He waved his hand in the air, as if that nugget of information didn't matter.

"Anyway, there's a hunt for her, and I snuck onto the scouting team. I was leading them another direction, but one of the dragons caught wind of her and so I had no choice but to come this way."

"But the book. The Dragon Rider said the king would be interested in it. How would he know?" Halcyon asked, and I raised my eyebrow at her. It was a valid question. The King's army certainly seemed to know more than they let on.

Galen sighed, a sliver of his exhaustion showing through his smile. "A few years ago, there was a string of thefts in Aurum. Ancient relics that had traces of magic in them were disappearing. We found out they were being transported to the mortal king. Which is why I'm here.

"I don't know *how* the King knows what to look for, but he does. He has been demanding soldiers to find any traces of Magi civilization for months. Even put a damn bounty on anything remotely tied to our roots. He says he wants to eradicate the world from evil. Luckily, no one seemed to remember a temple in these woods. Otherwise, it would have been raided a long time ago."

Galen pulled his sword from its sheath. It gleamed in the sunlight, but as I peered closer, the hilt was lined with delicate black gems, exactly like the ones that lined Halcyon's bow.

"I have a theory, though. It seems like ancient weapons like this sword—and your bow—are a key to triggering the bond. I also have a theory that it can only be activated in sacred places.

"I know someone else who has a black diamond-lined weapon, but she has no dragon bond. It wouldn't work without a dragon, either, but I digress."

Glancing back at the pile of rubble that used to be the temple, I pondered. The palace beneath would certainly be qualified as sacred.

Halcyon's brow pinched in thought. "So, in order to trigger the bond, you have to have a weapon and a sacred place. Do the mortal riders have these?"

Galen shook his head. "Not from what I can tell. The traditional bond also requires a sacrifice, but I don't think any of the men in the army have been required to do that, unless it's to the King himself."

"A sacrifice?" Halcyon and I asked at the same time.

"I didn't have to sacrifice anything. I just touched the bow, and the bond was sealed," she said.

Galen's eyes moved between the two of us. "It's not a sacrifice that would be so blatant. It's something bigger than anything with monetary value."

"But I would have to do so willingly?" Halcyon asked, and Galen shrugged.

"It's what was required of me." he said simply, but his eyes swirled with darkness, an underlying pain he wouldn't voice.

"The circumstances certainly are different. Maybe the sacrifice is required only if the sacred place doesn't hold enough magic," I noted, thinking about the raw magic filling the throne room when Halcyon triggered her bond.

My mind went elsewhere as Halcyon relayed all the information we had found about the massive castle below our feet. If the castle, palace—whatever it was—was hidden by magic and buried so deep underground, and we found it purely by luck, wouldn't it be possible there *were* places like this in Ambrose?

Glancing at the rubble behind us, he contemplated. "It seems like it *would* be the perfect place to activate the Dragon Bond. I got my sword and bond with Casimir in a similar type of sacred place, although it was administered by an overseer, so I didn't question the ritual."

I glanced at Halcyon, her eyes wide with questions as we took in Galen's revelation.

"What kind of overseer?" I asked, crossing my arms over my chest. Galen smirked but averted his gaze.

"The dragon kind," he said evasively, but a lump formed in my throat. Not only was he a Dragon Rider, but he had relationships with multiple dragons? Just how much power did he wield? And how much did Halcyon have now that she was in the same league as him?

"And what sort of sacred place did you get your bond?" I implored.

"The dragon kind," he repeated with a laugh.

Halcyon stepped to my side and threaded her fingers in my hand. It was more assuring than I even realized it could be.

"How did you find the others, anyway?" she asked, rubbing circles with her thumb on my palm. I felt my shoulders loosen from her touch and gave her a grateful smile.

"I saw your team at the mouth of the cave, and Sumyre connected with Casimir instantly. She certainly has some fight in her, even though she is still young," Galen told us as he recounted how he had found our group while we were fighting the Dragon Rider. "Thankfully, Maya recognized me straight away."

"Maya?" My brain froze. "How does Maya know you?"

"I've met her a handful of times. I work with her brother...more often than I would like," he admitted with a grimace.

"Who's her brother?" I asked. I didn't even know Maya *had* a brother. She never once brought him up to me. Not that any of us were very forthcoming about our lives previous to when we banded together, but still. I scoffed internally.

"Kasiel," Galen said simply. *Who?*

Halcyon sucked in a bit of air through her teeth. "The assassin?"

Galen grimaced. "The one and only."

I shook my head, shocked. I didn't know who the hell Kasiel was, and why the hell did Maya neglect to tell me her brother was a damned assassin? I sifted through dirt and rocks for a living, but I didn't live underneath one. A pit fell into my stomach for multiple reasons, and I gave one more pensive glance at Galen.

Assassins, Ambrosian Dragon Riders. It was too much; not my life at all. It reminded me I was nothing in the grand scheme of things. Just a man who liked to dig around the earth for old trinkets.

The ground was quick to turn into sloppy mud, but I wasn't in the mind to get irritated each time my boots squished beneath me. Halcyon followed Galen around, as he gave her instructions on how to further her bond with

Sumyre. I listened out of the corner of my ear, not wanting to get directly involved in their conversation but interested all the same.

"When the other dragons wake up," he told her, "Casimir is going to relay directions to the Dragon's Keep in Ambrose."

"The Dragon's Keep?" she asked. "Where is that? How haven't I heard of it before?"

"We aren't *supposed* to know about it," he whispered. "The dragons have their own community as much as we do. The un-bonded dragons have a haven there. But—and I cannot express this enough—you don't want to go there. They will eat you alive, Rider or not. Dragons are very much the 'act now, ask questions later', kind."

I saw Halcyon suppress a shiver, and so did I.

Galen shoved his hand out toward me, and I grasped it once again for a handshake. "I think it's time to go our separate ways. The dragons most likely won't know what's happening when they wake up, so for all of our safety, we must say goodbye."

"It was a pleasure to meet you." I replied with a tight smile.

"Thank you again, Galen. You truly are invaluable to Ambrose," Halcyon cut in, offering her own hand, and I was silently grateful she didn't offer him an embrace instead.

"The pleasure is all mine. Hopefully, I'll be seeing you sooner rather than later." Galen nodded to each of us before trudging through the mud back to Casimir.

We took our leave. All four of us and Sumyre made our way back through the woods toward the camp, where we would pack up and leave.

"I NEED A GOOD ale when we get back," Iris groaned from behind me. Somehow, we saved all our horses, the wagon, and everything in it.

The air was thick and somber as we traveled. We recovered Aceus' body, wrapped him in linens, and laid him gently in the back of the wagon. Halcyon was adamant we bring his body back to Ambrose, and no matter how much of a strong façade she wore, I could tell she was very near the breaking point.

Maya and Iris were similarly mourning in their own way. When they thought no one was looking, they whispered in each other's ears and held each other, silently crying. I was glad more than ever they had each other, but Aceus had become more than just a fixture for their passing time.

When Maya had soaked the linens that wrapped Aceus' body in a balm which would slow the decaying process, she had done so through endless tears. Even though she said nothing, her pain was visible.

I was at a loss for how to comfort her. What if it had been Halcyon? If she had died, I wouldn't have ever been able to forgive myself. Was that how she felt now? My heart ached at the thought.

I regretted not getting to know the man more. I had taken advantage of how protective he was over Halcyon, even though it was his job. Remembering the time he had stepped in front of wolves for her, and how he was fearless in the eye of death, I regarded him as one of the bravest mortals I had ever known. His death, while not in vain, left a gouge through all of us.

Halcyon grew more silent with each passing day, and I supposed I did the same. She would open her mouth to say something, then shake her head and close it. I didn't pry. Whatever she wanted to say, it would break me. Both of us were unwilling to bring up our inevitable end.

We were safe. I had the tome strapped to my side, a guarantee of payment and accolades, but it also meant the inevitable end between me and Hal. Each night we were wrapped in each other's arms, not mentioning the unavoidable conclusion of what we knew was coming.

Once we got through the cave system, there was a potent aura of relief. Green pine and evergreens greeted us with their spindly branches, and I couldn't help but think about how small they looked compared to the redwoods we had just spent the last week familiarizing ourselves with.

Halcyon took flight on Sumyre's back toward Dolan, wanting to arrive earlier than us to fill the Council in on our recent work. Her departure was hasty, and as I gave her a brief kiss on her pink lips, I couldn't decide if I was glad or upset to be back.

"A good ale, and a good bed," Maya agreed. I grunted my agreement, not quite feeling the return trip relief.

"Maya, why didn't you ever tell me you had a brother?" I asked, the question niggling in the back of my head for days. I trusted Maya with my life, and while we all rarely spoke of our lives before we banded together, it was still a shock I didn't know a piece of her.

Maya sighed and settled in her saddle a little more.

"My brother—" Maya looked up at the sky, gathering her thoughts. She pinched her lip between her bottom teeth. "—is complicated."

I nodded, and she sighed before she went on, "I see him every once in a while, but I can't exactly broadcast my relationship with him. He's an assassin, but he's a good person. He does what he does for his city, but if it got out we were related...well, it could be trouble for the both of us. Not to mention it could mean trouble for you."

"But we've been together for years. Don't you trust us?"

Iris let out a small laugh, and Maya threw daggers at her with her eyes.

"What?" I asked.

"I knew the whole time." Iris shrugged with mirth in her eyes.

"What the fuck, Maya? You told Iris before you told me?"

Maya groaned. "See, this is why I never wanted to have this conversation. Yes, Iris knows, but I'm not sorry I kept you in the dark. It is safer for all of us that way."

"But why did you tell Iris?" I pressed, feeling my blood boil. Iris only laughed again, and this time I was the one shooting daggers with my eyes.

"Caelum," Iris said, "I know about Maya and Kasiel because that's how we met. He was after me."

"*What?*" I couldn't believe my ears, and Maya groaned again.

"It was a false lead," Maya replied. "He was going after a killer, and the guy pinned evidence on Iris. Kasiel brought her to me to give her shelter while he went after the actual murderer." Maya glanced over at Iris, a small smile pulling at her lips.

"And for that, I am forever grateful to him. For two things. Saving my life, and giving me the love of my life on the same day," Iris said as she grinned widely at Maya.

I was happy they had each other, but my heart sank. If I knew what true love felt like, it was whatever I had with Halcyon, but I wouldn't allow myself to think about that with her since it was reaching the inevitable crash of the end.

The future was too muddled, my heart wanting to go in one direction, logic and reason telling me it needed to go another. Time was passing too quickly, the sands in my proverbial hourglass sifting through with no way to stop it.

"What are the plans for when this is all over? We'll have money. Should we consider finding another exploration job?" I asked, aiming my question broadly on purpose. I needed to research that tome, but being so close to Halcyon while I couldn't have her seemed impossible. Maybe there was somewhere else I could take it, even if they didn't have all the resources I needed.

"I need to go back to the Seaside Cliffs for the time being, I think," Maya groaned. "Speaking of the aforementioned brother, it really has been too long and I'm sure he's let my garden go to shit."

Iris gave her a small smile, and I knew Iris would follow Maya to the ends of the world if she desired to go there.

"We'll make sure it gets all fixed up," Iris reassured her with a passing hand squeeze.

"What about you, Cal?" Maya asked. "Will you be joining us at the Cliffs?"

A lump lodged in my throat, and I glanced away because I had no words to answer.

THE CITY OF DOLAN sprawled out before us as we trailed the familiar path we originally set out on.

Halcyon stood in the street, her head high, wearing a deep navy dress which made her eyes shine, and hugged her body until it flowed out around her knees. The small straps bared her smooth skin, and the sunlight bounced off her perfectly braided silver hair, combed back with small curls around her face.

My breath caught in my throat. I wanted to gallop toward her, sweep her off her feet and take her far, far away. Where no one would find us, and I could keep her to myself.

Instead, I mustered the best grin I could. Her lips upturned in response, but she quickly veered her gaze away. It was a whip cracking into my heart.

"Welcome back, travelers." She regarded us in a perfect demeanor. It was just a shell of the person I came to know. Seeing her like that was a mockery of who Halcyon was. There was no light in her eyes, nothing to give away the laughter which rang in my ears night after night. It was like I was staring at a completely different person, and I shifted uncomfortably in my saddle.

Niklaus stood next to her in all black, his shoulders squared. Sumyre wasn't around, and I could only guess she had been left back at the castle, tucked away from the townspeople's prying eyes.

There was a small crowd gathered behind Halcyon, curious gazes peeking around security guards.

"Please join me in my home as a congratulations for a successful mission," she announced.

There was no room for argument as Halcyon turned on her heel and climbed into a horse-drawn carriage. She embodied the ruler of the city, gracefully taking Niklaus' hand as he helped her up. Gone was the Halcyon from the mortal kingdom; instead a ghost of who I knew Halcyon to be rode elegantly toward the cold castle.

We followed her toward the castle like a damned procession. Citizens lined the street. Some even threw flowers at us and cheered for us. Like we were heroes.

A pang of sadness ricocheted through me. Did they know Aceus sacrificed his life for our return? How could they? Not when they beamed up at us with smiling faces.

The castle gates closed behind us, and I let out a shaking breath of relief. Animal handlers came out and took the reins of our horses, promising good care and getting them well-fed. I had no issues. I trusted Halcyon and her people, but Iris was hell-bent on listing out every single thing they needed to do to care for the horses.

When guards came out to retrieve Aceus' body, there was a stillness in the air that clogged my throat. Maya and Iris held each other with tears streaming down their faces as Aceus was carted off. Halcyon's face was downturned, and I didn't need to see to know there were tears rolling down her cheeks.

Niklaus had promised he would have a ceremonial burial—killed in the line of duty—but it didn't ease any of the pressure in my chest.

Halcyon watched as they disappeared into the castle, her face impassable. Niklaus strode over to us, but my attention was on Halcyon, and how she had turned her back toward me, trailing the guards with her eyes.

"Welcome back to Dolan." Niklaus smiled sadly. "I hope you can find this a warm welcome from your weary travels. Please, follow me."

I couldn't peel my eyes away from Halcyon as she greeted Iris and Maya. She wore a small smile and a grace that I hadn't seen her with since we had gone into the mortal kingdom.

She glanced over, and for a moment it was like the world stopped. Nothing existed between us. All the excited chatter around us faded away until there was absolutely nothing between us.

I didn't recall stepping toward her, but suddenly she was a hairsbreadth away from my chest, our eyes locking on each other.

"Halcyon..." I whispered, at a complete loss for words. The urge to run pounded through my heart, to take her and go to the ends of Ambrose, where no one else could reach us. My fingers twitched, wanting to tuck a loose strand of hair behind her ear, but I clenched my fists, remembering who she was, and who watched us. Just looking at her now, the absolute vision she made in her swaths of silk—she was made for the role of Lady, and I was just...just me. Just Cal.

"Caelum." She blew out a deep breath, peeling her gaze away from mine, and my breath caught, fearing the worst. Her soft hand took mine, and I nearly forgot how to breathe, and she looked at me again. "The castle is open to you. To everyone, but especially you." There was a question in her eyes, but I couldn't decipher what it was, and gods did I want to know, and my heart beat faster in anticipation. "Will you stay this one night with me?"

I wanted to. I wanted to feel my arms around her for one last time. It was something I craved so desperately, it was clawing out of me. Brushing away the loose curl hanging beside her rounded cheek, I gave in.

"I would..." The words got lodged in my throat, not wanting to voice them, but the heat in my face became unbearable. "I would do anything you asked of me, Hal. Anything and everything." I winced, knowing I was only digging myself deeper into this hole that I never should have started digging. "Of course I will stay with you. This one last time."

Chapter 25

HALCYON

Exhaustion was so heavy on me, I could barely keep my eyes open through dinner. Paired with the flow of wine, my limbs became laden and for the first time in what felt like forever, I felt truly relaxed. I was still reeling over Aceus' death, but Niklaus had helped secure his resting place, lifting a small weight from my shoulders.

Guilt still lingered in the back of my mind, but I knew he wouldn't have made any other choice. He died doing what he felt was right. He would have died in the mortal kingdom if I had gone or not. But if I hadn't been there—if I hadn't bonded with Sumyre—they could *all* be dead. I shivered at the thought and refused to allow those possibilities to even take root in my mind.

When I told Niklaus, he had taken the news well, but I knew it had still pained him from the tightness in his eyes. I wasn't sure what his relationship with Aceus was, but I knew he spent at least some time with him. As my father's advisor for so many years, he had to. But for now, we ate with gratitude. Our lives were spared.

Niklaus sat stunned as we recalled the latest events. His mouth hung open and, more than once, I thought I caught a spark of jealousy in his eyes.

"When the horse I provided you with came back, we feared the worst," Niklaus admitted. "I'm beyond grateful that it was nothing more than a mishap." The wolf attack was far more than a mere mishap, but I had no energy to fight him on it. After everything we had gone through since then, it felt miniscule. Besides, I was grateful he had kept up the ruse, sticking to the three-week timeline instead of jumping to conclusions.

"Too bad you insisted not to go," I prodded at him. "Sumyre could be your dragon right now." He shot me a playful glare and grumbled under his breath.

There was a deep rumbling growl behind me. Before dinner, Sumyre flew straight into the dining room through one of the large archways that looked down into the valley below.

What?

Do not jest about that. I wouldn't have picked him.

Why not?

Sumyre didn't answer and instead huffed a puff of smoke through her nose and flung her head in the opposite direction. Like the question I asked was offensive.

I shook my head at her dramatics, but she only lifted her heavy body and flew out into the open ravine below. I tugged at the bond and relaxed, knowing she loved the air here, and the ability to fly without the threat of the mortal army chasing after her. There was freedom for her in Ambrose, as there was for all of us.

The moon was high, our bellies were full, and my head buzzed pleasantly from wine when I noticed Iris leaning on Maya, her eyes heavy.

"Lady, should I show your guests to their chambers?" Shara materialized beside me, a sparkle in her eye.

When I arrived, she burst into tears, her yellow hair beginning to darken at the roots. I could never repay her for the gift she had given me by acting as my decoy.

After she had finished fawning over me in my room while I readied for tonight's dinner, rushed words recounting everything that happened while I was gone poured from her mouth.

Apparently, it was easy enough to keep hidden from prying eyes, as long as she made sure to take walks around the castle a few times a day. Questions that regarded my whereabouts otherwise were handled by Niklaus, and I couldn't help but observe her as she caught his eye more than a few times this evening. If I wasn't mistaken, a blush flushed her cheeks every time.

They had been spending quite some time together, since it was imperative to keep up appearances, and I made a mental note to ask her about it directly the next time we were alone.

"I supposed it is time for us to part ways," Niklaus said as he noticed Iris as well. The others nodded, and Maya roused Iris awake enough to stand. Shara patiently strode over to the table and invited everyone to follow her.

Caelum remained behind, a twinkle in his eye, but melancholy lined his face. I knew why, but I refused to acknowledge it. Reaching for his hand, I gripped his palm, threading his fingers through mine.

"Wait for me in the hall, Cal. I need to speak with my cousin for a moment."

He gave me a smirk and nodded before removing himself from the dining room. I waited until the doors banged shut behind him before turning to regard my cousin. Niklaus lounged in his seat, his eyes filled with mirth.

"You and the archeologist?" He raised his eyebrow at me, a smile playing on his lips.

"I need to talk to you about something." I breathed in a deep breath, running my hands down the front of my dress, the silk soft on my fingertips. Niklaus frowned and sat up in his chair. Nerves suddenly made my hands shake.

Was I perhaps being rash? Would the retaliation make Dolan look weak? But it was far too late for those questions now. I had plenty of time to think on the journey back, but now that I was making those daydreams a reality, it set my heart racing.

"What is it, Hal? Is there something wrong? Did the mortal army—"

"No," I interrupted. "Nothing of the sort." I shook my head. "With all the recent developments, my dragon bond, the bow..." My words trailed off as I really took in the castle walls.

Walls that I was born in and destined to die in. This place was supposed to be my legacy. Everything that happened within these walls and in this city was my destiny. Not anymore. My destiny changed the moment I touched the bow in the mortal kingdom. Possibly even before then.

"I think it's for the best that I step down from my Ladyship," I said resolutely.

Galen said I needed a sacrifice, something bigger than monetary value. If this wasn't my sacrifice, then I wasn't sure what else it could be.

Every waking moment since the time I could walk had been setting me up to rule this city, and I had never once doubted my place in it. But now, I knew I needed to give up everything I dedicated my life to. For Sumyre. For the good of Ambrose. It felt like I was cleaving my life in two. I had felt those bonds, the souls tied to my own, and I knew from that moment forward, I could not live my life the same way I always had.

Niklaus sat silently with wide eyes. I was expecting an argument, bracing myself for heated words.

Instead, he quietly asked, "Who would take your place?"

I swallowed, a lump forming in my throat not from sadness or regret, but at the potential of actual freedom. I looked upon the stone archways, so different from the archways in the palace we had found underground.

Even though they were tall and mighty, they were a fraction of the size, and yet, they felt like a prison cell.

"You did a wonderful job of fulfilling my duties while I was away. The people look up to you, the council respects you, even the staff loves you. I was hoping to implement more modern techniques such as an election, but until then, the Castle would need an interim Lord. I was hoping..."

Niklaus stood from his seat, and for the first time in our lives, he bowed to me. His black hair fell toward the ground, and he slowly rose with a soft smile on his otherwise hardened face. I thought he would protest. Assure me this was where I was supposed to be. Hadn't he been the one to insist that he wasn't prepared to take the role a few weeks ago? I was the heir, after all. It was something that hadn't changed in hundreds of years, but I was tired of living as my ancestors did. It was time for change.

Instead of protesting, Niklaus smiled. "I would be honored to take your place, Hal. Temporarily. But I must know, is this something that you really want to do? This isn't because of..." He nodded his head toward the hallway where Caelum was most likely standing, waiting for me. My heart skipped at the thought. I smiled as I responded, and Nik's face flashed with something like confusion.

"It's not because of him, and yes, it is something I really want to do." I paused. "No, it's something I *have* to do. I need to find answers," I told him, feeling lightness in my chest at my decision.

I raised my hand in front of my face, the golden band around my forearm glinting in the candlelight. "I'll go back to Neverwind Library. Commit my time to research and training with Sumyre. There's plenty of space for her there, in the mountains, where people won't get in the way."

Nik sighed. "I support your decision, Halcyon. I don't know how the Council will respond, but they don't have much of a choice, do they?"

The curls framing my face swayed as I shook my head. "None at all."

"It will take time to get everything passed over. I can't just fill the role immediately. It will take time to enforce new policies."

"I understand. I'll help you as much as I can before your title is accepted."

He swept past me, gripping my hand and squeezing as he passed by. "Dean William will be pleased." He chuckled and then stood still, looking at me with an expression that conveyed all the cousinly love he may have felt for me. "For the record, I don't think I have ever seen you smile like the way you smile at Caelum."

I bit my lip, and my cheeks heated.

"*Goodnight*, Lord Niklaus," I said, dismissing *that* conversation in its entirety. Nik released my hand and turned away with a gleam in his eye.

"Goodnight, Halcyon." He gave me a wave and turned to go back to his chambers.

I swung the door open to my bedchambers and breathed in the floral scent I had missed so very much. Shara must have kept watering my plants and dusting. It felt like I hadn't even left. The moonlight cast the room in a silvery glow, reminding me of the night I told Nik I would embark on this adventure. It felt like it had been ages, even if it was only a matter of weeks, and yet it altogether felt like no time at all. So much had changed since then, though.

I headed straight to the window, pulling back the white linens that covered the night landscape, admiring the endless tops of trees which eventually led into the Jagged Peaks where we crossed only a few days prior.

The stars shone brightly, each twinkling dot in the sky felt like they were looking down on me, blessing me with possibilities as vast as their numbers.

A low whistle had me turning on my feet to find Caelum looking around my room with a smirk on his lips, his dimple making an appearance.

"This is quite the room. I can't believe you traded this for dirt." He chuckled as he took everything in, his hands drifting over the back of my settee in front of the unlit fireplace.

"I did. And I would do it again, too," I said, meaning every word.

Cal stilled. His lips wavered for the tiniest second, but he was quick to hide his inner turmoil. A beat of silence passed through us, only the critters singing in the woods giving any sound before I cleared my throat.

"When is the last time you had a bath?" I asked, curious as to when he had last let himself indulge.

"This evening, when we all washed up before dinner. Why?"

I shook my head and smiled. "I don't mean *when did you last bathe*? I meant, when did you last have a nice, *hot* bath?" A sultry tone took over my voice, but Cal didn't seem to notice.

"Two nights ago, in the springs, when we came back through the caves." He scoffed. "You were there—" I raised a hand and sighed.

"I don't mean bathing in a dark pond where you don't know if something is going to nibble on your toes. I meant—" Pushing myself off of the dresser, I took deliberate steps toward him. Our chests touched and my nipples pebbled from the contact pressing against the silk of my dress. Slowly, I unbuttoned the top button on his tunic, revealing the hard planes of his chest. "When was the last time you sat in a wide tub, with an array of soaps to choose from, and just let yourself *relax*?"

Caelum let out a hiss of pleasure as I trailed my fingertips along the exposed skin, tracing along his collarbone and up his neck, where I could feel the pulse of his heartbeat.

"I'm not sure I remember, to be honest." His eyes darkened as he looked down at me, his hand wrapping around my wrist. I took my other hand and slowly peeled his fingers away, watching him through my eyelashes.

"Sounds like it's been a long time coming, then." I tugged Caelum by the hand to the bathing chambers, where a tub that was far too big for me alone sat along another tall arched window. The spigot gushed as I turned the handle, filling the bathtub to the brim with delightfully hot water.

"Lavender or sandalwood?" I held up two bottles of bathing oils. Caelum swallowed thickly, his throat bobbing as though if he made the choice between the two, he was choosing between life or death.

"Cal? Are you alright?" Settling for lavender, I poured a few drops into the water before placing the bottle down and reaching for Caelum's hands.

"Remember..." Caelum tore his gaze away from me, instead opting to stare out the window. "Remember when we were in the woods, and you and I had that conversation?"

I frowned, not liking the path of where this conversation was headed. Tonight was about celebration, and I certainly didn't want it ruined with whatever deals we had made in those trees.

"We had a lot of conversations in the woods, Cal. You'll need to be more specific," I said, biting the corner of my mouth.

Cal lowered his voice to a strained whisper. I winced, knowing exactly what he was going to say.

"You said this could never last. And I knew at the time what I agreed to, but Hal. We aren't out there anymore. We came back and we're supposed to be going our separate ways. If we do this—if *I* do this, I don't know if I can walk away. I'll exit these halls, I'll walk out of the gates, gallop from the city, but Halcyon"—he traced a knuckle over my cheekbone, his jaw flexed—"there will always be a piece of me stuck here. Stranded. Waiting and yearning for the one woman that I can never have. The woman that I would never deserve, but for some reason, got to spend the smallest amount of time with."

He let out a strangled sigh, and a single tear ran down my cheek. It was gone just as quickly as he brushed it away with his thumb and cradled the back of my head.

"A Magi's life is long, but even if I only ever get the memories of those few short weeks with you, it will forever be etched in my heart. I don't deserve you, Halcyon. I never have, and never will live up to what you need, what you deserve."

His hazel eyes studied me, memorized me. My lips parted in response to the way he made me feel naked as he looked at me.

The way he looked *through* me, down to the depths of my soul. He looked at me like *I* was the world's greatest treasure. As though he had spent his entire life looking for the diamonds in the rough, the great divinity, and he finally found it, and it was *me*. My heart swelled, and my heart thrummed erratically.

He had no idea I felt the exact same way about *him*.

"I stepped down," I blurted. I couldn't hold the information from him any longer. There was too much heartbreak written on his face.

Cal stiffened, but he didn't remove his hands from me or pull away. "What?"

"I stepped down. I am no longer the Lady of Dolan," I stated.

Conflicted emotions flashed over Caelum's face. Surprise, hope, confusion.

"Why would you do that?" he asked tentatively.

"I can't be the Lady of a growing city, experiment with my dragon bond, and find answers about the importance of these weapons all at the same time." My fingers traced along Cal's arm, wrapping them around the hand that held my head.

"I had to give up something for it to work, so I rescinded my duties. I'm going to the library, and I plan on spearheading research on the bond."

Caelum was so still I wasn't sure he was breathing. If it wasn't for the hazel eyes that bounced along my face, I would have been worried.

"I need...an assistant. Someone I can trust, preferably someone with experience and knowledge. *Preferably* someone who has also been inside the temple the bow came from." The words fell from my mouth too quickly. My stomach swooping with nerves of facing rejection. I pleaded with him through my eyes, hoping he could grasp the unspoken words I was trying to convey.

Stay with me.

Choose to be here.

Choose me.

Caelum opened and shut his mouth several times. "But what about—"

"If you dare to suggest anyone else, I will turn them down."

Caelum's grasp tightened, and he wrapped his other arm around my waist, pulling me closer to his chest.

"Are you asking me to stay?"

"I am." I had never been surer with any decision in my life. "Will you stay? You want to know more about the gods, right? I'm giving you that chance." The next word that came out of my mouth shook. "*Please.*" I chewed the bottom of my lip in anticipation. I wanted him to take it, needed him near me, and I thought he felt the same, but I still replayed all of his moments of hesitation.

What if he says no?

Cal's smirk made its reappearance, and I held back a sigh of relief. It meant nothing, and I refused to let myself hope.

"I'll stay. But not for the gods." Those first two words were the only words I cared about. My hands shook as I wrapped them around his neck. Cal pressed his lips against mine, his hands cradling my face, his thumbs tracing my cheekbones. He pulled back, leaving me breathless, and shrugged.

"Okay, maybe a little for the gods," he said, and I laughed. It was a genuine laugh, letting the weight on my chest fly free before Caelum claimed my mouth once again.

Reluctantly, I pulled away from Caelum, heading for the taps which were nearly overfilling the tub. The water was hot, steam filling the bathing chamber and fogging the mirror on the wall. The smell of lavender permeated the room, coaxing me to relax, and I turned toward Caelum.

His eyes were dark and hungry, but he made no move toward me as I gently slipped a shoulder of my dress down, exposing my collarbone. I turned slowly, drawing a shaky breath.

"Would you mind untying my dress? I have trouble getting it myself."

That was a lie, but I craved Cal's touch. Imagining his fingers trailing on my back made me clench my legs together with need. He shuffled behind me, and at the first touch of his skin against mine, I gasped.

His fingers were light as they traced the lace edge of my dress, the pad of his fingertip trailing a blazing fire against my skin.

The corset was tugged with excruciating slowness. His deft hands untied and loosened the ribbon methodically, allowing me to breathe in a little more with each flick of his wrist.

Quiet anticipation filled the room. Not a single word between us. The last drips of the tap were the only indication that time didn't stand still.

Caelum's breath brushed over my neck as he worked the corset undone. When it was untied, he raised his hands to my shoulders, brushing the loose strands of my braided hair away before placing gentle lips on my skin.

I let out a shuddered breath at the contact. Pins fell from my hair, making quiet pings against the tiles as he pulled each one out one-by-one. My hair fell down in silvery waves before he removed the other strap from my shoulder. The dress dropped around me, a pile of silks around my feet.

Removing my under garments, I turned, baring myself to him. He eyed me hungrily, a steady fire behind his hazel eyes.

"I wasn't lying, you know," he whispered as he devoured me with his eyes. There was no denying the lust and the reverence in his gaze.

"When you said what?" I asked, my voice husky and low, matching the heat pulsing through my core.

He didn't look away from me as he unbuttoned the rest of his shirt and then peeled it off of his arms, dropping it unceremoniously on the ground. I sucked in a sharp breath at his toned muscles, the humidity from the bath clinging to his skin and reflecting the moon's light.

"When I said you were a goddess. I am not worthy of this gift, and yet you bless me." His hands moved to his pants, where I watched raptly as he wrapped his hand around his very obvious erection. He let out a small groan, his half-lidded eyes grazing over every inch of me. My heart lodged in my throat and I stood still, unable to move through the pounding in my ears.

"Come here, Halcyon," he demanded with a fire in his eyes.

My breath hitched at his commanding tone, heat and desire flooding my body with memories of the last time he used that same voice, and the sheer bliss that was promised with it.

My feet padded along the cool floor as I walked toward him until I was close enough that our breaths mingled together. His eyes flickered down, noticing how my breasts pebbled and peaked in the air. Before I let him try to touch me, I fell to my knees.

I unbuttoned his pants with ease, sliding them down his thick thighs until he, too, stepped out of his garments, my face in perfect height with his hard cock. The desire to take him in my mouth again made my pulse beat faster. To watch from below as he came undone for me was a gift all on its own, but before that, I wanted to *feel* him.

Running my hands along his thighs, I moved them up before reaching the swell of his backside, round and taut with hard muscle. I squeezed, relishing in the flesh I held onto. Caelum hummed under his breath, closing his eyes as he reached behind him to lean on the vanity.

He hissed as I wrapped my hands around his hard length, and I ran my tongue along the bottom. Wetness coated my thighs, and I squeezed them together, telling myself not to rush, I would get my own soon. I was sure of it.

Caelum's hand wrapped around the back of my head, weaving his fingers through the strands of my hair, tugging just enough for it to sting. He pulled me back far enough for me to look at him, his eyes heavy with lust.

"Your lips on me are the essence of life. They are a rare joy that not everyone gets to experience in their lifetime. I don't know what I did to deserve you."

I preened under his praise, only making me more eager to take him. His grasp lessened for a fraction of a second, and I took my chances. Licking my lips, I descended on his cock. He hit the back of my throat as I pulled him in further, swirling my tongue along his length. He groaned as I bobbed up and down slowly, his hips undulated in time with my head.

Caelum tightened his grasp on my hair, stinging my scalp in the best way as he pulled me off of him. He crouched down in front of me, our eyes meeting, and a smile playing on his lips.

Gods, he was beautiful. The way his hair was dampening from the humid air, his eyes spearing into me with desire, the dimple on his left cheek. Just looking at him had me moaning without even touching me.

"While I appreciate all that you've done for me, this time it's my turn. Let me worship *you*."

I jolted as vines wrapped around my wrist and middle, emerging from the cracks in the walls and slithering across the floor. They pulled me down, weaving around my thighs until I was spread open. I was entirely exposed, my center wet and glistening, and when I tried to close my legs, the vines were unforgiving, not allowing me to hide away from Caelum's hungry gaze.

Caelum bent over me, running his hand along my sternum, where my chest was heaving from anticipation and nervous energy. My hands were bound above my head, and I was surprised to find that I loved the way I was at Caelum's disposal. This man had become my undoing, only to piece me together again. He knew what I needed before I even knew it myself.

I remembered how those vines had crept up in that tent, how they had prevented me from moving while Caelum gave everything to me, and it made me molten inside as the vines grew taut across my body.

A voracious grin slid over his features as he stared down at me, his fingers roaming along my ribs and stomach. Every point of contact made me shudder and whimper under his touch.

Caelum grabbed the wrinkled fabric of my dress and placed it gently under my head, creating a soft pillow enveloping me in blue, reprieving my head from the hard, cold stone underneath.

"Is this okay?" He tugged at one vine that wrapped around my thigh, and I nodded, my core suddenly feeling too empty. "You say the word, and I stop."

I stared at him, confused. "The word?"

"Whatever word you like, pick one. This way, I know you're comfortable and enjoying yourself. You use it and I know to stop."

I took a gulp of air, trying to think of a word that I would remember, one that would mean something to the both of us. "Treasure."

"Treasure." He sighed with a laugh. "You say 'treasure', and I stop. Deal?"

I nodded, eagerly. "Deal."

Caelum's hand traveled lower, and I bucked in response, eager to have him touch me, eager to have him fill me. A dark chuckle was my only warning before he slid a fingertip along my opening and groaned. I could hear how wet I was, the liquid coating his finger as he circled my clit. Warmth encompassed my body, but I needed more.

As if he could read my mind, Caelum slipped a second finger inside of me, and I threw my head back. I hadn't forgotten what his touch felt like, but apparently, I hadn't remembered how good it felt either.

Pumping his fingers into me, he curled them, and the sensation was overriding every single thought. I didn't even realize he shifted down until I felt the warm stroke of his tongue run straight through my center.

The vines dug into my skin as my legs tried to move of their own accord. They shook, and I bucked my hips, only to be met with more resistance from the vine around my middle.

I couldn't run from Caelum's tongue or pull away from his fingers as they heightened my pleasure, the heat in my body rising up and up and until I felt hot from the tips of my toes to the crown of my head. Nonsensical words came out of my mouth, meaning nothing and everything all at once.

Just when I thought I couldn't take it anymore, my climax crested. My voice echoed along the stone walls, and I found myself uncaring if the sound reverberated through the castle. Every muscle in my body tightened in the hold of the vines. Every inch of my body succumbed to Caelum's ministrations.

All the nerves in my body were firing off. My fingers and toes tingled; my head fuzzy and sated. I lay there on the cold tile of the floor, my chest rising and falling and my body completely languid. The vines were gone, retreated back into the earth, and Cal pulled me into his arms.

I hummed in satisfaction as he helped me stand, my legs still wobbly underneath me. The water was still plenty warm as I sank in and relished the heat. Crawling in after me, Caelum sat on the other end of the tub. His erection still stood, and my body reacted immediately, my core clenching at nothing.

Tension grew taut between us, but before I questioned myself, I pushed myself on my knees, crawling over Caelum's lap. Warm hands ran over my shoulders, pulling me closer. Water sloshed over the basin and splashed against the stone floors, but I couldn't be bothered by the mess.

Ice coated my fingers, and I could feel it warring with the hot bath water, threatening to melt if I let it go. When my ice-laden fingers pressed against his skin, Caelum gasped, and I watched as gooseflesh rose on his body. Following every frozen touch with a press of my lips, I trailed along his neck, over his jaw, and finally reaching his lips. The bite of my magic met my tongue as I pressed into his mouth, and he shuddered underneath me as he met me stroke for stroke.

Softly, he moaned, and I couldn't help myself from rocking myself over his hard length as I straddled him. His cock twitched against me, and I lifted myself up and eased onto his length.

"Cal," his name left my lips like a prayer as I seated myself on him. His hands wrapped around my hips, his fingers biting into my skin. The both of us let ourselves bathe in the essence of each other. Just breathing with our foreheads pressed together. He tucked a strand of my hair behind my ear, and I looked down at his hazel eyes. They were writhing and whirling with emotion.

Exhaling, I tapped into the words etched into my heart. "I love you. I know I shouldn't, and it's selfish of me to even expect you to return those feelings. But my heart belongs to you." Three steady beats of my heart went past, and Caelum said nothing.

"I love you too." Cal's voice cracked and then his lips were on mine, our tongues meshing together in a fervor until I was breathless. Relief flooded through me. Relief, and hope, and gratitude.

We rocked into each other gently, savoring our bodies pressed into each other, the steam muffling the panting we were both making as Caelum's fingers gripped my hips, his thrusts into me deliberate and agonizingly slow.

I grasped his shoulders for purchase, my nails biting into his skin hard enough to leave marks.

He said he would stay, but I wished to fuse myself to him to make sure he was telling the truth.

Each push and pull was a prayer and a plea with his slow and steady rhythm. There was nothing but raw energy between us now. It was the unbarring of our souls uniting us together at this moment. A cumulative crescendo from the very moment we met outside these walls.

I cried out as my body tightened around Caelum, my arms winding around his neck, pressing his face against my breast. Flicking my nipple with his tongue, he prolonged the coursing pleasure pouring through my body. I felt him strain beneath me, his hands splayed along my back, nails scratching down my skin as he shuddered, finding release for himself.

For a long moment, we didn't move, barely allowed ourselves to breathe as we held onto each other. It was like if we let go, our time would be up, promises or not.

I blinked my eyes open as a warmth spread through my chest, one which felt familiar yet foreign all at once. It was urgent, like a thread tightening around me. Bright gold light surrounded us with a golden cord wrapping around our bodies, tying us together, and I gasped.

Cal opened his eyes at my sound, and his hands clung to my back, his fingertips digging into my skin as he held his breath.

I laughed as tears streamed down my face, knowing exactly what this was. No longer did I have to wonder about the unwoven thread. Fear of what did or did not lie at the end of what I saw in my soul washed away at the sight of the magic around us. Fate tied us together, and now I knew for certain: Caelum was *mine*.

"We have a choice to make, Cal," my voice cracked on a smile, and I cradled his chin, forcing him to take his focus away from the gold cord around us and look at me.

"Caelum?" I asked in a whisper. His heart was pounding as our chests pressed together, and while I could see a thousand thoughts going through Caelum's mind, I had no idea *what* he was thinking.

He blinked several times before regarding me with his full attention. His throat bobbed, and a tear rolled down his cheek, my breath catching in my throat.

Gritting my teeth together, I ground them until I was sure they would crack, knowing we had to answer this call, but I would only agree if he was willing.

His arms fell slack in the water, and I wished I could drown at the sound of the splash as it fell against the stone floor. Fear swirled in his eyes, and I choked back the sob attempting to claw out of my chest.

"Halcyon," Cal whispered with the gentleness of a butterfly's wings, and I closed my eyes, bracing myself for this rejection, knowing now he was a part of me. I had seen the cord, seen it in the process of being woven as I hunted for more power. I had felt him through it, and I recognized it for what it was. Maybe, if I had told him, he would be more prepared. We could have talked about what our lives would look like, with or without each other.

Would he truly give up his way of life for me? Cal had repeatedly told me how unworthy he was, but it was *I* who was the unworthy one.

Gentle fingers drifted along my cheek, and I wanted to beg him to stop, but I couldn't.

"What kind of world would I live in if I knew that my soul bonded was right here, and I didn't seize the chance to be with them?"

Blinking my eyes open through wet lashes, I met a smile so bright it rivaled the divine light around us.

"You're choosing me?" I asked, breathless.

"I would choose you today, tomorrow, and for eternity, Halcyon. You are the air that I breathe, the stars in the night sky, the reason I live and the one person in this world that I would die for."

I sobbed into his chest, wrapping my arms around his neck. Uncontrollable fat tears rolled from my cheek down Caelum's chest as I clung onto him.

"I choose you, too. I choose you, I choose life, and I choose my happiness," I sniffled into his ear, feeling lighter than I could ever remember.

The gold light shined even brighter, and I peeled myself from Caelum's shoulder as I watched it spin around us. Blinding, pure light emanated from the solid cord that bound our souls together. As it grew closer, pressing in against our intertwined bodies, I felt the raw energy of the gods as they graced us in this moment.

The gods were very, very much alive, and all my doubts were now wiped away. The cord sank into our skin, and I gasped as Caelum and I became one in body and spirit.

Unbridled joy came out in a fit of laughter as I pressed my forehead to Caelum's, and when I raised my hand to brace his cheek, I noticed the shimmering gold bond mark wrapping around my wrist below my other bond mark to Sumyre. Cal raised his hand as he inspected himself, bearing the same mark.

We were united, joined together for eternity, mated in the most definitive fashion.

Chapter 26

CAELUM

I STARED AT THE horizon, rubbing my chest where it now felt empty. Watching Halcyon leave earlier that week on the back of Sumyre left me bereft in her absence.

I peeled my eyes away from the never-ending expanse of sky, the light blues and grays of the coming day only making me feel more hollow.

We both made our choices, and I had to live with that decision, even though I felt like it was going to rip my soul to shreds. Dramatics aside, the heart feels what the heart feels, and right now it felt empty.

Placing my hands in my pockets, I took a deep breath before turning into the woods where Olympia patiently awaited me. We rode through the trees until I reached the winding path I had recently become so familiar with.

Up ahead stood a round man dressed in a blue-collared shirt, blue tights, and a white jacket which came down to his knees. He carried a book stack so tall it looked about to topple over.

"Dean William, to what do I owe this pleasure?" I greeted him with a tight smile as I dismounted Olympia. I tied her off on a nearby hitching rail, giving her a solid pat on her rump before turning back to the Dean.

"My dear boy, I believe I've found some information that can help us decipher the tome. At least, in part." He gestured to the pile of books in his arms. "I've pulled all the books that might have more details, but it's imperative we go right away."

I followed after him into Neverwind Library. Large, cream marble columns paved the entrance to the library. It was an architectural wonder. A beauty the good citizens of Dolan upheld. But it was nothing but a herald of what lay deep in the ground beyond the border.

Still, the columns towered into the sky. Each column etched with stories of the gods and chosen gods-blessed in carvings which caught shadows in the sunlight. I followed the Dean through the winding, never-ending halls of the library. Students and scholars from around the world congregated here for their research. Dean William wove through the bodies in the halls, and I chased after him.

We hustled through the main portion of the library. Rows and rows and rows of books lined the walls from the floor to the tall ceiling. There were ladders sporadically placed around the library, all leading up to the domed ceiling, where a large painting portraying the last war between the gods artfully accented the room with constellations mapped out beneath them.

I could spend hours looking at that painting, trying to decipher what the artist meant with each brush stroke, but for now, there were more pressing matters to attend to.

Dean William halted at a pair of wooden double doors, which he swung open, revealing a wide spiral staircase leading up into the Dean's office. It was a cozy room, with a fireplace on one end and a heavy wooden desk on the other. In the middle sat a table with four chairs absolutely filled to the brim with books and loose parchments.

The Dean placed his stack of books on the table unceremoniously, and let out a long, whooshing breath. He gestured to the pile of papers, and I took a seat at the table, tugging at the large book which rested on top.

"Let's go through this quickly, and hopefully, by the time Halcyon gets back, we will have some answers." He paused as he took in my pained expression and laughed. "Boy, get that sorrowful look off your face. She only left four days ago."

I grunted in response, resigning to my now-scholarly duties. My head was stuck in a book rather than my hands in dirt. When I accepted Halcyon's offer, I was sure I would miss the great outdoors. The dirt in my fingers, the sun on my skin, but I found myself enjoying my new surroundings.

In the weeks I'd spent here, I never went a night without a good meal, never had to sleep on the unforgiving ground, and most importantly, I got to spend my free time with the woman I loved. She blossomed from the Lady of Dolan who was closed-off, distant, and unhappy, to someone with a drive and new passions.

I let myself get lost in the pages of the books William had laid out. The chances of finding anything were slim, but I still paid attention to every detail. The tome we found was filled with indecipherable text. An ancient alphabet or something written in code, we didn't know. When the candles on the table started turning into stubs, Dean William cleared his throat.

"Would you like to join me for dinner, my boy?"

I sighed, closing the book I was currently reading, and tossing it onto the pile of useless information.

"Actually, I think I'll take my dinner outside this evening, if that's all right?"

The Dean smiled at me and nodded before getting up and adjusting his lapels.

"Very well, son. I'll see you tomorrow morning."

And with that, he was off.

After snagging some food from the kitchens, I made my way up to the quiet landing where I had said goodbye to Halcyon. To her credit, she had asked if I wanted to go with her, and while I *wanted* to, I knew I was going to be of better use here.

The other Lords and Ladies of Ambrose demanded a session over her new dragon bond. Not to mention we broke a thousand laws just getting over the border and we needed to answer for our crimes.

We were lucky. They gave Halcyon enough grace to get Dolan in order with Lord Niklaus and the upcoming election before scheduling the session, and Galen was fortunately able to communicate with the other Lords, confirming we were not a danger to Ambrose.

Unfortunately, Halcyon wouldn't even entertain me taking any responsibility, saying it was her father who funded the excavation, and it would be her who answered in his stead. I just wish I could be there to defend her. Not that she needed anyone to do that. The woman was plenty headstrong herself.

I was about to take my second bite of some delightful soft cheese on a slice of bread when I heard a small *pop* behind me. A big black dragon maw appeared in my peripheral, and I let out a shout of alarm. Sumyre licked me, leaving a trail of dragon slobber on my cheek, and puffed out a plume of smoke.

"Caelum!" Halcyon stood next to her dragon, the last remnants of the sun bathing her in gold light. There wasn't a piece of art, an artifact, a sunset that could even begin to compare to the beauty of Halcyon, and she made my breath catch.

She strode up to me, wrapping her arms around my middle, before pulling away quickly. Warm incense and the heat of the desert overcame her usual floral scent. I took her face in the palm of my hands, wanting to squeeze her so tightly she would never leave my side again.

"Why are you here? What happened in Aurum? How did you even—"

My words were cut off as I looked over Halcyon's head to see two strangers. A tall, broad man with dark skin standing with his arms crossed, his eyes narrowed at a curvy woman with curly copper hair. She grinned at him.

"See? I *told* you it would work." She waved a small circular device in his face, which the man promptly snatched. I gave Halcyon a questioning glance as this man grimaced down at the woman.

"And I told *you* to stop stealing things from my pockets." He sighed and turned to me. The woman only laughed.

"Can't steal what's already mine." She shrugged.

Halcyon peeled herself from my side, the air already cold from her absence. "Caelum, this is Leoni. She's the elected Lady of Aurum, and the gentleman next to her is her husband, Riel. He's the General of Aurum's security."

Oh. My palms instantly grew clammy, so I wiped them on my pants.

"Pleasure to make your acquaintance," I greeted them with a nod.

Leoni had a smile tugging at the corner of her lip, while Riel still had his arms crossed, and it felt like his penetrating gaze was measuring me up.

"To what do we owe the honor of your presence?" I cleared my throat, having been a while since the last time I had to present myself in front of any part of Ambrose's Head Council—Halcyon aside.

"We have a vested interest in the research you are conducting." Riel spoke to me with directed attention, and I held back a nervous laugh.

"They have a bond blessed by the gods. Same as us," Halcyon explained. She gestured to their wrists, where a similar intricate band of weaving lines were embedded in gold. "We all have a Soulmate bond, and my other bond is with Sumyre—so obviously it's different—but, both are godly bonds and we are going to figure out why, in all these years, we have been chosen to be blessed."

I blew out a long breath. "What about Galen and his dragon? Surely it would be better to have his experience?"

"Unfortunately, Galen's position in Tantal is too important," Riel replied. "We are on our own for this." His gaze was scathing and skeptical, like he was trying to decide if I was a threat.

I stared at the three of them. All of whom who had been blessed by the gods, for reasons unknown. I felt a sharp sting of jealousy. These were all people who held positions of power. They all had experience navigating the politics of Ambrose, and then there was me. Nothing but a lowly archeologist who never practiced the customs of the elite.

But they still needed me, too. I was chosen in my own right. The gods recognized that Halcyon and I needed each other. Just as quickly, my self-conscious doubts evaporated.

There was nothing I wouldn't do to sate my curiosity. People from around the country called me crazy for wanting to go to the mortal kingdom. They said there was nothing there, but that wasn't good enough for me, and it would never be.

I nodded, taking Halcyon's hand in my own. "All right. Let's get started."

Thank you so much for reading The Temple of Frozen Fates. If you enjoyed this book, please consider leaving a review on Goodreads and Amazon. As an indie author, every review is crucial to a book's success.

Sign up for my newsletter to get sneak peeks and bonus content at www. authorjenniferkay.com

You can find me on TikTok and Instagram @jenniferkayauthor

Acknowledgements

Book two... The Temple of Frozen Fates... What can I say about this book other than that it was such a labor of love? There are a lot of things about this book—and Halcyon—that I identify with. When I first wrote Halcyon's character she was bitter and cold, much like my mindset at the time of the first draft. I learned a lot writing her character. How being strong doesn't necessarily mean being a bitch. How it's okay to be scared and excited at the same time. How to embrace big changes and learn from past mistakes. Caelum's unconditional support is stemmed a lot from my amazing support system, and the people that continue to encourage me every day.

To Marlon, who has supported me since the very first day I said I wanted to write a book and said, "fucking do it, that would be awesome!" You've been my biggest cheerleader in this whole endeavor and no matter what our future holds, you will always hold a piece of my heart. Thank you for allowing me to chase my dreams, and never once second guessing my abilities.

This book wouldn't be the same piece if it wasn't for my incredible Beta readers: Sarah D., Sara M., Cynthia, Ophelia, Kate, Ashley, Samantha, Kasey, Kristi, Elliot, and Ella. Your feedback, as always, is such a crucial part to my story-telling process and I truly don't know where I would be without you.

To my editor, Julie who always leaves the best notes! Thank you for fixing all my comma splices and also leaving me countless references to Chicago. You're the best!

To my love Keli, who read the very first draft, complete with [insert scene here] notes. I don't know how you manage to go through my first drafts while also keeping your sanity. May the gods forever bless you.

To Sarah and Jasmine, my besties who get to hear me vent with frustration and scream with joy. All of the emotions and it's never too much. I love y'all so much.

At lastly, but certainly not least, to you—my readers. I don't know how you found me, and I also don't know why you love me, but I am so grateful. Thank you for giving me a chance with Shadows in the Golden City and trusting me enough to read The Temple of Frozen Fates. I hope that this book gave you as much joy reading as it gave me writing it.